MVFOL

TRIPLE PURSUIT

Also by Graham Greene

NOVELS

The Man Within / Orient Express (Stamboul Train) / It's a Battlefield / The Shipwrecked (England Made Me) / Brighton Rock / The Power and the Glory / The Heart of the Matter / The End of the Affair / Three by Graham Greene: This Gun for Hire (A Gun for Sale), The Confidential Agent, The Ministry of Fear / The Quiet American / Loser Takes All / A Burnt-Out Case / The Comedians / Travels with My Aunt

SHORT STORIES

Twenty-one Stories / A Sense of Reality / May We Borrow Your Husband?

ESSAYS

Collected Essays (*including* The Lost Childhood)

TRAVEL

Journey without Maps / Another Mexico (The Lawless Roads) / In Search of a Character

PLAYS

The Living Room / The Potting Shed / The Complaisant Lover

TRIPLE PURSUIT

A GRAHAM GREENE OMNIBUS

THIS GUN FOR HIRE

THE THIRD MAN

OUR MAN IN HAVANA

NEW YORK · THE VIKING PRESS

Published in 1971 by The Viking Press, Inc.
625 Madison Avenue, New York, N.Y. 10022
SBN 670-73126-9
Library of Congress catalog card number: 70-146055
Printed in U.S.A.

CONTENTS

This
Gun
for Hire

One

1

Murder didn't mean much to Raven. It was just a new job. You had to be careful. You had to use your brains. It was not a question of hatred. He had seen the minister only once: he had been pointed out to Raven as he walked down the new housing estate between the little lit Christmas trees—an old, rather grubby man without any friends, who was said to love humanity.

The cold wind cut his face in the wide Continental street. It was a good excuse for turning the collar of his coat well up above his mouth. A harelip was a serious handicap in his profession. It had been badly sewn in infancy, so that now the upper lip was twisted and scarred. When you carried about you so easy an identification you couldn't help becoming ruthless in your methods. It had always, from the first, been necessary for Raven to eliminate the evidence.

He carried an attaché case. He looked like any other youngish man going home after his work; his dark overcoat had a clerical air. He moved steadily up the street like hundreds of his kind. A tram went by, lit up in the early dusk; he didn't take it. An economical young man, you might have thought, saving money for his home. Perhaps even now he was on his way to meet his girl.

But Raven had never had a girl. The harelip prevented that. He had learned when he was very young how repulsive it was. He turned into one of the tall grey houses and climbed the stairs, a sour, bitter, screwed-up figure.

Outside the top flat he put down his attaché case and put on gloves. He took a pair of clippers out of his pocket and cut through the telephone wire where it ran out from above the door to the lift shaft. Then he rang the bell.

He hoped to find the minister alone. This little top-floor flat was
the Socialist's home. He lived in a poor, bare solitary way, and
Raven had been told that his secretary always left him at half-past
six—he was very considerate with his employees. But Raven was a
minute too early and the minister half an hour too late. A woman
opened the door, an elderly woman with pince-nez and several gold
teeth. She had her hat on, and her coat was over her arm. She had
been on the point of leaving, and she was furious at being caught.
She didn't allow him to speak, but snapped at him in German, "The
minister is engaged."

He wanted to spare her, not because he minded a killing but because his employers might prefer him not to exceed his instructions.
He held the letter of introduction out to her silently; as long as she
didn't hear his foreign voice or see his harelip she was safe. She
took the letter bitterly and held it up close to her pince-nez. Good,
he thought, she's shortsighted. "Stay where you are," she said and
walked primly back up the passage. He could hear her disapproving
governess's voice, then she was back in the passage, saying, "The
minister will see you. Follow me, please." He couldn't understand
the foreign speech, but he knew what she meant from her behaviour.

His eyes, like little concealed cameras, photographed the room instantaneously: the desk, the easy chair, the map on the wall, the door
to the bedroom behind, the wide window above the bright cold
Christmas street. A little oilstove was all the heating, and the minister was using it now to boil a saucepan. A kitchen alarm clock on
the desk marked seven o'clock. A voice said, "Emma, put another
egg in the saucepan." The minister came out from the bedroom. He
had tried to tidy himself, but he had forgotten the cigarette ash on
his trousers. He was old and small and rather dirty. The secretary
took an egg out of one of the drawers in the desk. "And the salt.
Don't forget the salt," the minister said. He explained in slow English, "It prevents the shell cracking. Sit down, my friend. Make
yourself at home. Emma, you can go."

Raven sat down and fixed his eyes on the minister's chest. He
thought, I'll give her three minutes by the alarm clock to get well
away. He kept his eyes on the minister's chest. Just there I'll shoot.
He let his coat collar fall and saw with bitter rage how the old man
turned away from the sight of his harelip.

The minister said, "It's years since I heard from him. But I've
never forgotten him, never. I can show you his photograph in the

other room. It's good of him to think of an old friend. So rich and powerful too. You must ask him when you go back if he remembers the time—" A bell began to ring furiously. Raven thought, The telephone. I cut the wire. It shook his nerve. But it was only the alarm clock drumming on the desk. The minister turned it off. "One egg's boiled," he said and stooped for the saucepan. Raven opened his attaché case; in the lid he had fixed his automatic fitted with a silencer. The minister said, "I'm sorry the bell made you jump. You see, I like my egg just four minutes."

Feet ran along the passage. The door opened. Raven turned furiously in his seat, his harelip flushed and raw. It was the secretary. He thought, My God, what a household. They won't let a man do things tidily. He forgot his lip, he was angry; he had a grievance. She came in, flashing her gold teeth, prim and ingratiating. She said, "I was just going out when I heard the telephone." Then she winced slightly, looked the other way, showed a clumsy delicacy before his deformity which he couldn't help noticing. It condemned her. He snatched the automatic out of the case and shot the minister twice in the back.

The minister fell across the oilstove; the saucepan upset, and the two eggs broke on the floor. Raven shot the minister once more in the head, leaning across the desk to make quite certain, driving the bullet hard into the base of the skull, smashing it open like a china doll's. Then he turned on the secretary. She moaned at him; she hadn't any words; the old mouth couldn't hold its saliva. He supposed she was begging him for mercy. He pressed the trigger again; she staggered as if she had been kicked in the side by an animal. But he had miscalculated. Her unfashionable dress, the swathes of useless material in which she hid her body, perhaps confused him. And she was tough, so tough he couldn't believe his eyes: she was through the door before he could fire again, slamming it behind her.

But she couldn't lock it; the key was on his side. He twisted the handle and pushed. The elderly woman had amazing strength; it only gave two inches. She began to scream some word at the top of her voice.

There was no time to waste. He stood away from the door and shot twice through the woodwork. He could hear the pince-nez fall on the floor and break. The voice screamed again and stopped; there was a sound outside as if she were sobbing. It was her breath going out through her wounds. Raven was satisfied. He turned back to the minister.

There was a clue he had been ordered to leave; a clue he had to remove. The letter of introduction was on the desk. He put it in his pocket, and between the minister's stiffened fingers he inserted a scrap of paper. Raven had little curiosity; he had only glanced at the introduction, and the nickname at its foot conveyed nothing to him; he was a man who could be depended on. Now he looked round the small bare room to see whether there was any clue he had overlooked. The suitcase and the automatic he was to leave behind. It was all very simple.

He opened the bedroom door. His eyes again photographed the scene: the single bed, the wooden chair, the dusty chest of drawers, a photograph of a young Jew with a small scar on his chin as if he had been struck there with a club, a pair of brown wooden hairbrushes initialled *J. K.*, everywhere cigarette ash—the home of a lonely untidy old man, the home of the minister for war.

A low voice whispered an appeal quite distinctly through the door. Raven picked up the automatic again. Who would have imagined an old woman could be so tough? It touched his nerve a little just in the same way as the bell had done, as if a ghost were interfering with a man's job. He opened the study door—he had to push it against the weight of her body. She looked dead enough, but he made quite sure with his automatic almost touching her eyes.

It was time to be gone. He took the automatic with him.

2

They sat and shivered side by side as the dusk came down. They were borne in their bright small smoky cage above the streets. The bus rocked down to Hammersmith. The shop windows sparkled like ice and—"Look," she said, "it's snowing." A few large flakes went drifting by as they crossed the bridge, falling like paper scraps into the dark Thames.

He said, "I'm happy as long as this ride goes on."

"We're seeing each other tomorrow—Jimmy." She always hesitated before his name. It was a silly name for anyone of such bulk and gravity.

He said, "It's the nights that bother me, Anne."

She laughed. "It's going to be wearing." But immediately she became serious. "I'm happy too." About happiness she was always serious; she preferred to laugh when she was miserable. She couldn't avoid being serious about things she cared for, and happiness made her grave at the thought of all the things which might destroy it. She said, "It would be dreadful now if there was a war."

"There won't be a war."

"The last one started with a murder."

"That was an archduke. This is just an old politician."

She said, "Be careful. You'll break the record—Jimmy."

"Damn the record."

She began to hum the tune she'd bought it for, "It's Only Kew to You," and the large flakes fell past the window, melted on the pavement—"a snowflower a man brought from Greenland."

He said, "It's a silly song."

She said, "It's a lovely song—Jimmy. I simply can't call you Jimmy. You aren't Jimmy. You're outsize. Detective Sergeant Mather. You're the reason why people make jokes about policemen's boots."

"What's wrong with dear, anyway?"

"Dear, dear." She tried it out on the tip of her tongue, between lips as vividly stained as a winter berry. "Oh no," she decided, "it's cold. I'll call you that when we've been married ten years."

"Well—darling?"

"Darling, darling. I don't like it. It sounds as if I'd known you a long, long time." The bus went up the hill past the fish-and-chip shops. A brazier glowed, and they could smell the roasting chestnuts. The ride was nearly over; there were only two more streets and a turn to the left by the church, which was already visible, the spire lifted like a long icicle above the houses. The nearer they got to home the more miserable she became; the nearer they got to home the more lightly she talked. She was keeping things off and out of mind: the peeling wallpaper, the long flights to her room, cold supper with Mrs. Brewer, and next day the walk to the agent's, perhaps a job again in the provinces away from him.

Mather said heavily, "You don't care for me like I care for you. It's nearly twenty-four hours before I see you again."

"It'll be more than that if I get a job."

"You don't care. You simply don't care."

She clutched his arm. "Look. Look at that poster." But it was gone before he could see it through the steamy pane. "Europe Mobilizing" lay like a weight on her heart.

"What was it?"

"Oh, just the same old murder again."

"You've got that murder on your mind. It's a week old now. It's got nothing to do with us."

"No, it hasn't, has it?"

"If it had happened here, we'd have caught him by now."

"I wonder why he did it."

"Politics. Patriotism."

"Well. Here we are. It might be a good thing to get off. Don't look so miserable. I thought you said you were happy?"

"That was five minutes ago."

"Oh," she said out of her light and heavy heart, "one lives quickly these days." They kissed under the lamp; she had to stretch to reach him. He was comforting like a large dog, even when he was sullen and stupid, but one didn't have to send away a dog alone in the cold dark night.

"Anne," he said, "we'll be married, won't we, after Christmas?"

"We haven't a penny," she said, "you know. Not a penny— Jimmy."

"I'll get a rise."

"You'll be late for duty."

"Damn it, you don't care."

She jeered at him, "Not a scrap—dear," and walked away from him up the street to Number 54, praying, Let me get some money quick; let *this* go on *this* time. She hadn't any faith in herself. A man passed her, going up the road. He looked cold and strung-up as he passed in his black overcoat. He had a harelip. Poor devil, she thought, and forgot him, opening the door of 54, climbing the long flights to the top floor (the carpet stopped on the first), putting on the new record, hugging to her heart the silly, senseless words, the slow, sleepy tune:

> *It's only Kew*
> *To you,*
> *But to me* \
> *It's Paradise.*
> *They are only blue*
> *Petunias to you,*
> *But to me*
> *They are your eyes.*

The man with the harelip came back down the street. Fast walking hadn't made him warm; like Kay in "The Snow Queen," he bore the cold within him as he walked. The flakes went on falling, melting into slush on the pavement; the words of a song dropped from the lit room on the third floor, the scrape of a used needle.

> They say that's a snowflower
> A man brought from Greenland.
> I say it's the lightness, the coolness, the whiteness
> Of your hand.

The man hardly paused. He went on down the street, walking fast. He felt no pain from the chip of ice in his breast.

3

Raven sat at an empty table in the Corner House, near a marble pillar. He stared with distaste at the long list of sweet iced drinks, of parfaits and sundaes and coupes and splits. Somebody at the next little table was eating brown bread and butter and drinking Horlick's. He wilted under Raven's gaze and put up his newspaper. One word, "Ultimatum," ran across the top line.

Mr. Cholmondeley picked his way between the tables.

He was fat and wore an emerald ring. His wide square face fell in folds over his collar. He looked like a real-estate man or perhaps a man more than usually successful in selling women's belts. He sat down at Raven's table and said, "Good evening."

Raven said, "I thought you were never coming, Mr. Chol-mon-deley," pronouncing every syllable.

"Chumley, my dear man, Chumley," Mr. Cholmondeley corrected him.

"It doesn't matter how it's pronounced. I don't suppose it's your own name."

"After all, I chose it," Mr. Cholmondeley said. His ring flashed under the great inverted bowls of light as he turned the pages of the menu. "Have a parfait."

"It's odd wanting to eat ice in this weather. You've only got to stay outside if you're hot. I don't want to waste any time, Mr. Cholmon-deley. Have you brought the money? I'm broke."

Mr. Cholmondeley said, "They do a very good Maiden's Dream. Not to speak of Alpine Glow. Or the Knickerbocker Glory."

"I haven't had a thing since Calais."

"Give me the letter," Mr. Cholmondeley said. "Thank you." He told the waitress, "I'll have an Alpine Glow with a glass of kümmel over it."

"The money," Raven said.

"Here in this case."

"They are all fivers."

"You can't expect to be paid two hundred in small change. And it's nothing to do with me," Mr. Cholmondeley said; "I'm merely the agent." His eyes softened as they rested on a Raspberry Split at the next table. He confessed wistfully to Raven, "I've got a sweet tooth."

"Don't you want to hear about it?" Raven said. "The old woman—"

"Please, please," Mr. Cholmondeley said, "I want to hear nothing. I'm just an agent. I take no responsibility. My clients—"

Raven twisted his harelip at him with sour contempt. "That's a fine name for them."

"How long the waitress is with my parfait," Mr. Cholmondeley complained. "My clients are really quite the best people. These acts of violence—they regard them as war."

"And I and the old man—" Raven said.

"Are in the front trench." He began to laugh softly at his own humour. His great white open face was like a curtain on which you can throw grotesque images: a rabbit, a man with horns. His small eyes twinkled with pleasure at the mass of ice cream which was borne towards him in a tall glass. He said, "You did your work very well, very neatly. They are quite satisfied with you. You'll be able to take a long holiday now." He was fat, he was vulgar, he was false, but he gave an impression of great power as he sat there with the cream dripping from his mouth. He was prosperity, he was one of those who possessed things; but Raven possessed nothing but the contents of the wallet, the clothes he stood up in, the harelip, the automatic he should have left behind.

He said, "I'll be moving."

"Good-bye, my man, good-bye," Mr. Cholmondeley said, sucking through a straw.

Raven rose and went. Dark and thin and made for destruction, he wasn't at ease among the little tables, among the bright fruit drinks. He went out into the Circus and up Shaftesbury Avenue. The shop windows were full of tinsel and hard red Christmas berries. It maddened him, the sentiment of it. His hands clenched in his pockets. He leaned his face against a modiste's window and jeered silently through the glass. A Jewish girl with a neat curved figure bent over a dummy. He fed his eyes contemptuously on her legs and hips; so much flesh, he thought, on sale in the Christmas window.

A kind of subdued cruelty drove him into the shop. He let his harelip loose on the girl when she came towards him with the same pleasure that he might have turned a machine gun on a picture gallery. He said, "That dress in the window. How much?"

She said, "Five guineas." She wouldn't "sir" him. His lip was like a badge of class. It revealed the poverty of parents who couldn't afford a clever surgeon.

He said, "It's pretty, isn't it?"

She lisped at him genteelly, "It's been vewwy much admired."

"Soft. Thin. You'd have to take care of a dress like that, eh? Do for someone pretty and well off?"

She lied without interest, "It's a model." She was a woman; she knew all about it; she knew how cheap and vulgar the little shop really was.

"It's got class, eh?"

"Oh yes," she said, catching the eye of a dago in a purple suit through the pane, "it's got class."

"All right," he said. "I'll give you five pounds for it." He took a note from Mr. Cholmondeley's wallet.

"Shall I pack it up?"

"No," he said. "The girl'll fetch it." He grinned at her with his raw lip. "You see, she's class. This the best dress you have?" And when she nodded and took the note away he said, "It'll just suit Alice then."

And so out into the avenue with a little of his scorn expressed, out into Frith Street and round the corner into the German café where he kept a room. A shock awaited him there, a little fir tree in a tub hung with coloured glass, a crib. He said to the old man who owned the café, "You believe in this? This junk?"

"Is there going to be war again?" the old man said. "It's terrible what you read."

"All this business of no room in the inn. They used to give us plum pudding. A decree from Caesar Augustus. You see I know the stuff, I'm educated. We used to have it read us once a year."

"I have seen one war."

"I hate the sentiment."

"Well," the old man said, "it's good for business."

Raven picked up the bambino. The cradle came with it, all of a piece—cheap painted plaster. "They put him on the spot, eh? You see I know the whole story. I'm educated."

He went upstairs to his room. It hadn't been seen to: there was still dirty water in the basin, and the ewer was empty. He remembered the fat man saying, "Chumley, my man, Chumley. It's pronounced Chumley," flashing his emerald ring. He called furiously, "Alice," over the banisters.

She came out of the next room, a slattern, one shoulder too high, with wisps of fair bleached hair over her face. She said, "You needn't shout."

He said, "It's a pigsty in there. You can't treat me like that. Go in and clean it." He hit her on the side of the head, and she cringed away from him, not daring to say anything but, "Who do you think you are?"

"Get on," he said, "you humpbacked bitch." He began to laugh at her when she crouched over the bed. "I've bought you a Christmas dress, Alice. Here's the receipt. Go and fetch it. It's a lovely dress. It'll suit you."

"You think you're funny," she said.

"I've paid a fiver for this joke. Hurry, Alice, or the shop'll be shut." But she got her own back, calling up the stairs, "I won't look worse than what you do with that split lip." Everyone in the house could hear her: the old man in the café, his wife in the parlour, the customers at the counter. He imagined their smiles. "Go it, Alice, what an ugly pair you are." He didn't really suffer; he had been fed the poison from boyhood drop by drop; he hardly noticed its bitterness now.

He went to the window and opened it and scratched on the sill. The kitten came to him, making little rushes along the drainpipe, feinting at his hand. "You little bitch," he said, "you little bitch." He took a small twopenny carton of cream out of his overcoat pocket and spilled it in his soap dish. She stopped playing and rushed at him with a tiny cry. He picked her up by the scruff and put her on top of his chest of drawers with the cream. She wriggled from his hand; she was no larger than the rat he'd trained in the home, but softer. He scratched her behind the ear, and she struck back at him in a preoccupied way. Her tongue quivered on the surface of the milk.

Dinnertime, he told himself. With all that money he could go anywhere. He could have a slap-up meal at Simpson's with the businessmen—cut off the joint and any number of vegs.

When he got by the public call box in the dark corner below the stairs he caught his name, "Raven." The old man said, "He always has a room here. He's been away."

"You," a strange voice said, "what's your name—Alice—show me his room. Keep an eye on the door, Saunders."

Raven went on his knees inside the telephone box. He left the door ajar because he never liked to be shut in. He couldn't see out, but he had no need to see the owner of the voice to recognize police, plain clothes, the Yard accent. The man was so near that the floor of the box vibrated to his tread. Then he came down again. "There's no one there. He's taken his hat and coat. He must have gone out."

"He might have," the old man said. "He's a soft-walking sort of fellow."

The stranger began to question them. "What's he like?"

The old man and the girl both said in a breath, "A harelip."

"That's useful," the detective said. "Don't touch his room. I'll be sending a man round to take his fingerprints. What sort of a fellow is he?"

Raven could hear every word. He couldn't imagine what they were after. He knew he'd left no clues; he wasn't a man who imagined things, he knew. He carried the picture of that room and flat in his brain as clearly as if he had the photographs. They had nothing against him. It had been against his orders to keep the automatic, but he could feel it now safe under his armpit. Besides, if they had picked up any clue they'd have stopped him at Dover. He listened to the voices with a dull anger. He wanted his dinner; he hadn't had a square meal for twenty-four hours, and now with two hundred pounds in his pocket he could buy anything, anything.

"I can believe it," the old man said. "Why, tonight he even made fun of my poor wife's crib."

"A bloody bully," the girl said. "*I* shan't be sorry when you've locked him up."

He told himself with surprise, They hate me.

She said, "He's ugly through and through. That lip of his. It gives you the creeps."

"An ugly customer all right."

"I wouldn't have him in the house," the old man said. "But he pays. You can't turn away someone who pays. Not in these days."

"Has he friends?"

"You make me laugh," Alice said. "Him friends. What would he do with friends?"

He began to laugh quietly to himself on the floor of the little dark box. That's me they're talking about, me. He stared up at the pane of glass with his hand on his automatic.

"You seem kind of bitter. What's he been doing to you? He was going to give you a dress, wasn't he?"

"Just his dirty joke."

"You were going to take it, though."

"You bet I wasn't. Do you think I'd take a present from him? I was going to sell it back to them and show him the money, and wasn't I going to laugh!"

He thought again with bitter interest, They hate me. If they open this door I'll shoot the lot.

"I'd like to take a swipe at that lip of his. I'd laugh. I'd say I'd laugh."

"I'll put a man," the strange voice said, "across the road. Tip him the wink if our man comes in." The café door closed.

"Oh," the old man said. "I wish my wife was here. She would not miss this for ten shillings."

"I'll give her a ring," Alice said. "She'll be chatting at Mason's. She can come right over and bring Mrs. Mason too. Let 'em all join in the fun. It was only a week ago Mrs. Mason said she didn't want to see his ugly face in her shop again."

"Yes, be a good girl, Alice. Give her a ring."

Raven reached up his hand and took the bulb out of the fitment; he stood up and flattened himself against the wall of the box. Alice opened the door and shut herself in with him. He put his hand over her mouth before she had time to cry. He said, "Don't you put the pennies in the box. I'll shoot if you do. I'll shoot if you call out. Do what I say." He whispered in her ear. They were as close together as if they were in a single bed. He could feel her crooked shoulder pressed against his chest. He said, "Lift the receiver. Pretend you're talking to the old woman. Go on. I don't care a damn if I shoot you. Say, Hello, Frau Groener."

"Hello, Frau Groener."

"Spill the whole story."

"They are after Raven."

"Why?"

"That five-pound note. They were waiting at the shop."

"What do you mean?"

"They'd got its number. It was stolen."

He'd been double-crossed. His mind worked with mechanical accuracy like a ready-reckoner. You only had to supply it with the figures and it gave you the answer. He was possessed by a deep sullen rage. If Mr. Cholmondeley had been in the box with him he would have shot him; he wouldn't have cared a damn.

"Stolen from where?"

"You ought to know that."

"Don't give me any lip. Where from?"

He didn't even know who Cholmondeley's employers were. It was obvious what had happened: they hadn't trusted him. They had arranged this so that he might be put away. A newsboy went by outside, calling, "Ultimatum. Ultimatum." His mind registered the fact, but no more; it seemed to have nothing to do with him. He repeated, "Where from?"

"I don't know. I don't remember."

With the automatic stuck against her back he tried to plead with her. "Remember, can't you? It's important. I didn't do it."

"I bet you didn't," she said bitterly into the unconnected phone.

"Give me a break. All I want you to do is remember."

She said, "On your life I won't."

"I gave you that dress, didn't I?"

"You didn't. You tried to plant your money, that's all. You didn't know they'd circulated the numbers to every shop in town. We've even got them in the café."

"If I'd done it, why should I want to know where they came from?"

"It'll be a bigger laugh than ever if you get jugged for something you didn't do."

"Alice," the old man called from the café, "is she coming?"

"I'll give you ten pounds."

"Phony notes. No thank you, Mr. Generosity."

"Alice," the old man called again; they could hear him coming along the passage.

"Justice," he said bitterly, jabbing her between the ribs with the automatic.

"You don't need to talk about justice," she said. "Driving me like I was in prison. Hitting me when you feel like it. Spilling ash all over the floor. I've got enough to do with your slops. Milk in the soap dish. Don't talk about justice."

Pressed against him in the tiny dark box she suddenly came alive to him. He was so astonished that he forgot the old man till he had the door of the box open. He whispered passionately, out of the dark, "Don't say a word or I'll plug you." He had them both out of the box in front of him. He said, "Understand this. They aren't going to get me. I'm not going to prison. I don't care a damn if I plug one of you. I don't care if I hang. My father hanged. What's good enough for him— Get along in front of me up to my room. There's hell coming to somebody for this."

When he had them there he locked the door. A customer was ringing the café bell over and over again. He turned on them. "I've got a good mind to plug you. Telling them about my harelip. Why can't you play fair?" He went to the window; he knew there was an easy way down: that was why he had chosen the room. The kitten caught his eye, prowling like a toy tiger in a cage up and down the edge of the chest of drawers, afraid to jump. He lifted her up and threw her on his bed; she tried to bite his finger as she went. Then he got through onto the leads. The clouds were massing up across the moon, and the earth seemed to move with them, an icy barren globe, through the vast darkness.

4

Anne Crowder walked up and down the small room in her heavy tweed coat; she didn't want to waste a shilling on the gas meter, because she wouldn't get her shilling's worth before morning. She told herself, I'm lucky to have got that job. I'm glad to be going off to work again. But she wasn't convinced. It was eight now; they would have four hours together till midnight. She would have to deceive him and tell him she was catching the nine-o'clock, not the five-o'clock train, or he would be sending her back to bed early. He was like that. No romance. She smiled with tenderness and blew on her fingers.

The telephone at the bottom of the house was ringing. She thought it was the doorbell and ran to the mirror in the wardrobe. There wasn't enough light from the dull globe to tell her if her makeup would stand the brilliance of the Astoria Dance Hall. She began making up all over again; if she was pale he would take her home early.

The landlady stuck her head in at the door and said, "It's your gentleman. On the phone."

"On the phone?"

"Yes," the landlady said, sidling in for a good chat, "he sounded all of a jump. Impatient, I should say. Half barked my head off when I wished him good evening."

"Oh," she said despairingly, "it's only his way. You mustn't mind him."

"He's going to call off the evening, I suppose," the landlady said. "It's always the same. You girls who go travelling round never get a square deal. You said *Dick Whittington,* didn't you?"

"No, no; *Aladdin.*"

She pelted down the stairs. She didn't care a damn who saw her hurry. She said, "Is that you, darling?" There was always something wrong with their telephone. She could hear his voice so hoarsely vibrating against her ear she could hardly realize it was his. He said, "You've been ages. This is a public call box. I've put in my last pennies. Listen, Anne, I can't be with you. I'm sorry. It's work. We're onto the man in that safe robbery I told you about. I shall be out all night on it. We've traced one of the notes." His voice beat excitedly against her ear.

She said, "Oh, that's fine, darling. I know you wanted—" But she couldn't keep it up. "Jimmy," she said, "I shan't be seeing you again. For weeks."

He said, "It's tough, I know. I'd been dreaming of— Listen. You'd better not catch that early train; what's the point? There isn't a nine-o'clock. I've been looking them up."

"I know. I just said—"

"You'd better go tonight. Then you can get a rest before rehearsals. Midnight from Euston."

"But I haven't packed."

He took no notice. It was his favourite occupation, planning things, making decisions. He said, "If I'm near the station, I'll try—"

"Your two minutes up."

He said, "Oh hell, I've no coppers. Darling, I love you."

She struggled to bring it out herself, but his name stood in the way, impeded her tongue. She could never bring it out without hesitation. "Ji—" The line went dead on her. She thought bitterly, He oughtn't to go out without coppers. She thought, It's not right, cutting off a detective like that. Then she went back up the stairs. She wasn't crying; it was just as if somebody had died and left her alone and scared, scared of the new faces and the new job, the harsh provincial jokes, the fellows who were fresh; scared of herself, scared of not being able to remember clearly how good it was to be loved.

The landlady said, "I just thought so. Why not come down and have a cup of tea and a good chat? It does you good to talk. Really good. A doctor said to me once it clears the lungs. Stands to reason, don't it? You can't help getting dust up, and a good talk blows it out. I wouldn't bother to pack yet. There's hours and hours. My old man would never of died if he'd talked more. Stands to reason. It was something poisonous in his throat cut him off in his prime. If he'd talked more he'd have blown it out. It's better than spitting."

5

The crime reporter couldn't make himself heard. He kept on trying to say to the chief reporter, "I've got some stuff on that safe robbery."

The chief reporter had had too much to drink. They'd all had too much to drink. He said, "You can go home and read *The Decline and Fall—*"

The crime reporter was a young earnest man who didn't drink and didn't smoke; it shocked him when someone was sick in one of the telephone boxes. He shouted at the top of his voice, "They've traced one of the notes."

"Write it down, write it down, old boy," the chief reporter said, "and then smoke it."

"The man escaped—held up a girl. It's a terribly good story," the earnest young man said. He had an Oxford accent; that was why they had made him crime reporter: it was the news editor's joke.

"Go home and read Gibbon."

The earnest young man caught hold of someone's sleeve. "What's the matter? Are you all crazy? Isn't there going to be any paper or what?"

"War in forty-eight hours," somebody bellowed at him.

"But this is a wonderful story I've got. He held up a girl and an old man, climbed out of a window—"

"Go home. There won't be any room for it."

"They've killed the annual report of the Kensington Kitten Club."

"No 'Round the Shops.' "

"They've made the Limehouse Fire a News in Brief."

"Go home and read Gibbon."

"He got clean away with a policeman watching the front door. The Flying Squad's out. He's armed. The police are taking revolvers. It's a lovely story."

The chief reporter said, "Armed. Go away and put your head in a glass of milk. We'll all be armed in a day or two. They've published their evidence. It's clear as daylight a Serb shot him. Italy's supporting the ultimatum. They've got forty-eight hours to climb down. If you want to buy armament shares hurry and make your fortune."

"You'll be in the army this day week," somebody said.

"Oh no," the young man said; "no, I won't be that. You see, I'm a pacifist."

The man who was sick in the telephone box said, "I'm going home. There isn't any more room in the paper if the Bank of England's blown up."

A little thin piping voice said, "My copy's going in."

"I tell you there isn't any room."

"There'll be room for mine. Gas Masks for All. Special Air Raid Practices for Civilians in every town of more than fifty thousand inhabitants." He giggled.

"The funny thing is—it's—it's—" But nobody ever heard what it was. A boy opened the door and flung them in a pull of the middle page: damp letters on a damp grey sheet; the headlines came off on your hands. "Yugoslavia Asks for Time. Adriatic Fleet at War Stations. Paris Rioters Break into Italian Embassy." Everyone was suddenly quite quiet as an airplane went by, driving low overhead through the dark, heading south, a scarlet tail-lamp, pale transparent wings in the moonlight. They watched it through the great glass ceiling, and suddenly nobody wanted to have another drink.

The chief reporter said, "I'm tired. I'm going to bed."

"Shall I follow up this story?" the crime reporter said.

"If it'll make you happy, but *that's* the only news from now on."

They stared up at the glass ceiling, the moon, the empty sky.

6

The station clock marked three minutes to midnight. The ticket collector at the barrier said, "There's room in the front."

"A friend's seeing me off," Anne Crowder said. "Can't I get in at this end and go up front when we start?"

"They've locked the doors."

She looked desperately past him. They were turning out the lights in the buffet; no more trains from that platform.

"You'll have to hurry, miss."

The poster of an evening paper caught her eye, and as she ran down the train, looking back as often as she was able, she couldn't help remembering that war might be declared before they met again. He would go to it. He always did what other people did, she told herself with irritation, but she knew that that was the reliability she loved. She wouldn't have loved him if he'd been queer, had his own opinions about things; she lived too closely to thwarted genius, to second-touring-company actresses who thought they ought to be Cochran stars, to admire difference. She wanted her man to be ordinary; she wanted to be able to know what he'd say next.

A line of lamp-struck faces went by her. The train was full, so full that in the first-class carriages you saw strange shy awkward people who were not at ease in the deep seats, who feared the ticket collector would turn them out. She gave up the search for a third-class carriage, opened a door, dropped her *Woman and Beauty* on the only seat, and struggled back to the window over legs and protruding suitcases. The engine was getting up steam, the smoke blew back up the platform; it was difficult to see as far as the barrier.

A hand pulled at her sleeve. "Excuse me," a fat man said, "if you've quite finished with that window. I want to buy some chocolate."

She said, "Just one moment, please. Somebody's seeing me off."

"He's not here. It's too late. You can't monopolize the window like that. I must have some chocolate." He swept her to one side and waved an emerald ring under the light. She tried to look over his shoulder to the barrier; he almost filled the window. He called, "Boy, boy," waving the emerald ring. He said, "What chocolate have you got? No, not Motorist's, not Mexican. Something sweet."

Suddenly through a crack she saw Mather. He was past the barrier, he was coming down the train, looking for her, looking in all the third-class carriages, running past the first-class. She implored the fat man, "Please, please do let me come. I can see my friend."

"In a moment. In a moment. Have you Nestlé's? Give me a shilling packet."

"Please let me."

"Haven't you anything smaller," the boy said, "than a ten-shilling note?"

Mather went by, running past the first-class. She hammered on the window, but he didn't hear her among the whistles and the beat of trolley wheels, the last packing cases rolling into the van. Doors slammed, a whistle blew, the train began to move.

"Please. Please."

"I must get my change," the fat man said, and the boy ran beside the carriage, counting the shillings into his palm. When she got to the window and leaned out they were past the platform; she could only see on a wedge of asphalt a small figure who couldn't see her. An elderly woman said, "You oughtn't to lean out like that. It's dangerous."

She trod on their toes getting back to her seat; she felt unpopularity well up all around her; everyone was thinking, She oughtn't to be in the carriage. What's the good of our paying first-class fares when— But she wouldn't cry; she was fortified by all the conventional remarks which came automatically to her mind about spilled milk and it will all be the same in fifty years. Nevertheless she noted with deep dislike, on the label dangling from the fat man's suitcase his destination, which was the same as hers, Nottwich. He sat opposite her with the *Spectator* and the *Evening News* and the *Financial Times* on his lap, eating sweet milk chocolate.

Two

1

Raven walked with his handkerchief over his lip across Soho Square, Oxford Street, up Charlotte Street. It was dangerous, but not so dangerous as showing his harelip. He turned to the left and then to the right into a narrow street, where big-breasted women in aprons called across to each other and a few solemn children scooted up the gutter. He stopped by a door with a brass plate: Dr. Alfred Yogel on the second floor, on the first floor the North American Dental Company. He went upstairs and rang the bell. There was a smell of greens from below, and somebody had drawn a naked torso in pencil on the wall.

A woman in nurse's uniform opened the door, a woman with a mean lined face and untidy grey hair. Her uniform needed washing; it was spotted with grease marks and what might have been blood or iodine. She brought with her a harsh smell of chemicals and disinfectants. When she saw Raven holding his handkerchief over his mouth she said, "The dentist's on the floor below."

"I want to see Doctor Yogel."

She looked him over closely, suspiciously, running her eyes down his dark coat. "He's busy."

"I can wait."

One naked globe swung behind her head in the dingy passage. "He doesn't generally see people as late as this."

"I'll pay for the trouble," Raven said. She judged him with just the same appraising stare as the doorkeeper at a shady night club. She said, "You can come in." He followed her into a waiting room: the same bare globe, a chair, a round oak table splashed with dark paint. She shut him in, and he heard her voice start in the next room. It went on and on. He picked up the only magazine, *Good Housekeeping* of eighteen months back, and began mechanically to read. "Bare walls are very popular today, perhaps one picture to give the necessary point of colour . . ."

The nurse opened the door and jerked her hand. "He'll see you." Dr. Yogel was washing his hands in a fixed basin behind his long yellow desk and swivel chair. There was no other furniture in the room except a kitchen chair, a cabinet, and a long couch. His hair was jet black. It looked as if it had been dyed, and there was not much of it. It was plastered in thin strands across the scalp. When he turned he showed a plump, hard, bonhomous face, a thick sensual mouth. He said, "And what can we do for you?" You felt he was more accustomed to deal with women than with men. The nurse stood harshly behind, waiting.

Raven lowered his handkerchief. He said, "Can you do anything about this lip quickly?"

Dr. Yogel came up and prodded it with a little fat forefinger. "I'm not a surgeon."

Raven said, "I can pay."

Dr. Yogel said, "It's a job for a surgeon. It's not in my line at all."

"I know that," Raven said and caught the quick flicker of glances between the nurse and Dr. Yogel. Dr. Yogel lifted up the lip on each side; his fingernails were not quite clean. He watched Raven carefully and said, "If you come back tomorrow at ten . . ." His breath smelled faintly of brandy.

"No," Raven said. "I want it done now, at once."

"Ten pounds," Dr. Yogel said quickly.

"All right."

"In cash."

"I've got it with me."

Dr. Yogel sat down at his desk. "And now if you'll give me your name . . ."

"You don't need to know my name."

Dr. Yogel said gently, "Any name."

"Chumley, then."

"C-h-o-l-m-o —"

"No. Spell it C-h-u-m-l-e-y."

Dr. Yogel filled up a slip of paper and handed it to the nurse. She went outside and closed the door behind her. Dr. Yogel went to the cabinet and brought out a tray of knives. Raven said, "The light's bad."

"I'm used to it," Dr. Yogel said. "I've a good eye." But as he held up a knife to the light his hand very slightly trembled. He said softly, "Lie down on the couch, old man."

Raven lay down. He said, "I knew a girl who came to you. Name of Page. She said you did her trick fine."

Dr. Yogel said, "She oughtn't to talk about it."

"Oh," Raven said, "you are safe with me. I don't go back on a fellow who treats me right." Dr. Yogel took a case like a portable gramophone out of his cabinet and carried it over to the couch. He produced a long tube and a mask. He smiled gently and said, "We don't run to anesthetists here, old man."

"Stop," Raven said; "you're not going to give me gas."

"It would hurt without it, old man," Dr. Yogel said, approaching with the mask; "it would hurt like hell."

Raven sat up and pushed the mask aside. "I won't have it," he said, "not gas. I've never had gas. I've never passed out yet. I like to see what's going on."

Dr. Yogel laughed gently and pulled at Raven's lip in a playful way. "Better get used to it, old man. We'll all be gassed in a day or two."

"What do you mean?"

"Well, it looks like war, doesn't it?" Dr. Yogel said, talking rapidly and unwinding more tube, turning screws in a soft, shaking, inexorable way. "The Serbs can't shoot a minister of war like that and get away with it. Italy's ready to come in. And the French are warming up. We'll be in it ourselves inside a week."

Raven said, "All that because an old man—" He explained, "I haven't read the papers."

"I wish I'd known beforehand," Dr. Yogel said, making conversation, fixing his cylinder. "I'd have made a fortune in munitions shares. They've gone up to the sky, old man. Now lean back. It won't take a moment." He again approached the mask. He said, "You've only got to breathe deep, old man."

Raven said, "I told you I wouldn't have gas. Get that straight. You can cut me about as much as you like, but I won't have gas."

"It's very silly of you, old man," Dr. Yogel said. "It's going to hurt." He went back to the cabinet and again picked up a knife, but his hand shook more than ever. He was frightened of something. And then Raven heard from outside the tiny tinkle a telephone makes when the receiver is lifted. He jumped up from the couch. It was bitterly cold, but Dr. Yogel was sweating. He stood by the cabinet holding his surgical knife, unable to say a word. Raven said, "Keep quiet. Don't speak." He flung the door suddenly open, and there was the nurse in the little dim hall with the telephone at her ear. Raven stood sideways so that he could keep his eye on both of them. "Put back that receiver," he said. She put it back, watching him with her little mean conscienceless eyes. He said furiously, "You double-crossing — !" He said, "I've got a mind to shoot you both."

"Old man," Dr. Yogel said, "old man, you've got it all wrong"; but the nurse said nothing. She had all the guts in their partnership; she was toughened by a long career of illegalities, by not a few deaths.

Raven said, "Get away from that phone." He took the knife out of Dr. Yogel's hand and hacked and sawed at the telephone wire. He was touched by something he had never felt before; a sense of injustice stammered on his tongue. These people were of his own kind; they didn't belong inside the legal borders; for the second time in one day he had been betrayed by the lawless. He had always been alone, but never as alone as this. The telephone wire gave. He wouldn't speak another word for fear his temper might master him and he might shoot. This wasn't the time for shooting. He went downstairs in a dark loneliness of spirit, his handkerchief over his face, and from the little wireless shop at the street corner heard, "We have received the following notice . . ." The same voice followed him down the street from the open windows of the little impoverished homes, the suave, expressionless voice from every house,

"New Scotland Yard. Wanted. James Raven. Aged about twenty-eight. Easily recognizable by his harelip. A little above the middle height. Last seen wearing a dark overcoat and a black felt hat. Any information leading to the arrest . . ." Raven walked away from the voice, out into the traffic of Oxford Street, bearing south.

There were too many things he didn't understand—this war they were talking of, why he had been double-crossed. He wanted to find Cholmondeley. Cholmondeley was of no account: he was acting under orders; but if he found Cholmondeley he could squeeze out of him— He was harassed, hunted, lonely; he bore with him a sense of great injustice and a curious pride. Going down the Charing Cross Road, past the music shops and the rubber-goods shops, he swelled with it; after all it needed a man to start a war as he was doing.

He had no idea where Cholmondeley lived; the only clue he had was an accommodation address. It occurred to him that there was a faint chance that if he watched the small shop to which Cholmondeley's letters were sent he might see him—a very faint chance, but it was strengthened by the fact of his escape. Already the news was on the air; it would be in the evening papers. Cholmondeley might want to clear out of the way for a while, and there was just a possibility that before he went he would call for letters. But that depended on whether he used that address for other letters besides Raven's. Raven wouldn't have believed there was one chance in a thousand if it were not that Cholmondeley was a fool. You didn't have to eat many ices with him to learn that.

The shop was in a side street opposite a theatre. It was a tiny one-roomed place in which was sold nothing above the level of *Film Fun* and *Breezy Stories*. There were postcards from Paris in sealed envelopes, American and French magazines, and books on flagellation in paper jackets for which the pimply youth or his sister, whoever was in the shop, charged twenty shillings—fifteen shillings back if you returned the book.

It wasn't an easy shop to watch. A woman policeman kept an eye on the tarts at the corner, and opposite there was just the long blank theatre wall, the gallery door. Against the wall you were as exposed as a fly against wallpaper, unless, he thought, waiting for the lights to flash green and let him pass, unless the play was popular.

And it was popular. Although the doors wouldn't open for another hour, there was quite a long queue for the gallery. Raven hired a camp stool with almost his last small change and sat down. The shop was only just across the way. The youth wasn't in charge, but his sister. She sat there just inside the door in an old green dress that might have been stripped from one of the billiard tables in the pub next door. She had a square face that could never have looked young, a squint that her heavy steel spectacles did nothing to disguise. She might have been any age from twenty to forty; a parody of a woman, dirty and depraved, crouched under the most lovely figures, the most beautiful vacant faces, the smut photographers could hire.

Raven watched; with a handkerchief over his mouth, one of sixty in the gallery queue, he watched. He saw a young man stop and eye *Plaisirs de Paris* furtively and hurry on; he saw an old man go into the shop and come out again with a brown paper parcel. Somebody from the queue went across and bought cigarettes.

An elderly woman in pince-nez sat beside him. She said over her shoulder, "That's why I always liked Galsworthy. He was a gentleman. You knew where you were, if you know what I mean."

"It always seems to be the Balkans."

"I liked *Loyalties*."

"He was such a humane man."

A man stood between Raven and the shop, holding up a little square of paper. He put it in his mouth and held up another square. A tart ambled by on the other side of the road and said something to the girl in the shop. The man put the second piece of paper in his mouth.

"They say the fleet—"

"He makes you *think*. That's what I like."

Raven thought, If he doesn't come before the queue begins to move I'll have to go.

"Anything in the papers?"

"Nothing new."

The man in the road took the papers out of his mouth and began to tear them and fold them and tear them. Then he opened them out, and it was a paper St. George's Cross, blowing flimsily in the cold wind.

"He used to subscribe heavily to the Antivivisection Society. Mrs. Milbanke told me. She showed me one of his cheques with his signature."

"He was really humane."

"And a *really* great writer."

A girl and a boy who looked happy applauded the man with the paper flag, and he took off his cap and began to come down the queue, collecting coppers. A taxi drew up at the end of the street, and a man got out. It was Cholmondeley. He went into the bookshop, and the girl got up and followed him. Raven counted his money. He had two and sixpence and a hundred and ninety-five pounds in stolen notes he could do nothing with. He sank his face deeper in his handkerchief and got up hurriedly like a man taken ill. The paper tearer reached him, held out his cap, and Raven saw with envy the odd dozen pennies, a sixpence, a threepenny bit. He would have given a hundred pounds for the contents of that cap. He pushed the man roughly and walked away.

At the other end of the road there was a taxi rank. He stood there bowed against the wall, a sick man, until Cholmondeley came out.

He said, "Follow that taxi," and sank back with a sense of relief, moving back up Charing Cross Road, Tottenham Court Road, the Euston Road, where all the bicycles had been taken in for the night and the secondhand-car dealers from that end of Great Portland Street were having a quick one before they bore their old school ties and their tired, tarnished bonhomie back to their lodgings. He wasn't used to being hunted; this was better, to hunt.

Nor did the metre fail him. He had a shilling to spare when Mr. Cholmondeley led the way in by the Euston war memorial to the great smoky entrance, and rashly he gave it to the driver; rashly because there was a long wait ahead of him with nothing but his hundred and ninety-five pounds to buy a sandwich with. For Mr. Cholmondeley led the way with two porters behind him to the left-luggage counter, depositing there three suitcases, a portable typewriter, a bag of golf clubs, a small attaché case, and a hatbox. Raven heard him ask from which platform the midnight train went.

Raven sat down in the great hall beside a model of Stephenson's Rocket. He had to think. There was only one midnight train. If Cholmondeley was going to report, his employers were somewhere in the smoky industrial north, for there wasn't a stop before Nottwich. But again he was faced with his wealthy poverty; the numbers of the notes had been circulated everywhere; the booking clerks would almost certainly have them. The trail for a moment seemed to stop at the barrier to number 3 platform.

But slowly a plan did form in Raven's mind as he sat under the Rocket among the bundles and crumbs of sandwich eaters. He *had* a chance, for it was possible that the ticket collectors on the trains had not been given the numbers. It was the kind of loophole the authorities might forget. There remained, of course, this objection: that the note would eventually give away his presence on the north-bound train. He would have to take a ticket to the limit of the journey, and it would be easy enough to trace him to the town where he alighted. The hunt would follow him, but there might be a time lag of half a day in which his own hunt could get nearer to *his* prey. Raven could never realize other people; they didn't seem to him to live in the same way as he lived; and though he bore a grudge against Mr. Cholmondeley, hated him enough to kill him, he couldn't imagine Mr. Cholmondeley's own fears and motives. He was the greyhound and Mr. Cholmondeley only the mechanical hare; only in this case the greyhound was chased in its turn by another mechanical hare.

He was hungry, but he couldn't risk changing a note. He hadn't even a copper to pass him into the lavatory. After a while he got up and walked the station to keep warm among the frozen smuts, the icy turbulence. At eleven-thirty he saw from behind a chocolate machine Mr. Cholmondeley fetch his luggage, followed him at a distance until he passed through the barrier and down the length of the lit train. The Christmas crowds had begun. They were differ-ent from the ordinary crowd: you had a sense of people going home. Raven stood back in the shadow of an indicator and heard their laughter and calls, saw smiling faces raised under the great lamps. The pillars of the station had been decorated to look like enormous crackers. The suitcases were full of presents; a girl had a sprig of holly in her coat; high up under the roof dangled a bough of mistletoe lit by floodlamps. When Raven moved he could feel the automatic rubbing beneath his arm.

At two minutes to twelve Raven ran forward. The engine smoke was blowing back along the platform, the doors were slammed. He said to the collector at the barrier, "I haven't time to get a ticket. I'll pay on the train."

He tried the first carriages. They were full and locked. A porter shouted to him to go up front, and he ran on. He was only just in time. He couldn't find a seat but stood in the corridor with his face pressed against the pane to hide his harelip, watching London re-cede from him: a signal box lit up so that you could see the sauce-pan of cocoa heating on the stove, a signal going green, a long line of blackened houses standing rigid against the cold-starred sky;

watching because there was nothing else to do to keep his lip hidden, but like a man watching something he loves slide back from him out of his reach.

2

Mather walked back up the platform. He was sorry to have missed Anne, but it wasn't important. He would be seeing her again in a few weeks. It was not that his love was any less than hers but that his mind was more firmly anchored. He was on a job. If he pulled it off, he might be promoted: they could marry. Without any difficulty at all he wiped his mind clear of her.

Saunders was waiting on the other side of the barrier. Mather said, "We'll be off."

"Where next?"

"Charlie's."

They sat in the back seat of a car and dived back into the narrow dirty streets behind the station. A prostitute put her tongue out at them. Saunders said, "What about J-J-J-Joe's?"

"I don't think so, but we'll try it."

The car drew up two doors away from a fried fish shop. A man sitting beside the driver got down and waited for orders. "Round to the back, Frost," Mather said. He gave him two minutes and then hammered on the door of the fish shop. A light went on inside, and Mather could see through the window the long counter, the stock of old newspapers, the dead grill. The door opened a crack. He put his foot in and pushed it wide. He said, "Evening, Charlie," looking round.

"Mr. Mather," Charlie said. He was as fat as an eastern eunuch, and he swayed his great hips coyly when he walked, like a street woman.

"I want to talk to you," Mather said.

"Oh, I'm delighted," Charlie said. "Step this way, Mr. Mather. I was just off to bed."

"I bet you were," Mather said. "Got a full house down there tonight?"

"Oh, Mr. Mather. What a wag you are. Just one or two Oxford boys."

"Listen. I'm looking for a fellow with a harelip. About twenty-eight years old."

"He's not here."

"Dark coat, black hat."

"I don't know him, Mr. Mather."

"I'd like to take a look over your basement."

"Of course, Mr. Mather. There are just one or two Oxford boys. Do you mind if I go down first? Just to introduce you, Mr. Mather." He led the way down the stone stairs. "It's safer."

"I can look after myself," Mather said. "Saunders, stay in the shop."

Charlie opened a door. "Now, boys, don't be scared. Mr. Mather's a friend of mine." They faced him in an ominous line at the end of the room, the Oxford boys, with their broken noses and their cauliflower ears, the dregs of pugilism.

"Evening," Mather said. The tables had been swept clear of drink and cards. He plodded down the last steps into the stone-floored room.

Charlie said, "Now, boys, you don't need to get scared."

"Why don't you get a few Cambridge boys into this club?" Mather said.

"Oh, what a wag you are, Mr. Mather."

They followed him with their eyes as he crossed the floor. They wouldn't speak to him; he was the Enemy. They didn't have to be diplomats like Charlie, they could show their hatred. They watched every move he made. Mather said, "What are you keeping in that cupboard?" Their eyes followed him as he went towards the cupboard door.

Charlie said, "Give the boys a chance, Mr. Mather. They don't mean any harm. This is one of the best-run clubs—" Mather pulled open the door of the cupboard. Four women fell into the room. They were like toys turned from the same mould with their bright, brittle hair.

Mather laughed. He said, "The joke's on me. That's a thing I never expected in one of your clubs, Charlie. Good night all." The girls got up and dusted themselves. None of the men spoke.

"Really, Mr. Mather," Charlie said, blushing all the way upstairs, "I do wish this hadn't happened in my club. I don't know what you'll think. But the boys didn't mean any harm. Only you know how it is. They don't like to leave their sisters alone."

"What's that?" Saunders said at the top of the stairs.

"So I said they could bring their sisters, and the dear girls just sit around . . ."

"What's that?" Saunders said. "G-g-g-girls?"

"Don't forget, Charlie," Mather said. "Fellow with a harelip. You'd better let me know if he turns up here. You don't want your club closed up."

"Is there a reward?"

"There'd be a reward for you all right."

They got back into the car. "Pick up Frost," Mather said. "Then Joe's." He took his notebook out and crossed off another name. "And after Joe's six more—"

"We shan't be f-f-finished till three," Saunders said.

"Routine. He's out of town by now. But sooner or later he'll cash another note."

"Fingerprints?"

"Plenty. There was enough on his soap dish to stock an album. Must be a clean sort of fellow. Oh, he doesn't stand a chance. It's just a question of time."

The lights of Tottenham Court Road flashed across their faces. The windows of the big shops were still lit up. "That's a nice bedroom suite," Mather said.

"It's a lot of f-fuss, isn't it?" Saunders said. "About a few notes, I mean. When there may be a w-w-w-w—"

Mather said, "If those fellows over there had our efficiency there mightn't be a war. We'd have caught the murderer by now. Then all the world could see whether the Serbs— Oh," he said softly, as Heal's went by, a glow of soft colour, a gleam of steel, allowing himself about the furthest limits of his fancy, "I'd like to be tackling a job like that. A murderer with all the world watching."

"Just a few n-notes," Saunders complained.

"No, you are wrong," Mather said. "It's the routine which counts. Five-pound notes today. It may be something better next time. But it's the routine which matters. That's how I see it," he said, letting his anchored mind stretch the cable as far as it could go as they drove round St. Giles's Circus and on towards Seven Dials, stopping every hole the thief might take, one by one. "It doesn't matter to me if there is a war. When it's over I'll still want to be going on with this job. It's the organization I like. I always want to be on the side that organizes. On the other you get your geniuses, of course, but you get all your shabby tricksters, you get all the cruelty and the selfishness and the pride."

You got it all, except the pride, in Joe's, where they looked up from their bare tables and let him run the place through, the extra aces back in the sleeve, the watered spirit out of sight, facing him each with his individual mark of cruelty and egotism. Even pride was perhaps there in a corner, bent over a sheet of paper, playing an endless game of double noughts and crosses against himself because there was no one else in that club he deigned to play with.

Mather again crossed off a name and drove southwest towards Kensington. All over London there were other cars doing the same: he was part of an organization. He did not want to be a leader, he did not even wish to give himself up to some God-sent fanatic of a leader. He liked to feel that he was one of thousands, more or less equal, working for a concrete end: not equality of opportunity, not government by the people or by the richest or by the best, but simply to do away with crime, which meant uncertainty. He liked to be certain, to feel that one day quite inevitably he would marry Anne Crowder.

The loud speaker in the car said, "Police cars proceed back to the King's Cross area for intensified search. Raven driven to Euston Station about seven P.M. May not have left by train." Mather leaned across to the driver. "Right about and back to Euston." They were by Vauxhall. Another police car came past them through the Vauxhall tunnel. Mather raised his hand. They followed it back over the river. The floodlit clock on the Shell-Mex building showed half-past one. The light was on in the clock tower at Westminster: Parliament was having an all-night sitting as the opposition fought their losing fight against mobilization.

It was six o'clock in the morning when they drove back towards the Embankment. Saunders was asleep. He said, "That's fine." He was dreaming: he had no impediment in his speech; he had an independent income; he was drinking champagne with a girl; everything was fine. Mather totted things up in his notebook. He said to Saunders, "He got on a train for sure, I'd bet you—" Then he saw that Saunders was asleep and slipped a rug across his knees and began to consider again. They turned in at the gates of New Scotland Yard.

Mather saw a light in the chief inspector's room and went up.

"Anything to report?" Kusack asked.

"Nothing. He must have caught a train, sir."

"We've got a little to go on at this end. Raven followed somebody to Euston. We are trying to find the driver of the first car. And another thing, he went to a doctor called Yogel to try and get his lip altered. Offered some more of those notes. Still handy, too, with that automatic. We've got him taped. As a kid he was sent to an industrial school. He's been smart enough to keep out of our way since. I can't think why he's broken out like this. A smart fellow like that. He's blazing a trail."

"Has he much money besides the notes?"

"We don't think so. Got an idea, Mather?"

Colour was coming into the sky above the city. Kusack switched off his table lamp and left the room grey. "I think I'll go to bed."

"I suppose," Mather said, "that all the booking offices have the numbers of those notes."

"Every one."

"It looks to me," Mather said, "that if you had nothing but phony notes and wanted to catch an express—"

"How do we know it was an express?"

"Yes, I don't know why I said that, sir. Or perhaps—if it was a slow train with plenty of stops near London, surely someone would have reported by this time."

"You may be right."

"Well, if I wanted to catch an express, I'd wait till the last minute and pay on the train. I don't suppose the ticket collectors carry the numbers."

"I think you're right. Are you tired, Mather?"

"No."

"Well, I am. Would you stay here and ring up Euston and King's Cross and St. Pancras, all of them. Make a list of all the outgoing expresses after seven. Ask them to telephone up the line to all stations to check up on any man travelling without a ticket who paid on the train. We'll soon find out where he stepped off. Good night, Mather."

"Good morning, sir." He liked to be accurate.

3

There was no dawn that day in Nottwich. Fog lay over the city like a night sky with no stars. The air in the streets was clear. You had only to imagine that it was night. The first tram crawled out of its shed and took the steel track down towards the market. An old piece of newspaper blew up against the door of the Royal Theatre and flattened out. In the streets on the outskirts of Nottwich nearest the pits an old man plodded by with a pole, tapping at the windows. The stationer's window in the High Street was full of prayer books and Bibles. A printed card remained among them, a relic of Armistice Day, like the old drab wreath of Haig poppies by the War Memorial: "Look up, and swear by the slain of the war that you'll never forget." Along the line a signal lamp winked green in the dark day, and the lit carriages drew slowly in past the cemetery, the glue factory, over the wide, tidy, cement-lined river. A bell began to ring from the Roman Catholic cathedral. A whistle blew.

The packed train moved slowly into another morning; smuts were thick on all the faces; everyone had slept in his clothes. Mr. Cholmondeley·had eaten too many sweets: his teeth needed cleaning; his breath was sweet and stuffy. He put his head into the corridor, and Raven at once turned his back and stared out at the sidings, the trucks heaped with local coal. A smell of bad fish came in from the glue factory. Mr. Cholmondeley dived back across the carriage to the other side, trying to make out at which platform the train was drawing in. He said, "Excuse me," trampling on the feet. Anne smiled softly to herself and hacked his ankle. Mr. Cholmondeley glared at her. She said, "I'm sorry," and began to mend her face with her Pond's tissues and her powder, to bring it up to standard so that she could bear the thought of the Royal Theatre, the little dressing rooms and the oil heating, the rivalry and the scandals.

"If you'll let me by," Mr. Cholmondeley said fiercely, "I'm getting down here."

Raven saw his ghost in the windowpane getting down. But he didn't dare follow him closely. It was almost as if a voice blown over many foggy miles, over the long swelling fields of the hunting counties, the villaed suburbs creeping up to town, had spoken to him. "Any man travelling without a ticket," he thought, with the slip of white paper the collector had given him in his hand. He opened the door and watched the passengers flow by him to the barrier. He needed time, and the paper in his hand would so quickly identify him. He needed time, and he realized now that he wouldn't have even so much as a twelve-hour start. They would visit every boarding house, every lodging in Nottwich; there was nowhere for him to stay.

Then it was that the idea struck him—by the slot machine on number 2 arrival platform—which thrust him finally into other people's lives, broke the world in which he walked alone.

Most of the passengers had gone now, but one girl waited for a returning porter by the buffet door. He went up to her and said, "Can I help and carry your bags?"

"Oh, if you would," she said. He stood with his head a little bent, so that she mightn't see his lip.

"What about a sandwich?" he said. "It's been a hard journey."

"Is it open," she said, "this early?"

He tried the door. "Yes, it's open."

"Is it an invitation?" she said. "You're standing treat?"

He gazed at her with faint astonishment: her smile, the small neat face with the eyes rather too wide apart. He was more used to the absent-minded routine endearments of prostitutes than to this natural friendliness, this sense of rather lost and desperate amusement. He said, "Oh yes. It's on me." He carried the bags inside and hammered on the counter. "What'll you have?" he said. In the pale light of the electric globe he kept his back to her: he didn't want to scare her yet.

"There's a rich choice," she said. "Bath buns, penny buns, last year's biscuits, ham sandwiches. I'd like a ham sandwich and a cup of coffee. Or will that leave you broke? If so, leave out the coffee."

He waited till the girl behind the counter had gone again, till the other's mouth was full of sandwich so that she couldn't have screamed if she'd tried. Then he turned his face on her. He was disconcerted when she showed no repulsion but smiled as well as she could with her mouth full. He said, "I want your ticket. The police are after me. I'll do anything to get your ticket."

She swallowed the bread in her mouth and began to cough. She said, "For God's sake, hit me on the back." He nearly obeyed her; she'd got him rattled: he wasn't used to normal life, and it upset his nerve. He said, "I've got a gun," and added lamely, "I'll give you this in return." He laid the paper on the counter, and she read it with interest between the coughs. "First class. All the way to . . . Why, I'll be able to get a refund on this. I call that a fine exchange; but why the gun?"

He said, "The ticket."

"Here."

"Now," he said, "you are going out of the station with me. I'm not taking any chances."

"Why not eat your ham sandwich first?"

"Be quiet," he said. "I haven't the time to listen to your jokes."

She said, "I like he-men. My name's Anne. What's yours?" The train outside whistled; the carriage began to move, a long line of light going back into the fog; the steam blew along the platform. Raven's eyes left her for a moment. She raised her cup and dashed the hot coffee at his face. The pain drove him backwards with his hands to his eyes; he moaned like an animal; this was pain. This was what the old war minister had felt, the woman secretary, his father when the trap sprang and the neck took the weight. His right hand felt for the automatic, his back was against the door. People were driving him to do things, to lose his head. He checked himself; with an effort he conquered the agony of the burns, the agony which drove him to kill. He said, "I've got you covered. Pick up those cases. Go out in front of me with that paper."

She obeyed him, staggering under the weight. The ticket collector said, "Changed your mind? This would have taken you to Edinburgh. Do you want to break the journey?"

"Yes," she said, "yes. That's it." He took out a pencil and began to write on the paper. An idea came to Anne: she wanted him to remember her and the ticket. There might be enquiries. "No," she said, "I'll give it up. I don't think I'll be going on. I'll stay here," and she went out through the barrier, thinking, He won't forget that in a hurry.

The long street ran down between the small dusty houses. A milk float clattered round a corner out of sight. She said, "Well, can I go now?"

"You think me a fool," he said bitterly. "Keep on walking."

"You might take one of these bags." She dropped one in the road and went on; he had to pick it up. It was heavy. He carried it in his left hand; he needed his right for the automatic.

She said, "This isn't taking us into Nottwich. We ought to have turned right at that corner."

"I know where I'm going."

"I wish I did."

The little houses went endlessly on under the fog. It was very early. A woman came to a door and took in the milk. Through a window Anne saw a man shaving. She wanted to scream to him, but he might have been in another world. She could imagine his stupid stare, the slow working of the brain before he realized anything was wrong. On they went, Raven a step behind. She wondered if he were bluffing her; he must be wanted for something very serious if he was really ready to shoot.

She spoke her thoughts aloud, "Is it murder?" and the lapse of her flippancy, the whispered fear, came to Raven like something familiar, friendly: he was used to fear. It had lived inside him for twenty years. It was normality he couldn't cope with. He answered her without strain, "No. I'm not wanted for that."

She challenged him. "Then you wouldn't dare to shoot," but he had the answer pat, the answer which never failed to convince because it was the truth. "I'm not going to prison. I'd rather hang. My father hanged."

She said again, "Where are we going?" watching all the time for her chance. He didn't answer.

"Do you know this place?" But he had said his say. And suddenly the chance was there: outside a little stationer's, where the morning posters leaned, looking in the window filled with cheap notepaper, pens, and ink bottles—a policeman. She felt Raven come up behind her. It was all too quick: she hadn't time to make up her mind; they were past the policeman and on down the mean road. It was too late to scream now: he was twenty yards away; there'd be no rescue. She said in a low voice, "It *must* be murder."

The repetition stung him into speech. "That's justice for you. Always thinking the worst. They've pinned a robbery onto me, and I don't even know where the notes were stolen." A man came out of a public house and began to wipe the steps with a wet cloth; they could smell frying bacon; the suitcases weighed on their arms. Raven couldn't change his hands for fear of leaving hold of the automatic. He said, "If a man's born ugly, he doesn't stand a chance. It begins at school. It begins before that."

"What's wrong with your face?" she said with bitter amusement. There seemed hope while he talked. It must be harder to murder anyone with whom you'd had any kind of relationship.

"My lip, of course."

"What's up with your lip?"

He said with astonishment, "Do you mean you haven't noticed—"

"Oh," Anne said, "I suppose you mean your harelip. I've seen worse things than that." They had left the little dirty houses behind them. She read the name of the new street: Shakespeare Avenue. Bright red bricks and Tudor gables and half-timbering, doors with stained glass, names like Restholme. These houses represented something worse than the meanness of poverty, the meanness of the spirit. They were on the very edge of Nottwich now, where the speculative builders were running up their hire-purchase houses. It occurred to Anne that he had brought her here to kill her in the scarred fields behind the housing estate, where the grass had been trampled into the clay and the stumps of trees showed where an old wood had been. Plodding on, they passed a house with an open door, which at any hour of the day visitors could enter and inspect, from the small square parlour to the small square bedroom and the bathroom and water closet off the landing. A big placard said:

COME IN AND INSPECT A COZYHOLME
TEN POUNDS DOWN AND A HOUSE IS YOURS

"Are you going to buy a house?" she said with desperate humour.

He said, "I've got a hundred and ninety pounds in my pocket, and I couldn't buy a box of matches with them. I tell you, I was double-crossed. I never stole these notes. A fellow gave them to me."

"That was generous."

He hesitated outside Sleepy Nuik. It was so new that the builder's paint had hardly been removed from the panes. He said, "It was for a piece of work I did. I did the work well. He ought to have paid me properly. I followed him here. A fellow called Chol-mon-deley."

He pushed her through the gate of Sleepy Nuik, up the unmade path and round to the back door. They were at the edge of the fog here: it was as if they were at the boundary between night and day; it faded out in long streamers into the grey winter sky. He put his shoulder against the back door, and the little doll's house lock snapped at once out of the cheap rotten wood. They stood in the kitchen, a place of wires waiting for bulbs, of tubes waiting for the gas cooker. "Get over to the wall," he said, "where I can watch you."

He sat down on the floor with the pistol in his hand. He said, "I'm tired. All night standing in that train. I can't think properly. I don't know what to do with you."

Anne said, "I've got a job here. I haven't a penny if I lose it. I'll give you my word I'll say nothing if you'll let me go." She added hopelessly, "But you wouldn't believe me."

"People don't trouble to keep their word to me," Raven said. He brooded darkly in his dusty corner by the sink. He said, "I'm safe here for a while as long as you are here too." He put his hand to his face and winced at the soreness of the burns. Anne made a movement. He said, "Don't move. I'll shoot if you move."

"Can't I sit down?" she said. "I'm tired too. I've got to be on my feet all the afternoon." But while she spoke she saw herself bundled into a cupboard with the blood still wet. She said, "Dressed up as a Chink. Singing." But he wasn't listening to her; he was making his own plans in his own darkness. She tried to keep her courage up with the first song that came into her head, humming it because it reminded her of Mather, the long bus ride home, the "see you to-morrow."

> It's only Kew
> To you,
> But to me
> It's Paradise.

He said, "I've heard that tune." He couldn't remember where. He remembered a dark night and a cold wind and hunger and the scratch of a needle. It was as if something sharp and cold were breaking in his heart with great pain. He sat there under the sink with the automatic in his hand and began to cry. He made no sound: the tears seemed to run like flies of their own will from the corners of his eyes. Anne didn't notice for a while, humming the song, "They say that's a snowflower a man brought from Greenland." Then she saw. She said, "What's the matter?"

Raven said, "Keep back against that wall, or I'll shoot."

"You're all in."

"That doesn't matter to you."

"Well, I suppose I'm human," Anne said. "You haven't done me any harm yet."

He said, "This doesn't mean anything. I'm just tired." He looked along the bare, dusty boards of the unfinished kitchen. He tried to swagger. "I'm tired of living in hotels. I'd like to fix up this kitchen. I learned to be an electrician once. I'm educated." He said, "Sleepy Nuik. It's a good name when you are tired. But they've gone and spelled Nook wrong."

"Let me go," Anne said. "You can trust me. I'll not say a thing. I don't even know who you are."

He laughed miserably. "Trust you! I'd say I can. When you get into the town you'll see my name in the papers and my description, what I'm wearing, how old I am. I never stole the notes, but *I* can't put a description in of the man I want: name Chol-mon-deley, profession double-crosser, fat, wears an emerald ring—"

"Why," she said, "I believe I travelled down with a man like that. I wouldn't have thought he'd have the nerve—"

"Oh, he's only the agent," Raven said, "but if I could find him I'd squeeze the names—"

"Why don't you give yourself up? Tell the police what happened?"

"That's a great idea, that is. Tell them it was Cholmondeley's friends got the old Czech killed. You're a bright girl."

"The old Czech?" she exclaimed. A little more light came into the kitchen as the fog lifted over the housing estate, the wounded fields. She said, "You don't mean what the papers are so full of?"

"That's it," he said with gloomy pride.

"You know the man who shot him?"

"As well as myself."

"And Cholmondeley's mixed up in it. . . . Doesn't that mean —that everyone's all wrong?"

"They don't know a thing about it, these papers. They can't give credit where credit's due."

"And you know and Cholmondeley. Then there won't be a war at all if you find Cholmondeley."

"I don't care a damn whether there's a war or not. I only want to know who it is who double-crossed me. I want to get even," he explained, looking up at her across the floor, with his hand over his mouth, hiding his lip, noticing that she was young and flushed and lovely, with no more personal interest than a mangy wolf will show from the cage in the groomed, well-fed bitch beyond the bars. "A war won't do people any harm," he said. "It'll show them what's what, it'll give them a taste of their own medicine. I know. There's always been a war for me." He touched the automatic. "All that worries me is what to do with you to keep you quiet for twenty-four hours."

She said under her breath, "You wouldn't kill me, would you?"

"It is the only way," he said. "Let me think a bit."

"But I'd be on your side," she implored him, looking this way and that for anything to throw, for a chance of safety.

"Nobody's on my side," Raven said. "I've learned that. Even a crook doctor . . . You see—I'm ugly. I don't pretend to be one of your handsome fellows. But I'm educated. I've thought things out." He said quickly, "I'm wasting time. I ought to get started."

"What are you going to do?" she said, scrambling to her feet.

"Oh," he said in a tone of disappointment, "you are scared again. You were fine when you weren't scared." He faced her across the kitchen with the automatic pointed at her breast. He pleaded with her. "There's no need to be scared. This lip—"

"I don't mind your lip," she said desperately. "You aren't bad-looking. You ought to have a girl. She'd stop you worrying about that lip."

He shook his head. "You're talking that way because you are scared. You can't get round me that way. But it's hard luck on you, my picking on you. You shouldn't be so afraid of death. We've all got to die. If there's a war, you'll die anyway. It's sudden and quick; it doesn't hurt," he said, remembering the smashed skull of the old man. Death was like that: no more difficult than breaking an egg.

She whispered, "Are you going to shoot me?"

"Oh no, no," he said, trying to calm her; "turn your back and go over to that door. We'll find a room where I can lock you up for a few hours." He fixed his eyes on her back; he wanted to shoot her clean: he didn't want to hurt her.

She said, "You aren't so bad. We might have been friends if we hadn't met like this. If this was the stage door. Do you meet girls at stage doors?"

"Me?" he said. "No. They wouldn't look at me."

"You aren't ugly," she said. "I'd rather you had that lip than a cauliflower ear like all those fellows have who think they are tough. The girls go crazy on them when they are in shorts. But they look silly in a dinner jacket." Raven thought, If I shoot her here anyone may see her through a window; I'll shoot her upstairs in the bathroom. He said, "Go on. Walk."

She said, "Let me go this afternoon. Please. I'll lose my job if I'm not at the theatre."

They came out into the little glossy hall, which smelled of paint. She said, "I'll give you a seat for the show."

"Go on," he said, "up the stairs."

"It's worth seeing. Alfred Bleek as the Widow Twankey." There were only three doors on the little landing; one had ground-glass panes. "Open the door," he said, "and go in there." He decided that he would shoot her in the back as soon as she was over the threshold. Then he would only have to close the door, and she would be out of sight. A small aged voice whispered agonizingly in his memory through a closed door. Memories had never troubled him. He didn't mind death: it was foolish to be scared of death in this bare, wintry world. He said hoarsely, "Are you happy? I mean, you like your job?"

"Oh, not the job," she said. "But the job won't go on forever. Don't you think someone might marry me? I'm hoping."

He whispered, "Go in. Look through that window," his finger touching the trigger. She went obediently forward. He brought the automatic up; his hand didn't tremble; he told himself that she would feel nothing. Death wasn't a thing she need be scared about. She had taken her handbag from under her arm. He noticed the odd, sophisticated shape; a circle of twisted glass on the side and within it chromium initials, A. C. She was going to make her face up.

A door closed, and a voice said, "You'll excuse me bringing you here this early, but I have to be at the office till late—"

"That's all right, that's all right, Mr. Graves. Now don't you call this a snug little house?"

He lowered the pistol as Anne turned. She whispered breathlessly, "Come in here quick." He obeyed her. He didn't understand; he was still ready to shoot her if she screamed. She saw the automatic and said, "Put it away. You'll only get into trouble with that."

Raven said, "Your bags are in the kitchen."

"I know. They've come in by the front door."

"Gas and electric," a voice said, "laid on. Ten pounds down, and you sign along the dotted line and move in the furniture."

A precise voice which went with pince-nez and a high collar and thin flaxen hair said, "Of course I shall have to think it over."

"Come and look upstairs, Mr. Graves."

They could hear them cross the hall and climb the stairs, the agent talking all the time. Raven said, "I'll shoot if you—"

"Be quiet," Anne said. "Don't talk. Listen, have you those notes? Give me two of them." When he hesitated she whispered urgently, "We've got to take a risk." The agent and Mr. Graves were in the best bedroom now.

"Just think of it, Mr. Graves," the agent was saying, "with flowered chintz."

"Are the walls soundproof?"

"By a special process. Shut the door—" The door closed, and the agent's voice went thinly, distinctly on—"and in the passage you couldn't hear a thing. These houses were specially made for family men."

"And now," Mr. Graves said, "I should like to see the bathroom."

"Don't move," Raven threatened her.

"Oh, put it away," Anne said, "and be yourself." She closed the bathroom door behind her and walked to the door of the bedroom. It opened, and the agent said with the immediate gallantry of a man known in all the Nottwich bars, "Well, well, what have we here?"

"I was passing," Anne said, "and saw the door open. I'd been meaning to come and see you, but I didn't think you'd be up this early."

"Always on the spot for a young lady," the agent said.

"I want to buy this house."

"Now look here," Mr. Graves said, a young-old man in a black suit who carried about with him in his pale face and irascible air the idea of babies in small, sour rooms, of insufficient sleep, "you can't do that. I'm looking over this house."

"My husband sent me here to buy it."

"I'm here first."

"Have you bought it?"

"I've got to look it over first, haven't I?"

"Here," Anne said, showing two five-pound notes. "Now all I have to do—"

"Is sign along the dotted line," the agent said.

"Give me time," Mr. Graves said. "I like this house." He went to the window. "I like the view." His pale face stared out at the damaged fields stretching under the fading fog to where the slag heaps rose along the horizon. "It's quite country," Mr. Graves said. "It'll be good for the children and the wife."

"I'm sorry," Anne said, "but you see I'm ready to pay and sign."

"References?" the agent said.

"I'll bring them this afternoon."

"Let me show you another house, Mr. Graves." The agent belched slightly and apologized, "I'm not used to business before breakfast."

"No," Mr. Graves said, "if I can't have this I won't have any." Pallid and aggrieved, he planted himself in the best bedroom of Sleepy Nuik and presented his challenge to fate, a challenge which he knew from long and bitter experience was always accepted.

"Well," the agent said, "you can't have this. First come, first served."

Mr. Graves said, "Good morning"; carried his pitiful, narrow-chested pride downstairs. At least he could claim that, if he had been always too late for what he really wanted, he had never accepted substitutes.

"I'll come with you to the office," Anne said, "straight-away," taking the agent's arm, turning her back on the bathroom where the dark, pinched man stood waiting with his pistol, going downstairs into the cold overcast day, which smelled to her as sweet as summer because she was safe again.

4

> *"What did Aladdin say*
> *When he came to Pekin?"*

Obediently the long, shuffling row of them repeated with tired vivacity, bending forward, clapping their knees, "Chin chin." They had been rehearsing for five hours.

"It won't do. It hasn't got any sparkle. Start again, please."

"What did Aladdin say . . ."

"How many of you have they killed so far?" Anne said under her breath. "Chin chin."

"Oh, half a dozen."

"I'm glad I got in at the last minute. A fortnight of this! No thank you."

"Can't you put some Art into it?" the producer implored them. "Have some pride. This isn't just any panto."

"What did Aladdin say . . ."

"You look washed out," Anne said.

"You don't look too good yourself."

"Things happen quick in this place."

"Once more, girls, and then we'll go on to Miss Maydew's scene."

> *"What did Aladdin say*
> *When he came to Pekin?"*

"You won't think that when you've been here a week."

Miss Maydew sat sideways in the front row with her feet up on the next stall. She was in tweeds and had a golf and grouse-moor air about her. Her real name was Binns, and her father was Lord Fordhaven. She said in a voice of penetrating gentility to Alfred Bleek, "I said I won't be presented."

"Who's the fellow at the back of the stalls?" Anne whispered. He was only a shadow to her.

"I don't know. Hasn't been here before. One of the men who put up the money, I expect, waiting to get an eyeful." She began to mimic an imaginary man. "Won't you introduce me to the girls, Mr. Collier? I want to thank them for working so hard to make this panto a success. What about a little dinner, missy?"

"Stop talking, Ruby, and make it snappy," said Mr. Collier.

"What did Aladdin say
When he came to Pekin?"

"All right. That'll do."

"Please, Mr. Collier," Ruby said, "may I ask you a question?"

"Now, Miss Maydew, your scene with Mr. Bleek. Well, what is it you want to know?"

"What *did* Aladdin say?"

"I want discipline," Mr. Collier said, "and I'm going to have discipline." He was rather undersized, with a fierce eye and straw-coloured hair and a receding chin. He was continually glancing over his shoulder in fear that somebody was getting at him from behind. He wasn't a good producer: his appointment was due to more wheels within wheels than you could count. Somebody owed money to somebody else who had a nephew . . . but Mr. Collier was not the nephew: the chain of causes went much further before you reached Mr. Collier. Somewhere it included Miss Maydew, but the chain was so long you couldn't follow it. You got a confused idea that Mr. Collier must owe his position to merit. Miss Maydew didn't claim that for herself. She was always writing little articles in the cheap women's paper on "Hard Work the only Key to Success on the Stage." She lit a new cigarette and said, "Are you talking to *me?*" She said to Alfred Bleek, who was in a dinner jacket with a red knitted shawl round his shoulders, "It was to get away from all that: royal garden parties . . ."

Mr. Collier said, "Nobody's going to leave this theatre." He looked nervously over his shoulder at the stout gentleman emerging into the light from the back of the stalls, one of the innumerable wheels within wheels that had spun Mr. Collier into Nottwich, into this exposed position at the front of the stage, into this fear that nobody would obey him.

"Won't you introduce me to the girls, Mr. Collier?" the stout gentleman said. "If you are finishing. I don't want to interrupt."

"Of course," Mr. Collier said. He said, "Girls, this is Mr. Davenant, one of our chief backers."

"Davis, not Davenant," the fat man said. "I bought out Davenant." He waved his hand: the emerald ring on his little finger flashed and caught Anne's eye. He said, "I want to have the pleasure of taking every one of you girls out to dinner while this show lasts. Just to tell you how I appreciate the way you are working to make the panto a success. Who shall I begin with?" He had an air of desperate jollity. He was like a man who suddenly finds he has nothing to think about and somehow must fill the vacuum.

"Miss Maydew," he said half-heartedly, as if to show to the chorus the honesty of his intentions by inviting the principal boy.

"Sorry," Miss Maydew said, "I'm dining with Bleek."

Anne walked out on them. She didn't want to high hat Davis, but his presence there shocked her. She believed in Fate and God and Vice and Virtue, Christ in the stable, all the Christmas stuff; she believed in unseen powers that arranged meetings, drove people along ways they didn't mean to go; but she, she was quite determined, wouldn't help. She wouldn't play God's or the Devil's game. She had evaded Raven, leaving him there in the bathroom of the little empty house, and Raven's affairs no longer concerned her. She wouldn't give him away—she was not yet on the side of the big organized battalions—but she wouldn't help him either. It was a strictly neutral course she steered out of the changing room, out of the theatre door into Nottwich High Street.

But what she saw there made her pause. The street was full of people; they stretched along the southern pavement, past the theatre entrance, as far as the market. They were watching the electric bulbs above Wallace's, the big drapers, spelling out the night's news. She had seen nothing like it since the last election, but this was different, because there were no cheers. They were reading of the troop movements over Europe, of the precautions against gas raids. Anne was not old enough to remember how the last war began; but she had read of the crowds outside the palace, the enthusiasm, the queues at the recruiting offices, and that was how she had pictured every war beginning. She had feared it only for herself and Mather. She had thought of it as a personal tragedy played out against a background of cheers and flags. But this was different: this silent crowd wasn't jubilant, it was afraid. The white faces were turned towards the sky with a kind of secular entreaty; they weren't praying to any God, they were just willing that the electric bulbs would tell a different story. They were caught there, on the way back from work with tools and attaché cases, by the rows of bulbs spelling out complications they simply didn't understand.

Anne thought, Can it be true that that fat fool—that the boy with the harelip *knows*— Well, she told herself, I believe in fate; I suppose I can't just walk out and leave them. I'm in it up to the neck. If only Jimmy were here. But Jimmy, she remembered with pain, was on the other side; he was among those hunting Raven down. And Raven must be given his chance to finish *his* hunt first. She went back into the theatre.

Mr. Davenant—Davis—Cholmondeley, whatever his name was, was telling a story. Miss Maydew and Alfred Bleek had gone. Most of the girls had gone too, to change. Mr. Collier watched and listened nervously: he was trying to remember who Mr. Davis was. Mr. Davenant had been silk stockings and had known Callitrope, who was the nephew of the man Dreid owed money to. Mr. Collier had been quite safe with Mr. Davenant, but he wasn't certain about Davis. This panto wouldn't last forever, and it was as fatal to get *in* with the wrong people as to get *out* with the right. It was possible that Davis was the man Cohen had quarrelled with, or he might be the uncle of the man Cohen had quarrelled with. The echoes of that quarrel were still faintly reverberating through the narrow backstage passages of provincial theatres in the second-class touring towns. Soon they would reach the third companies, and everyone would either move up one or move down one, except those who couldn't move down any lower. Mr. Collier laughed nervously and glared in a miserable attempt to be in and out simultaneously.

"I thought somebody breathed the word dinner," Anne said. "I'm hungry."

"First come, first served," Mr. Davis-Cholmondeley said cheerily. "Tell the girls I'll be seeing them. Where shall it be, miss?"

"Anne."

"That's fine," Mr. Davis-Cholmondeley said. "I'm Willie."

"I bet you know this town well," Anne said. "I'm new." She came close to the footlights and deliberately showed herself to him —she wanted to see whether he recognized her—but Mr. Davis never looked at a face. He looked past you. His large square face didn't need to show its force by any eye-to-eye business. Its power lay in its existence at all. You couldn't help wondering, as you wondered with an outsize mastiff, how much sheer weight of food had daily to be consumed to keep him fit.

Mr. Davis winked at Mr. Collier, who decided to glare back at

him, and said, "Oh yes, Í know this town. In a manner of speaking
I made this town." He said, "There isn't much choice. There's the
Grand or the Metropole. The Metropole's more intimate."

"Let's go to the Metropole."

"They have the best sundaes, too, in Nottwich."

The street was no longer crowded; just the usual number of
people looking in the windows, strolling home, going into the Imperial Cinema. Anne thought, Where is Raven now? How can I find
Raven?

"It's not worth taking a taxi," Mr. Davis said, "the Metropole's
only just round the corner. You'll like the Metropole," he repeated.
"It's more intimate than the Grand." But it wasn't the kind of hotel
you associated with intimacy. It came in sight at once all along one
side of the market place; as big as a railway station, of red and
yellow stone, with a big clock face in a pointed tower.

"Kind of Hotel-de-Ville, eh?" Mr. Davis said. You could tell
how proud he was of Nottwich.

There were sculptured figures in between every pair of windows;
all the historic worthies of Nottwich stood in stiff neo-Gothic at-
titudes, from Robin Hood up to the Mayor of Nottwich in 1864.
"People come a long way to see this," Mr. Davis said.

"And the Grand? What's the Grand like?"

"Oh, the Grand," Mr. Davis said. "The Grand's gaudy."

He pushed her in ahead of him through the swing doors, and
Anne saw how the porter recognized him. It wasn't going to be
hard, she thought, to trace Mr. Davis in Nottwich. But how to find
Raven?

The restaurant had room for the passengers of a liner; the roof
was supported on pillars painted in stripes of sage green and gold.
The curved ceiling was blue, scattered with gold stars arranged in
their proper constellations. "It's one of the sights of Nottwich," Mr.
Davis said. "I always keep a table under Venus." He laughed nervously, settling in his seat, and Anne noticed that they weren't under
Venus at all, but under Jupiter.

"You ought to be under the Great Bear," she said.

"Ha ha, that's good," Mr. Davis said. "I must remember that."
He bent over the wine list. "I know you ladies always like a sweet
wine." He confessed, "I've a sweet tooth myself." He sat there
studying the card, lost to everything. He wasn't interested in her.
He seemed interested at that moment in nothing but a series of
tastes, beginning with the lobster he had ordered. This was his

chosen home, the huge stuffy palace of food; this was his idea of intimacy, one table set among two hundred tables.

Anne thought he had brought her there for a flirtation. She had imagined that it would be easy to get on terms with Mr. Davis, even though the ritual a little scared her. Five years of provincial theatres had not made her adept at knowing how far she could go without arousing in the other more excitement than she could easily cope with. Her retreats were always sudden and dangerous. Over the lobster she thought of Mather, of security, of loving one man. Then she put out her knee and touched Mr. Davis's. Mr. Davis took no notice, cracking his way through a claw. He might just as well have been alone. It made her uneasy, to be so neglected. It didn't seem natural. She touched his knee again and said, "Anything on your mind, Willie?"

The eyes he raised were like the lenses of a large, powerful microscope focused on an empty slide. He said, "What's that? This lobster all right, eh?" He stared past her over the wide, rather empty restaurant, all the tables decorated with holly and mistletoe. He called, "Waiter, I want an evening paper," and set to again at his claw. When the paper was brought he turned first of all to the financial page. He seemed satisfied: what he read there was as good as a lollipop.

Anne said, "Would you excuse me a moment, Willie?" She took three coppers out of her bag and went to the ladies' lavatory. She stared at herself in the glass over the wash basin: there didn't seem to be anything wrong. She said to the old woman there, "Do I look all right to you?"

The woman grinned. "Perhaps he doesn't like so much lipstick."

"Oh no," Anne said, "he's the lipstick type. A change from home. Hubbie on the razzle." She said, "Who is he? He calls himself Davis. He says he made this town."

"Excuse me, dear, but your stocking's laddered."

"It's not his doing anyway. Who is he?"

"I've never heard of him, dear. Ask the porter."

"I think I will."

She went to the front door. "The restaurant's so hot," she said. "I had to get a bit of air." It was a peaceful moment for the porter of the Metropole. Nobody came in, nobody went out. He said, "It's cold enough outside." A man with one leg stood on the curb and sold matches. The trams went by, little lighted homes full of smoke and talk and friendliness. A clock struck half-past eight, and you could hear from one of the streets outside the square the shrill voices of children singing a tuneless carol. Anne said, "Well, I must be getting back to Mr. Davis." She said; "Who *is* Mr. Davis?"

"He's got plenty," the porter said.

"He says he made this town."

"That's boasting," the porter said. "It's Midland Steel made this town. You'll see their offices in the Tanneries. But they're ruining the town now. They *did* employ fifty thousand. Now they don't have ten thousand. I was a doorkeeper there once myself. But they even cut down the doorkeepers."

"It must have been cruel," Anne said.

"It was worse for him," the porter said, nodding through the door at the one-legged man. "He had twenty years with them. Then he lost his leg, and the court brought it in wilful negligence, so they didn't give him a tanner. They economized there too, you see. It was negligence, all right: he fell asleep. If you tried watching a machine do the same thing once every second for eight hours, you'd feel sleepy yourself."

"But Mr. Davis?"

"Oh, I don't know anything about Mr. Davis. He may have something to do with the boot factory. Or he may be one of the directors of Wallace's. They've got money to burn."

A woman came through the door carrying a Pekingese. She wore a heavy fur coat. She said, "Has Mr. Alfred Piker been in here?"

"No, ma'am."

"There. It's just what his uncle was always doing. Disappearing," she said. "Keep hold of the dog," and she rolled away across the square.

"That's the mayoress," the porter said.

Anne went back. But something had happened. The bottle of wine was almost empty, and the paper lay on the floor at Mr. Davis's feet. Two sundaes had been laid, but Mr. Davis hadn't touched his. It wasn't politeness; something had put him out. He growled at her, "Where have you been?" She tried to see what he had been reading. It wasn't the financial page any more, but she could make out only the main headlines. "Decree Nisi for Lady——" the name was too complicated to read upside down; "Manslaughter Verdict on Motorist." Mr. Davis said, "I don't know what's wrong with this place. They've put salt or something in the sundaes." He turned his furious, dewlapped face at the passing waiter. "Call this a Knickerbocker Glory?"

"I'll bring you another, sir."

"You won't. My bill."

"So we call it a day," Anne said.

Mr. Davis looked up from the bill with something very like fear. "No, no," he said, "I didn't mean that. You won't go and leave me flat now?"

"Well, what do you want to do, the flickers?"

"I thought," Mr. Davis said, "you might come back with me to my place and have a tune on the radio and a glass of something good. We might foot it together a bit, eh?" He wasn't looking at her; he was hardly thinking of what he was saying. He didn't look dangerous. Anne thought she knew his type: you could pass them off with a kiss or two, and when they were drunk tell them a sentimental story until they began to think you were their sister. This would be the last: soon she would be Mather's; she would be safe. But first she was going to learn where Mr. Davis lived.

As they came out into the square the carol singers broke on them —six small boys without an idea of a tune among them. They wore wool gloves and mufflers, and they stood across Mr. Davis's path, chanting, "Mark my footsteps well, my page."

"Taxi, sir?" the porter asked.

"No." Mr. Davis explained to Anne, "It saves threepence to take one from the rank in the Tanneries." But the boys got in his way, holding out their caps for money. "Get out of the way," Mr. Davis said. With the intuition of children they recognized his uneasiness and baited him, pursuing him along the curb, singing, "Follow in them boldly." The loungers outside the Crown turned to look. Somebody clapped. Mr. Davis suddenly turned and seized the hair of the boy nearest him. He pulled it till the boy screamed; pulled it till a tuft came out between his fingers. He said, "That will teach you," and sinking back a moment later in the taxi from the rank in the Tanneries, he said with pleasure, "They can't play with me." His mouth was open, and his lip was wet with saliva; he brooded over his victory in the very same way as he had brooded over the lobster; he didn't look to Anne as safe as he had done. She reminded herself that he was only an agent. He *knew* the murderer, Raven said; he hadn't committed it himself.

"What's that building?" she asked, seeing a great black glass front stand out from the Victorian street of sober offices where once the leather-workers had tanned their skins.

"Midland Steel," Mr. Davis said.

"Do you work there?"

Mr. Davis for the first time returned look for look. "What made you think that?"

"I don't know," Anne said and recognized with uneasiness that Mr. Davis was only simple when the wind stood one way.

"Do you think you could like me?" Mr. Davis said, fingering her knee.

"I daresay I might."

The taxi had left the Tanneries. It heaved over a net of tramlines and came out into the station approach. "Do you live out of town?"

"Just at the edge," Mr. Davis said.

"They ought to spend more on lighting in this place."

"You're a cute little girl," Mr. Davis said. "I bet you know what's what."

"It's no good looking for eggshell, if that's what you mean," Anne said, as they drove under the great steel bridge that carried the line on to York. There were only two lamps on the whole of the long, steep gradient to the station. Over a wooden fence you could see the shunted trucks on the side line, the stacked coal ready for entrainment. An old taxi and a bus waited for passengers outside the small dingy station entrance. Built in 1860, it hadn't kept pace with Nottwich.

"You've got a long way to go to work," Anne said.

"We are nearly there."

The taxi turned to the left. Anne read the name of the road: Khyber Avenue, a long row of mean villas showing apartment cards. The taxi stopped at the end of the road. Anne said, "You don't mean you live *here?*" Mr. Davis was paying off the driver. "Number sixty-one," he said (Anne noticed there was no card in this window between the pane and the thick lace curtains). He smiled in a soft, ingratiating way and said, "It's really nice inside, dear." He put a key in the lock and thrust her firmly forward into a little dimly lit hall with a hatstand. He hung up his hat and walked softly towards the stairs on his toes. There was a smell of gas and greens. A blue fan of flame lit up a dusty plant.

"We'll turn on the wireless," Mr. Davis said, "and have a tune."

A door opened in the passage, and a woman's voice said, "Who's that?"

"Just Mr. Cholmondeley."

"Don't forget to pay before you go up."

"The first floor," Mr. Davis said. "The room straight ahead of you. I won't be a moment," and he waited on the stairs till she passed him. The coins chinked in his pocket as his hand groped for them.

There *was* a wireless in the room, standing on a marble washstand, but there was certainly no space to dance in, for the big double bed filled the room. There was nothing to show the place was ever lived in; there was dust on the wardrobe mirror, and the ewer beside the loudspeaker was dry. Anne looked out of the window behind the bedposts on a little dark yard. Her hand trembled against the sash; this was more than she had bargained for. Mr. Davis opened the door.

She was badly frightened. It made her take the offensive. She said at once, "So you call yourself Mr. Cholmondeley?"

He blinked at her, closing the door softly behind him. "What if I do?"

"And you said you were taking me home. This isn't your home."

Mr. Davis sat down on the bed and took off his shoes. He said, "We mustn't make a noise, dear. The old woman doesn't like it." He opened the door of the washstand and took out a cardboard box; it spilled soft icing sugar out of its cracks all over the bed and the floor as he came towards her. "Have a piece of Turkish Delight."

"This isn't your home," she persisted.

Mr. Davis, with his fingers halfway to his mouth, said, "Of course it isn't. You don't think I'd take you to my home, do you? You aren't as green as that. I'm not going to lose my reputation." He said "We'll have a tune, shall we, first?" And turning the dials, he set the instrument squealing and moaning. "Lot of atmospherics about," Mr. Davis said, twisting and turning the dials until very far away you could hear a dance band playing, a dreamy rhythm underneath the shrieking in the air. You could just discern the tune: "Night light, Love light." "It's our own Nottwich programme," Mr. Davis said. "There isn't a better band on the Midland Regional. From the Grand. Let's do a step or two," and, grasping her round the waist, he began to shake up and down between the bed and the wall.

"I've known better floors," Anne said, trying to keep up her spirits with her own hopeless form of humour, "but I've never known a worse crush." And Mr. Davis said, "That's good. I'll remember that." Quite suddenly, blowing off the relics of icing sugar which clung round his mouth, he grew passionate. He fastened his lips on her neck. She pushed him away and laughed at him at the same time. She had to keep her head. "Now I know what a rock feels like," she said, "when the sea amen—anem— Damn, I can never say that word."

"That's good," Mr. Davis said mechanically, driving her back.

She began to talk rapidly about anything which came into her head. She said, "I wonder what this gas practice will be like. Wasn't it terrible the way they shot the old woman through her eyes?"

He loosed her at that, though she hadn't really meant anything by it. He said, "Why do you bring that up?"

"I was just reading about it," Anne said. "The man must have made a proper mess in that flat."

Mr. Davis implored her, "Stop. Please stop." He explained weakly, leaning back for support against the bedpost, "I've got a weak stomach. I don't like horrors."

"I like thrillers," Anne said. "There was one I read the other day—"

"I've got a very vivid imagination," Mr. Davis said.

"I remember once when I cut my finger—"

"Don't. Please don't."

Success made her reckless. She said, "I've got a vivid imagination too. I thought someone was watching this house."

"What do you mean?" Mr. Davis said. He was scared all right. But she went too far. She said, "There was a dark fellow watching the door. He had a harelip."

Mr. Davis went to the door and locked it. He turned the wireless low. He said, "There's no lamp within twenty yards. You couldn't have seen his lip."

"I just thought—"

"I wonder how much he told you," Mr. Davis said. He sat down on the bed and looked at his hands. "You wanted to know where I lived, whether I worked—" He cut his sentence short and looked up at her with horror. But she could tell from his manner that he was no longer afraid of her: it was something else that scared him. He said, "They'd never believe you."

"Who wouldn't?"

"The police. It's a wild story." To her amazement he began to sniffle, sitting on the bed, nursing his great hairy hands. "There must be some way out. I don't want to hurt you. I don't want to hurt anyone. I've got a weak stomach."

Anne said, "I don't know a thing. Please open the door."

Mr. Davis said in a low, furious voice, "Be quiet. You've brought it on yourself."

She said again, "I don't know anything."

"I'm only an agent," Mr. Davis said. "I'm not responsible." He explained gently, sitting there in his stockinged feet with tears in his deep, selfish eyes. "It's always been our policy to take no risks. It's not my fault that fellow got away. I did my best. I've always done my best. But he won't forgive me again."

"I'll scream if you don't open the door."

"Scream away. You'll only make the old woman cross."

"What are you going to do?"

"There's more than half a million at stake," Mr. Davis said. "I've got to make sure this time." He got up and came towards her with his hands out. She screamed and shook the door, then fled from it because there was no reply and ran around the bed. He just let her run: there was no escape in the tiny cramped room. He stood there muttering to himself, "Horrible. Horrible." You could tell he was on the verge of sickness, but the fear of somebody else drove him on.

Anne implored him, "I'll promise anything."

He shook his head. "He'd never forgive me." He sprawled across the bed and caught her wrist. He said thickly, "Don't struggle. I won't hurt you if you don't struggle," pulling her to him across the bed, feeling with his other hand for the pillow. She told herself even then, It isn't me. It's other people who are murdered. Not me. The urge to life which made her disbelieve that this could possibly be the end of everything for her, for the loving, enjoying I, comforted her even when the pillow was across her mouth, never allowed her to realize the full horror as she fought against his hands, strong and soft and sticky with icing sugar.

5

The rain blew up along the River Weevil from the east. It turned to ice in the bitter night and stung the asphalt walks, pitted the paint on the wooden seats. A constable came quietly by in his heavy raincoat gleaming like wet macadam, moving his lantern here and there in the dark spaces between the lamps. He said "Good night" to Raven without another glance. It was couples he expected to find, even in December under the hail, the signs of poor, cooped provincial passion.

Raven, buttoned to the neck, went on, looking for any shelter. He wanted to keep his mind on Cholmondeley, on how to find the man in Nottwich. But continually he found himself thinking instead of the girl he had threatened that morning. He remembered the kitten he had left behind in the Soho café. He had loved that kitten. It had been sublimely unconscious of his ugliness. "My name's Anne." "You aren't ugly." She never knew, he thought, that he had meant to kill her; she had been as innocent of his intention as a cat he had once been forced to drown. And he remembered with astonishment that she had not betrayed him, although he had told her that the police were after him. It was even possible that she had believed him.

These thoughts were colder and more uncomfortable than the hail. He wasn't used to any taste that wasn't bitter on the tongue. He had been made by hatred; it had constructed him into this thin, smoky, murderous figure in the rain, hunted and ugly. His mother had borne him when his father was in jail, and six years later, when his father was hanged for another crime, she had cut her own throat with a kitchen knife. Afterwards there had been the home. He had never felt the least tenderness for anyone; he was made in this image, and he had his own odd pride in the result; he didn't want to be unmade. He had a sudden terrified conviction that he must be himself now as never before if he was to escape. It was not tenderness that made you quick on the draw.

Somebody in one of the larger houses on the river front had left his garage gate ajar. It was obviously not used for a car, but only to house a pram, a child's playground, and a few dusty dolls and bricks. Raven took shelter there: he was cold through and through except in the one spot that had lain frozen all his life. That dagger of ice was melting with great pain. He pushed the garage gate a little farther open: he had no wish to appear furtively hiding if anyone passed along the river beat. Anyone might be excused for sheltering in a stranger's garage from *this* storm, except, of course, a man with a harelip wanted by the police.

These houses were only semidetached. They were joined by their garages. Raven was closely hemmed in by the red brick walls. He could hear the wireless playing in both houses. In the one house it switched and changed as a restless finger turned the screw and beat up the wave lengths, bringing a snatch of rhetoric from Berlin, of opera from Stockholm. On the National Programme from the other house an elderly critic was reading verse. Raven couldn't help but hear, standing in the cold garage by the baby's pram, staring out at the black hail.

> "A shadow flits before me,
> Not thou, but like to thee;
> Ah Christ, that it were possible
> For one short hour to see
> The souls we loved, that they might tell us
> What and where they be."

He dug his nails into his hands, remembering his father who had been hanged and his mother who had killed herself in the basement kitchen, and all the long parade of those who had done him down. The elderly cultured Civil Service voice read on:

> "And I loathe the squares and streets,
> And the faces that one meets,
> Hearts with no love for me . . ."

He thought, Give her time, and she too will go to the police. That's what always happens in the end with a skirt—

> "My whole soul out to thee . . ."

—trying to freeze again as hard and safe as ever the icy fragment.

"That was Mr. Druce Winton, reading a selection from *Maud* by Lord Tennyson. This ends the National Programme. Good night, everybody."

Three

1

Mather's train got in at eleven that night, and with Saunders he drove straight through the almost empty streets to the police station. Nottwich went to bed early; the cinemas closed at ten-thirty, and a quarter of an hour later everyone had left the middle of Nottwich by tram or bus. Nottwich's only tart hung round the market place, cold and blue under her umbrella, and one or two businessmen were having a last cigar in the hall of the Metropole. The car slid on the icy road. Just before the police station Mather noticed the posters of *Aladdin* outside the Royal Theatre. He said to Saunders, "My girl's in that show." He felt proud and happy.

The chief constable had come down to the police station to meet
Mather. The fact that Raven was known to be armed and desperate
gave the chase a more serious air than it would otherwise have had.
The chief constable was fat and excited. He had made a lot of
money as a tradesman and during the war had been given a commission and the job of presiding over the local military tribunal.
He prided himself on having been a terror to pacifists. It atoned a
little for his own home life and a wife who despised him. That was
why he had come down to the station to meet Mather: it would be
something to boast about at home.

Mather said, "Of course, sir, we don't *know* he's here. But he
was on the train all right, and his ticket was given up. By a woman."

"Got an accomplice, eh?" the chief constable said.

"Perhaps. Find the woman, and we may have Raven."

The chief constable belched behind his hand. He had been
drinking bottled beer before he came out, and it always repeated
itself. The superintendent said, "Directly we heard from the Yard
we circulated the number of the notes to all shops, hotels, and
boarding houses."

"That a map, sir," Mather asked, "with your beats marked?"

They walked over to the wall, and the superintendent pointed
out the main points in Nottwich with a pencil: the railway station,
the river, the police station.

"And the Royal Theatre," Mather said, "will be about there?"

"That's right."

"What's brought 'im to Nottwich?" the chief constable asked.

"I wish we knew, sir. Now these streets round the station, are
they hotels?"

"A few boarding houses. But the worst of it is," the superintendent said, absent-mindedly turning his back on the chief constable,
"a lot of these houses take occasional boarders."

"Better circulate them all."

"Some of them wouldn't take much notice of a police request.
Houses of call, you know. Quick ten minutes and the door always
open."

"Nonsense," the chief constable said, "we don't 'ave that kind
of place in Nottwich."

"If you wouldn't mind my suggesting it, sir, it wouldn't be a bad
thing to double the constables on any beats of that kind. Send the
sharpest men you've got. I suppose you've had his description in
the evening paper. He seems to be a pretty smart safe-breaker."

"There doesn't seem to be much more we can do tonight," the superintendent said. "I'm sorry for the poor devil if he's found nowhere to sleep."

"Keep a bottle of whisky here, Super?" the chief constable asked. "Do us all good to 'ave a drink. Had too much beer. It returns. Whisky's better, but the wife doesn't like the smell." He leaned back in his chair with his fat thighs crossed and watched the inspector with a kind of childlike happiness; he seemed to be saying, What a spree this is, drinking again with the boys. Only the superintendent knew what an old devil he was with anyone weaker than himself. "Just a splash, Super." He said over his glass, "You caught that old swine Baines out nicely," and explained to Mather, "Street betting. He's been a worry for months."

"He was straight enough. I don't believe in harrying people. Just because he was taking money out of Macpherson's pocket."

"Ah," the chief constable said, "but that's legal. Macpherson's got an office and a telephone. He's got expenses to carry. Cheerio, boys. To the ladies." He drained his glass. "Just another two fingers, Super." He blew out his chest. "What about some more coal on the fire? Let's be snug. There's no work we can do tonight."

Mather was uneasy. It was quite true there wasn't much one could do, but he hated inaction. He stayed by the map. It wasn't such a large place, Nottwich. They ought not to take long to find Raven, but here he was a stranger. He didn't know what dives to raid, what clubs and dance halls. He said, "We think he's followed someone here. I'd suggest, sir, that first thing in the morning we interview the ticket collector again. See how many local people he can remember leaving the train. We might be lucky."

"Do you know that story about the Archbishop of York?" the chief constable asked. "Yes, yes. We'll do that. But there's no hurry. Make yourself at 'ome, man, and take some scotch. You're in the Midlands now. The slow Midlands—eh, Super? We don't 'ustle, but we get there just the same."

Of course, he was right. There *was* no hurry, and there wasn't anything anyone could do at this hour, but as Mather stood beside the map it was just as if someone were calling to him, "Hurry. Hurry. Hurry. Or you may be too late." He traced the main streets with his finger; he wanted to be as familiar with them as he was with central London. Here was the G.P.O., the market, the Metropole, the High Street. What was this? The Tanneries. "What's this big block in the Tanneries, sir?" he asked.

"That'll be Midland Steel," the superintendent said and, turning to the chief constable, he went on patiently, "No, sir. I hadn't heard that one. That's a good one, sir."

"The mayor told me that," the chief constable said. "He's a sport, old Piker. You'd think he wasn't a day under forty. Do you know what he said when we had that committee on the gas practice? He said, 'This'll give us a chance to get into a strange bed.' He meant the women couldn't tell who was who in a gas mask. You see?"

"Very witty man, Mr. Piker, sir."

"Yes, Super, but I was too smart for him there. I was on the spot that day. Do you know what I said?"

"No, sir."

"I said, 'You won't be able to find a strange bed, Piker.' Catch me meaning? He's a dog, old Piker."

"What are your arrangements for the gas practice, sir?" Mather asked with his finger jabbed on the Town Hall.

"You can't expect people to buy gas masks at twenty-five bob a time, but we're having a raid the day after tomorrow with smoke bombs from Hanlow aerodrome, and anyone found in the street without a mask will be carted off by ambulance to the General Hospital. So anyone who's too busy to stop indoors will have to buy a mask. Midland Steel are supplying all their people with masks, so it'll be business as usual there."

"Kind of blackmail," the inspector said. "Stay in or buy a mask. The transport companies have spent a pretty penny on masks."

"What hours, sir?"

"We don't tell them that. Sirens hoot. You know the idea. Boy Scouts on bicycles. They've been lent masks. But of course we know it'll be all over before noon."

Mather looked back at the map. "These coal yards," he said, "round the station. You've got them well covered?"

"We are keeping an eye on those," the superintendent said. "I saw to that as soon as the Yard rang through."

"Smart work, boys, smart work," the chief constable said, swallowing the last of his whisky. "I'll be off home. Busy day before us all tomorrow. You'd like a conference with me in the morning, I daresay, Super?"

"Oh, I don't think we'll trouble you that early, sir."

"Well, if you do need any advice, I'm always at the end of the phone. Good night, boys."

"Good night, sir. Good night."

"The old boy's right about one thing." The superintendent put the whisky away in his cupboard. "We can't do anything more tonight."

"I won't keep you up, sir," Mather said. "You mustn't think I'm fussy. Saunders will tell you I'm as ready to knock off as any man, but there's something about this case . . . I can't leave it alone. It's a queer case. I was looking at this map, sir, and trying to think where I'd hide. What about these dotted lines out here on the east?"

"It's a new housing estate."

"Half-built houses?"

"I've put two men on special beat out there."

"You've got everything taped pretty well, sir. You don't really need us."

"You mustn't judge us by *him*."

"I'm not quite easy in my mind. He's followed someone here. He's a smart lad. We've never had anything on him before, and yet for the last twenty-four hours he's done nothing but make mistakes. The chief said he's blazing a trail, and it's true. It strikes me that he's desperate to get someone."

The superintendent glanced at the clock.

"I'm off, sir," Mather said. "See you in the morning. Good night, Saunders. I'm just going to take a stroll around a bit before I come to the hotel. I want to get this place clear."

He walked out into the High Street. The rain had stopped and was freezing in the gutters. He slipped on the pavement and had to put his hand on the lamp standard. They turned the lights very low in Nottwich after eleven. Over the way, fifty yards down towards the market, he could see the portico of the Royal Theatre. No lights at all to be seen there. He found himself humming, "But to me it's Paradise," and thought, It's good to love, to have a centre, a certainty, not just to be *in* love floating around. He liked organization. He wanted that too to be organized as soon as possible; he wanted love stamped and sealed and signed and the license paid for. He was filled with a dumb tenderness he would never be able to express outside marriage. He wasn't a lover; he was already like a married man, but a married man with years of happiness and confidence to be grateful for.

He did the maddest thing he'd done since he had known her: he went and took a look at her lodgings. He had the address. She'd given it to him over the phone, and it fitted in with his work to find his way to All Saints Road. He learned quite a lot of things on the way, keeping his eyes open; it wasn't really a waste of time. He learned, for instance, the name and address of the local papers, the Nottwich *Journal* and the Nottwich *Guardian,* two rival papers facing each other across Chatton Street, one of them next a great gaudy cinema. From their posters he could even judge their publics: the *Journal* was popular; the *Guardian* was "class." He learned too where the best fish-and-chip shops were and the public houses where the pitmen went. He discovered the park, a place of dull wilted trees and palings and gravel paths for perambulators. Any of these facts might be of use, and they humanized the map of Nottwich so that he could think of it in terms of people, just as he thought of London, when he was on a job, in terms of Charlie's and Joe's.

All Saints Road was two rows of stone-tiled neo-Gothic houses lined up as carefully as a company on parade. He stopped outside Number 14 and wondered if she were awake. She'd get a surprise in the morning: he had posted a card at Euston, telling her he was putting up at the Crown, the commercial house. There was a light on in the basement: the landlady was still awake. He wished that he could send a quicker message than that card: he knew the dreariness of new lodgings, of waking to the black tea and the unfriendly face. It seemed to him that life couldn't treat her well enough.

The wind froze him, but he lingered there on the opposite pavement, wondering whether she had enough blankets on her bed, whether she had any shillings for the gas metre. Encouraged by the light in the basement, he nearly rang the bell to ask the landlady whether Anne had all she needed. But he made his way instead towards the Crown. He wasn't going to look silly; he wasn't even going to tell her that he'd been and had a look at where she slept.

2

A knock on the door woke him. It was barely seven. A woman's voice said, "You're wanted on the phone," and he could hear her trailing away downstairs, knocking a broom handle against the banisters. It was going to be a fine day.

Mather went downstairs to the telephone, which was behind the bar in the empty saloon. He said, "Mather. Who's that?" and heard the station sergeant's voice: "We've got some news for you. He slept last night in St. Mark's, the Roman Catholic cathedral. And someone reports he was down by the river earlier."

But by the time he was dressed and at the station more evidence had come in. The agent of a housing estate had read in the local paper about the stolen notes and brought to the station two notes he had received from a girl who said she wanted to buy a house. He'd thought it odd because she had never turned up to sign the papers.

"That'll be the girl who gave up his ticket," the superintendent said. "They are working together on this."

"And the cathedral?" Mather asked.

"A woman saw him come out early this morning. Then when she got home (she was on the way to chapel) and read the paper, she told a constable on point duty. We'll have to have the churches locked."

"No, watched," Mather said. He warmed his hand over the iron stove. "Let me talk to this house agent."

The man came breezily in in plus fours from the outer room. "Name of Green," he said.

"Could you tell me, Mr. Green, what this girl looked like?"

"A nice little thing," Mr. Green said.

"Short? Below five-feet four?"

"No, I wouldn't say that."

"You said little?"

"Oh," Mr. Green said, "term of affection, you know. Easy to get on with."

"Fair? Dark?"

"Oh, I couldn't say that. Don't look at their hair. Good legs."

"Anything strange in her manner?"

"No, I wouldn't say that. Nicely spoken. She could take a joke."

"Then you wouldn't have noticed the colour of her eyes?"

"Well, as a matter of fact, I did. I always look at a girl's eyes. They like it. 'Drink to me only,' you know. A bit of poetry. That's my gambit. Kind of spiritual, you know."

"And what colour were they?"

"Green with a spot of gold."

"What was she wearing? Did you notice that?"

"Of course I did," Mr. Green said. He moved his hands in the air. "It was something dark and soft. You know what I mean."

"And the hat? Straw?"

"No. It wasn't straw."

"Felt?"

"It might have been a kind of felt. That was dark too. I noticed that."

"Would you know her again if you saw her?"

"Of course I would," Mr. Green said. "Never forget a face."

"Right," Mather said. "You can go. We may want you later to identify the girl. We'll keep these notes."

"But I say," Mr. Green said, "those are good notes. They belong to the company."

"You can consider the house is still for sale."

"I've had the ticket collector here," the superintendent said. "Of course he doesn't remember a thing that helps. In these stories you read people always remember *something,* but in real life they just say she was wearing something dark or something light."

"You've sent someone up to look at the house? Is this the man's story? It's odd. She must have gone there straight from the station. Why? And why pretend to buy the house and pay him with a stolen note?"

"It looks as if she was desperate to keep the other man from buying. As if she'd got something hidden there."

"Your man had better go through that house with a comb, sir. But of course they won't find anything. If there was still anything to find she'd have turned up to sign the papers."

"No, she'd have been afraid," the superintendent said, "in case he'd found out they were stolen notes."

"You know," Mather said, "I wasn't much interested in this case. It seemed sort of petty—chasing down a small thief when the whole world will soon be fighting because of a murderer those fools in Europe couldn't catch. But now it's getting me. There's something odd about it. I told you what my chief said about Raven? He said he was blazing a trail. But he's managed so far to keep just ahead of us. Could I see the ticket collector's statement?"

"There's nothing in it."

"I don't agree with you, sir," Mather said, while the superintendent turned it up from the file of papers on his desk. "The books are right. People generally do remember something. If they remembered nothing at all it would look very queer. It's only spooks that don't leave any impression. Even that agent remembered the colour of her eyes."

"Probably wrong," the superintendent said. "Here you are. All he remembers is that she carried two suitcases. It's something, of course, but it's not worth much."

"Oh, one could make guesses from that," Mather said. "Don't you think so?" He didn't believe in making himself too clever in front of the provincial police: he needed their cooperation. "She was coming for a long stay (a woman can get a lot in one suitcase), or else, if she was carrying his case too, he was the dominant one. Believes in treating her rough and making her do all the physical labour. That fits in with Raven's character. As for the girl—"

"In these gangster stories," the superintendent said, "they call her a moll."

"Well, this moll," Mather said, "is one of those girls who like being treated rough. Sort of clinging and avaricious, I picture her. If she had more spirit he'd carry one of the suitcases or else she'd split on him."

"I thought this Raven was about as ugly as they are made."

"That fits too," Mather said. "Perhaps she likes 'em ugly. Perhaps it gives her a thrill."

The superintendent laughed. "You've got a lot out of those suitcases. Read the report and you'll be giving me her photograph. Here you are. But he doesn't remember a thing about her, not even what she was wearing."

Mather read it. He read it slowly. He said nothing, but something in his manner of shock and incredulity was conveyed to the superintendent. He said, "Is anything wrong? There's nothing *there,* surely?"

"You said I'd be giving you her photograph," Mather said. He took a slip of newspaper from the back of his watch. "There it is, sir. You'd better circulate that to all stations in the city and to the press."

"But there's nothing in the report," the superintendent said.

"Everybody remembers something. It wasn't anything you could have spotted. I seem to have private information about this crime, but I didn't know it till now."

The superintendent said, "He doesn't remember a thing. Except the suitcases."

"Thank God for those," Mather said. "It may mean— You see he says here that one of the reasons he remembers her—he calls it remembering her—is that she was the only woman who got out of the train at Nottwich. And this girl I happen to know was travelling by it. She'd got an engagement at the theatre here."

The superintendent said bluntly—he didn't realize the full extent of the shock, "And is she of the type you said? Likes 'em ugly?"

"I thought she liked them plain," Mather said, staring out through the window at a world going to work through the cold early day.

"Sort of clinging and avaricious?"

"No, damn it."

"But if she'd had more spirit—" the superintendent mocked. He thought Mather was disturbed because his guesses were wrong.

"She had all the spirit there was," Mather said. He turned back from the window. He forgot the superintendent was his superior officer; he forgot you had to be tactful to these provincial police officers; he said, "Goddam it, don't you see? He didn't carry his suitcase because he had to keep her covered. He *made* her walk out to that housing estate." He said, "I've got to go there. He meant to murder her."

"No, no," the superintendent said. "You are forgetting: she paid the money to Green and walked out of the house with him alone. He saw her off the estate."

"But I'd swear," Mather said, "she isn't in this. It's absurd. It doesn't make sense." He said, "We're engaged to be married."

"That's tough," the superintendent said. He hesitated, picked up a dead match and cleaned a nail, then he pushed the photograph back. "Put it away," he said. "We'll go about this differently."

"No," Mather said. "I'm on this case. Have it printed. It's a bad smudged photo." He wouldn't look at it. "It doesn't do her justice. But I'll wire home for a better likeness. I've got a whole strip of Photomatons at home. Her face from every angle. You couldn't have a better lot of photos for newspaper purposes."

"I'm sorry, Mather," the superintendent said. "Hadn't I better speak to the Yard? Get another man sent?"

"You couldn't have a better on the case," Mather said. "I know her. If she's to be found, I'll find her. I'm going out to the house now. You see, your man may miss something. I *know* her."

"There may be an explanation," the superintendent said.

"Don't you see," Mather said, "that if there's an explanation it means—why, that she's in danger. She may even be—"

"We'd have found her body."

"We haven't even found a living man," Mather said. "Would you ask Saunders to follow me out? What's the address?" He wrote it carefully down: he always noted facts; he didn't trust his brain for more than theories, guesses.

It was a long drive out to the housing estate. He had time to think of many possibilities. She might have fallen asleep and been carried on to York. She might not have taken the train . . . and there was nothing in the hideous little house to contradict him. He found a plain-clothes man in what would one day be the best front room. In its flashy fireplace, its dark-brown picture rail and the cheap oak of its wainscotting, it bore already the suggestion of heavy unused furniture, dark curtains, and Gosse china. "There's nothing," the detective said, "nothing at all. You can see, of course, that someone's been here. The dust has been disturbed. But there wasn't enough dust to take a footprint. There's nothing to be got here."

"There's always something," Mather said. "Where did you find traces? All the rooms?"

"No, not all of them. But that's not evidence. There was no sign in this room, but the dust isn't as thick here. Maybe the builders swept up better. You can't say no one was in here."

"How did she get in?"

"The lock of the back door's busted."

"Could a girl do that?"

"A cat could do it. A determined cat."

"Green says he came in at the front. Just opened the door of this room and then took the other fellow straight upstairs, into the best bedroom. The girl joined them there just as he was going to show the rest of the house. Then they all went straight down and out of the house, except the girl went into the kitchen and picked up her suitcases. He'd left the front door open and thought she'd followed them in."

"She was in the kitchen all right. And in the bathroom."

"Where's that?"

"Up the stairs and round to the left."

The two men—they were both large—nearly filled the cramped bathroom. "Looks as if she heard them coming," the detective said, "and hid in here."

"What brought her up? If she was in the kitchen she had only to slip out at the back." Mather stood in the tiny room between the bath and the lavatory seat and thought, *She* was here yesterday. It was incredible. It didn't fit in at any point with what he knew of her. They had been engaged for six months: she couldn't have disguised herself so completely. On the bus ride from Kew that evening, humming the song—what was it?—something about a snowflower; the night they sat two programmes round at the cinema because he'd spent his week's pay and hadn't been able to give her dinner. She never complained as the hard, mechanized voices began all over again: "A wise guy, huh?" "Baby, you're swell," "Siddown, won't you?" "Thenks" at the edge of their consciousness. She was straight, she was loyal, he could swear that, but the alternative was a danger he hardly dared contemplate. Raven was desperate. He heard himself saying with harsh conviction, "Raven was here. He drove her up at the point of his pistol. He was going to shut her in here—or maybe shoot her. Then he heard voices. He gave her the notes and told her to get rid of the other fellows. If she'd tried anything on, he'd have shot her. Damn it, isn't it plain?" But the detective only repeated the substance of the superintendent's criticism: "She walked right out of the place alone with Green. There was nothing to prevent her going to the police station."

"He may have followed at a distance."

"It looks to me," the detective said, "as if you are taking the most *unlikely* theory," and Mather could tell from his manner how puzzled he was at the Yard man's attitude: these Londoners were a little too ingenious; he believed in good sound Midland common sense. It angered Mather in his professional pride; he even felt a small chill of hatred against Anne for putting him in a position where his affection warped his judgment. He said, "We've no proof that she didn't try to tell the police," and wondered, Do I want her dead and innocent or alive and guilty? He began to examine the bathroom with meticulous care. He even pushed his finger up the taps in case . . . He had a wild idea that if it were really Anne who had stood here she would have wanted to leave a message. He straightened himself impatiently. "There's nothing here." He remembered there was a test; she might have missed her train. "I want a telephone," he said.

"There'll be one down the road at the agent's."

Mather rang up the theatre. There was no one there except a caretaker, but as it happened she could tell him that no one had been absent from rehearsal. The producer, Mr. Collier, always posted absentees on the board inside the stage door. He was great on discipline, Mr. Collier. Yes, and she remembered that there *was* a new girl. She happened to see her going out with a man at dinnertime after the rehearsal just as she came back to the theatre to tidy up a bit, and thought, That's a new face. She didn't know who the man was. He must be one of the backers. "Wait a moment, wait a moment," Mather said. He had to think what to do next. She *was* the girl who had given the agent the stolen notes; he had to forget that she was Anne, who had so wildly wished that they could marry before Christmas, who had hated the promiscuity of her job, who had promised him that night on the bus from Kew that she would keep out of the way of all rich business backers and stage-door loungers. He said, "Mr. Collier? Where can I find him?"

"He'll be at the theatre tonight. There's a rehearsal at eight."

"I want to see him at once."

"You can't. He's gone up to York with Mr. Bleek."

"Where can I find any of the girls who were at the rehearsal?"

"I dunno. I don't have the address book. They'll be all over the town."

"There must be *someone* who was there last night."

"You could find Miss Maydew, of course."

"Where?"

"I don't know where she's staying. But you've only got to look at the posters of the jumble."

"The jumble? What do you mean?"

"She's opening the jumble up at St. Luke's at two."

Through the window of the agent's office Mather saw Saunders coming up the frozen mud of the track between the Cozyholmes. He rang off and intercepted him. "Any news come in?"

"Yes," Saunders said. The superintendent had told him everything. He was deeply distressed. He loved Mather. He owed everything to Mather; it was Mather who had brought him up every stage of promotion in the police force, who had persuaded the authorities that a man who stammered could be as good a policeman as the champion reciter at police concerts. But he would have loved him anyway for a quality of idealism, for believing so implicitly in what he did.

"Well? Let's have it."

"It's about your g-girl. She's disappeared." He took the news at a run, getting it out in one breath. "Her landlady rang up the station, said she was out all night and never came back."

"Run away," Mather said.

Saunders said, "D-Don't you believe it. You t-t-told her to take that train. She wasn't going till the m-m-m-m-morning."

"You're right," Mather said. "I'd forgotten that. Meeting him must have been an accident. But it's a miserable choice, Saunders. She may be dead now."

"Why should he do that? We've only got a theft on him. What are you going to do next?"

"Back to the station. And then at two—" he smiled miserably— "a jumble sale."

3

The vicar was worried. He wouldn't listen to what Mather had to say; he had too much to think about himself. It was the curate, the new, bright, broad-minded curate from a London East End parish, who had suggested inviting Miss Maydew to open the jumble sale. He thought it would be a draw, but as the vicar explained to Mather, holding him pinned there in the pitch-pine anteroom of St. Luke's Hall, a jumble was always a draw. There was a queue fifty yards long of women with baskets waiting for the door to open. They hadn't come to see Miss Maydew; they had come for bargains. St. Luke's jumble sales were famous all over Nottwich.

A dry, perky woman with a cameo brooch put her head in at the door. "Henry," she said, "the committee are rifling the stalls again. Can't you *do* something about it? There'll be nothing left when the sale starts."

"Where's Mander? It's *his* business," the vicar said.

"Mr. Mander, of course, is off fetching Miss Maydew." The perky woman blew her nose and disappeared into the hall, crying, "Constance, Constance."

"You can't really do anything about it," the vicar said. "It happens every year. These good women give their time voluntarily. The Altar Society would be in a very bad way without them. They *expect* to have first choice of everything that's sent in. Of course the trouble is, *they* fix the prices."

"Henry," the perky woman said, appearing again in the doorway, "you *must* interfere. Mrs. Penny has priced that very good hat Lady Cundifer sent at eighteenpence and bought it herself."

"My dear, how can I say anything? They'd never volunteer again. You must remember they've given time and trouble—" but he was addressing a closed door. "What worries me," he said to Mather, "is that this young lady will expect an ovation. She won't understand that nobody's interested in *who* opens a jumble sale. Things are so different in London."

"She's late," Mather said.

"They are quite capable of storming the doors," the vicar said with a nervous glance through the window at the lengthening queue. "I must confess to a little stratagem. After all she is our guest. She is giving time and trouble." Time and trouble were the gifts of which the vicar was always most conscious. They were given more readily than coppers in the collection. He went on, "Did you see any young boys outside?"

"Only women," Mather said.

"Oh dear, oh dear. I *told* Troop Leader Lance. You see, I thought if one or two Scouts, in plain clothes of course, brought up autograph books, it would please Miss Maydew, seem to show we appreciated—the time and trouble." He said miserably, "The St. Luke's Troop is always the least trustworthy."

A grey-haired man with a carpet bag put his head in at the door. He said, "Mrs. 'Arris said as there was something wrong with the 'eating."

"Ah, Mr. Bacon," the vicar said, "so kind of you. Step into the hall. You'll find Mrs. Harris there. A little stoppage, so I understand."

Mather looked at his watch. He said, "I must speak to Miss Maydew directly—"

A young man entered at a rush. He said to the vicar, "Excuse me, Mr. Harris, but will Miss Maydew be speaking?"

"I hope not. I profoundly hope not," the vicar said. "It's hard enough as it is to keep the women from the stalls till after I've said a prayer. Where's my prayer book? Who's seen my prayer book?"

"Because I'm covering it for the *Journal,* and if she's not, you see, I can get away . . ."

Mather wanted to say, Listen to me. Your damned jumble is of no importance. My girl's in danger. She may be dead. He wanted to do things to people, but he stood there heavy, immobile, patient, even his private passion and fear subdued by his training: one didn't give way to anger, one plodded on calmly, adding fact to fact. If one's girl was killed, one had the satisfaction of knowing one had done one's best according to the standards of the best police force in the world. He wondered bitterly, as he watched the vicar search for his prayer book, whether that would be any comfort.

Mr. Bacon came back and said, "She'll 'eat now," and disappeared with a clank of metal. A boisterous voice said, "Upstage a little, upstage, Miss Maydew," and the curate entered. He wore suede shoes, he had a shiny face and plastered hair, and he carried an umbrella under his arm like a cricket bat; he might have been returning to the pavilion after scoring a duck in a friendly, taking his failure noisily, as a good sportsman should. "Here is my C.O., Miss Maydew, on the O.P. side." He said to the vicar, "I've been telling Miss Maydew about our dramatics."

Mather said, "May I speak to you a moment privately, Miss Maydew?"

But the vicar swept her away. "A moment, a moment; first our little ceremony. Constance. Constance," and almost immediately the anteroom was empty, except for Mather and the journalist, who sat on the table swinging his legs, biting his nails. An extraordinary noise came from the next room; it was like the trampling of a herd of animals, a trampling suddenly brought to a standstill at a fence. In the sudden silence one could hear the vicar hastily finishing off the Lord's Prayer, and then Miss Maydew's clear, immature, principal boy's voice saying, "I declare this jumble well and truly . . ." and then the trampling again. She had got her words wrong: it had always been foundation stones her mother laid, but no one noticed. Everyone was relieved because she hadn't made a speech. Mather went to the door. Half a dozen boys were queued up in front of Miss Maydew with autograph albums; the St. Luke's Troop hadn't failed after all. A hard, astute woman in a toque said to Mather, "This stall will interest *you*. It's a Man's Stall," and Mather looked down at a dingy array of penwipers and pipe cleaners and hand-embroidered tobacco pouches. Somebody had even presented a lot of old pipes. He lied quickly, "I don't smoke."

The astute woman said, "You've come here to spend money, haven't you, as a duty? You may as well take *some*thing that will be of use. You won't find anything on any of the other stalls," and between the women's shoulders, as he craned to follow the movements of Miss Maydew and the St. Luke's Troop, he caught a few grim glimpses of discarded vases, chipped fruit stands, yellowing piles of babies' napkins. "I've got several pairs of braces. You may just as well take a pair of braces."

Mather, to his own astonishment and distress, said, "She may be dead."

The woman said, "Who dead?" and bristled over a pair of mauve suspenders.

"I'm sorry," Mather said. "I wasn't thinking." He was horrified at himself for losing grip. He thought, I ought to have let them exchange me. It's going to be too much. He said, "Excuse me," seeing the last Scout shut his album.

He led Miss Maydew into the anteroom. The journalist had gone. He said, "I'm trying to trace a girl in your company called Anne Crowder."

"Don't know her," Miss Maydew said.

"She only joined the cast yesterday."

"They all look alike," Miss Maydew said; "like Chinamen. I never can learn their names."

"This one's fair. Green eyes. She has a good voice."

"Not in *this* company," Miss Maydew said, "not in *this* company. I can't listen to them. It sets my teeth on edge."

"You don't remember her going out last night with a man at the end of rehearsal?"

"Why should I? Don't be so sordid."

"He invited you out too."

"The fat fool," Miss Maydew said.

"Who was he?"

"I don't know. Davenant, I think Collier said, or did he say Davis? Never saw him before. I suppose he's the man Cohen quarrelled with. Though somebody said something about Callitrope."

"This is important, Miss Maydew. The girl's disappeared."

"It's always happening on these tours. If you go into their dressing room it's always *men* they are talking about. How can they ever hope to act? So sordid."

"You can't help me at all? You've no idea where I can find this man Davenant?"

"Collier will know. He'll be back tonight. Or perhaps he won't. I don't think he knew him from Adam. It's coming back to me now. Collier called him Davis, and he said No, he was Davenant. He'd bought out Davis."

Mather went sadly away. Some instinct that always made him go where people were, because clues were more likely to be found among a crowd of strangers than in empty rooms or deserted streets, drove him through the hall. You wouldn't have known among these avid women that England was on the edge of war. "I said to Mrs. 'Opkinson, if you are addressing me, I said." "That'll look tasty on Dora." A very old woman said across a pile of artificial silk knickers, " 'E lay for five hours with 'is knees drawn up." A girl giggled and said in a hoarse whisper, "Artful. I'd say so. 'E put 'is fingers right down." Why should these people worry about war?

They moved from stall to stall in an air thick with their own deaths and sicknesses and loves. A woman with a hard, driven face touched Mather's arm. She must have been about sixty years old. She had a way of ducking her head when she spoke, as if she expected a blow, but up her head would come again with a sour unconquerable malice. He had watched her without really knowing it as he walked down the stalls. Now she plucked at him; he could smell fish on her fingers. "Reach me that bit of stuff, dear," she said. "You've got long arms. No, not that. The pink," and began to fumble for money —in Anne's bag.

4

Mather's brother had committed suicide. More than Mather he had needed to be part of an organization, to be trained and disciplined and given orders, but unlike Mather he hadn't found his organization. When things went wrong he had killed himself, and Mather was called to the mortuary to identify the body. He had hoped it was a stranger until they exposed the pale, drowned, lost face. All day he had been trying to find his brother, hurrying from address to address, and the first feeling he had when he saw him there was not grief. He thought, I needn't hurry, I can sit down. He went out to an A.B.C. and ordered a pot of tea. He began to feel his grief only after the second cup.

It was the same now. He thought, I needn't have hurried; I needn't have made a fool of myself before that woman with the braces. She must be dead. I needn't have felt so rushed.

The old woman said, "Thank you, dear," and thrust the little piece of pink material away. He couldn't feel any doubt whatever about the bag. He had given it her himself. It was an expensive bag, not of a kind you would expect to find in Nottwich, and to make it quite conclusive you could still see, within a little circle of twisted glass, the place where two initials had been removed. It was all over forever; he hadn't got to hurry any more. A pain was on its way worse than he had felt in the A.B.C. (a man at the next table had been eating fried plaice, and now, he didn't know why, he associated a certain kind of pain with the smell of fish). But first it was a perfectly cold, calculating satisfaction he felt, that he had the devils in his hands already. Someone was going to die for this. The old woman had picked up a small brassière and was testing the elastic with a malicious grin because it was meant for someone young and pretty with breasts worth preserving. "The silly things they wear," she said.

He could have arrested her at once, but already he had decided that wouldn't do; there were more in it than the old woman. He'd get them all, and the longer the chase lasted the better: he wouldn't have to begin thinking of the future till it was over. He was thankful now that Raven was armed, because he himself was forced to carry a gun, and who could say whether chance might not allow him to use it?

He looked up, and there on the other side of the stall, with his eyes fixed on Anne's bag, was the dark, bitter figure he had been seeking, the harelip imperfectly hidden by a few days' growth of moustache.

Four

1

Raven had been on his feet all the morning. He had to keep moving; he couldn't use the little change he had on food, because he did not dare to stay still, to give anyone the chance to study his face. He bought a paper outside the post office and saw his own description there, printed in black type inside a frame. He was angry because it was on a back page; the situation in Europe filled the front page. By midday, moving here and moving there with his eyes always open for Cholmondeley, he was dog-tired. He stood for a moment and stared at his own face in a barber's window. Ever since his flight from the café he had remained unshaven. A moustache might hide his deformity, but he knew from experience how his hair grew in patches, strong on the chin, weak on the lip, and not at all on either side the red deformity. Now the scrubby growth on his chin was making him conspicuous, and he didn't dare go into the barber's for a shave. He passed a chocolate machine, but it would take only sixpenny or shilling pieces, and his pocket held nothing but half-crowns, florins, halfpennies. If it had not been for his bitter hatred he would have given himself up—they couldn't give him more than five years—but the death of the old minister lay, now that he was so tired and harried, like an albatross round his neck. It was hard to realize that he was wanted only for theft.

He was afraid to haunt alleys, to linger in culs-de-sac, because

if a policeman passed and he was the only man in sight he felt conspicuous—the man might give him a second glance—and so he
walked all the time in the most crowded streets and took the risk
of innumerable recognitions. It was a dull, cold day, but at least it
wasn't raining. The shops were full of Christmas gifts; all the absurd useless junk which had lain on back shelves all the year was
brought out to fill the windows: foxhead brooches, book rests in
the shape of the Cenotaph, woollen cosies for boiled eggs, innumerable games with counters and dice, and absurd patent variations on
darts or bagatelle, "Cats on a Wall," the old shooting game, and
"Fishing for Gold Fish." In a religious shop by the Catholic cathedral he found himself facing again the images that had angered
him in the Soho café: the plaster mother and child, the wise men,
and the shepherds. They were arranged in a cavern of brown paper
among the books of devotion, the little pious scraps of St. Theresa.
"The Holy Family"—he pressed his face against the glass with a
kind of horrified anger that that tale still went on. "Because there
was no room for them in the inn . . ." He remembered how they
had sat in rows on the benches, waiting for Christmas dinner, while
the thin precise voice read on about Caesar Augustus and how
everyone went up to his own city to be taxed. Nobody was beaten
on Christmas Day; all punishments were saved for Boxing Day.
Love, Charity, Patience, Humility: he was educated, he knew all
about those virtues; he'd seen what they were worth. They twisted
everything, even that story in there. It was historical, it had happened, but they twisted it to their own purposes. They made him a
god because they could feel fine about it all; they didn't have to
consider themselves responsible for the raw deal they'd given him.
He'd consented, hadn't he? That was the argument, because he
could have called down "a legion of angels" if he'd wanted to escape hanging there. On your life he could, he thought, with bitter
lack of faith; just as easily as his own father, taking the drop at
Wandsworth, could have saved himself when the trap opened. He
stood there, with his face against the glass, waiting for somebody
to deny *that* reasoning, staring at the swaddled child with a horrified
tenderness—"the little bastard"—because he was educated and
knew what the child was in for: the damned Jews and the double-
crossing Judas, with no one even to draw a knife on his side when
the soldiers came for him in the garden.

A policeman came up the street as Raven stared into the window,
and passed without a glance. It occurred to him to wonder how

much they knew. Had the girl told them her story? He supposed she had by this time. It would be in the paper, and he looked. There was not a word about her there. It shook him. He'd nearly killed her, and she hadn't gone to them; that meant she had believed what he'd told her. He was momentarily back in the garage again beside the Weevil in the rain and dark with the dreadful sense of desolation, of having missed something valuable, of having made an irretrievable mistake, but he could no longer comfort himself with any conviction with his old phrase, "Give her time—it always happens with a skirt." He wanted to find her, but he thought, What a chance. I can't even find Cholmondeley. He said bitterly to the tiny scrap of plaster in the plaster cradle, "If you were a god you'd know I wouldn't harm her. You'd give me a break—you'd let me turn and see her on the pavement," and he turned with a half a hope, but of course there was nothing there.

As he moved away he saw a sixpence in the gutter. He picked it up and went back the way he had come, to the last chocolate slot machine he had passed. It was outside a sweet shop and next a church hall, where a queue of women waited along the pavement for some kind of sale to open. They were getting noisy and impatient; it was after the hour when the doors should have opened; and he thought what fine game they would be for a really expert bag picker. They were pressed against each other and would never notice a little pressure on the clasp. There was nothing personal in the thought; he had never fallen quite so low, he believed, as picking women's bags. But it made him idly pay attention to them as he walked along the line. One stood out from the others. Carried by an old, rather dirty woman, the bag was new, expensive, sophisticated, of a kind he had seen before. He remembered at once the occasion: the little bathroom, the raised pistol, the compact she had taken from the bag.

The door was opened, and the women pushed in. Almost at once he was alone on the pavement beside the slot machine and the jumble-sale poster: "Entrance 6d." It couldn't be her bag, he told himself, there must be hundreds like it; but nevertheless he pursued it through the pitch-pine door. "And lead us not into temptation," the vicar was saying from a dais at one end of the hall above the old hats and the chipped vases and the stacks of women's underwear. When the prayer was finished Raven was flung by the pressure of the crowd against a stall of fancy goods: little framed amateur water colours of lakeland scenery, gaudy cigarette boxes from Italian holidays, brass ash trays, and a row of discarded novels. Then the crowd lifted him and pushed him on towards the favourite stall. There was nothing he could do about it. He couldn't seek for any individual in the crowd, but that didn't matter, for he found himself pressed against a stall on the other side of which the old woman stood. He leaned across and stared at the bag. He remembered how the girl had said, "My name's Anne," and there, impressed on the leather, was a faint initial *A*, where a chromium letter had been removed. He looked up. He didn't notice that there was another man beside the stall; his eyes were filled with the image of a dusty, wicked face.

He was shocked by it just as he had been shocked by Mr. Cholmondeley's duplicity. He felt no guilt about the old war minister. He was one of the great ones of the world, one of those who "sat." He knew all the right words, he was educated, "in the chief seats at the synagogues," and if he was sometimes a little worried by the memory of the secretary's whisper through the imperfectly shut door, he could always tell himself that he had shot her in self-defence. But this was evil, that people of the same class should prey on each other. He thrust himself along the edge of the stall until he was by her side. He bent down. He whispered, "How did you get that bag?" but an arrowhead of predatory women forced themselves between; she couldn't even have seen who had whispered to her. As far as she knew it might have been a woman mistaking it for a bargain on one of the stalls, but nevertheless the question had scared her. He saw her elbowing her way to the door, and he fought to follow her.

When he got out of the hall she was just in sight, trailing her long old-fashioned skirt round a corner. He walked fast. He didn't notice in his hurry that he in his turn was followed by a man whose clothes he would immediately have recognized, the soft hat and overcoat worn like a uniform. Very soon he began to remember the road they took; he had been this way with the girl. It was like retracing in mind an old experience. A newspaper shop would come in sight next moment. A policeman had stood just there. He had intended to kill her, to take her out somewhere beyond the houses and shoot her quite painlessly in the back. The wrinkled, deep malice in the face he had seen across the stall seemed to nod at him, "You needn't worry; we have seen to all that for you."

It was incredible how quickly the old woman scuttled.

She held the bag in one hand, lifted the absurd long skirt with the other; she was like a female Rip van Winkle who had emerged from her sleep in the clothes of fifty years ago. He thought, They've done something to her, but who are "they"? She hadn't been to the police; she'd believed his story; it was only to Cholmondeley's benefit that she should disappear. For the first time since his mother died he was afraid for someone else, because he knew only too well that Cholmondeley had no scruples.

Past the station she turned to the left up Khyber Avenue, a line of dingy apartment houses. Coarse grey lace quite hid the interior of little rooms save when a plant in a jardinière pressed glossy green palms against the glass between the lace. There were no bright geraniums lapping up the air behind closed panes; those scarlet flowers belonged to a poorer class than the occupants of Khyber Avenue—to the exploited. In Khyber Avenue they had progressed to the aspidistra of the small exploiters. They were all Cholmondeleys on a tiny scale. Outside Number 61 the old woman had to wait and fumble for her key; it gave Raven time to catch her up. He put his foot against the closing door and said, "I want to ask you some questions."

"Get out," the old woman said. "We don't 'ave anything to do with your sort."

He pressed the door steadily open. "You'd better listen," he said. "It'd be good for you." She stumbled backwards among the crowded litter of the little dark hall. He noted it all with hatred: the glass case with a stuffed pheasant, the moth-eaten head of a stag picked up at a country auction to act as a hatstand, the black metal umbrella holder painted with gold stars, the little pink glass shade over the gas jet. He said, "Where did you get that bag? Oh," he said, "it wouldn't take much to make me squeeze your old neck."

"Acky," the old woman screamed. "Acky."

"What do you do here, eh?" He opened one of the two doors at random off the hall and saw a long cheap couch with the ticking coming through the cover, a large gilt mirror, a picture of a naked girl knee-deep in the sea. The place reeked of scent and stale gas.

"Acky," the old woman screamed again. "Acky."

He said, "So that's it, eh? You old bawd," and turned back into the hall. But she was supported now. She had Acky with her; he had come through to her side from the back of the house on rubber-soled shoes, making no sound. Tall and bald, with a shifty pious look, he faced Raven.

"What d'you want, my man?" He belonged to a different class

altogether: a good school and a theological college had formed his accent; something else had broken his nose.

"What names," the old woman said, turning on Raven from under Acky's protecting arm.

Raven said, "I'm in a hurry. I don't want to break up this place. Tell me where you got that bag."

"If you refer to my wife's reticule," the bald man said, "it was given her—was it not, Tiny?—by a lodger."

"When?"

"A few nights ago."

"Where is she now?"

"She only stayed one night."

"Why did she give her bag to you?"

"We only pass this way once," Acky said, "and therefore—you know the quotation."

"Was she alone?"

"Of course she wasn't alone," the old woman said. Acky coughed, put his hand over her face, and pushed her gently behind him. "Her betrothed," he said, "was with her." He advanced towards Raven. "That face," he said, "is somehow familiar. Tiny, my dear, fetch me a copy of the *Journal*."

"No need," Raven said. "It's me all right." He said, "You've lied about that bag. If the girl was here, it was last night. I'm going to search this bawdy house of yours."

"Tiny," her husband said, "go out at the back and call the police." Raven's hand was on his gun, but he didn't move, he didn't draw it. His eyes were on the old woman as she trailed indeterminately through the kitchen door. "Hurry, Tiny, my dear."

Raven said, "If I thought she was going, I'd shoot you straight, but she's not going to any police. You're more afraid of them than I am. She's in the kitchen now, hiding in a corner."

Acky said, "Oh no, I assure you she's gone; I heard the door. You can see for yourself," and as Raven passed him he raised his hand and struck with a knuckle-duster at a spot behind Raven's ear.

But Raven had expected that. He ducked his head and was safely through in the kitchen doorway with his gun out. "Stay put," he said. "This gun doesn't make any noise. I'll plug you where you'll feel it if you move." The old woman was where he had expected her to be, between the dresser and the door, squeezed in a corner. She moaned, "Oh, Acky, you ought to 'ave 'it 'im."

Acky began to swear. The obscenity trickled out of his mouth effortlessly like dribble, but the tone, the accent never changed; it was still the good school, the theological college. There were a lot of Latin words Raven didn't understand. He said impatiently, "Now where's the girl?" But Acky simply didn't hear. He stood there in a kind of nervous seizure with his pupils rolled up almost under the lids. He might have been praying; for all Raven knew some of the Latin words might be prayers: "saccus stercoris," "fauces." He said again, "Where's the girl?"

"Leave 'im alone," the old woman said. " 'E can't 'ear you. Acky," she moaned from her corner by the dresser, "it's all right, love, you're at 'ome." She said fiercely to Raven, "The things they did to 'im."

Suddenly the obscenity stopped. He moved and blocked the kitchen door. The hand with the knuckle-duster grasped the lapel of Raven's coat. Acky said softly, "After all, my lord Bishop, you too, I am sure—in your day—among the haycocks . . ." and tittered.

Raven said, "Tell him to move. I'm going to search this house." He kept his eye on both of them. The little stuffy house wore on his nerves; madness and wickedness moved in the kitchen. The old woman watched him with hatred from her corner. Raven said, "My God, if you've killed her . . ." He said, "Do you know what it feels like to have a bullet in your belly? You'll just lie there and bleed." It seemed to him that it would be like shooting a spider. He suddenly shouted at her husband, "Get out of my way."

Acky said, "Even St. Paul . . ." watching him with glazed eyes, barring the door. Raven struck him in the face, then backed out of reach of the flailing arm. He raised the pistol, and the woman screamed at him.

"Stop. I'll get 'im out." She said, "Don't you dare to touch Acky. They've treated 'im bad enough in 'is day." She took her husband's arm; she only came halfway to his shoulder, grey and soiled and miserably tender. "Acky dear," she said, "come into the parlour." She rubbed her old wicked wrinkled face against his sleeve. "Acky, there's a letter from the bishop."

His pupils moved down again like those of a doll. He was almost himself again. He said, "Tut tut, I gave way, I think, to a little temper." He looked at Raven with half-recognition. "That fellow's still here, Tiny."

"Come into the parlour, Acky dear. I've got to talk to you." He

let her pull him away into the hall, and Raven followed them and
mounted the stairs. All the way up he heard them talking: they
were planning something between them. As like as not, when he
was out of sight and round the corner, they'd slip out and call the
police. If the girl was really not here or if they had disposed of her,
they had nothing to fear from the police. On the first-floor landing
there was a tall cracked mirror; he came up the stairs into its reflection—unshaven chin, harelip, and ugliness. His heart beat against
his ribs; if he had been called on to fire now, quickly, in self-
defence, his hand and eye would have failed him. He thought hopelessly, This is ruin . . . I'm losing grip . . . a skirt's got me
down. He opened the first door to hand and came into what was
obviously the best bedroom: a wide double bed with a flowery
eiderdown, veneered walnut furniture, a little embroidered bag for
hair combings, a tumbler of Lysol on the washstand for someone's
false teeth. He opened the big wardrobe door, and a musty smell
of old clothes and camphor balls came out at him. He went to the
closed window and looked out at Khyber Avenue, and all the while
he looked he could hear the whispers from the parlour: Acky and
Tiny plotting together. His eye for a moment noted a large, rather
clumsy-looking man in a soft hat chatting to a woman at the house
opposite; another man came up the road and joined him, and they
strolled together out of sight. He recognized at once: the police.
They mightn't, of course, have seen him there; they might be engaged on a purely routine inquiry. He went quickly out onto the
landing and listened; Acky and Tiny were quite silent now. He
thought at first they might have left the house, but when he listened
carefully he could hear the faint whistling of the old woman's breath
somewhere near the foot of the stairs.

There was another door on the landing. He tried the handle. It
was locked. He wasn't going to waste any more time with the old
people downstairs. He shot through the lock and crashed the door
open. But there was no one there. The room was empty. It was a
tiny room almost filled by its double bed, its dead fireplace hidden
by a smoked brass trap. He looked out of the window and saw
nothing but a small stone yard, a dustbin, a high sooty wall keeping
out neighbours, the grey, waning afternoon light. On the washstand
was a wireless set, and the wardrobe was empty. He had no doubt
what this room was used for.

But something made him stay—some sense uneasily remaining
in the room, of someone's terror. He couldn't leave it, and there

was the locked door to be accounted for. Why should they have locked up an empty room unless it held some clue, some danger to themselves? He turned over the pillows of the bed and wondered, his hand loose on the pistol, his brain stirring with another's agony. Oh, to know, to know. He felt the painful weakness of a man who had depended always on his gun. I'm educated, aren't I?—the phrase came mockingly into his mind, but he knew that one of the police out there could discover in this room more than he. He knelt down and looked under the bed. Nothing there. The very tidiness of the room seemed unnatural, as if it had been tidied after a crime. Even the mats looked as if they had been shaken.

He asked himself whether he had been imagining things. Perhaps the girl had really given the old woman her bag. But he couldn't forget that they had lied about the night she'd stayed with them, had picked the initial off the bag. And they had locked this door. But people did lock doors—against burglars, against sneak thieves. Oh, there was an explanation, he was only too aware of that, for everything; why should you leave another person's initials on a bag? When you had many lodgers, naturally you forgot which night . . . There were explanations, but he couldn't get over the impression that something had happened here, that something had been tidied away; and it came over him with a sense of great desolation that only he could not call in the police to find his girl. Because he was an outlaw she had to be an outlaw too. "Ah, Christ, if it were possible . . ." The rain beating on the Weevil, the plaster child, the afternoon light draining from the little stone yard, the image of his own ugliness fading in the mirror, and from belowstairs Tiny's whistling breath. "For one short hour to see . . ."

He went back onto the landing, but something all the time pulled him back, as if he were leaving a place which had been dear to him. It dragged on him as he went upstairs to the second floor and into every room in turn. There was nothing in any of them but beds and wardrobes and the stale smell of scent and toilet things, and in one cupboard a broken cane. They were all of them more dusty, less tidy, more used than the room he'd left. He stood up there among the empty rooms, listening. There wasn't a sound to be heard now: Tiny and her Acky were quite silent below him, waiting for him to come down. He wondered again if he had made a fool of himself and risked everything. But if they had nothing to hide, why hadn't they tried to call the police? He had left them alone, they had nothing to fear while he was upstairs, but something kept them to the house just as something kept him tied to the room on the first floor.

It took him back to it. He was happier when he had closed the door behind him and stood again in the small cramped space between the big bed and the wall. The drag at his heart ceased. He was able to think again. He began to examine the room thoroughly, inch by inch. He even moved the radio on the washstand. Then he heard the stairs creak and, leaning his head against the door, he listened to someone he supposed was Acky mounting the stairs step by step with clumsy caution. Then he was crossing the landing, and there he must be, just outside the door, waiting and listening. It was impossible to believe that those old people had nothing to fear. Raven went along the walls, squeezing by the bed, touching the glossy, flowery paper with his fingers; he had heard of people before now papering over a cavity. He reached the fireplace and unhooked the brass trap.

Propped up inside the fireplace was a woman's body, the feet in the grate, the head out of sight in the chimney. The first thought he had was of revenge: if it's the girl, if she's dead, I'll shoot them both. I'll shoot them where it hurts most so that they die slow. Then he went down on his knees to ease the body out.

The hands and feet were roped; an old cotton vest had been tied between the teeth as a gag; the eyes were closed. He cut the gag away first. He couldn't tell whether she was alive or dead. He cursed her. "Wake up, you bitch, wake up." He leaned over her, imploring her. "Wake up." He was afraid to leave her; there was no water in the ewer; he couldn't do a thing. When he had cut away the ropes he just sat on the floor beside her with his eyes on the door and one hand on his pistol and the other on her breast. When he could feel her breathing under his hand it was like beginning life over again.

She didn't know where she was. She said, "Please. The sun. It's too strong." There was no sun in the room—it would soon be too dark to read. He thought, What ages have they had her buried there? and held his hand over her eyes to shield them from the dim winter light of early evening. She said in a tired voice, "I could go to sleep now. There's air."

"No, no," Raven said, "we've got to get out of here," but he wasn't prepared for her simple acquiescence. "Yes, where to?"

He said, "You don't remember who I am. I haven't anywhere. But I'll leave you some place where it's safe."

She said, "I've been finding out things." He thought she meant things like fear and death, but as her voice strengthened she explained quite clearly. "It was the man you said. Cholmondeley."

"So you know me," Raven said. But she took no notice. It was as if all the time in the dark she had been rehearsing what she had to say when she was discovered, at once, because there was no time to waste.

"I made a guess at somewhere where he worked. Some company. It scared him. He must work there. I don't remember the name. I've got to remember."

"Don't worry," Raven said. "You're fine. It'll come back. But how it is you aren't crazy—Christ, you've got nerve."

She said, "I remembered till just now. I heard you looking for me in the room, and then you went away and I forgot everything."

"Do you think you could walk now?"

"Of course I could walk. We've got to hurry."

"Where to?"

"I had it all planned. It'll come back. I had plenty of time to think things out."

"You sound as if you weren't scared at all."

"I knew I'd be found all right. I was in a hurry. We haven't got much time. I thought about the war all the time."

He said again admiringly, "You've got nerve."

She began to move her hands and feet up and down quite methodically as if she was following a programme she had drawn up for herself. "I thought a lot about that war. I read somewhere, but I'd forgotten, about how babies can't wear gas masks because there's not enough air for them." She knelt up with her hand on his shoulder. "There wasn't much air there. It made things sort of vivid. I thought, We've got to stop it. It seems silly, doesn't it?—us two, but there's nobody else." She said, "My feet have got pins and needles bad. That means they are coming alive again." She tried to stand up, but it wasn't any good.

Raven watched her. He said, "What else did you think?"

She said, "I thought about you. I wished I hadn't had to go away like that and leave you."

"I thought you'd gone to the police."

"I wouldn't do that." She managed to stand up this time with her hands on his shoulders. "I'm on your side."

Raven said, "We've got to get out of here. Can you walk?"

"Yes."

"Then leave go of me. There's someone outside." He stood by the door with his gun in his hand, listening. They'd had plenty of time, those two, to think up a plan, longer than he. He pulled the door open. It was very nearly dark. He could see no one on the landing. He thought, The old devil's at the side, waiting to get a hit at me with the poker. I'll take a run for it. And immediately he tripped across the string they had tied across the doorway. He was on his knees with the gun on the floor. He couldn't get up in time, and Acky's blow got him on the left shoulder. It staggered him; he couldn't move; he had just time to think, It'll be the head next time; I've gone soft; I ought to have thought of a string—when he heard Anne speak. "Drop the poker."

He got painfully to his feet. The girl had snatched the gun as it fell and had Acky covered.

He said with astonishment, "You're fine."

At the bottom of the stairs the old woman cried out, "Acky, where are you?"

"Give me the gun," Raven said. "Get down the stairs; you needn't be afraid of the old bitch." He backed after her, keeping Acky covered, but the old couple had shot their bolt. He said regretfully, "If he'd only rush I'd put a bullet in him."

"It wouldn't upset *me*," Anne said. "I'd have done it myself."

He said again, "You're fine." He nearly forgot the detectives he had seen in the street, but with his hand on the door he remembered. He said, "I may have to make a bolt for it if the police are outside." He hardly hesitated before he trusted her. "I've found a hideout for the night. In the goods yard. A shed they don't use any longer. I'll be waiting by the wall tonight fifty yards down from the station." He opened the door. Nobody moved in the street. They walked out together and down the middle of the road into a vacant dusk.

Anne said, "Did you see a man in the doorway opposite?"

"Yes," Raven said. "I saw him."

"I thought it was like—but how could it—?"

"There was another at the end of the street. They were police all right, but they didn't know who I was. They'd have tried to get me if they'd known."

"And you'd have shot?"

"I'd have shot all right. But they didn't know it was me." He laughed with the night damp in his throat. "I've fooled them properly." The lights went on in the city beyond the railway bridge, but where they were it was just a grey dusk with the sound of an engine shunting in the yard.

"I can't walk far," Anne said. "I'm sorry. I suppose I'm a bit sick after all."

"It's not far now," Raven said. "There's a loose plank. I got it all fixed up for myself early this morning. Why, there's even sacks —lots of sacks. It's going to be like home," he said.

"Like home?"

He didn't answer, feeling along the tarred wall of the goods yard, remembering the kitchen in the basement and the first thing very nearly he could remember, his mother bleeding across the table. She hadn't even troubled to lock the door—that was all she had cared about him. He'd done some ugly things in his time, he told himself, but he'd never been able to equal that ugliness. Someday he would. It would be like beginning life over again, to have something else to look back to when somebody spoke of death or blood or wounds or home.

"A bit bare for a home," Anne said.

"You needn't be scared of me," Raven said. "I won't keep you. You can sit down a bit and tell me what he did to you, what Cholmon-deley did, and then you can be getting along anywhere you want."

"I couldn't go any farther if you paid me." He had to put his hands under her shoulders and hold her up against the tarred wood, while he put more will into her from his own inexhaustible reserve. He said, "Hold on. We're nearly there." He shivered in the cold, holding her with all his strength, trying in the dusk to see her face. He said, "You can rest in the shed. There are plenty of sacks there." He was like somebody describing with pride some place he lived in, that he'd bought with his own money or built with his own labour, stone by stone.

2

Mather stood back in the shadow of the doorway. It was worse in a way than anything he'd feared. He put his hand on his revolver. He had only to go forward and arrest Raven—or stop a bullet in the attempt. He was a policeman; he couldn't shoot first. At the end of the street Saunders was waiting for him to move. Behind, a uniformed constable waited on them both. But he made no move.

He let them go off down the road in the belief that they were alone. Then he followed as far as the corner and picked up Saunders. Saunders said, "The d-d-devil."

"Oh no," Mather said, "it's only Raven—and Anne." He struck a match and held it to the cigarette which he had been holding between his lips for the last twenty minutes. They could hardly see the man and woman going off down the dark road by the goods yard, but beyond them another match was struck. "We've got them covered," Mather said. "They won't be able to get out of our sight now."

"W-will you take them b-b-both?"

"We can't have shooting with a woman there," Mather said. "Can't you see what they'd make of it in the papers if a woman got hurt? It's not as if he was wanted for murder."

"We've got to be careful of your girl," Saunders brought out in a breath.

"Get moving again," Mather said. "We don't want to lose touch. I'm not thinking about *her* any more. I promise you that's over. She's led me up the garden properly. I'm just thinking of what's best with Raven—and any accomplice he's got in Nottwich. If we've got to shoot, we'll shoot."

Saunders said, "They've stopped." He had sharper eyes than Mather. Mather said, "Could you pick him off from here if I rushed him?"

"No," Saunders said. He began to move forward quickly. "He's loosened a plank. They are getting through."

"Don't worry," Mather said. "I'll follow. Bring up three more men and post one of them at the gap where I can find him. We've got all the gates into the yard picketed already. Bring the rest inside. But keep it quiet." He could hear the slight shuffle of cinders where the two were walking. It wasn't so easy to follow them because of the sound his own feet made. They disappeared round a stationary truck, and the light failed more and more. He caught a glimpse of their moving shadows, and then an engine hooted and belched a grey plume of steam round him; for a moment it was like walking in a mountain fog. A warm, dirty spray settled on his face. When he was clear he had lost them. He began to realize the difficulty of finding anyone in the yard at night. There were trucks everywhere; they could slip into one and lie down. He barked his shin and swore softly. Then quite distinctly he heard Anne whisper, "I can't make it."

There were only a few trucks between them. Then the movements began again, heavier movements, as if someone was carrying a weight. Mather climbed onto the truck and stared across a dark, desolate waste of cinders and points, a tangle of lines and sheds and piles of coal and coke. It was like a no man's land full of torn iron across which one soldier picked his way with a wounded companion in his arms. Mather watched them with an odd sense of shame, as if he were a spy. The thin limping shadow became a human being who knew the girl he loved. There was a kind of relationship between them. He thought, How many years will he get for that robbery? He no longer wanted to shoot. He thought, Poor devil, he must be pretty driven by now. He's probably looking for a place to sit down in, and there the place was—a small wooden workman's shed between the lines.

Mather struck a match again, and presently Saunders was below him, waiting for orders. "They are in that shed," Mather said. "Get the men posted. If they try to get out, nab them quick. Otherwise wait for daylight. We don't want any accidents."

"You aren't s-staying?"

"You'll be easier without me," Mather said. "I'll be at the station tonight." He said gently, "Don't think about me. Just go ahead. And look after yourself. Got your gun?"

"Of course."

"I'll send the men along to you. It's going to be a cold watch, I'm afraid, but it's no good trying to rush that shed. He might shoot his way clear out."

"It's t-t-t-tough on you," Saunders said. The dark had quite come, healing the desolation of the yard. Inside the shed there was no sign of life, no glimmer of light. Soon Saunders couldn't have told that it existed, sitting there with his back to a truck, out of the wind's way, hearing the breathing of the policeman nearest him, and saying over to himself to pass the time (his mind's words free from any impediment) the line of a poem he had learned at school about a dark tower: "He must be wicked to deserve such pain." It was a comforting line, he thought. Those who followed his profession couldn't be taught a better; that's why he had remembered it.

3

"Who's coming to dinner, dear?" the chief constable asked, putting his head in at the bedroom door.

"Never you mind," Mrs. Calkin said, "you'll change."

The chief constable said, "I was thinking, dear, as·'ow—"

"As how," Mrs. Calkin said firmly.

"The new maid. You might teach her that I'm *Major* Calkin."

Mrs. Calkin said, "You'd better hurry."

"It's not the mayoress again, is it?" He trailed drearily out towards the bathroom, but on second thought nipped quietly downstairs to the dining room. Must see about the drinks. But if it was the mayoress there wouldn't be any. Piker never turned up; didn't blame him. While there he might just as well take a nip. He took it neat for speed and cleaned the glass afterwards with a splash of soda and his handkerchief. He put the glass, as an afterthought, where the mayoress would sit. Then he rang up the police station.

"Any news?" he asked hopelessly. He knew there was no real hope that they'd ask him down for a consultation.

The inspector's voice said, "We know where he is. We've got him surrounded. We are just waiting till daylight."

"Can I be of any use? Like me to come down, eh, and talk things over?"

"It's quite unnecessary, sir."

He put the receiver down miserably, sniffed the mayoress's glass (she'd never notice that), and went upstairs. Major Calkin, he thought wistfully, Major Calkin. The trouble is, I'm a man's man. Looking out of the window of his dressing room at the spread gleam of Nottwich, he remembered for some reason the war, the tribunal, the fun it had all been giving hell to the conchies. His uniform still hung there, next the tails he wore once a year at the Rotarian dinner, when he was able to get among the boys. A faint smell of mothballs came out at him. His spirits suddenly lifted. He thought, My God, in a week's time we may be at it again. Show the devils what we are made of. I wonder if the uniform will fit? He couldn't resist trying on the jacket over his evening trousers. It was a bit tight, he couldn't deny that, but the general effect in the glass was not too bad—a bit pinched; it would have to be let out. With his influence in the county he'd be back in uniform in a fortnight. With any luck he'd be busier than ever in this war.

"Joseph," his wife said, "whatever are you doing?" He saw her in the mirror, posed statuesquely in the doorway in her new black-and-sequined evening dress like a shop-window model of an outsize matron. She said, "Take it off at once. You'll smell of mothballs now all dinnertime. The mayoress is taking off her things, and any moment Sir Marcus—"

"You might have told me," the chief constable said. "If I'd known Sir Marcus was coming— How did you snare the old boy?"

"He invited himself," Mrs. Calkin said proudly. "So I rang up the mayoress."

"Isn't old Piker coming?"

"He hasn't been home all day."

The chief constable slipped off his uniform jacket and put it away carefully. If the war had gone on another year they'd have made him a colonel; he had been getting on the very best terms with the regimental headquarters, supplying the mess with groceries at very little more than the cost price. In the next war he'd make the grade. The sound of Sir Marcus's car on the gravel brought him downstairs. The mayoress was looking under the sofa for her Pekingese, which had gone to ground defensively to escape strangers; she was on her knees with her head under the fringe, saying, "Chinky, Chinky," ingratiatingly. Chinky growled invisibly.

"Well, well," the chief constable said, trying to put a little warmth into his tones, "and how's Alfred?"

"Alfred," the mayoress said, coming out from under the sofa. "It's not Alfred, it's Chinky. Oh," she said, talking very fast, for it was her habit to work towards another person's meaning while she talked, "you mean how is he? Alfred? He's gone again."

"Chinky?"

"No, Alfred." One never got much further with the mayoress.

Mrs. Calkin came in. She said, "Have you got him, dear?"

"No, he's gone again," the chief constable said, "if you mean Alfred."

"He's under the sofa," the mayoress said. "He won't come out."

Mrs. Calkin said, "I ought to have warned you, dear. I thought of course you knew the story of how Sir Marcus hates the very sight of dogs. Of course, if he stays there quietly—"

"The poor dear," Mrs. Piker said; "so sensitive, he could tell at once he wasn't wanted."

The chief constable suddenly could bear it no longer. He said, "Alfred Piker's my best friend. I won't have you say he wasn't wanted," but no one took any notice of him. The maid had announced Sir Marcus.

Sir Marcus entered on the tips of his toes. He was a very old and very sick man with a little wisp of white beard on his chin like chicken fluff. He gave the effect of having withered inside his clothes like a kernel in a nut. He spoke with the faintest foreign accent, and it was difficult to determine whether he was Levantine or of an old English family. He gave the impression that very many cities had rubbed him smooth. If there was a touch of Alexandria, there was also a touch of St. James's; if of Vienna or some Central European slum, there were also marks of the most exclusive clubs in Cannes.

"So good of you, Mrs. Calkin," he said, "to give me this opportunity." It was difficult to hear what he said; he spoke in a whisper. His old scaly eyes took them all in. "I have always been hoping to make the acquaintance—"

"May I introduce the Lady Mayoress, Sir Marcus?"

He bowed with the very slightly servile grace of a man who might have been pawnbroker to the Pompadour. "So famous a figure in the city of Nottwich." There was no sarcasm or patronage in his manner. He was just old. Everyone was alike to him. He didn't trouble to differentiate.

"I thought you were on the Riviera, Sir Marcus," the chief constable said breezily. "Have a sherry. It's no good asking the ladies."

"I don't drink, I'm afraid," Sir Marcus whispered. The chief constable's face fell. "I came back two days ago."

"Rumours of war, eh? Dogs delight to bark—"

"Joseph," Mrs. Calkin said sharply, and glanced with meaning at the sofa.

The old scaly eyes cleared a little. "Yes. Yes," Sir Marcus repeated. "Rumours."

"I see you've been taking on more men at Midland Steel, Sir Marcus."

"So they tell me," Sir Marcus whispered.

The maid announced dinner. The sound startled Chinky, who growled under the sofa, and there was an agonizing moment while they all watched Sir Marcus. But he had heard nothing, or else the noise had just faintly stirred his subconscious mind, for as he took Mrs. Calkin into the dining room he whispered venomously, "The dogs drove me away."

"Some lemonade for Mrs. Piker, Joseph," Mrs. Calkin said. The chief constable watched her drink with some nervousness. She seemed a little puzzled by the taste. She sipped and tried again.

"Really," she said, "what delicious lemonade. It has quite an aroma."

Sir Marcus passed the soup. He passed the fish. When the entree was served he leaned across the large silver-plated flower bowl inscribed "To Joseph Calkin from the assistants in Calkin and Calkin's on the occasion . . ." (the inscription ran round the corner out of sight) and whispered, "Might I have a dry biscuit and a little hot water?" He explained, "My doctor won't allow me anything else at night."

"Well, that's hard luck," the chief constable said. "Food and drink as a man gets older . . ." He glared at his empty glass. What a life! Oh, for a chance to get away for a bit among the boys, throw his weight about and know that he was a man.

The Lady Mayoress said suddenly, "How Chinky would love those bones," and choked.

"Who is Chinky?" Sir Marcus whispered.

Mrs. Calkin said quickly, "Mrs. Piker has the most lovely cat."

"I'm glad it isn't a dog," Sir Marcus whispered. "There is something about a dog—" the old hand gestured hopelessly with a piece of cheese biscuit—"and of all dogs the Pekingese." He said with extraordinary venom, "Yap, yap, yap," and sucked up some hot water. He was a man almost without pleasures. His most vivid emotion was venom, his main object defence—defence of his fortune, of the pale flicker of vitality he gained each year in the Cannes sun, of his life. He was quite content to eat cheese biscuits to the end of them if eating biscuits would extend his days.

The old boy couldn't have many left, the chief constable thought, watching Sir Marcus wash down the last dry crumb and then take a white tablet out of a little flat gold box in his waistcoat pocket. He had a heart; you could tell it in the way he spoke, from the special coaches he travelled in when he went by rail, the bath chairs which propelled him softly down the long passages in Midland Steel. The chief constable had met him several times at civic receptions; after the general strike Sir Marcus had given a fully equipped gymnasium to the police force in recognition of their services; but never before had Sir Marcus visited him at home.

Everyone knew a lot about Sir Marcus. The trouble was, what they knew was contradictory. There were people who, because of his Christian name, believed that he was a Greek; others were quite as certain that he had been born in a ghetto. His business associates said that he was of an old English family. His face was no evidence either way—you found plenty of faces like that in Cornwall and the west country. His name did not appear at all in Who's Who, and an enterprising journalist who had once tried to write his life found extraordinary gaps in registers; it wasn't possible to follow any rumour to its source. There was even a gap in the legal records of Marseilles, where one rumour said that Sir Marcus as a youth had been charged with theft from a visitor to a bawdy house. Now he sat there in the heavy Edwardian dining room, brushing biscuit crumbs from his waistcoat, one of the richest men in Europe.

No one even knew his age, unless perhaps his dentist; the chief constable had an idea that you could tell the age of a man by his teeth. But then they probably were *not* his teeth at his age—another gap in the records.

"Well, we shan't be leaving them to their drinks, shall we?" Mrs. Calkin said in a sprightly way, rising from the table and fixing her husband with a warning glare. "But I expect they have a lot to talk about together."

When the door closed Sir Marcus said, "I've seen that woman somewhere with a dog. I'm sure of it."

"Would you mind if I gave myself a spot of port?" the chief constable said. "I don't believe in lonely drinking, but if you really won't— Have a cigar?"

"No," Sir Marcus whispered, "I don't smoke." He said, "I wanted to see you—in confidence—about this fellow Raven. Davis is worried. The trouble is he caught a glimpse of the man. Quite by chance. At the time of the robbery at a friend's office in Victoria Street. This man called on some pretext. He has an idea that the wild fellow wants to put him out of the way. As a witness."

"Tell him," the chief constable said proudly, pouring himself out another glass of port, "that he needn't worry. The man's as good as caught. We know where he is at this very moment. He's surrounded. We are only waiting till daylight, till he shows himself."

"Why wait at all? Wouldn't it be better," Sir Marcus whispered, "if the silly, desperate fellow were taken at once?"

"He's armed, you see. In the dark anything might happen. He might shoot his way clear. And there's another thing. He has a girl friend with him. It wouldn't do if he escaped and the girl got shot."

Sir Marcus bowed his old head above the two hands that lay idly, with no dry biscuit or glass of warm water or white tablet to occupy them, on the table. He said gently, "I want you to understand. In a way it is our responsibility. Because of Davis. If there were any trouble, if the girl were killed, all our money would be behind the police force. If there had to be an inquiry the best counsel—I have friends too, as you may suppose."

"It would be better to wait till daylight, Sir Marcus. Trust me. I know how things stand. I've been a soldier, you know.."

"Yes, I understood that," Sir Marcus said.

"Looks as if the old bulldog will have to bite again, eh? Thank God for a government with guts."

"Yes, yes," Sir Marcus said. "I should say it was almost certain now." The old scaly eyes shifted to the decanter. "Don't let me stop you having your glass of port, Major."

"Well, if you say so, Sir Marcus, I'll just have one more glass for a nightcap."

Sir Marcus said, "I'm very glad that you have such good news for me. It doesn't look well to have an armed ruffian loose in Nott-wich. You mustn't risk any of your men's lives, Major. Better that this—waste product should be dead than one of your fine fellows." He suddenly leaned back in his chair and gasped like a landed fish. He said, "A tablet. Please. Quick."

The chief constable picked the gold box from his pocket, but Sir Marcus had already recovered. He took the tablet himself. The chief constable said, "Shall I order your car, Sir Marcus?"

"No, no," Sir Marcus whispered, "there's no danger. It's simply pain." He stared with dazed old eyes down at the crumbs on his trousers. "What were we saying? Fine fellows, yes; you mustn't risk *their* lives. The country will need them."

"That's very true."

Sir Marcus whispered with venom, "To me this—ruffian is a traitor. This is a time when every man is needed. I'd treat him like a traitor."

"It's one way of looking at it."

"Another glass of port, Major."

"Yes, I think I will."

"To think of the number of able-bodied men this fellow will take from their country's service even if he shoots no one. Warders. Police guards. Fed and lodged at his country's expense when other men—"

"Are dying. You're right, Sir Marcus." The pathos of it all went deeply home. He remembered his uniform jacket in the cupboard; the buttons needed shining, the king's buttons. The smell of moth-balls lingered round him still. He said, "Somewhere there's a cor-ner of a foreign field that is forever—Shakespeare knew. Old time-honoured Gaunt when he said that—"

"It would be so much better, Major Calkin, if your men take no risks. If they shoot on sight. One must take up weeds—by the roots."

"It would be better."

"You're the father of your men."

"That's what old Piker said to me once. God forgive him, he meant it differently. I wish you'd drink with me, Sir Marcus. You're an understanding man. You know how an officer feels. I was in the Army once."

"Perhaps in a week you will be in it again."

"You know how a man feels. I don't want anything to come between us, Sir Marcus. There's one thing I'd like to tell you. It's on my conscience. There *was* a dog under the sofa."

"A dog?"

"A Pekingese called Chinky. I didn't know as 'ow—"

"She said it was a cat."

"She didn't want you to know."

Sir Marcus said, "I don't like being deceived. I'll see to Piker at the elections." He gave a small tired sigh as if there were too many things to be seen to, to be arranged, revenges to be taken, stretching into an endless vista of time, and so much time already covered— since the ghetto, the Marseilles brothel, if there had ever been a ghetto or a brothel. He whispered abruptly, "So you'll telephone now to the station and tell them to shoot at sight? Say you'll take the responsibility. I'll look after you."

"I don't see as 'ow, as how—"

The old hands moved impatiently; so much to be arranged. "Listen to me. I never promise anything I can't answer for. There's a training depot ten miles from here. I can arrange for you to have nominal charge of it, with the rank of colonel, directly war's declared."

"Colonel Banks?"

"He'll be shifted."

"You mean if I telephone?"

"No. I mean if you are successful."

"And the man's dead?"

"He's not important. A young scoundrel. There's no reason to hesitate. Take another glass of port."

The chief constable stretched out his hand for the decanter. He thought with less relish than he would have expected, "Colonel Calkin," but he couldn't help remembering other things. He was a sentimental middle-aged man. He remembered his appointment; it had been "worked," of course, no less than his appointment to the training depot would be worked, but there came vividly back to him his sense of pride at being head of one of the best police forces in the country. "I'd better not have any more port," he said lamely. "It's bad for my sleep, and the wife—"

Sir Marcus said, "Well, Colonel," blinking his old eyes, "you'll be able to count on me for anything."

"I'd like to do it," the chief constable said imploringly. "I'd like to please you, Sir Marcus. But I don't see as how— The police couldn't do that."

"It would never be known."

"I don't suppose they'd take my orders. Not on a thing like that."

Sir Marcus whispered, "Do you mean in your position you haven't any *hold?*" He spoke with the astonishment of a man who had always been careful to secure his hold on the most junior of his subordinates.

"I'd like to please you."

"There's the telephone," Sir Marcus said. "At any rate, you can use your influence. I never ask a man for more than he can do."

The chief constable said, "They are a good lot of boys. I've been down often to the station of an evening and had a drink or two. They're keen. You couldn't have keener men. They'll get him. You needn't be afraid, Sir Marcus."

"You mean dead?"

"Alive or dead. They won't let him escape. They are good boys."

"But he has got to be dead," Sir Marcus said. He sneezed. The intake of breath seemed to have exhausted him. He lay back again, panting gently.

"I couldn't ask them, Sir Marcus, not like that. Why, it's like murder."

"Nonsense."

"Those evenings with the boys mean a lot to me. I wouldn't even be able to go down there again after doing that. I'd rather stay what I am. They'll give me a tribunal. As long as there's wars there'll be conchies."

"There'd be no commission of any kind for you," Sir Marcus said. "I could see to that." The smell of mothballs came up from Calkin's evening shirt to mock him. "I can arrange, too, that you shan't be chief constable much longer. You and Piker." He gave a queer little whistle through the nose. He was too old to laugh, to use his lungs wastefully. "Come. Have another glass."

"No. I don't think I'd better. Listen, Sir Marcus, I'll put detectives at your office. I'll have Davis guarded."

"I don't much mind about Davis," Sir Marcus said. "Will you get my chauffeur?"

"I'd like to do what you want, Sir Marcus. Won't you come back and see the ladies?"

"No, no," Sir Marcus whispered, "not with that dog there." He had to be helped to his feet, and his stick brought him. A few dry crumbs lay in his beard. He said, "If you change your mind tonight you can ring me up. I shall be awake." A man at his age, the chief constable thought charitably, would obviously think differently of death; it threatened him every moment on the slippery pavement, in a piece of soap at the bottom of a bath. It must seem quite a natural thing he was asking. Great age was an abnormal condition; you had to make allowances. But watching Sir Marcus helped down the drive and into his deep, wide car, he couldn't help saying over to himself, "Colonel Calkin. Colonel Calkin." After a moment he added, "C.B."

The dog was yapping in the drawing room. They must have lured it out. It was very highly bred and nervous, and if a stranger spoke to it too suddenly or sharply it would rush round in circles, foaming at the mouth and crying out in a horribly human way, its low fur sweeping the carpet like a vacuum cleaner. I might slip down, the chief constable thought, and have a drink with the boys. But the idea brought no lightening of his gloom and indecision. Was it possible that Sir Marcus could rob him of even that? But he had robbed him of it already. He couldn't face the superintendent or the inspector with this on his mind. He went into his study and sat down by the telephone. In five minutes Sir Marcus would be home. So much stolen from him already, surely there was little more he could lose by acquiescence. But he sat there doing nothing, a small, plump, bullying, henpecked profiteer.

His wife put her head in at the door. "Whatever are you doing, Joseph?" she said. "Come at once and talk to Mrs. Piker."

4

Sir Marcus lived with his valet, who was also a trained nurse, at the top of the big building in the Tanneries. It was his only home. In London he stayed at Claridge's, in Cannes at the Ritz. His valet met him at the door of the building with his bath chair and pushed him into the lift, then out along the passage to his study. The heat of the room had been turned up to the right degree, the tape machine was gently ticking beside his desk. The curtains were not drawn, and through the wide double panes the night sky spread out over Nottwich, striped by the searchlights from Hanlow aerodrome.

"You can go to bed, Mollison. I shan't be sleeping."

Sir Marcus slept very little these days. In the little time left him to live a few hours of sleep made a distinct impression. And he didn't really need the sleep. No physical exertion demanded it. Now, with the telephone within reach, he began to read first the memorandum on his desk, then the strips of tape. He read the arrangements for the gas drill in the morning. All the clerks on the ground floor who might happen to be needed for outside work were already supplied with gas masks. The sirens were expected to go almost immediately the rush hour was over and work in the offices had begun. Members of the transport staff, lorry drivers, and special messengers would wear their masks immediately they started work. It was the only way to ensure that they wouldn't leave them behind somewhere and be caught unprotected during the hours of the practice and so waste in hospital the valuable hours of Midland Steel.

More valuable than they had ever been since November 1918. Sir Marcus read the tape prices. Armament shares continued to rise, and with them steel. It made no difference at all that the British government had stopped all export licenses; the country itself was now absorbing more armaments than it had ever done since the peak year of Haig's assaults on the Hindenburg Line. Sir Marcus had many friends, in many countries; he wintered with them regularly at Cannes or in Soppelsa's yacht off Rhodes; he was the intimate friend of Mrs. Cranbeim. It was impossible now to export arms, but it was still possible to export nickel and most of the other metals which were necessary to the arming of nations. Even when war was declared, Mrs. Cranbeim was able to say quite definitely that evening, when the yacht pitched a little and Rosen was so distressingly sick over Mrs. Ziffo's black satin, that the British government would not forbid the export of nickel to Switzerland or other neutral countries so long as the British requirements were first met. So the future really was very rosy indeed, for you could trust Mrs. Cranbeim's word. She spoke directly from the horse's mouth, if you could so describe the elder statesman whose confidence she shared.

It seemed quite certain now; Sir Marcus read in the tape messages that the two governments chiefly concerned would not either amend or accept the terms of the ultimatum. Probably within five days at least four countries would be already at war and the consumption of munitions have risen to a million pounds a day.

And yet Sir Marcus was not quite happy. Davis had bungled things. When he had told Davis that a murderer ought not to be allowed to benefit from his crime, he had never expected all this silly business of the stolen notes. Now he must wait up all night for the telephone to ring. The old thin body made itself as comfortable as it could on the air-blown cushion—Sir Marcus was as painfully aware of his bones as a skeleton must be, wearing itself away against the leaden lining of its last suit. A clock struck midnight; he had lived one more whole day.

Five

1

Raven groped through the dark of the small shed till he had found the sacks. He piled them up, shaking them as one shakes a pillow. He whispered anxiously, "You'll be able to rest there a bit?" Anne let his hand guide her to the corner. She said, "It's freezing."

"Lie down, and I'll find more sacks." He struck a match, and the tiny flame went wandering through the close, cold darkness. He brought the sacks and spread them over her, dropping the match.

"Can't we have a little light?" Anne said.

"It's not safe. Anyway," he said, "it's a break for me. You can't see me in the dark. You can't see *this*." He touched his lip secretly. He was listening at the door; he heard feet stumble on the tangle of metal and cinders, and after a time a low voice speak. He said, "I've got to think. They know I'm here. Perhaps you'd better go. They've got nothing on you. If they come there's going to be shooting."

"Do you think they know I'm here?"

"They must have followed us all the way."

"Then I'll stay," Anne said. "There won't be any shooting while I'm here. They'll wait till morning, till you come out."

"That's friendly of you," he said with sour incredulity, all his suspicion of friendliness coming back.

"I've told you. I'm on your side."

"I've got to think of a way," he said.

"You may as well rest now. You've all the night to think in."

"It *is* sort of—good in here," Raven said, "out of the way of the whole damned world of them. In the dark." He wouldn't come near her, but sat down in the opposite corner with the automatic in his lap. He said suspiciously, "What are you thinking about?" He was astonished and shocked by the sound of a laugh. "Kind of homey," Anne said.

"I don't take any stock in homes," Raven said. "I've been in one."

"Tell me about it. What's your name?"

"You know my name. You've seen it in the papers."

"I mean your Christian name."

"Christian. That's a good joke, that one. Do you think anyone ever turns the other cheek these days?" He tapped the barrel of the automatic resentfully on the cinder floor. "Not a chance." He could hear her breathing there in the opposite corner, out of sight, out of reach, and he was afflicted by the odd sense that he had missed something. He said, "I'm not saying you aren't fine. I daresay you're Christian all right."

"Search me," Anne said.

"I took you out to that house to kill you."

"To kill me?"

"What did you think it was for? I'm not a lover, am I? Girl's dream? Handsome as the day?"

"Why didn't you?"

"Those men turned up. That's all. I didn't fall for you. I don't fall for girls. I'm saved that. You won't find me ever going soft on a skirt." He went desperately on, "Why didn't you tell the police about me? Why don't you shout to them now?"

"Well," she said, "you've got a gun, haven't you?"

"I wouldn't shoot."

"Why not?"

"I'm not all that crazy," he said. "If people go straight with me, I'll go straight with them. Go on. Shout. I won't do a thing."

"Well," Anne said, "I don't have to ask your leave to be grateful, do I? You saved me tonight."

"That lot wouldn't have killed you. They haven't the nerve to kill. It takes a man to kill."

"Well, your friend Cholmondeley came pretty near it. He nearly throttled me when he guessed I was in with you."

"In with me?"

"To find the man you're after."

"The double-crossing bastard." He brooded over his pistol, but his thoughts always disturbingly came back from hate to this dark safe corner; he wasn't used to that. He said, "You've got sense all right. I like you."

"Thanks for the compliment."

"It's no compliment. You don't have to tell me. I've got something I'd like to trust you with, but I can't."

"What's the dark secret?"

"It's not a secret. It's a cat I left back in my lodgings in London when they chased me out. You'd have looked after her."

"You disappoint me, Mr. Raven. I thought it was going to be a few murders at least." She exclaimed with sudden seriousness, "I've got it! The place where Davis works."

"Davis?"

"The man you call Cholmondeley. I'm sure of it. Midland Steel. In a street near the Metropole. A big palace of a place."

"I've got to get out of here," Raven said, beating the automatic on the freezing ground.

"Can't you go to the police?"

"Me?" Raven said. "Me go to the police?" He laughed. "That'd be fine, wouldn't it? Hold out my hands for the cuffs—"

"I'll think of a way," Anne said. When her voice ceased it was as if she had gone. He said sharply, "Are you there?"

"Of course I'm here," she said. "What's worrying you?"

"It feels odd to be alone." The sour incredulity surged back. He struck a couple of matches and held them to his face, close to his disfigured mouth. "Look," he said, "take a long look." The small flames burned steadily down. "You aren't going to help *me*, are you? Me?"

"You are all right," she said. "I like you." The flames touched his skin, but he held the two matches rigidly up and they burned out against his fingers; the pain was like joy. But he rejected it; it had come too late. He sat in the dark, feeling tears like heavy weights behind his eyes, but he couldn't weep. He had never known the particular trick that opened the right ducts at the right time. He crept a little way out of his corner towards her, feeling his way along the floor with the automatic. He said, "Are you cold?"

"I've been in warmer places," Anne said.

There were only his own sacks left. He pushed them over to her. "Wrap 'em round," he said.

"Have you got enough?"

"Of course I have. I can look after myself," he said sharply, as if he hated her. His hands were so cold that he would have found it hard to use the automatic. "I've got to get out of here."

"We'll think of a way. Better have a sleep."

"I can't sleep," he said; "I've been dreaming bad dreams lately."

"We might tell each other stories? It's about the children's hour."

"I don't know any stories."

"Well, I'll tell you one. What kind? A funny one?"

"They never seem funny to me."

"The three bears might be suitable."

"I don't want anything financial. I don't want to hear anything about money."

She could just see him now that he had come closer, a dark, hunched shape that couldn't understand a word she was saying. She mocked at him gently, secure in the knowledge that he would never realize she was mocking him. She said, "I'll tell you about the fox and the cat. Well, this cat met a fox in a forest, and she'd always heard the fox cracked up for being wise. So she passed him the time of day politely and asked how he was getting along. But the fox was proud. He said, 'How dare you ask me how I get along, you hungry mousehunter? What do you know about the world?' 'Well, I do know one thing,' the cat said. 'What's that?' said the fox. 'How to get away from the dogs,' the cat said. 'When they chase me, I just jump into a tree.' Then the fox went all high and mighty and said, 'You've only one trick, and I've a hundred. I've got a sackful of tricks. Come along with me, and I'll show you.' Just then a hunter ran quietly up with four hounds. The cat sprang into the tree and cried, 'Open your sack, Mr. Fox, open your sack.' But the dogs held him with their teeth. So the cat laughed at him, saying, 'Mr. Know-all, if you'd had just this one trick in your sack you'd be safe up the tree with me now.'" Anne stopped. She whispered to the dark shape beside her, "Are you asleep?"

"No," Raven said, "I'm not asleep."

"It's your turn now."

"I don't know any stories," Raven said sullenly, miserably.

"No stories like that? You haven't been brought up properly."

"I'm educated all right," he protested, "but I've got things on my mind. Plenty of them."

"Cheer up. There's someone who's got more."

"Who's that?"

"The fellow who began all this, who killed the old man—you know who I mean. Davis's friend."

"What do you say?" he said furiously. "Davis's friend?" He held his anger in. "It's not the killing I mind, it's the double-crossing."

"Well, of course," Anne said cheerily, making conversation under the pile of sacks, "I don't mind a little thing like killing myself."

He looked up and tried to see her through the dark, hunting a hope. "You don't mind that?"

"But there are killings and killings," Anne said. "If I had the man here who killed—what was the old man's name?"

"I don't remember."

"Nor do I. We couldn't pronounce it anyway."

"Go on. If he was here . . ."

"Why, I'd let you shoot him without raising a finger. And I'd say, 'Well done' to you, afterwards." She warmed to the subject. "You remember what I told you, that they can't invent gas masks for babies to wear? That's the kind of thing he'll have on his mind. The mothers alive in their masks, watching the babies cough up their insides."

He said stubbornly, "The poor ones'll be lucky. And what do I care\about the rich? This isn't a world I'd bring children into." She could just see his tense, crouching figure. "It's just their selfishness," he said. "They have a good time, and what do they mind if someone's born ugly? Mother love—" He began to laugh, seeing quite clearly the kitchen table, the carving knife on the linoleum, the blood all over his mother's dress. He explained, "You see, I'm educated. I. one of His Majesty's own homes. They call them that —homes. What do you think a home means?" But he didn't allow her time to speak. "You are wrong. You think it means a husband in work, a nice gas cooker and a double bed, carpet-slippers and cradles and the rest. That's not a home. A home's solitary confinement for a kid that's caught talking in the chapel, and the birch for almost anything you do. Bread and water. A sergeant knocking you around if you try to lark a bit. That's a home."

"Well, he was trying to alter all that, wasn't he? He was poor like we are."

"Who are you talking about?"

"Old What's-his-name. Didn't you read about him in the papers? How he cut down all the army expenses to help clear the slums?

There were photographs of him opening new flats, talking to the children. He wasn't one of the rich. He wouldn't have gone to war. That's why they shot him. You bet there are fellows making money now out of him being dead. And he'd done it all himself too, the obituaries said. His father was a thief and his mother committed—"

"Suicide?" Raven whispered. "Did you read how she—"

"She drowned herself."

"The things you read," Raven said. "It's enough to make a fellow think."

"Well, I'd say the fellow who killed old What's-his-name had something to think about."

"Maybe," Raven said, "he didn't know all the papers know. The men who paid him, they knew. Perhaps if we knew all there was to know—the kind of breaks the fellow had had—we'd see his point of view."

"It'd take a lot of talking to make me see that. Anyway, we'd better sleep now."

"I've got to think," Raven said.

"You'll think better after you've had a nap."

But it was far too cold for him to sleep; he had no sacks to cover himself with, and his black, tight overcoat was worn almost as thin as cotton. Under the door came a draught which might have travelled down the frosty rails from Scotland, a northeast wind bringing icy fogs from the sea. He thought to himself, I didn't mean the old man any harm; there was nothing personal . . . "I'd let you shoot him, and afterwards I'd say, 'Well done.'" He had a momentary crazy impulse to get up and go through the door with his automatic in his hand and let them shoot. "Mr. Know-all," she could say then, "if you'd only had this one trick in your sack, the dogs wouldn't . . ." But then it seemed to him that this knowledge he had gained of the old man was only one more count against Chol-mon-deley. Chol-mon-deley had known all this. There'd be one more bullet in his belly for this, and one more for Chol-mon-deley's master. But how was he to find the other man? He had only the memory of a photograph to guide him, a photograph which the old minister had somehow connected with the letter of introduction Raven had borne: a young, scarred boy's face which was probably an old man's now.

Anne said, "Are you asleep?"

"No," Raven said. "What's troubling you?"

"I thought I heard someone moving."

He listened. It was only the wind tapping a loose board outside. He said, "You go to sleep. You needn't be scared. They won't come till it's light enough to see." He thought, Where would those two have met when they were young? Surely not in the kind of home he'd known—the cold stone stairs, the cracked commanding bell, the tiny punishment cells. Quite suddenly he fell asleep, and the old minister was coming towards him, saying, "Shoot me. Shoot me in the eyes," and Raven was a child with a catapult in his hands. He wept and wouldn't shoot, and the old minister said, "Shoot, dear child. We'll go home together. Shoot."

Raven woke again as suddenly. In his sleep his hand had gripped the automatic tight. It was pointed at the corner where Anne slept. He gazed with horror into the dark, hearing a whisper like the one he had heard through the door when the secretary tried to call out. He said, "Are you asleep? What are you saying?"

Anne said, "I'm awake." She said defensively, "I was just praying."

"Do you believe in God?" Raven said.

"I don't know," Anne said. "Sometimes, maybe. It's a habit, praying. It doesn't do any harm. It's like crossing your fingers when you walk under a ladder. We all need any luck that's going."

Raven said, "We did a lot of praying in the home. Twice a day, and before meals too."

"It doesn't prove anything."

"No, it doesn't prove anything. Only you get sort of mad when everything reminds you of what's over and done with. Sometimes you want to begin fresh, and then someone praying or a smell or something you read in the paper, and it's all back again, the places and the people." He came a little nearer in the cold shed for company; it made you feel more than usually alone to know that they were waiting for you outside, waiting for daylight so that they could take you without any risk of your escaping or of your firing first. He had a good mind to send her out directly it was day and stick where he was and shoot it out with them. But that meant leaving Cholmon-deley and his employer free; it was just what would please them most. He said, "I was reading once—I like reading, I'm educated—something about psicko—psicko—"

"Leave it at that," Anne said. "I know what you mean."

"It seems as how your dreams mean things. I don't mean like tea leaves or cards."

"I knew someone once," Anne said. "She was so good with the

cards it gave you the creeps. She used to have those cards with queer pictures on them. The Hanged Man—"

"It wasn't like that," Raven said. "It was— Oh, I don't know properly. I couldn't understand it all. But it seems if you told your dreams— It was like you carrying a load around with you; you are born with some of it because of what your father and mother were and their fathers—seems as if it goes right back, like it says in the Bible about the sins being visited. Then when you're a kid the load gets bigger: all the things you need to do and can't, and then all the things you do. They get you either way." He leaned his sad, grim, killer's face on his hands. "It's like confessing to a priest. Only when you've confessed you go and do it all over again. I mean you tell these doctors everything, every dream you have, and afterwards you don't *want* to do it. But you have to tell them everything."

"Even the flying pigs?" Anne said.

"Everything. And when you've told everything it's gone."

"It sounds phony to me," Anne said.

"I don't suppose I've told it right. But it's what I read. I thought that maybe sometime it would be worth a trial."

"Life's full of funny things. Me and you being here. You thinking you wanted to kill me. Me thinking we can stop a war. Your psicko isn't any funnier than that."

"You see, it's the getting rid of it all that counts," Raven said. "It's not what the doctor does. That's how it seemed to me. Like when I told you about the home, about the bread and water and the prayers, they didn't seem so important afterwards." He swore softly and obscenely under his breath. "I'd always said I wouldn't go soft on a skirt. I always thought my lip'd save me. It's not safe to go soft. It makes you slow. I've seen it happen to other fellows. They've always landed in jail or got a razor in their guts. Now I've gone soft, as soft as all the rest."

"I like you," Anne said. "I'm your friend—"

"I'm not asking anything," Raven said. "I'm ugly, and I know it. Only one thing. Be different. Don't go to the police. Most skirts do. I've seen it happen. But maybe you aren't a skirt. You're a girl."

"I'm *someone's* girl."

"That's all right with me," he exclaimed with painful pride in the coldness and the dark. "I'm not asking anything but that, that you don't double-cross me."

"I'm not going to the police," Anne said. "I promise you I won't. I like you as well as any man—except my friend."

"I thought as how perhaps I could tell you a thing or two—dreams—just as well as any doctor. You see I know doctors. You can't trust them. I went to one before I came down here. I wanted him to alter this lip. He tried to put me to sleep with gas. He was going to call the police. You can't trust them. But I could trust you."

"You can trust me all right," Anne said. "I won't go to the police. But you'd better sleep first and tell me your dreams after, if you want to. It's a long night."

His teeth suddenly chattered uncontrollably with the cold, and Anne heard him. She put out a hand and touched his coat. "You're cold," she said. "You've given me all the sacks."

"I don't need 'em. I've got a coat."

"We're friends, aren't we?" Anne said. "We are in this together. You take two of these sacks."

He said, "There'll be some more about. I'll look," and he struck a match and felt his way round the wall. "Here are two," he said, sitting down farther away from her, empty-handed, out of reach. He said, "I can't sleep. Not properly. I had a dream just now. About the old man."

"What old man?"

"The old man that got murdered. I dreamed I was a kid with a catapult, and he was saying, 'Shoot me through the eyes,' and I was crying and he said, 'Shoot me through the eyes, dear child.' "

"Search *me* for a meaning," Anne said.

"I just wanted to tell it you."

"What did he look like?"

"Like he did look." Hastily he added, "Like I've seen in the photographs." He brooded over his memories with a low passionate urge towards confession. There had never in his life been anyone he could trust till now. He said, "You don't mind hearing these things?" and listened with a curious deep happiness to her reply—"We are friends." He said, "This is the best night I've ever had." But there were things he still couldn't tell her. His happiness was incomplete till she knew everything, till he had shown his trust completely. He didn't want to shock or pain her; he led slowly towards the central revelation. He said, "I've had other dreams of being a kid. I've dreamed I opened a door, a kitchen door, and there was my mother—she'd cut her throat—she looked ugly—her head nearly off—she'd sawn at it—with a breadknife."

Anne said, "That wasn't a dream."

"No," he said, "you're right, that wasn't a dream." He waited. He could feel her sympathy move silently towards him in the dark. He said, "That was ugly, wasn't it? You'd think you couldn't beat that for ugliness, wouldn't you? She hadn't even thought enough of me to lock the door so as I shouldn't see. And after that, there was a home. You know all about that. You'd say that was ugly too, but it wasn't as ugly as that other was. And they educated me, too, properly, so as I could understand the things I read in the papers. Like this psicko business. And write a good hand and speak the King's English. I got beaten a lot at the start, solitary confinement, bread and water, all the rest of the homey stuff. But that didn't go on when they'd educated me. I was too clever for them after that. They could never put a thing on me. They suspected all right, but they never had the proofs. Once the chaplain tried to frame me. They were right when they told us the day we left about it was like life. Jim and me and a bunch of soft kids." He said bitterly, "This is the first time they've had anything on me, and I'm innocent."

"You'll get away," Anne said. "We'll think up something together."

"It sounds good, your saying 'together' like that, but they've got me this time. I wouldn't mind if I could get that Chol-mon-deley and his boss first." He said with a kind of nervous pride, "Would you be surprised if I told you I'd killed a man?" It was like the first fence; if he cleared that he would have confidence. . . .

"Who?"

"Did you ever hear of Battling Kite?"

"No."

He laughed with a scared pleasure. "I'm trusting you with my life now. If you'd told me twenty-four hours ago that I'd trust my life to— But of course I haven't given you any *proof*. I was doing the races then. Kite had a rival gang. There wasn't anything else to do. He'd tried to bump my boss off on the course. Half of us took a fast car back to town. He thought we were on the train with him. But we were on the platform, see, when the train came in. We got round him directly he got outside the carriage. I cut his throat, and the others held him up till we were all through the barrier in a bunch. Then we dropped him by the bookstall and did a bolt." He said, "You see it was his lot or our lot. They'd had razors out on the course. It was war."

After a while Anne said, "Yes. I can see that. He had his chance."

"It sounds ugly," Raven said. "Funny thing is, it wasn't ugly. It was natural."

"Did you stick to that game?"

"No. It wasn't good enough. You couldn't trust the others. They either went soft or else they got reckless. They didn't use their brains." He said, "I wanted to tell you that about Kite. I'm not sorry. I haven't got religion. Only you said about being friendly, and I don't want you to get any wrong ideas. It was that mix-up with Kite brought me up against Chol-mon-deley. I can see now he was only in the racing game so as he could meet people. I thought he was a mug."

"We've got a long way from dreams."

"I was coming back to them," Raven said. "I suppose killing Kite like that made me nervous." His voice trembled very slightly from fear and hope, hope because she had accepted one killing so quietly and might, after all, take back what she had said ("Well done," "I wouldn't raise a finger"); fear because he didn't really believe that you could put such perfect trust in another and not be deceived. But it'd be fine, he thought, to be able to tell everything, to know that another person knew and didn't care; it would be like going to sleep for a long while. He said, "That spell of sleep I had just now was the first for two—three—I don't know how many nights. It looks as if I'm not tough enough after all."

"You seem tough enough to me," Anne said. "Don't let's hear any more about Kite."

"No one will hear any more about Kite. But if I was to tell you—" He ran away from the revelation. "I've been dreaming a lot lately it was an old woman I killed, not Kite. I heard her calling out through a door, and I tried to open the door, but she held the handle. I shot at her through the wood, but she held the handle tight. I had to kill her to open the door. Then I dreamed she was still alive and I shot her through the eyes. But even that—it wasn't *ugly*."

"You are tough enough in your dreams," Anne said.

"I killed an old man, too, in that dream. Behind his desk. I had a silencer. He fell behind it. I didn't want to hurt him. He didn't mean anything to me. I pumped him full. Then I put a bit of paper in his hand. I didn't have to take anything."

"What do you mean—you didn't have to take?"

Raven said. "They hadn't paid me to take anything. Chol-mon-deley and his boss."

"It wasn't a dream."

"No. It wasn't a dream." The silence frightened him. He began to talk rapidly to fill it. "I didn't know the old fellow was one of us. I wouldn't have touched him if I'd known he was like that. All this talk of war. It doesn't mean a thing to me. Why should I care if there's a war? There's always been a war for me. You talk a lot about the babies. Can't you have a bit of pity for the men? It was me or him. Two hundred pounds when I got back and fifty pounds down. It's a lot of money. It was only Kite over again. It was just as easy as it was with Kite." He said, "Are you going to leave me now?" and in the silence Anne could hear his rasping, anxious breath.

She said at last, "No. I'm not going to leave you."

He said, "That's good. Oh, that's good," putting out his hand, feeling hers cold as ice on the sacking. He put it for a moment against his unshaven cheek—he wouldn't touch it with his malformed lip. He said, "It feels good to trust someone with everything."

2

Anne waited for a long time before she spoke again. She wanted her voice to sound right, not to show her repulsion. Then she tried it on him, but all she could think of to say was again, "I'm not going to leave you." She remembered very clearly in the dark all she had read of the crime: the old woman secretary shot through the eyes, lying in the passage, the brutally smashed skull of the old Socialist. The papers had called it the worst political murder since the day when the king and queen of Serbia were thrown through the windows of their palace to ensure the succession of the wartime hero king.

Raven said again, "It's good to be able to trust someone like this," and suddenly his mouth, which had never before struck her as particularly ugly, came to mind, and she could have retched at the memory. Nevertheless, she thought, I must go on with this, I mustn't let him know. He must find Cholmondeley and Cholmondeley's boss, and then— She shrank from him into the dark.

He said, "They are out there waiting now. They've got cops down from London."

"From London?"

"It was all in the papers," he said with pride. "Detective Sergeant Mather from the Yard."

She could hardly restrain a cry of desolation and horror. "Here?"

"He may be outside now."

"Why doesn't he come in?"

"They'd never get me in the dark. And they'll know by now that *you* are here. They wouldn't be able to shoot."

"And you—you would?"

"There's no one *I* mind hurting," Raven said.

"How are you going to get out when it's daylight?"

"I shan't wait till then. I only want just light enough to see my way. And see to shoot. *They* won't be able to fire first; they won't be able to shoot to kill. That's what gives me a break. I only want a few clear hours. If I get away they'll never guess where to find me. Only you'll know I'm at Midland Steel."

She felt a desperate hatred. "You'll just shoot like that in cold blood?"

"You said you were on my side, didn't you?"

"Oh yes," she said warily, "yes," trying to think. It was getting too much to have to save the world—*and* Jimmy. If it came to a showdown the world would have to take second place. And what, she wondered, is Jimmy thinking? She knew his heavy, humourless rectitude; it would take more than Raven's head on a platter to make him understand why she had acted as she had with Raven and Cholmondeley. It sounded weak and fanciful even to herself to say that she wanted to stop a war.

"Let's sleep now," she said. "We've got a long, long day ahead."

"I think I could sleep now," Raven said. "You don't know how good it seems . . ." It was Anne now who could not sleep. She had too much to think about. It occurred to her that she might steal his pistol before he woke and call the police in. That would save Jimmy from danger, but what was the use? They'd never believe her story; they had no proof that he had killed the old man. And even then he might escape. She needed time, and there was no time. She could hear very faintly, droning up from the south, where the military aerodrome was, a troop of planes. They passed very high on special patrol, guarding the Nottwich mines and the key industry of Midland Steel, tiny specks of light the size of fireflies travelling fast in formation, over the railway, over the goods yard, over the shed where Anne and Raven lay, over Saunders beating his arms for warmth behind a truck out of the wind's way, over Acky dreaming that he was in the pulpit of St. Luke's, over Sir Marcus, sleepless beside the tape machine.

Raven slept heavily for the first time for nearly a week, holding the automatic in his lap. He dreamed that he was building a great bonfire on Guy Fawkes Day. He threw in everything he could find: a saw-edged knife, a lot of racing cards, the leg of a table. It burned warmly, deeply, beautifully. A lot of fireworks were going off all round him, and again the old war minister appeared on the other side of the fire. He said, "It's a good fire," stepping into it himself. Raven ran to the fire to pull him out, but the old man said, "Let me be. It's warm here," and then he sagged like a Guy Fawkes in the flames.

A clock struck. Anne counted the strokes, as she had counted them all through the night; it must be nearly day, and she had no plan. She coughed—her throat was stinging—and suddenly she realized with joy that there was fog outside—not one of the black upper fogs, but a cold, damp, yellow fog from the river, through which it would be easy, if it were thick enough, for a man to escape. She put out her hand unwillingly, because he was now so repulsive to her, and touched Raven. He woke at once. She said, "There's a fog coming up."

"What a break," he said, "what a break," laughing softly. "It makes you believe in Providence, doesn't it?" They could just see each other in the pale, earliest light. He was shivering now that he was awake. He said, "I dreamed of a big fire." She saw that he had no sacks to cover him, but she felt no pity at all. He was just a wild animal who had to be dealt with carefully and then destroyed. Let him freeze, she thought. He was examining the automatic; she saw him put down the safety catch. He said, "What about you? You've been straight with me. I don't want you to get into any trouble. I don't want them to think"—he hesitated and went on with questioning humility—"to know that we are in this together."

"I'll think up something," Anne said.

"I ought to knock you out. They wouldn't know then. But I've gone soft. I wouldn't hurt you, not if I was paid."

She couldn't resist saying, "Not for two hundred and fifty pounds?"

"He was a stranger," Raven said. "It's not the same. I thought he was one of the high and mighties. You're"—he hesitated again, glowering dumbly down at the automatic—"a friend."

"You needn't be afraid," Anne said. "I'll have a tale to tell."

He said with admiration, "You're clever." He watched the fog coming in under the badly fitting door, filling the small shed with its

freezing coils. "It'll be nearly thick enough now to take a chance."
He held the automatic in his left hand and flexed the fingers of the
right. He laughed to keep his courage up. "They'll never get me
now in this fog."

"You'll shoot?"

"Of course I'll shoot."

"I've got an idea," Anne said. "We don't want to take any risks.
Give me your overcoat and hat. I'll put them on and slip out first
and give them a run for their money. In this fog they'll never notice
till they've caught me. Directly you hear the whistles blow count
five slowly and make a bolt. I'll run to the right. You run to the
left."

"You've got nerve," Raven said. He shook his head. "No. They
might shoot."

"You said yourself they wouldn't shoot first."

"That's right. But you'll get a couple of years for this."

"Oh," Anne said, "I'll tell them a tale. I'll say you forced me."
She said with a trace of bitterness, "This'll give me a lift out of the
chorus. I'll have a speaking part."

Raven said shyly, "If you made out you were my girl, they
wouldn't pin it on you. I'll say that for them. They'd give a man's
girl a break."

"Got a knife?"

"Yes." He felt in all his pockets. It wasn't there; he must have
left it on the floor of Acky's best guest chamber.

Anne said, "I wanted to cut up my skirt. I'd be able to run
easier."

"I'll try and tear it," Raven said, kneeling in front of her, taking
a grip; but it wouldn't tear. Looking down, she was astonished at
the smallness of his wrists; his hands had no more strength or substance than a delicate boy's. The whole of his strength lay in the
mechanical instrument at his feet. She thought of Mather and felt
contempt now as well as repulsion for the thin, ugly body kneeling
at her feet.

"Never mind," she said. "I'll do the best I can. Give me the
coat."

He shivered, taking it off, and seemed to lose some of his sour
assurance without the tight black tube which had hidden a very
old, very flamboyant check suit in holes at both the elbows. It hung
on him uneasily. He looked undernourished. He wouldn't have impressed anyone as dangerous now. He pressed his arms to his sides

to hide the holes. "And your hat," Anne said. He picked it from the sacks and gave it her. He looked humiliated, and he had never accepted humiliation before without rage. "Now," Anne said, "remember. Wait for the whistles and then count."

"I don't like it," Raven said. He tried hopelessly to express the deep pain it gave him to see her go; it felt too much like the end of everything. He said, "I'll see you again—sometime," and when she mechanically reassured him, "Yes," he laughed with his aching despair. "Not likely, after I've killed—" But he didn't even know the man's name.

Six

1

Saunders had half fallen asleep. A voice at his side woke him. "The fog's getting thick, sir."

It was already dense, with the first light touching it with dusty yellow, and he would have sworn at the policeman for not waking him earlier if his stammer had not made him chary of wasting words. He said, "Pass the word round to move in."

"Are we going to rush the place, sir?"

"No. There's the girl there. We can't have any s-s-shooting. Wait till he comes out."

But the policeman hadn't left his side when he noticed, "The door's opening." Saunders put his whistle in his mouth and lowered his safety catch. The light was bad and the fog deceptive, but he recognized the dark coat as it slipped quickly to the right into the shelter of the coal trucks. He blew his whistle and was after it. The black coat had half a minute's start and was moving quickly into the fog. It was impossible to see at all more than twenty feet ahead. But Saunders kept doggedly just in sight, blowing his whistle continuously. As he hoped, a whistle blew in front. It confused the fugitive; he hesitated for a moment, and Saunders gained on him. They had him cornered, and this Saunders knew was the dangerous moment. He blew his whistle urgently three times into the fog to bring the police round in a complete circle, and the whistle was taken up in the yellow obscurity, passing in a wide invisible circle.

But he had lost pace; the fugitive spurted forward and was lost. Saunders blew two blasts: "Advance slowly and keep in touch." To the right and in front a single long whistle announced that the man had been seen, and the police converged on the sound. Each kept in touch with a policeman on either hand. It was impossible, as long as the circle was kept closed, for the man to escape. But the circle drew in, and there was no sign of him. The short, single, explanatory blasts sounded petulant and lost. At last Saunders, gazing ahead, saw the faint form of a policeman come out of the fog a dozen yards away. He halted them all with a whistled signal; the fugitive must be somewhere just ahead in the tangle of trucks in the center. Revolver in hand, Saunders advanced, and a policeman took his place and closed the circle.

Suddenly Saunders spied his man. He had taken up a strategic position where a pile of coal and an empty truck at his back made a wedge which guarded him from surprise. He was invisible to the police behind him, and he had turned sidewise, like a duellist, and presented only a shoulder to Saunders, while a pile of old sleepers hid him to the knees. It seemed to Saunders that it meant only one thing—that he was going to shoot it out. The man must be mad and desperate. The hat was pulled down over the face; the coat hung in an odd, loose way; the hands were in the pockets. Saunders called at him through the yellow coils of fog, "You'd better come quietly." He raised his pistol and advanced, his finger ready on the trigger. But the immobility of the figure scared him. It was in shadow, half hidden in the swirl of fog. It was he who was exposed, with the east, and the pale penetration of early light behind him. It was like waiting for execution, for he could not fire first. But all the same, knowing what Mather felt, knowing that this man was mixed up with Mather's girl, he did not want much excuse to fire. Mather would stand by him. A movement would be enough. He said sharply, without a stammer, "Put up your hands." The figure didn't move. He told himself again, with a kindling hatred for the man who had injured Mather, I'll plug him if he doesn't obey. They'll all stand by me. One more chance. "Put up your hands," and when the figure stayed as it was, with its hands hidden, a hardly discernible menace, he fired.

But as he pressed the trigger a whistle blew, a long urgent blast which panted and gave out like a rubber animal, from the direction of the wall and the road. There could be no doubt whatever what that meant, and suddenly he saw it all—he had shot at Mather's girl; she'd drawn them off. He screamed at the men behind him, "Back to the gate," and ran forward. He had seen her waver at his shot. He said, "Are you hurt?" and knocked the hat off her head to see her better.

"You're the third person who's tried to kill me," Anne said weakly, leaning hard against the truck. "Come to sunny Nottwich. Well, I've got six lives left."

Saunders' stammer came back. "W-w-w-w—"

"This is where you hit," Anne said, "if that's what you want to know," showing the long yellow sliver on the edge of the truck. "It was only an outer. You don't even get a box of chocolates."

Saunders said, "You'll have to c-c-come along with me."

"It'll be a pleasure. Do you mind if I take off this coat? I feel kind of silly."

At the gate four policemen stood round something on the ground. One of them said, "We've sent for an ambulance."

"Is he dead?"

"Not yet. He's shot in the stomach. He must have gone on whistling—"

Saunders had a moment of vicious rage. "Stand aside, boys," he said, "and let the lady see." They drew back in an embarrassed, unwilling way, as if they'd been hiding a dirty chalk picture on the wall, and showed the white, drained face, which looked as if it had never been alive, never known the warm circulation of blood. You couldn't call the expression peaceful; it was just nothing at all. The blood was all over the trousers the men had loosened, was caked on the charcoal of the path. Saunders said, "Two of you take this lady to the station. I'll stay here till the ambulance comes."

2

Mather said, "If you want to make a statement I must warn you that anything you say may be used in evidence."

"I haven't got a statement to make," Anne said. "I want to talk to you, Jimmy."

Mather said, "If the superintendent had been here, I should have asked him to take the case. I want you to understand that I'm not letting personal—that my not having charged you doesn't mean—"

"You might give a girl a cup of coffee," Anne said. "It's nearly breakfast time."

Mather struck the table furiously. "Where was he going?"

"Give me time," Anne said. "I've got plenty to tell. But you won't believe it."

"You saw the man he shot," Mather said. "He's got a wife and two children. They've rung up from the hospital. He's bleeding internally."

"What's the time?" Anne said.

"Eight o'clock. It won't make any difference, your keeping quiet. He can't escape us now. In an hour the air-raid signals go. There won't be a soul on the streets without a mask. He'll be spotted at once. What's he wearing?"

"If you'd give me something to eat. I haven't had a thing for twenty-four hours. I could think then."

Mather said, "There's only one chance you won't be charged with complicity. If you make a statement."

"Is this third degree?" Anne said.

"Why do you want to shelter him? Why keep your word to him when you don't—?"

"Go on," Anne said. "Be personal. No one can blame you. I don't. But I don't want you to think I'd keep my word to him. He killed the old man. He told me so."

"What old man?"

"The war minister."

"You've got to think up something better than that," Mather said.

"But it's true. He never stole those notes. They double-crossed him. It was what they'd paid him to do the job."

"He spun you a fancy yarn," Mather said. "But *I* know where those notes came from."

"So do I. I can guess. From somewhere in this town."

"He told you wrong. They came from United Rail Makers in Victoria Street."

Anne shook her head. "They didn't start from there. They came from Midland Steel."

"So that's where he's going, to Midland Steel—in the Tanneries?"

"Yes," Anne said. There was a sound of finality about the word which daunted her. She hated Raven now. The policeman she had seen bleeding on the ground called at her heart for Raven's death, but she couldn't help remembering the hut, the cold, the pile of sacks, his complete and hopeless trust. She sat with bowed head while Mather lifted the receiver and gave his orders.

"We'll wait for him there," he said. "Who is it he wants to see?"

"He doesn't know."

"There might be something in it," Mather said. "Some connection between the two. He's probably been double-crossed by some clerk."

"It wasn't a clerk who paid him all that money, who tried to kill me just because I knew—"

Mather said, "Your fairy tale can wait." He rang a bell and told the constable who came, "Hold this girl for further inquiries. You can give her a sandwich and a cup of coffee now."

"Where are you going?"

"To bring in your boy friend," Mather said.

"He'll shoot. He's quicker than you are. Why can't you let the others . . ." she implored him. "I'll make a full statement. How he killed Kite, too."

"Take it," Mather said to the constable. He put on his coat. "The fog's clearing."

She said, "Don't you see that if it's true—only give him time to find his man and there won't be—war."

"He was telling you a fairy story."

"He was telling me the truth—but, of course, you weren't there, you didn't hear him. It sounds different to you. I thought I was saving—everyone."

"All you did," Mather said brutally, "was get a man killed."

"The whole thing sounds so different in here. Kind of fantastic. But he believed. Maybe," she said hopelessly, "he was mad."

Mather opened the door. She suddenly cried to him, "Jimmy, he wasn't mad. They tried to kill *me*."

He said, "I'll read your statement when I get back," and closed the door.

Seven

1

They were all having the hell of a time at the hospital. It was the biggest rag they'd had since the day of the street collection when they kidnapped old Piker and ran him to the edge of the Weevil and threatened to duck him if he didn't pay a ransom. Good old Fergusson, good old Buddy, was organizing it all. They had three ambulances out in the courtyard, and one had a death's head banner on it for the dead ones. Somebody shrieked that Mike was tak-

ing out the petrol with a nasal syringe, so they began to pelt him
with flour and soot—they had it ready in great buckets. It was the
unofficial part of the programme; all the casualties were going to be
rubbed with it, except the dead ones the death's-head ambulance
picked up. *They* were going to be put in the cellar where the re-
frigerating plant kept the corpses for dissection fresh.

One of the senior surgeons passed rapidly and nervously across
a corner of the courtyard. He was on the way to a Caesarian operation, but he had no confidence whatever that the students wouldn't
pelt him or duck him. Only five years ago there had been a scandal
and an inquiry because a woman had died on the day of a rag.
The surgeon attending her had been kidnapped and carried all over
town dressed as Guy Fawkes. Luckily she wasn't a paying patient,
and, though her husband had been hysterical at the inquest, the
coroner had decided that one must make allowance for youth. The
coroner had been a student himself once and remembered with
pleasure the day when they had pelted the vice-chancellor of the
university with soot.

The senior surgeon had been present that day too. Once safely
inside the glass corridor he could smile at the memory. The vice-
chancellor had been unpopular; he had been a classic, which wasn't
very suitable for a provincial university. He had translated Lucan's
Pharsalia into some complicated metre of his own invention. The
senior surgeon remembered something vaguely about stresses. He
could still see the little wizened, frightened Liberal face trying to
smile when his pince-nez broke, trying to be a good sportsman. But
anyone could tell that he wasn't really a good sportsman. That's
why they pelted him so hard.

The senior surgeon, quite safe now, smiled tenderly down at the
rabble in the courtyard. Their white coats were already black with
soot. Somebody had got hold of a stomach pump. Very soon they'd
be raiding the shop in the High Street and seizing their mascot, the
stuffed and rather moth-eaten tiger. Youth, youth, he thought,
laughing gently when he saw Mander, the treasurer, scuttle from
door to door with a scared expression. Perhaps they'll catch him—
no, they've let him by. What a joke it all was, "trailing clouds of
glory," "turn as swimmers into cleanness leaping."

Buddy was having the hell of a time. Everyone was scampering
to obey his orders. He was the leader. They'd duck or pelt anyone
he told them to. He had an enormous sense of power; it more than
atoned for unsatisfactory examination results, for surgeons' sar-

casms. Even a surgeon wasn't safe today if *he* gave an order. The soot and water and flour were his idea. The whole gas practice would have been a dull, sober, official piece of routine if he hadn't thought of making it a "rag." The very word "rag" was powerful; it conferred complete freedom from control. He'd called a meeting of the brighter students and explained, "If anyone's on the street without a gas mask he's a conchie. There are people who want to crab the practice. So when we get 'em back to the hospital we'll give 'em hell."

They boiled round him. "Good old Buddy." "Look out with that pump." "Who's the bastard who's pinched my stethoscope?" "What about Tiger Tim?" They surged round Buddy Fergusson, waiting for orders, and he stood superbly above them on the step of an ambulance, his white coat apart, his fingers in the pockets of his double-breasted waistcoat, his square, squat figure swelling with pride, while they shouted, "Tiger Tim. Tiger Tim. Tiger Tim."

"Friends, Romans, and Countrymen," he said, and they roared with laughter. Good old Buddy. Buddy always had the right word. He could make any party go. You never knew what Buddy would say next. "Lend me your—" They shrieked with laughter. He was a dirty dog, old Buddy. Good old Buddy.

Like a great beast which is in need of exercise, which has fed on too much hay, Buddy Fergusson was aware of his body. He felt his biceps; he strained for action. Too many exams, too many lectures. Buddy Fergusson wanted action. While they surged round him he imagined himself a leader of men. No Red Cross work for him when war broke: Buddy Fergusson, company commander; Buddy Fergusson, the daredevil of the trenches. The only exam he had ever successfully passed was Certificate A in the school O.T.C.

"Some of our friends seem to be missing," Buddy Fergusson said. "Simmons, Aitkin, Mallowes, Watt. They are bloody conchies, every one, grubbing up anatomy while we are serving our country. We'll pick 'em up in town. The Flying Squad will go to their lodgings."

"What about the women, Buddy?" someone screamed, and everyone laughed and began to hit at each other, wrestle and mill. For Buddy had a reputation with the women. He spoke airily to his friends of even the super-barmaid at the Metropole, calling her Juicy Juliet and suggesting to the minds of his hearers amazing scenes of abandonment over high tea at his digs.

Buddy Fergusson straddled across the ambulance step. "Deliver 'em to me. In wartime we need more mothers." He felt strong, coarse, vital, a town bull. He hardly remembered himself that he was virgin, guilty only of a shamefaced unsuccessful attempt on the old Nottwich tart. He was sustained by his reputation; it bore him magically in imagination into every bed. He knew women, he was a realist.

"Treat 'em rough," they shrieked at him, and, "You're telling me," he said magnificently, keeping well at bay any thought of the future: the small, provincial G.P.'s job, the panel patients in dingy consulting rooms, innumerable midwife cases, a lifetime of hard, underpaid fidelity to one dull wife. "Got your gas masks ready?" he called to them, the undisputed leader, daredevil Buddy. What the hell did examinations matter when you were a leader of men? He could see several of the younger nurses watching him through the panes. He could see the little brunette called Milly. She was coming to tea with him on Saturday. He felt his muscles taut with pride. What scenes, he told himself, there would be *this* time of disreputable revelry, forgetting the inevitable truth known only to himself and each girl in turn: the long silence over the muffins, the tentative references to League results, the peck at empty air on the doorstep.

The siren at the glue factory started its long mounting whistle rather like a lap dog with hysteria, and everyone stood still for a moment with a vague reminiscence of Armistice Day silences. Then they broke into three milling mobs, climbing onto the ambulance roofs, fixing their gas masks, and drove out into the cold, empty Nottwich streets. The ambulances shed a lot of them at each corner, and small groups formed and wandered down the streets with a predatory, disappointed air. The streets were almost empty. Only a few errand boys passed on bicycles, looking in their gas masks like bears doing a trick cycle act in a circus. They all shrieked at each other because they didn't know how their voices sounded outside. It was as if each of them were enclosed in a separate soundproof telephone cabinet. They stared hungrily through their big mica eyepieces into the doorways of shops, wanting a victim. A little group collected round Buddy Fergusson and proposed that they should seize a policeman who, being on point duty, was without a mask. But Buddy vetoed the proposal. He said this wasn't an ordinary rag. What they wanted were people who thought so little about their country that they wouldn't even take the trouble to put on a gas mask. "They are the people," he said, "who avoid boat drill. We had great fun with a fellow once in the Mediterranean who didn't turn up to boat drill."

That reminded them of all the fellows who weren't helping, who were probably getting ahead with their anatomy at that moment. "Watt lives near here," Buddy Fergusson said. "Let's get Watt and debag him." A feeling of physical well being came over him just as if he had drunk a couple of pints of bitter. "Down the Tanneries," Buddy said. "First left. First right. Second left. Number Twelve. First floor." He knew the way, he said, because he'd been to tea several times with Watt their first term before he'd learned what a hound Watt was. The knowledge of his early mistake made him unusually anxious to do something to Watt physically, to mark the severance of their relationship more completely than with sneers.

They ran down the empty Tanneries, half-a-dozen masked monstrosities in white coats smutted with soot. It was impossible to tell one from another. Through the great glass door of Midland Steel they saw three men standing by the lift, talking to the porter. There were a lot of uniformed police about, and in the square ahead they saw a rival group of fellow students, who had been luckier than they, carrying a little man (he kicked and squealed) towards an ambulance. The police watched and laughed, and a troop of planes zoomed overhead, diving low over the centre of the town to lend the practice verisimilitude. First left. First right. The centre of Nottwich, to a stranger, was full of sudden contrasts. Only on the edge of the town to the north, out by the park, were you certain of encountering street after street of well-to-do middle-class houses. Near the market you changed at a corner from modern chromium offices to little cats'-meat shops; from the luxury of the Metropole to seedy lodgings and the smell of cooking greens. There was no excuse in Nottwich for one half of the world being ignorant of how the other half lived.

Second left. The houses on one side gave way to bare rock, and the street dived steeply down below the Castle. It wasn't really a castle any longer; it was a yellow brick municipal museum full of flint arrowheads and pieces of broken brown pottery and a few stags' heads in the zoological section, suffering from moths, and one mummy brought back from Egypt by the Earl of Nottwich in 1843. The moths left that alone, but the custodian thought he had heard mice inside. Mike, with a nasal douche in his breast pocket, wanted to climb up the rock. He shouted to Buddy Fergusson that the custodian was outside without a mask, signalling to enemy aircraft. But Buddy and the others ran down the hill to Number Twelve.

The landlady opened the door to them. She smiled winningly and said Mr. Watt was in—she thought he was working. She button-holed Buddy Fergusson and said she was sure it would be good for Mr. Watt to be taken away from his books for half an hour. Buddy said, "We'll take him away."

"Why, that's Mr. Fergusson," the landlady said. "I'd know your voice anywhere, but I'd never 'ave known you without you spoke to me, not in them respiratorories. I was just going out when Mr. Watt reminded me as 'ow it was the gas practice."

"Oh, he remembers, does he?" Buddy said. He was blushing in-side the mask at having been recognized by the landlady. It made him want to assert himself more than ever.

"He said I'd be taken to the 'ospital."

"Come on, men," Buddy said and led them up the stairs. But their number was an embarrassment. They couldn't all charge through Watt's door and seize him in a moment from the chair in which he was sitting. They had to go through one at a time after Buddy and then bunch themselves in a shy silence beside the table. This was the moment when an experienced man could have dealt with them, but Watt was aware of his unpopularity. He was afraid of losing dignity. He was a man who worked hard because he liked the work—he hadn't the excuse of poverty. He played no games because he didn't like games, without the excuse of physical weak-ness. He had a mental arrogance which would ensure his success. If he suffered agony from his unpopularity now, as a student, it was the price he paid for the baronetcy, the Harley Street consult-ing room, the fashionable practice of the future. There was no reason to pity him; it was the others who were pitiable, living in their vivid, vulgar way for five years before the long provincial in-terment of a lifetime.

Watt said, "Close the door, please. There's a draught," and his scared sarcasm gave them the chance they needed to resent him.

Buddy said, "We've come to ask why you weren't at the hospital this morning."

"That's Fergusson, isn't it?" Watt said. "I don't know why you want to know."

"Are you a conchie?"

"How old-world your slang is," Watt said. "No. I'm not a conchie. Now I'm just looking through some old medical books, and as I don't suppose they'd interest you, I'll ask you to show yourself out."

"Working? That's how fellows like you get ahead, working while others are doing a proper job."

"It's just a different idea of fun, that's all," Watt said. "It's my pleasure to look at these folios, it's yours to go screaming about the streets in that odd costume."

That let them loose on him. He was as good as insulting the king's uniform. "We're going to debag you," Buddy said.

"That's fine. It'll save time," Watt said, "if I take them off myself," and he began to undress. He said, "This action has an interesting psychological significance. A form of castration. My own theory is that sexual jealousy in some form is at the bottom of it."

"You dirty tyke," Buddy said. He took an inkpot and splashed it on the wallpaper. He didn't like the word "sex." He believed in barmaids and nurses and tarts, and he believed in love—something rather maternal with deep breasts. The word sex suggested that there was something in common between the two; it outraged him. "Wreck the room," he bawled, and all were immediately happy and at ease, exerting themselves physically like young bulls. Because they were happy again they didn't do any real damage, just pulled the books out of the shelves and threw them on the floor. They broke the glass of a picture frame in puritanical zeal because it contained the reproduction of a nude girl by Munke. Watt watched them. He was scared, and the more scared he was the more sarcastic he became. Buddy suddenly saw him as he was, standing there in his pants, marked from birth for distinction, for success, and hated him. He felt impotent; he hadn't "class" like Watt, he hadn't the brains. In a very few years nothing he could do or say would affect the fortunes or the happiness of the Harley Street specialist, the woman's physician, the baronet. What was the good of talking about free will? Only war and death could save Buddy from the confinements, the provincial practice, the one dull wife, and the bridge parties. It seemed to him that he could be happy if he had the strength to impress himself on Watt's memory. He took an inkpot and poured it over the open title page of the old folio on the table.

"Come on, men," he said. "This room stinks," and led his party out and down the stairs. He felt an immense exhilaration; it was as if he had proved his manhood.

Almost immediately they picked up an old woman. She didn't

in the least know what it was all about. She thought it was a street collection and offered them a penny. They told her she had to come along to the hospital. They were very courteous, and one offered to carry her basket; they reacted from violence to a more than usual gentility. She laughed at them. She said, "Well I never, what you boys will think up next." And when one took her arm and began to lead her gently up the street, she said, "Which of you's Father Christmas?" Buddy didn't like that; it hurt his dignity. He had suddenly been feeling rather noble: "women and children first," "although bombs were falling all round he brought the woman safely . . ." He stood still and let the others go on up the street with the old woman. She was having the time of her life; she cackled and dug them in the ribs—her voice carried a long distance in the cold air. She kept on telling them to "take off them things and play fair," and just before they turned a corner out of sight she was calling them Mormons. She meant Mohammedans, because she had an idea that Mohammedans went about with their faces covered up and had a lot of wives. An airplane zoomed overhead, and Buddy was alone in the street with the dead and dying until Mike appeared. Mike said he had a good idea. Why not pinch the mummy in the castle and take it to the hospital for not wearing a gas mask? The fellows with the death's-head ambulance had already got Tiger Tim and were driving round the town, crying out for old Piker.

"No," Buddy said, "this isn't an ordinary rag. This is serious." And suddenly, at the entrance to a side street, he saw a man without a mask double back at the sight of him. "Quick. Hunt him down," Buddy cried. "Tally-ho," and they pelted up the street in pursuit. Mike was the faster runner—Buddy was already a little inclined to fatness—and Mike was soon leading by ten yards. The man had a start, he was round one corner and out of sight. "Go on," Buddy shouted, "hold him till I come." Mike was out of sight too when a voice from a doorway spoke as he passed. "Hi," it said, "you. What's the hurry?"

Buddy stopped. The man stood there with his back pressed to a house door. He had simply stepped back, and Mike in his hurry had gone by. There was something serious and planned and venomous about his behaviour. The street of little Gothic villas was quite empty.

"You were looking for me, weren't you?" the man said.

Buddy demanded sharply, "Where's your gas mask?"

"Is this a game?" the man said angrily.

"Of course it's not a game," Buddy said. "You're a casualty. You'll have to come along to the hospital with me."

"I will, will I?" the man said, pressed back against the door, thin and undersized and out-at-elbows.

"You'd better," Buddy said. He inflated his chest and made his biceps swell. Discipline, he thought, discipline. The little brute didn't recognize an officer when he saw one. He felt the satisfaction of superior physical strength. He'd punch his nose for him if he didn't come quietly.

"All right," the man said, "I'll come." He emerged from the dark doorway, mean vicious face, harelip, a crude check suit, ominous and aggressive in his submission.

"Not that way," Buddy said, "to the left."

"Keep moving," the small man said, covering Buddy through his pocket, pressing the pistol against his side. *"Me* a casualty," he said, "that's a good one," laughing without mirth. "Get in through that gate or you'll be the casualty." (They were opposite a small garage. It was empty. The owner had driven to his office, and the little bare box stood open at the end of a few feet of drive.)

Buddy blustered, "What the hell," but he had recognized the face of which the description had appeared in both the local papers, and there was a control in the man's actions which horribly convinced Buddy that he wouldn't hesitate to shoot. It was a moment in his life that he never forgot; he was not allowed to forget it by friends who saw nothing wrong in what he did. All through his life the tale cropped up in print in the most unlikely places: serious histories, symposiums of famous crimes. It followed him from obscure practice to obscure practice. Nobody saw anything important in what he did. Nobody doubted that he would have done the same—walked into the garage, closed the gates at Raven's orders. But friends didn't realize the crushing nature of the blow; they hadn't just been standing in the street under a hail of bombs, they had not looked forward with pleasure and excitement to war, they hadn't been Buddy, the daredevil of the trenches, one minute before real war in the shape of an automatic in a thin, desperate hand broke on him.

"Strip," Raven said, and obediently Buddy stripped. But he was stripped of more than his gas mask, his white coat, his green tweed suit. When it was over he hadn't a hope left. It was no good hoping for a war to prove him a leader of men. He was just a stout, flushed, frightened young man shivering in his pants in the cold garage.

There was a hole in the seat of his pants, and his knees were pink and hairless. You could tell that he was strong, but you could tell too in the curve of his stomach, the thickness of his neck, that he was beginning to run to seed. Like a mastiff, he needed more exercise than the city could afford him, even though several times a week, undeterred by the frost, he would put on shorts and a singlet and run slowly and obstinately round the park, a little red in the face but undeterred by the grins of nursemaids and the shrill, veracious comments of unbearable children in prams. He was keeping fit, but it was a dreadful thought that he had been keeping fit for this, to stand shivering and silent in a pair of holey pants while the mean, thin, undernourished city rat, whose arm he could have snapped with a single twist, put on his clothes, his white coat and, last of all, his gas mask.

"Turn round," Raven said, and Buddy Fergusson obeyed. He was so miserable now that he would have missed a chance even if Raven had given him one—miserable and scared as well. He hadn't much imagination; he had never really visualized danger as it now gleamed at him under the garage globe in a long, grey, wicked-looking piece of metal charged with pain and death. "Put your hands behind you." Raven tied together the pink, strong, hamlike wrists with Buddy's tie—the striped chocolate-and-yellow old boys' tie of one of the obscurer public schools. "Lie down," and meekly Buddy Fergusson obeyed, and Raven tied his feet together with a handkerchief and gagged him with another. It wasn't very secure, but it would have to do. He'd got to work quickly. He left the garage and pulled the doors softly to behind him. He could *hope* for several hours' start now, but he couldn't count on as many minutes.

He came quietly and cautiously up under the castle rock, keeping his eye open for students. But the gangs had moved on; some were picketing the station for train arrivals, and the others were sweeping the streets which led out northwards towards the mines. The chief danger now was that at any moment the sirens might blow the all-clear. There were a lot of police about—he knew why —but he moved unhesitantly past them and on towards the Tanneries. His plan carried him no farther than the big glass doors of Midland Steel. He had a kind of blind faith in destiny, in a poetic justice; somehow when he was inside the building he would find the way to the man who had double-crossed him. He came safely round into the Tanneries and moved across the narrow roadway, where there was only room for a single stream of traffic, towards the great

functional building of black glass and steel. He hugged the automatic to his hip with a sense of achievement and exhilaration. There
was a kind of lightheartedness now about his malice and hatred that
he had never known before; he had lost his sourness and bitterness,
he was less personal in his revenge. It was almost as if he were
acting for someone else.

Behind the door of Midland Steel a man peered out at the parked
cars and the deserted street. He looked like a clerk. Raven crossed
the pavement. He peered back through the panes of the mask at the
man behind the door. Something made him hesitate—the memory
of a face he had seen for a moment in the Soho café where he had
lodged. He suddenly started away again from the door, walking in
a rapid, scared way down the Tanneries. The police were there
before him.

It meant nothing, Raven told himself, coming out into a silent
High Street, empty except for a telegraph boy in a gas mask getting
onto a bicycle by the post office. It merely meant that the police
too had noted a connection between the office in Victoria Street
and Midland Steel. It didn't mean that the girl was just another skirt
who had betrayed him. Only the faintest shadow of the old sourness and isolation touched his spirits. She's straight, he swore with
almost perfect conviction; *she* wouldn't double-cross. We are together in this—and he remembered with a sense of doubtful safety
how she had said, "We are friends."

2

The producer had called a rehearsal early. He wasn't going to
add to the expenses by buying everyone gas masks. They would be
in the theatre by the time the practice started, and they wouldn't
leave until the all-clear had sounded. Mr. Davis had said he wanted
to see the new number, and so the producer had sent him notice of
the rehearsal. He had it stuck under the edge of his shaving mirror
next a card with the telephone numbers of all his girls.

It was bitterly cold in the modern central-heated bachelor's flat.
Something, as usual, had gone wrong with the oil engines, and the
constant hot water was barely warm. Mr. Davis cut himself shaving
several times and stuck little tufts of cotton wool all over his chin.
His eye caught Mayfair 632 and Museum 798. Those were Coral
and Lucy. Dark and fair, nubile and thin. His fair and his dark
angel. A little early fog still yellowed the panes, and the sound of a

car backfiring made him think of Raven safely isolated in the railway yard surrounded by armed police. He knew that Sir Marcus was arranging everything, and he wondered how it felt to be waking to your last day. "We know not the hour," Mr. Davis thought happily, plying his styptic pencil, sticking the cotton wool on the larger wounds, but if one knew, as Raven must know, would one still feel irritation at the failure of central heating, at a blunt blade? Mr. Davis's mind was full of great dignified abstractions, and it seemed to him a rather grotesque idea that a man condemned to death should be aware of something so trivial as a shaving cut. But then, of course, Raven would not be shaving in his shed.

Mr. Davis made a hasty breakfast: two pieces of toast, two cups of coffee, four kidneys and a piece of bacon, sent up by lift from the restaurant, some sweet silver-shred marmalade. It gave him a good deal of pleasure to think that Raven would not be eating such a breakfast; a condemned man in prison, possibly, but not Raven. Mr. Davis did not believe in wasting anything. He had paid for the breakfast, so on the second piece of toast he piled up all the remains of the butter and the marmalade. A little of the marmalade fell off onto his tie.

There was really only one worry left, apart from Sir Marcus's displeasure, and that was the girl. He had lost his head badly, first in trying to kill her and then in not killing her. It had all been Sir Marcus's fault. He had been afraid of what Sir Marcus would do to him if he learned of the girl's existence. But now everything should be all right. The girl had come out into the open as an accomplice; no court would take a criminal's story against Sir Marcus's. He forgot about the gas practice, hurrying down to the theatre for a little relaxation now that everything really seemed to have been tidied up. On the way he got a sixpenny packet of toffee out of a slot machine.

He found Mr. Collier worried. They'd already had one rehearsal of the new number, and Miss Maydew, who was sitting at the front of the stalls in a fur coat, had said it was vulgar. She said she didn't mind sex, but this wasn't in the right class. It was music-hall, it wasn't revue. Mr. Collier didn't care a damn what Miss Maydew thought, but it might mean that Mr. Cohen . . . He said, "If you'd tell me what's vulgar—I just don't see—"

Mr. Davis said, "I'll tell you if it's vulgar. Have it again," and he sat back in the stalls just behind Miss Maydew with the warm smell of her fur and her rather expensive scent in his nostrils, sucking a toffee. It seemed to him that life could offer nothing better than this. And the show was his. At any rate forty per cent of it was his. He picked out his forty per cent as the girls came on again in diminutive blue shorts with a red stripe and postmen's caps, and brassières, carrying cornucopias: the dark girl with the oriental eyebrows on the right, the fair girl with the rather plump legs and the big mouth (a big mouth was a good sign in a girl). They danced between two pillar boxes, wriggling their little neat hips, and Mr. Davis sucked his toffee.

"It's called 'Christmas for Two,' " Mr. Collier said.

"Why?"

"Well, you see, those cornucops are meant to be Christmas presents made sort of classical. And 'for Two' just gives it a little sex. Any number with 'for Two' in it goes."

"We've already got 'An Apartment for Two,' " Miss Maydew said, "and 'Two Make a Dream.' "

"You can't have too much of 'for Two,' " Mr. Collier said. He appealed pitiably, "Can't you tell me what's vulgar?"

"Those cornucopias, for one thing."

"But they are classical," Mr. Collier said. "Greek."

"And the pillar boxes for another."

"The pillar boxes!" Mr. Collier exclaimed hysterically. "What's wrong with the pillar boxes?"

"My dear man," Miss Maydew said, "if you don't know what's wrong with the pillar boxes, I'm not going to tell you. If you'd like to get a committee of matrons I wouldn't mind telling *them*. But if you *must* have them, paint them blue and let them be air mail."

Mr. Collier said, "Is this a game or what is it?" He added bitterly, "What a time you must have when you write a letter." The girls went patiently on behind his back to the jingle of the piano, offering the cornucopias, offering their collar-stud tails. He turned on them fiercely. "Stop that, can't you, and let me think!"

Mr. Davis said, "It's fine. We'll have it in the show." It made him feel good to contradict Miss Maydew, whose perfume he was now luxuriously taking in. It gave him in a modified form the pleasure of beating her or sleeping with her—the pleasure of mastery over a woman of superior birth. It was the kind of dream he had indulged in in adolescence, while he carved his name on the desk and seat in a grim Midland board school.

"You really think that, Mr. Davenant?"

"My name's Davis."

"I'm sorry, Mr. Davis." Horror on horror, Mr. Collier thought; he was alienating the new backer now.

"I think it's lousy," Miss Maydew said.

Mr. Davis took another piece of toffee. "Go ahead, old man," he said. "Go ahead." They went ahead. The songs and dances floated agreeably through Mr. Davis's consciousness, sometimes wistful, sometimes sweet and sad, sometimes catchy. Mr. Davis liked the sweet ones best. When they sang, "You have my mother's way," he really did think of his mother; he was the ideal audience.

Somebody came out of the wings and bellowed at Mr. Collier. Mr. Collier screamed, "What do you say?" and a young man in a pale-blue jumper went on mechanically singing:

> *"Your photograph*
> *Is just the sweetest half . . ."*

"Did you say Christmas tree?" Mr. Collier yelled.

> *"In your December*
> *I shall remember . . ."*

Mr. Collier screamed, "Take it away."

The song came abruptly to an end with the words "Another mother." The young man said, "You took it too fast," and began to argue with the pianist.

"I can't take it away," the man in the wings said. "It was ordered." He wore an apron and a cloth cap. He said, "It took a van and two horses. You'd better come and have a look."

Mr. Collier disappeared and returned immediately. "My God!" he said, "it's fifteen feet high. Who can have played this fool trick?" Mr. Davis was in a happy dream; his slippers had been warmed by a log fire in a big baronial hall, a little exclusive perfume like Miss Maydew's was kind of hovering in the air, and he was just going to go to bed with a good but aristocratic girl to whom he had been properly married that morning by a bishop. She reminded him a little of his mother. "In your December . . ."

He was suddenly aware that Mr. Collier was saying, "And there's a crate of glass balls and candles."

"Why," Mr. Davis said, "has my little gift arrived?"

"*Your*—little—?"

"I thought we'd have a Christmas party on the stage," Mr. Davis said. "I like to get to know all you artists in a friendly, homey way.

A little dancing, a song or two"— there seemed to be a visible lack of enthusiasm—"plenty of pop."

A pale smile lit Mr. Collier's face. "Well," he said, "it's very kind of you, Mr. Davis. We shall certainly appreciate it."

"Is the tree all right?"

"Yes, Mr. Daven—Davis, it's a magnificent tree." The young man in the blue jumper looked as if he were going to laugh, and Mr. Collier scowled at him. "We all thank you very much, Mr. Davis, don't we, girls?" Everybody said in refined and perfect chorus as if the words had been rehearsed, *"Rather,* Mr. Collier," except Miss Maydew, and a dark girl with a roving eye who was two seconds late and said, "You bet."

That attracted Mr. Davis's notice. Independent, he thought approvingly, stands out from the crowd. He said, "I think I'll step behind and look at the tree. Don't let me be in the way, old man. Just you carry on," and made his way into the wings, where the tree stood blocking the way to the changing rooms. An electrician had hung some of the baubles on for fun, and among the litter of properties under the bare globes it sparkled with icy dignity. Mr. Davis rubbed his hands, a buried childish delight came alive. He said, "It looks lovely." A kind of Christmas peace lay over his spirit; the occasional memory of Raven was only like the darkness pressing round the little lighted crib.

"That's a tree, all right," a voice said. It was the dark girl. She had followed him into the wings; she wasn't wanted on the stage for the number they were rehearsing. She was short and plump and not very pretty. She sat on a case and watched Mr. Davis with gloomy friendliness.

"Gives a Christmas feeling," Mr. Davis said.

"So will a bottle of pop," the girl said.

"What's your name?"

"Ruby."

"What about meeting me for a spot of lunch after the rehearsal's over?"

"Your girls sort of disappear, don't they?" Ruby said. "I could do with a steak and onions, but I don't want any conjuring. I'm not a detective's girl."

"What's that?" Mr. Davis said sharply.

"She's the Yard man's girl. He was round here yesterday."

"That's all right," Mr. Davis said crossly, thinking hard, "you're safe with me."

"You see, I'm unlucky."

Mr. Davis, in spite of his new anxiety, felt alive, vital. This wasn't *his* last day; the kidneys and bacon he had had for breakfast returned a little in his breath. The music came softly through to them: "Your photograph is just the sweetest half . . ." He licked a little grain of toffee on a back tooth as he stood under the tall, dark, gleaming tree and said, "You're in luck now. You couldn't have a better mascot than me."

"You'll have to do," the girl said with her habitual gloomy stare.

"The Metropole? At one, sharp?"

"I'll be there. Unless I'm run over. I'm the kind of girl who *would* get run over before a free feed."

"It'll be fun."

"It depends what you call fun," the girl said and made room for him on the packing case. They sat side by side staring at the tree. *In your December, I shall remember . . .* Mr. Davis put his hand on her bare knee. He was a little awed by the tune, the Christmas atmosphere. His hand fell flatly, reverently, like a bishop's hand on a choirboy's head.

"Sinbad," the girl said.

"Sinbad?"

"I mean Bluebeard. These pantos get one all mixed up."

"You aren't frightened of *me?*" Mr. Davis protested, leaning his head against the postman's cap.

"If any girl's going to disappear, it'll be me for sure."

"She shouldn't have left me," Mr. Davis said softly, "so soon after dinner. Made me go home alone. She'd have been safe with me." He put his arm tentatively round Ruby's waist and squeezed her, then loosed her hastily as an electrician came along. "You're a clever girl," Mr. Davis said, "you ought to have a part. I bet you've got a good voice."

"Me a voice? I've got as much voice as a peahen."

"Give me a little kiss?"

"Of course I will." They kissed rather wetly. "What do I call you?" Ruby said. "It sounds silly to me to call a man who's standing me a free feed Mister."

Mr. Davis said, "You could call me—Willy?"

"Well," Ruby said, sighing gloomily, "I hope I'll be seeing you, Willy. At the Metropole. At one. I'll be there. I only hope *you'll* be there, or bang'll go a good steak and onions." She drifted back towards the stage. She was needed. *What did Aladdin say . . .*

She said to the girl next her, "He fed out of my hand." *When he came to Pekin . . .* "The trouble is," Ruby said, "I can't keep them. There's too much of this love and ride away business. But it looks as if I'll get a good lunch, anyway." She said, "There I go again. Saying that and forgetting to cross my fingers."

Mr. Davis had seen enough. He had got what he'd come for. All that had to be done now was to shed a little light and comradeship among the electricians and other employees. He made his way slowly out by way of the dressing rooms, exchanging a word here and there, offering his gold cigarette case. One never knew. He was fresh to this backstage theatre, and it occurred to him that even among the dressers he might find—well, youth and talent, something to be encouraged, and fed too, of course, at the Metropole. He soon learned better: all the dressers were old; they couldn't understand what he was after, and one followed him round everywhere to make sure that he didn't hide in any of the girls' rooms. Mr. Davis was offended, but he was always polite. He departed through the stage door into the cold, tainted street, waving his hand. It was about time, anyway, that he looked in at Midland Steel and saw Sir Marcus. There should be good news for all of them this Christmas morning.

The High Street was curiously empty, except that there were more police about than was usual; he had quite forgotten the gas practice. No one attempted to interfere with Mr. Davis: his face was well known to all the force, though none of them could have said what Mr. Davis's occupation was. They would have said, without a smile at the thin hair, the heavy paunch, the plump and wrinkled hands, that he was one of Sir Marcus's young men. With an employer so old you could hardly avoid being one of the young men by comparison. Mr. Davis waved gaily to a sergeant on the other pavement and took a toffee. It was not the job of the police to take casualties to hospital, and no one would willingly have obstructed Mr. Davis. There was something about his fat good nature which easily turned to malevolence. They watched him, with covert amusement and hope, sail down the pavement towards the Tanneries, rather as one watches a man of some dignity approach an icy slide. Up the street from the Tanneries a medical student in a gas mask was approaching.

It was some while before Mr. Davis noticed the student, and the sight of the gas mask for a moment quite shocked him. He thought, These pacifists are going too far; sensational nonsense; and when

the man halted Mr. Davis and said something which he could not
catch through the heavy mask, Mr. Davis drew himself up and said
haughtily, "Nonsense. We're well prepared." Then he remembered
and became quite friendly again; it wasn't pacifism after all, it was
patriotism. "Well, well," he said, "I quite forgot. Of course, the
practice." The anonymous stare through the thickened eyepieces,
the muffled voice, made him uneasy. He said jocularly, "You won't
be taking *me* to the hospital now, will you? I'm a busy man." The
student seemed lost in thought, with his hand on Mr. Davis's arm.
Mr. Davis saw a policeman go grinning down the opposite pavement, and he found it hard to restrain his irritation. There was a
little fog still left in the upper air, and a troop of planes drove
through it, flying low, filling the street with their deep murmur, out
towards the south and the aerodrome. "You see," Mr. Davis said,
keeping his temper, "the practice is over. The sirens will be going
any moment now. It would be too absurd to waste a morning at the
hospital. You know me. Davis is the name. Everyone in Nottwich
knows me. Ask the police that. No one can accuse *me* of being a
bad patriot."

"You think it's nearly over?" the man said.

"I'm glad to see you boys enthusiastic," Mr. Davis said. "I expect we've met sometime at the hospital. I'm up there for all the big
functions, and I never forget a voice. Why," Mr. Davis said, "it was
me who gave the biggest contribution to the new operating theatre."
Mr. Davis would have liked to walk on, but the man blocked his
way, and it seemed a bit undignified to step into the road and go
round him. The man might think he was trying to escape. There
might be a tussle, and the police were looking on from the corner.
A sudden venom spurted up into Mr. Davis's mind like the ink a
cuttlefish shoots, staining his thoughts with its dark poison. That
grinning ape in uniform—I'll have him dismissed, I'll see Calkin
about it. He talked on cheerily to the man in the gas mask, a thin
figure, little more than a boy's figure, on whom the white medical
coat hung loosely. "You boys," Mr. Davis said, "are doing a splen-
did work. There's no one appreciates that more than I do. If war
comes—"

"You call yourself Davis," the muffled voice said.

Mr. Davis said with sudden irritation, "You're wasting my time.
I'm a busy man. Of course I'm Davis." He checked his rising temper with an effort. "Look here. I'm a reasonable man. I'll pay anything you like to the hospital. Say, ten pounds' ransom."

"Yes," the man said, "where is it?"

"You can trust me," Mr. Davis said. "I don't carry that much on me," and was amazed to hear what sounded like a laugh. This was going too far. "All right," Mr. Davis said, "you can come with me to my office, and I'll pay you the money. But I shall expect a proper receipt from your treasurer."

"You'll get your receipt," the man said in his odd, toneless, mask-muffled voice and stood on one side to let Mr. Davis lead the way. Mr. Davis's good humour was quite restored. He prattled on. "No good offering you a toffee in that thing," he said. A messenger boy passed in a gas mask with his cap cocked absurdly on the top of it; he whistled derisively at Mr. Davis. Mr. Davis went a little pink. His fingers itched to tear the hair, to pull the ear, to twist the wrist. "The boys enjoy themselves," he said. He became confiding; a doctor's presence always made him feel safe and oddly important: one could tell the most grotesque things to a doctor about one's digestion, and it was as much material for them as an amusing anecdote was for a professional humorist. He said, "I've been getting hiccups badly lately. After every meal. It's not as if I eat fast—but, of course, you're only a student still. Though you know more about these things than I do. Then too I get spots before my eyes. Perhaps I ought to cut down my diet a bit But it's difficult. A man in my position has a lot of entertaining to do. For instance"—he grasped his companion's unresponsive arm and squeezed it knowingly—"it would be no good, my promising you that I'd go without my lunch today. You medicos are men of the world, and I don't mind telling you I've got a little girl meeting me. At the Metropole. At one." Some association of ideas made him feel in his pocket to make sure his packet of toffee was safe.

They passed another policeman, and Mr. Davis waved his hand. His companion was very silent. The boy's shy, Mr. Davis thought, he's not used to walking about town with a man like me. It excused a certain roughness in his behaviour; even the suspicion Mr. Davis had resented was probably only a form of gawkiness. Mr. Davis, because the day was proving fine after all, a little sun sparkling through the cold, obscured air; because the kidneys and bacon had really been done to a turn; because he had asserted himself in the presence of Miss Maydew, who was the daughter of a peer; because he had a date at the Metropole with a little girl of talent; because, too, by this time Raven's body would be safely laid out on its icy slab in the mortuary—for all these reasons Mr. Davis felt kindness and Christmas in his spirit. He exerted himself to put the boy at his ease. He said, "I feel sure we've met somewhere. Perhaps the house surgeon introduced us." But his companion remained glumly unforthcoming. "A fine singsong you all put on at the opening of the new ward." He glanced again at the delicate wrists. "You weren't by any chance the boy who dressed up as a girl and sang that naughty song?" Mr. Davis laughed thickly at the memory, turning into the Tanneries, laughed as he had laughed more times than he could count over the port, at the club, among the good fellows, at the smutty masculine jokes. "I was tickled to death." He put his hand on his companion's arm and pushed through the glass door of Midland Steel.

A stranger stepped out from round a corner, and the clerk behind the inquiries counter told him in a strained voice, "That's all right. That's Mr. Davis."

"What's all this?" Mr. Davis asked in a harsh no-nonsense voice now that he was back where he belonged.

The detective said, "We are just keeping an eye open."

"Raven?" Mr. Davis asked in a rather shrill voice. The man nodded. Mr. Davis said, "You let him escape? What fools—"

The detective said, "You needn't be scared. He'll be spotted at once if he comes out of hiding. He can't escape this time."

"But why," Mr. Davis said, "are you here? Why do you expect—"

"We've got our orders," the man said.

"Have you told Sir Marcus?"

"He knows."

Mr. Davis looked tired and old. He said sharply to his companion, "Come with me, and I'll give you the money. I haven't any time to waste." He walked with lagging, hesitating feet down a passage paved with some black shining composition to the glass lift shaft. The man in the gas mask followed him down the passage and into the lift. They moved slowly and steadily upwards together, as intimate as two birds caged. Floor by floor the great building sank below them, a clerk in a black coat, hurrying on some mysterious errand which required a pot of bulbs; a girl standing outside a closed door with a file of papers, whispering to herself, rehearsing some excuse; an errand boy walking erratically along a passage, balancing a bundle of new pencils on his head. They stopped at an empty floor.

There was something on Mr. Davis's mind. He walked slowly,

turned the handle of his door softly, almost as if he feared that someone might be waiting for him inside. But the room was quite empty. An inner door opened, and a young woman with fluffy gold hair and exaggerated horn spectacles said, "Willy," and then saw his companion. She said, "Sir Marcus wants to see you, Mr. Davis."

"That's all right, Miss Connett," Mr. Davis said. "You might go and find me an A.B.C."

"Are you going away—at once?"

Mr. Davis hesitated. "Look me up what trains there are for town —after lunch."

"Yes, Mr. Davis." She withdrew, and the two of them were alone. Mr. Davis shivered slightly and turned on his electric fire. The man in the gas mask spoke, and again the muffled, coarse voice pricked at Mr. Davis's memory.

"Are you scared of something?"

"There's a madman loose in this town," Mr. Davis said. His nerves were alert at every sound in the corridor outside—a footstep, the ring of a bell. It had needed more courage than he had been conscious of possessing to say "after lunch"; he wanted to be away at once, clear away from Nottwich. He started at the scrape of a little cleaner's platform, which was being lowered down the wall of the inner courtyard. He padded to the door and locked it; it gave him a better feeling of security to be locked into his familiar room, with his desk, his swivel chair, the cupboard where he kept two glasses and a bottle of sweet port, the bookcase which contained a few technical works on steel, a Whitaker's, a Who's Who, and a copy of *His Chinese Concubine,* than to remember the detective in the hall. He took everything in like something seen for the first time, and it was true enough that he had never so realized the peace and comfort of his small room. Again he started at the creak of the ropes from which the cleaner's platform hung. He shut down his double window. He said in a tone of nervous irritation, "Sir Marcus can wait."

"Who's Sir Marcus?"

"My boss." Something about the open door of his secretary's room disturbed him with the idea that anyone could enter that way. He was no longer in a hurry, he wasn't busy any more, he wanted companionship. He said, "You aren't in any hurry. Take that thing off, it must be stuffy, and have a glass of port." On his way to the cupboard he shut the inner door and turned the key. He sighed with relief, fetching out the port and the glasses. "Now we are *really*

alone, I want to tell you about these hiccups." He poured two brim-
ming glasses, but his hand shook and the port ran down the sides.
He said, "Always just after a meal—"

The muffled voice said, "The money."

"Really," Mr. Davis said, "you are rather impudent. You can
trust *me*. I'm Davis." He went to his desk and unlocked a drawer,
took out two five-pound notes, and held them out. "Mind," he said,
"I shall expect a proper receipt from your treasurer."

The man put them away. His hand stayed in his pocket. He said,
"Are these phony notes too?" A whole scene came back to Mr.
Davis's mind: a Lyons' Corner House, the taste of an Alpine Glow,
the murderer sitting opposite him, trying to tell him of the old
woman he had killed. Mr. Davis screamed—not a word, not a plea
for help, just a meaningless cry such as a man gives under an anes-
thetic when the knife cuts the flesh. He ran, bolted, across the room
to the inner door and tugged at the handle. He struggled uselessly
as if he were caught on barbed wire between trenches.

"Come away from there," Raven said. "You've locked the door."

Mr. Davis came back to the desk. His legs gave way, and he sat
on the floor beside the wastepaper basket. He said, "I'm sick.
You wouldn't kill a sick man." The idea really gave him hope. He
retched convincingly.

"I'm not going to kill you yet," Raven said. "Maybe I won't kill
you if you keep quiet and do what I say. This Sir Marcus, he's
your boss?"

"An old man," Mr. Davis protested, weeping beside the wastepaper basket.

"He wants to see you," Raven said. "We'll go along." He said,
"I've been waiting days for this—to find the two of you. It almost
seems too good to be true. Get up. Get up!" he repeated furiously
to the weak, flabby figure on the floor. "Remember this: If you
squeal I'll plug you so full of lead they'll be able to use you as a
doorstop."

Mr. Davis led the way. Miss Connett came down the passage,
carrying a slip of paper. She said, "I've got the trains down, Mr.
Davis. The best is the three-five. The two-seven is really so slow
that you wouldn't be up more than ten minutes earlier. Then there's
only the five-ten before the night train."

"Put them on my desk," Mr. Davis said. He hung about there in
front of her in the shining modern plutocratic passage as if he
wanted to say good-bye to a thousand things if only he dared: to

this wealth, this comfort, this authority. Lingering there ("Yes, put them on my desk, May"), he might even have been waiting to express at the last some tenderness that had never before entered his mind in connection with "little girls." Raven stood just behind him with his hand in his pocket. Her employer looked so sick that Miss Connett said, "Are you feeling well, Mr. Davis?"

"Quite well," Mr. Davis said. Like an explorer going into strange country, he felt the need of leaving some record behind at the edge of civilization, to say to the last chance comer, "I shall be going towards the north" or "the west." He said, "We are going to see Sir Marcus, May."

"He's in a hurry for you," Miss Connett said. A telephone bell rang. "I shouldn't be surprised if that's him now." She pattered down the corridor to her room on very high heels, and Mr. Davis felt again the remorseless pressure on his elbow to advance, to enter the lift. They rose another floor, and when Mr. Davis pulled the gates apart he retched again. He wanted to fling himself to the floor and take the bullets in his back. The long gleaming passage to Sir Marcus's study was like a mile-long stadium track to a winded and defeated runner.

Sir Marcus was sitting in his bath chair with a kind of bed table on his knees. He had his valet with him, and his back was to the door, but the valet could see with astonishment Mr. Davis's exhausted entrance in the company of a medical student in a gas mask. "Is that Davis?" Sir Marcus whispered. He broke a dry biscuit and sipped a little hot milk. He was fortifying himself for a day's work.

"Yes, sir." The valet watched with astonishment Mr. Davis's sick progress across the hygienic rubber floor; he looked as if he needed support, as if he was about to collapse at the knees.

"Get out then," Sir Marcus whispered.

"Yes, sir." But the man in the gas mask had turned the key of the door. A faint expression of joy, a rather hopeless expectation, crept into the valet's face, as if he were wondering whether something at last was going to happen, something different from pushing bath chairs along rubber floors, dressing and undressing an old man not strong enough to keep himself clean, bringing him the hot milk or the hot water or the dry biscuits.

"What are you waiting for?" Sir Marcus whispered.

"Get back against the wall," Raven suddenly commanded the valet.

Mr. Davis cried despairingly, "He's got a gun. Do what he says." But there was no need to tell the valet that. The gun was out now and had them all three covered, the valet against the wall, Mr. Davis dithering in the middle of the room, Sir Marcus, who had twisted the bath chair round to face them.

"What do you want?" Sir Marcus said.

"Are you the boss?"

Sir Marcus said, "The police are downstairs. You can't get away from here unless I—" The telephone began to ring. It rang on and on and on, and then ceased.

Raven said, "You've got a scar under that beard, haven't you? I don't want to make a mistake. He had your photograph. You were in the home together," and he glared angrily round the large, rich office room, comparing it in mind with his own memories of cracked bells and stone stairs and wooden benches, and of the small flat, too, with the egg boiling in the ring. This man had moved farther than the old minister.

"You're mad," Sir Marcus whispered. He was too old to be frightened; the revolver represented no greater danger to him than a false step in getting into his chair, a slip in his bath. He seemed to feel only a faint irritation, a faint craving for his interrupted meal. He bent his old lip forward over the bed table and sucked loudly at the rim of hot milk.

The valet spoke suddenly from the wall. "He's got a scar," he said. But Sir Marcus took no notice of any of them, sucking up his milk untidily over his thin beard.

Raven twisted his gun on Mr. Davis. "It was him," he said. "If you don't want a bullet in your guts tell me it was him."

"Yes, yes," Mr. Davis said in horrified subservient haste, "the thought of it. It was his idea. We were on our last legs here. We'd got to make money. It was worth more than half a million to him."

"Half a million," Raven said. "And he paid me two hundred phony pounds."

"I said to him we ought to be generous. He said, 'Stop your mouth.'"

"I wouldn't have done it," Raven said, "if I'd known the old man was like he was. I smashed his skull for him. And the old woman, a bullet in both eyes." He shouted at Sir Marcus, "That was your doing. How do you like that?" But the old man sat there apparently unmoved; old age had killed the imagination. The deaths he had ordered were no more real to him than the deaths he read about in the newspapers. A little greed (for his milk), a little vice (occasionally to put his old hand inside a girl's blouse), a little avarice and calculation (half a million against a death), a very small, persistent, almost mechanical, sense of self-preservation—these were his only passions. The last made him edge his chair imperceptibly towards the bell at the edge of his desk. He whispered gently, "I deny it all. You are mad."

Raven said, "I've got you now where I want you. Even if the police kill me"—he tapped the gun—"here's my evidence. This is the gun I used. They can pin the murder to this gun. You told me to leave it behind, but here it is. It would put you away a long, long time even if I didn't shoot you."

Sir Marcus whispered gently, imperceptibly twisting his silent, rubbered wheels, "A Colt number seven. The factories turn out thousands."

Raven said angrily, "There's nothing the police can't do now with a gun. There are experts." He wanted to frighten Sir Marcus before he shot him; it seemed unfair to him that Sir Marcus should suffer less than the old woman he hadn't wanted to kill. He said, "Don't you want to pray? Better people than you," he said, "believe in a God," remembering how the girl had prayed in the dark, cold shed. The wheel of Sir Marcus's chair touched the desk, touched the bell, and the dull ringing came up the well of the lift, going on and on. It conveyed nothing to Raven until the valet spoke. "The old bastard," he said, with the hatred of years, "he's ringing the bell." Before Raven could decide what to do someone was at the door, shaking the handle.

Raven said to Sir Marcus, "Tell them to keep back or I'll shoot."

"You fool," Sir Marcus whispered, "they'll only get you for theft. If you kill me, you'll hang." But Mr. Davis was ready to clutch at any straw. He screamed to the man outside, "Keep away. For God's sake keep away."

Sir Marcus said venomously, "You're a fool, Davis. If he's going to kill us anyway—" While Raven stood, pistol in hand, before the two men, an absurd quarrel broke out between them.

"He's got no cause to kill me," Mr. Davis screamed. "It's you who've got us into this. I only acted for you."

The valet began to laugh. "Two to one on the field," he said.

"Be quiet," Sir Marcus whispered venomously back at Mr. Davis. "I can put you out of the way at any time."

"I defy you," Mr. Davis screamed in a high peacock voice. Somebody flung himself against the door.

"I have the West Rand Goldfields filed," Sir Marcus said, "the East African Petroleum Company."

A wave of impatience struck Raven. They seemed to be disturbing some memory of peace and goodness which had been on the point of returning to him when he had told Sir Marcus to pray. He raised his pistol and shot Sir Marcus in the chest. It was the only way to silence them. Sir Marcus fell forward across the bed table, upsetting the glass of warm milk over the papers on his desk. Blood came out of his mouth.

Mr. Davis began to talk very rapidly. He said, "It was all him, the old devil. You heard him. What could I do? He had me. You've got nothing against me." He shrieked, "Go away from that door. He'll kill me if you don't go," and immediately began to talk again, while the milk dripped from the bed table to the desk, drop by drop. "I wouldn't have done a thing if it hadn't been for him. Do you know what he did? He went and told the chief constable to order the police to shoot you on sight." He tried not to look at the pistol which remained pointed at his chest. The valet was white and silent by the wall; he watched Sir Marcus's life bleeding away with curious fascination. So this was what it would have been like, he seemed to be thinking, if he himself had had courage—any time, during all these years.

A voice outside said, "You had better open this door at once, or we'll shoot through it."

"For God's sake," Mr. Davis screamed, "leave me alone. He'll shoot me," and the eyes watched him intently through the panes of the gas mask with satisfaction. "There's not a thing I've done to you," he began to protest. Over Raven's head he could see the clock; it hadn't moved more than three hours since his breakfast; the hot, stale taste of the kidneys and bacon was still on his palate. He couldn't believe that this was really the end. At one o'clock he had a date with a girl—you didn't die before a date. "Nothing," he murmured, "nothing at all."

"It was you," Raven said, "who tried to kill—"

"Nobody. Nothing." Mr. Davis moaned.

Raven hesitated. The word was still unfamiliar on his tongue "—my friend."

"I don't know. I don't understand."

"Keep back," Raven cried through the door. "I'll shoot him if you fire." He said, "The girl."

Mr. Davis shook all over. He was like a man with St. Vitus' dance. He said, "She wasn't a friend of yours. Why are the police here if she didn't—who else could have known—"

Raven said, "I'll shoot you for that and nothing else. She's straight."

"Why," Mr. Davis screamed at him, "she's a policeman's girl. She's the Yard man's girl. She's Mather's girl."

Raven shot him. With despair and deliberation he shot his last chance of escape, plugged two bullets in where one would do, as if he were shooting the whole world in the person of stout, moaning, bleeding Mr. Davis. And so he was. For a man's world is his life, and he was shooting that: his mother's suicide, the long years in the home, the race-course gangs, Kite's death, and the old man's and the woman's. There was no other way; he had tried the way of confession, and it had failed him for the usual reason. There was no one outside your own brain whom you could trust—not a doctor, not a priest, not a woman. A siren blew up over the town, its message that the sham raid was over, and immediately the church-bells broke into a noisy Christmas carol—the foxes have their holes, but the son of man . . . A bullet smashed the lock of the door. Raven, with his gun pointed stomach-high, said, "Is there a bastard called Mather out there? He'd better keep away."

While he waited for the door to open he couldn't help remembering many things. He did not remember them in detail; they fogged together and formed the climate of his mind as he waited there for the chance of a last revenge: a voice singing above a dark street as the sleet fell, "They say that's a snowflower a man brought from Greenland"; the cultivated, unlived voice of the elderly critic reading *Maud:* "Oh,, that 'twere possible after long grief . . ." While he stood in the garage and felt the ice melt at his heart with a sense of pain and strangeness as if he were passing the customs of a land he had never entered before and would never be able to leave; the girl in the café, saying, "He's bad and ugly . . ." the little plaster child lying in its mother's arms, waiting the double-cross, the whips, the nails. She had said to him, "I'm your friend. You can trust me." Another bullet burst in the lock.

The valet, white-faced by the wall, said, "For God's sake, give it up. They'll get you anyway. He was right. It *was* the girl. I heard them on the phone."

I've got to be quick, Raven thought, when the door gives. I must shoot first. But too many ideas besieged his brain at once. He couldn't see clearly enough through the mask, and he undid it clumsily with one hand and dropped it on the floor. The valet could see now the raw, inflamed lip, the dark and miserable eyes. He said, "There's the window. Get onto the roof." He was talking to a man whose understanding was dulled, who didn't know whether he wished to make an effort or not, who moved his face so slowly to see the window that it was the valet who noticed first the painter's platform swinging down the wide, tall pane. Mather was on the platform; it was a desperate attempt to catch Raven in the rear, but the detective had not allowed for his own inexperience. The little platform swung this way and that; he held a rope with one hand and reached for the window with the other; he had no hand free for his revolver as Raven turned. He dangled outside the window six floors above the narrow Tanneries, a defenceless mark for Raven's pistol.

Raven watched him with bemused eyes, trying to take aim. It wasn't a difficult shot, but it was almost as if he had lost interest in killing. He was only aware of a pain and despair which was more like a complete weariness than anything else. He couldn't work up any sourness, any bitterness, at his betrayal. The dark Weevil under the storm of frozen rain flowed between him and any human enemy. "Ah, Christ that it were possible," but he had been marked from his birth for this end, to be betrayed in turn by everyone until every avenue into life was safely closed: by his mother bleeding in the basement, by the chaplain at the home, by the soft kids who had left it with him, by the shady doctor off Charlotte Street. How could he have expected to escape the commonest betrayal of all, to go soft on a skirt? Even Kite would have been alive now if it hadn't been for a skirt. They all went soft at some time or another: Penrith and Carter, Jossy and Ballard, Barker and the Great Dane. He took aim slowly, absent-mindedly, with a curious humility, with almost a sense of companionship in his loneliness: the trooper and Mayhew. They had all thought at one time or another that their skirt was better than other men's skirts, that there was something exalted in *their* relation The only problem when you were once born was to get out of life more neatly and expeditiously than you had entered it For the first time the idea of his mother's suicide came to him without bitterness, as he fixed his aim at the long reluctant last and Saunders shot him in the back through the opening door Death came to him in the form of unbearable pain It was as if he had to deliver this pain as a woman delivers a child, and he sobbed and moaned in the effort. At last it came out of him, and he followed his only child into a vast desolation.

Eight

1

The smell of food came through into the lounge whenever somebody passed in or out of the restaurant. The local Rotarians were having a lunch in one of the private rooms upstairs, and when the door opened Ruby could hear a cork pop and the scrap of a limerick. It was five past one. Ruby went out and chatted to the porter. She said, "The worst of it is I'm one of the girls who turn up on the stroke. One o'clock, he said, and here I am, panting for a good meal. I know a girl ought to keep a man waiting, but what do you do if you're hungry? He might go in and start." She said, "The trouble is I'm unlucky. I'm the kind of girl who daren't have a bit of fun because she'd be dead sure to get a baby Well, I don't mean I've had a baby, but I did catch mumps once. Would you believe a grown man could give a girl mumps? But I'm that kind of girl." She said, "You look fine in all that gold braid with those medals. You might say something."

The market was more than usually full, for everyone had come out late to do their shopping now that the gas practice was over Only Mrs. Alfred Piker, as Lady Mayoress, had set an example by shopping in a mask. Now she was walking home, and Chinky trotted beside her, trailing his low fur and the feathers on his legs in the cold slush, carrying her mask between his teeth. He stopped by a lamp post and dropped it in a puddle "Oh, Chinky, you bad little thing," Mrs. Piker said. The porter in his uniform glared out over the market. He wore the Mons medal and the Military medal. He had been three times wounded. He swung the glass door as the businessmen came in for their lunch, the head traveller of Crosthwaite and Crosthwaite, the managing director of the big grocery business in the High Street. Once he darted out into the road and disentangled a fat man from a taxi. Then he came back and stood beside Ruby and listened to her with expressionless good humour

"Ten minutes late," Ruby said. "I thought he was a man a girl could trust. I ought to have touched wood or crossed my fingers It serves me right. I'd rather have lost my honour than that steak. Do you know him? He flings his weight about a lot. Called Davis."

"He's always in here with girls," the porter said.

A little man in pince-nez bustled by. "A merry Christmas, Hallows."

"A merry Christmas to you, sir." The porter said, "You wouldn't have got very far with him."

"I haven't got as far as the soup," Ruby said.

A newsboy went by, calling out a special midday edition of the *News,* the evening edition of the *Journal;* and a few minutes later another newsboy went past with a special edition of the *Post,* the evening edition of the more aristocratic *Guardian.* It was impossible to hear what they were shouting, and the northeast wind flapped their posters so that on one it was only possible to read the syllable "gedy" and on the other the syllable "der."

"There are limits," Ruby said. "A girl can't afford to make herself cheap. Ten minutes' wait is the outside limit."

"You've waited more than that now," the porter said.

Ruby said, "I'm like that. You'd say I flung myself at men, wouldn't you? That's what I think, but I never seem to hit them." She added with deep gloom, "The trouble is, I'm the kind that's born to make a man happy. It's written all over me. It keeps them away. I don't blame them. I shouldn't like it myself."

"There goes the chief constable," the porter said. "Off to get a drink at the police station. His wife won't let him have them at home. The best of the season to you, sir."

"He seems in a hurry." A newspaper poster flapped "Trag—" at them. "Is he the kind that would buy a girl a good rump steak with onions and fried potatoes?"

"I tell you what," the porter said. "You wait around another five minutes and then I shall be going off for lunch."

"That's a date," Ruby said. She crossed her fingers and touched wood. Then she went and sat inside and carried on a long conversation with an imaginary theatrical producer whom she imagined rather like Mr. Davis, but a Mr. Davis who kept his engagements. The producer called her a little woman with talent, asked her to dinner, took her back to a luxurious flat, and gave her several cocktails. He asked her what she would think of a West End engagement at fifteen pounds a week and said he wanted to show her his flat. Ruby's dark, plump, gloomy face lightened. She swung one leg excitedly and attracted the angry attention of a businessman who was making notes of the midday prices. He found another chair and muttered to himself. Ruby, too, muttered to herself. She was saying, "This is the dining room. And through here is the bathroom. And this—elegant, isn't it?—is the bedroom." Ruby said promptly that she'd like the fifteen pounds a week, but need she have the West End engagement? Then she looked at the clock and went outside. The porter was waiting for her.

"What?" Ruby said. "Have I got to go out with that uniform?"

"I only get twenty minutes," the porter said.

"No rump steak then," Ruby said. "Well, I suppose sausages would do."

They sat at a lunch counter on the other side of the market and had sausages and coffee. "That uniform," Ruby said, "makes me embarrassed. Everyone'll think you're a guardsman going with a girl for a change."

"Did you hear the shooting?" the man behind the counter said.

"What shooting?"

"Just round the corner from you at Midland Steel. Three dead. That old devil Sir Marcus, and two others." He laid the midday paper open on the counter, and the old wicked face of Sir Marcus, the plump anxious features of Mr. Davis, stared up at them beyond the sausages, the coffee cups, the pepper pot, beside the hot-water urn.

"So that's why he didn't come," Ruby said. She was silent for a while, reading.

"I wonder what this Raven was after," the porter said. "Look here," and he pointed to a small paragraph at the foot of the column, which announced that the head of the special political department of Scotland Yard had arrived by air and gone straight to the offices of Midland Steel.

"It doesn't mean a thing to me," Ruby said.

The porter turned the pages, looking for something. He said, "Funny thing, isn't it? Here we are just going to war again, and they fill up the front page with a murder. It's driven the war onto a back page."

"Perhaps there won't be a war."

They were silent over their sausages. It seemed odd to Ruby that Mr. Davis, who had sat on the box with her and looked at the Christmas tree, should be dead, so violently and painfully dead. Perhaps he had meant to keep the date. He wasn't a bad sort. She said, "I feel kind of sorry for him."

"Who? Raven?"

"Oh no, not him. Mr. Davis, I mean."

"I know how you feel. I almost feel sorry too—for the old man. I was in Midland Steel myself once. He had his moments. He used to send round turkeys at Christmas. He wasn't too bad. It's more than they do at the hotel."

"Well," Ruby said, draining her coffee, "life goes on."

"Have another cup."

"I don't want to sting you."

"That's all right." Ruby leaned against him on the high stool; their heads touched. They were a little quietened because each had known a man who was suddenly dead; but the knowledge they shared gave them a sense of companionship which was oddly sweet and reassuring. It was like feeling safe, like feeling in love without the passion, the uncertainty, the pain.

2

Saunders asked a clerk in Midland Steel the way to a lavatory. He washed his hands and thought, "That job's over." It hadn't been a satisfactory job; what had begun as a plain robbery had ended with two murders and the death of the murderer. There was a mystery about the whole affair—everything hadn't come out. Mather was up there on the top floor now with the head of the political department. They were going through Sir Marcus's private papers. It really seemed as if the girl's story might be true.

The girl worried Saunders more than anything. He couldn't help admiring her courage and impertinence at the same time as he hated her for making Mather suffer. He was ready to hate anyone who hurt Mather. "She'll have to be taken to the Yard," Mather had said. "There may be a charge against her. Put her in a locked carriage on the three-five. I don't want to see her until this thing's cleared up." The only cheerful thing about the whole business was that the constable whom Raven had shot in the coal yard was pulling through.

Saunders came out of Midland Steel into the Tanneries with an odd sensation of having nothing to do. He went into a public house at the corner of the market and had half a pint of bitter and two cold sausages. It was as if life had sunk again to the normal level, was flowing quietly by once more between its banks. A card hanging behind the bar next a few cinema posters caught his eye: "A

New Cure for Stammerers." Mr. Montague Phelps, M.A., was
holding a public meeting in the Masonic Hall to explain his new
treatment. Entrance was free, but there would be a silver collection.
Two o'clock sharp. At one cinema Eddie Cantor. At another
George Arliss. Saunders didn't want to go back to the police station
until it was time to take the girl to the train. He had tried a good
many cures for stammering; he might as well try one more.

It was a large hall. On the walls hung large photographs of Masonic dignitaries. They all wore ribbons and badges of strange significance. There was an air of oppressive well-being, of successful
groceries, about the photographs. They hung, the well fed, the successful, the assured, over the small gathering of misfits in old mack-
intoshes, in rather faded mauve felt hats, in school ties. Saunders
entered behind a fat, furtive woman, and a steward stammered at
him, "T-t-t—?" "One," Saunders said. He sat down near the front
and heard a stammered conversation going on behind him, like the
twitters of two Chinamen. Little bursts of impetuous talk and then
the fatal impediment. There were about fifty people in the hall.
They eyed each other rather as an ugly man eyes himself in shop
windows: from this angle, he thinks, I am really not too bad. They
gained a sense of companionship; their mutual lack of communication was in itself like a communication. They waited together for a
miracle.

Saunders waited with them; waited as he had waited on the wind-
less side of the coal truck, with the same patience. He wasn't unhappy. He knew that he probably exaggerated the value of what he
lacked. Even if he could speak freely, without care to avoid the
dentals which betrayed him, he would probably find it no easier to
express his admiration and his affection. The power to speak didn't
give you words.

Mr. Montague Phelps, M.A., came onto the platform. He wore a
frock coat, and his hair was dark and oiled. His blue chin was
lightly powdered, and he carried himself with a rather aggressive
sangfroid, as much as to say to the depressed, inhibited gathering,
"See what you too might become, with a little more self-confidence,
after a few lessons from me." He was a man of about forty-two who
had lived well, who obviously had a private life. One thought in his
presence of comfortable beds and heavy meals and Brighton hotels.
For a moment he reminded Saunders of Mr. Davis, who had
bustled so importantly into the offices of Midland Steel that morning and had died very painfully and suddenly half an hour later. It

almost seemed as if Raven's act had had no consequences; as if to kill was just as much an illusion as to dream. Here was Mr. Davis all over again; they were turned out of a mould, and you couldn't break the *mould*. And suddenly, over Mr. Montague Phelps's shoulder, Saunders saw the photograph of the Grand Master of the Lodge above the platform—an old face and a crooked nose and a tuft of beard: Sir Marcus.

3

Major Calkin was very white when he left Midland Steel. He had seen for the first time the effect of violent death. That was war. He made his way as quickly as he could to the police station and was glad to find the superintendent in. He asked quite humbly for a spot of whisky. He said, "It shakes you up. Only last night he had dinner at my house. Mrs. Piker was there with her dog. What a time we had, stopping him knowing the dog was there."

"That dog," the superintendent said, "gives us more trouble than any man in Nottwich. Did I ever tell you the time it got in the women's lavatory in Higham Street? That dog isn't much to look at, but every once in a while it goes crazy. If it wasn't Mrs. Piker's we'd have had it destroyed many a time."

Major Calkin said, "He wanted me to give orders to your men to shoot this fellow on sight. I told him I couldn't. Now I can't help thinking we might have saved two lives."

"Don't you worry, sir," the superintendent said, "we couldn't have taken orders like that. Not from the Home Secretary himself."

"He was an odd fellow," Major Calkin said. "He seemed to think I'd be certain to have a hold over some of you. He promised me all kinds of things. I suppose he was what you'd call a genius. We shan't see his like again. What a waste." He poured himself out some more whisky. "Just at a time too when we need men like him. War." Major Calkin paused with his hand on his glass. He stared into the whisky, seeing things: the remount depot, his uniform in the cupboard. He would never be a colonel now, but on the other hand Sir Marcus could not prevent— But curiously he felt no elation at the thought of once more presiding over the tribunal. He said, "The gas practice seems to have gone off well. But I don't know that it was wise to leave so much to the medical students. They don't know where to stop."

"There was a pack of them," the superintendent said, "went

howling past here looking for the mayor. I don't know how it is Mr. Piker seems to be like catmint to those students."

"Good old Piker," Major Calkin said mechanically.

"They go too far," the superintendent said. "I had a ring from Higginbotham, the cashier at the Westminster. He said his daughter went into the garage and found one of these students there without his trousers."

Life began to come back to Major Calkin. He said, "That'll be Rose Higginbotham, I suppose. Trust Rose. What did she do?"

"He said she gave him a dressing down."

"Dressing down's good," Major Calkin said. He twisted his glass and drained his whisky. "I must tell that to old Piker. What did you say?"

"I told him his daughter was lucky not to find a murdered man in the garage. You see, that's where Raven must have got his clothes and his mask."

"What was the boy doing at the Higginbothams' anyway?" Major Calkin asked. "I think I'll go and cash a cheque and ask old Higginbotham that." He began to laugh. The air was clear again; life was going on quite in the old way: a little scandal, a drink with the super, a story to tell old Piker. On his way to the Westminster he nearly ran into Mrs. Piker. He had to dive hastily into a shop to avoid her, and for a horrible moment he thought Chinky, who was some way ahead of her, was going to follow him inside. He made motions of throwing a ball down the street, but Chinky was not a sporting dog, and anyway he was trailing a gas mask in his teeth. Major Calkin had to turn his back abruptly and lean over a counter. He found it was a small haberdasher's. He had never been in the shop before.

"What can I get you, sir?"

"Suspenders," Major Calkin said desperately. "A pair of suspenders."

"What colour, sir?" Out of the corner of his eye Major Calkin saw Chinky trot on past the shop door, followed by Mrs. Piker.

"Mauve," he said with relief.

4

The old woman shut the front door softly and trod on tiptoe down the little dark hall. A stranger could not have seen his way, but she knew exactly the position of the hatrack, of the whatnot table, and the staircase. She was carrying an evening paper, and when she opened the kitchen door with the very minimum of noise so as not to disturb Acky, her face was alight with exhilaration and excitement. But she held it in, carrying her basket over to the draining board and unloading there her burden of potatoes, a tin of pineapple chunks, two eggs, and a slab of cod.

Acky was writing a long letter on the kitchen table. He had pushed his wife's mauve ink to one side and was using the best blue-black and a fountain pen which had long ceased to hold ink. He wrote slowly and painfully, sometimes making a rough copy of a sentence on another slip of paper. The old woman stood beside the sink, watching him, waiting for him to speak, holding her breath in, so that sometimes it escaped in little whistles. At last Acky laid down his pen. "Well, my dear?" he said.

"Oh, Acky," the old woman said with glee, "what do you think? That Mr. Cholmondeley is dead. Killed." She added, "It's in the paper. And that Raven too."

Acky looked at the paper. "Quite horrible," he said with satisfaction. "Another death as well. A holocaust." He read the account slowly.

"Fancy a thing like that 'appening 'ere in Nottwich."

"He was a bad man," Acky said, "though I wouldn't speak ill of him now that he's dead. He involved us in something of which I was ashamed. I think perhaps now it will be safe for us to stay in Nottwich." A look of great weariness passed over his face as he looked down at the three pages of small, neat, classical handwriting.

"Oh, Acky, you've been tiring yourself."

"I think," Acky said, "this will make it clear."

"Read it to me, love," the old woman said. Her little old vicious face was heavily creased with tenderness as she leaned back against the sink in an attitude of infinite patience. Acky began to read. He spoke at first in a low, hesitating way, but he gained confidence from the sound of his own voice; his hand went up to the lapel of his coat.

" 'My Lord Bishop—' " He said, "I thought it best to begin formally, not to trespass at all on my former acquaintanceship."

"That's right, Acky, you are worth the whole bunch."

" 'I am writing to you for the fourth time, after an interval of some eighteen months.' "

"Is it so long, love? It was after we took the trip to Clacton."

"Sixteen months. 'I am quite aware what your previous answers have been, that my case has been tried already in the proper church court, but I cannot believe, my Lord Bishop, that your sense of justice, if once I convince you of what a deeply injured man I am, will not lead you to do all that is in your power to have my case reheard. I have been condemned to suffer all my life for what in the case of other men is regarded as a peccadillo, a peccadillo of which I am not even guilty.' "

"It's written lovely, love."

"At this point, my dear, I come down to particulars. 'How, my Lord Bishop, could the hotel domestic swear to the identity of a man seen once, a year before the trial, in a darkened chamber, for in her evidence she agreed that he had not allowed her to draw up the blind? As for the evidence of the porter, my Lord Bishop, I asked in court whether it was not true that money had passed from Colonel and Mrs. Mark Egerton into his hands, and my question was disallowed. Is this justice, founded on scandal, misapprehension, and perjury?' "

The old woman smiled with tenderness and pride. "This is the best letter you've written, Acky, so far."

" 'My Lord Bishop, it was well known in the parish that Colonel Mark Egerton was my bitterest enemy on the church council, and it was at his instigation that the inquiry was held. As for Mrs. Mark Egerton, she was a bitch.' "

"Is that wise, Acky?"

"Sometimes, dear, one reaches an impasse when there is nothing to be done but to speak out. At this point I take the evidence in detail as I have done before, but I think I have sharpened my arguments more than a little. And at the end, my dear, I address the worldly man in the only way he can understand." He knew this passage by heart. He reeled it fierily off at her, raising his crazy, sunken, flawed saint's eyes. " 'But even assuming, my Lord Bishop, that this perjured and bribed evidence were accurate, what then? Have I committed the unforgivable sin that I must suffer all my life long, be deprived of my livelihood, depend on ignoble methods to raise enough money to keep myself and my wife alive? Man, my Lord Bishop—and no one knows it better than yourself; I have seen you among the fleshpots at the palace—is made up of body as well as soul. A little carnality may be forgiven even to a man of my cloth. Even you, my Lord Bishop, have in your time no doubt sported among the haycocks.' " He stopped; he was a little out of breath. They stared back at each other with awe and affection.

Acky said, "I want to write a little piece, dear, now, about you."
He took in with what could only have been the deepest and the
purest love the black, sagging skirt, the soiled blouse, the yellow
wrinkled face. "My dear," he said, "what I should have done without—" He began to make a rough draft of yet another paragraph,
speaking the phrases aloud as he wrote them. " 'What I should have
done during this long trial—no, martyrdom—I do not know—I
cannot conceive—if I had not been supported by the trust and the
unswerving fidelity—no, fidelity and unswerving trust of my dear
wife, a wife whom Mrs. Mark Egerton considered herself in a position to despise. As if Our Lord had chosen the rich and well-born
to serve Him. At least this trial—has taught me to distinguish between my friends and enemies. And yet at my trial *her* word, the
word of the woman who loved and believed in me, counted—for
nought beside the word—of that—that—trumpery and deceitful
scandalmonger.' "

The old woman leaned forward with tears of pride and importance in her eyes. She said, "That's lovely. Do you think the bishop's
wife will read it? Oh dear, I know I ought to go and tidy the
room upstairs (we might be getting some young people in), but
some'ow, Acky dear, I'd just like to stay right 'ere with you awhile.
What you write makes me feel kind of 'oly." She slumped down on
the kitchen chair beside the sink and watched his hand move on, as
if she were watching some unbelievably lovely vision passing
through the room, something which she had never hoped to see and
now was hers.

"And finally, my dear," Acky said, "I propose to write, 'In a
world of perjury and all manner of uncharitableness one woman
remains my sheet anchor, one woman I can trust until death and beyond.' "

"They ought to be ashamed of themselves. Oh, Acky, my dear"
—she wept—"to think they've treated you that way. But you've
said true. I won't ever leave you. I won't leave you, not even when
I'm dead. Never, never, never," and the two old vicious faces regarded each other with the complete belief, the awe and mutual
suffering of a great love, while they affirmed their eternal union.

5

Anne cautiously felt the door of the compartment in which she
had been left alone. It was locked, as she had thought it would be

in spite of Saunders' tact and his attempt to hide what he was doing. She stared out at the dingy Midland station with dismay. It seemed to her that everything which made her life worth the effort of living was lost—she hadn't even got a job—and she watched between an advertisement of Horlick's for night starvation and a bright blue-and-yellow picture of the Yorkshire coast the weary pilgrimage which lay before her from agent to agent. The train began to move past the waiting rooms, the lavatories, the sloping concrete, into a waste of rails.

What a fool, she thought, I have been, thinking I could save us from a war. Three men are dead, that's all. Now that she was herself responsible for so many deaths, she could no longer feel the same repulsion towards Raven. In this waste through which she travelled, between the stacks of coal, the tumbledown sheds, abandoned trucks in sidings where a little grass had poked up and died between the cinders, she thought of him again with pity and distress. They had been on the same side, he had trusted her, she had given her word to him, and then she had broken it without even the grace of hesitation. He must have known of her treachery before he died; in that dead mind she was preserved forever with the chaplain who had tried to frame him, with the doctor who had telephoned to the police.

Well, she had lost the only man she cared a damn about—it was always regarded as some kind of atonement, she thought, to suffer too—lost him for no reason at all. For *she* couldn't stop a war. Men were fighting beasts; they needed war. In the paper that Saunders had left for her on the opposite seat she could read how the mobilization in four countries was complete, how the ultimatum expired at midnight; it was no longer on the front page, but that was only because to Nottwich readers there was a war nearer at hand, fought out to a finish in the Tanneries. How they love it, she thought bitterly, as the dusk came up from the dark wounded ground and the glow of furnaces became visible beyond the long black ridge of slag heaps. This was war too—this chaos through which the train moved slowly, grinding over point after point like a dying creature dragging itself painfully away through no man's land from the scene of battle.

She pressed her face against the window to keep her tears away; the cold pressure of the frosting pane stiffened her resistance. The train gathered speed by a small neo-Gothic church, a row of villas, and then the country, the fields, a few cows making for an open gate, a hard, broken lane, and a cyclist lighting his lamp. She began to hum to keep her spirits up, but the only tunes she could remember were "Aladdin" and "It's Only Kew." She thought of the long bus ride home, the voice on the telephone, and how she couldn't get to the window to wave to him and he had stood there with his back to her while the train went by. It was Mr. Davis even then who had ruined everything.

And it occurred to her, staring out at the bleak, frozen countryside, that perhaps, even if she had been able to save the country from a war, it wouldn't have been worth the saving. She thought of Mr. Davis and Acky and his old wife, of the producer and Miss Maydew and the landlady at her lodging with the bead of liquid on her nose. What had made her play so absurd a part? If she had not offered to go out to dinner with Mr. Davis, Raven probably would be in jail and the others alive. She tried to remember the watching, anxious faces studying the sky signs in Nottwich High Street, but she couldn't remember them with any vividness.

The door into the corridor was unlocked, and, staring through the window into the grey, fading winter light, she thought, More questions. Will they never stop worrying me? She said aloud, "I've made my statement, haven't I?"

Mather's voice said, "There are still a few things to discuss."

She turned hopelessly towards him. "Need *you* have come?"

"I'm in charge of this case," Mather said, sitting down opposite her with his back to the engine, watching the country which she could see approach flow backward over her shoulder and disappear. He said, "We've been checking what you told us. It's a strange story."

"It's true," she repeated wearily.

He said, "We've had half the legations in London on the phone. Not to speak of Geneva. And the commissioner."

She said with a flicker of malice, "I'm sorry you've been troubled." But she couldn't keep it up. Her formal indifference was ruined by his presence—the large, clumsy, once friendly hands, the bulk of the man. "Oh, I'm sorry," she said. "I've said that before, haven't I? What else can I—? I'd say it if I'd spilled your coffee, and I've got to say it after all these people are killed. There are no other words, are there, which mean more? It all worked out wrong. I thought everything was clear. I've failed. I didn't mean to hurt you ever. I suppose the commissioner—" She began to cry without tears; it was as if those ducts were frozen.

He said, "I'm to have promotion. I don't know why. It seems to me as if I'd bungled it." He added gently and pleadingly, leaning forward across the compartment. "We could get married—at once —though I daresay if you don't want to now, you'll do all right. They'll give you a grant."

It was like going into the manager's office expecting dismissal and getting a rise instead—or a speaking part; but it never had happened that way. She stared silently back at him.

"Of course," he said gloomily, "you'll be the rage now. You'll have stopped a war. I know I didn't believe you. I've failed. I thought I'd always trust— We've found enough already to prove what you told me and I thought was lies. They'll have to withdraw their ultimatum now. They won't have any choice." He added with a deep hatred of publicity, "It'll be the sensation of a century," sitting back with his face heavy and sad.

"You mean," she said with incredulity, "that when we get in— we can go off straightaway and be married?"

"Will you?"

She said, "The taxi won't be fast enough."

"It won't be as quick as all that. It takes three weeks. We can't afford a special licence."

She said, "Didn't you tell me about a grant? I'll blow it on the licence," and suddenly, as they simultaneously laughed, it was as if the past three days left the carriage, were whirled backward down to the metals to Nottwich. It had all happened there, and they need never go back to the scene of it. Only a shade of disquiet remained, a fading spectre of Raven. If his immortality was to be on the lips of living men, he was fighting now his last losing fight against extinction.

"All the same," Anne said, as Raven covered her with his sack, as Raven touched her icy hand, "I failed."

"Failed?" Mather said. "You've been the biggest success," and it seemed to Anne for a few moments that this sense of failure would never die from her brain, that it would cloud a little every happiness. It was something she could never explain; her lover would never understand it. But already, as his face lost its gloom, she was failing again—failing to atone. The cloud was blown away by his voice; it evaporated under his large and clumsy and tender hand.

"Such a success." He was as inarticulate as Saunders, now that he was realizing what it meant. It was worth a little publicity. This darkening land, flowing backwards down the line, was safe for a few more years. He was a countryman, and he didn't ask for more than a few years' safety at a time for something he so dearly loved. The precariousness of its safety made it only the more precious. Somebody was burning winter weeds under a hedge, and down a dark lane a farmer rode home alone from the hunt in a queer old-fashioned bowler hat on a horse that would never take a ditch. A small lit village came up beside his window and sailed away like a little pleasure steamer hung with lanterns. He had just time to notice the grey English church squatted among the yews and graves, the thick deaths of centuries, like an old dog who will not leave his corner. On the little wooden platform as they whirled by a porter was reading the label on a tall Christmas tree.

"You haven't failed," he said.

London had its roots in her heart; she saw nothing in the dark countryside. She looked away from it to Mather's happy face. "You don't understand," she said, sheltering the ghost for a very short while longer. "I *did* fail." But she forgot it herself completely when the train drew into London over a great viaduct under which the small, bright, shabby streets ran off like the rays of a star with their sweet shops, their Methodist chapels, their messages chalked on the paving stones. Then it was she who thought, This is safe, and, wiping the glass free from steam, she pressed her face against the pane and happily and avidly and tenderly watched, as a child whose mother has died watches the family *she* must rear without being aware at all that the responsibility is too great. A mob of children went screaming down a street—she could tell they screamed because she was one of them; she couldn't hear their voices or see their mouths. A man was selling hot chestnuts at a corner, and it was on *her* face that his little fire glowed. The sweet shops were full of white gauze stockings crammed with cheap gifts. "Oh," she said, with a sigh of unshadowed happiness, "we're home."

The
Third
Man

To Carol Reed
in admiration and affection
and in memory of so many early morning
Vienna hours
at Maxim's, the Casanova, the Oriental

Preface

The Third Man was never written to be read but only to be seen.
Like many love affairs it started at a dinner table and continued
with many headaches in many places: Vienna, Venice, Ravello,
London, Santa Monica.

Most novelists, I suppose, carry round in their heads or in their
notebooks the first ideas for stories that have never come to be
written. Sometimes one turns them over after many years and
thinks regretfully that they would have been good once, in a time
now dead. So, twenty years back, on the flap of an envelope, I had
written an opening paragraph: "I had paid my last farewell to
Harry a week ago, when his coffin was lowered into the frozen
February ground, so that it was with incredulity that I saw him
pass by, without a sign of recognition, among the host of strangers
in the Strand." I, no more than my hero, had pursued Harry, so
when Sir Alexander Korda asked me to write a film for Carol
Reed—to follow our *Fallen Idol*—I had nothing more to offer
than this paragraph. Though Korda wanted a film about the four-
power occupation of Vienna, he was prepared to let me pursue
the tracks of Harry Lime.

To me it is almost impossible to write a film play without first
writing a story. Even a film depends on more than plot, on a certain measure of characterization, on mood and atmosphere; and
these seem to me almost impossible to capture for the first time in
the dull shorthand of a script. One can reproduce an effect caught
in another medium, but one cannot make the first act of creation
in script form. One must have the sense of more material than one
needs to draw on. *The Third Man,* therefore, though never intended for publication, had to start as a story before it began

those apparently interminable transformations from one treatment to another.

On these treatments Carol Reed and I worked closely together, covering so many feet of carpet a day, acting scenes at each other. No third ever joined our conferences; so much value lies in the clear cut-and-thrust of argument between two people. To the novelist, of course, his novel is the best he can do with a particular subject; he cannot help resenting many of the changes necessary for turning it into a film or a play; but *The Third Man* was never intended to be more than the raw material for a picture. The reader will notice many differences between the story and the film, and he should not imagine these changes were forced on an unwilling author: as likely as not they were suggested by the author. The film, in fact, is better than the story because it is in this case the finished state of the story.

Some of these changes have obvious superficial reasons. The choice of an American instead of an English star involved a number of alterations. For example, Mr. Joseph Cotten quite reasonably objected to the name Rollo. The name had to be an absurd one, and the name Holley occurred to me when I remembered that figure of fun, the America poet Thomas Holley Chivers. An American, too, could hardly have been mistaken for the great English writer Dexter, whose literary character bore certain echoes of the gentle genius of Mr. E. M. Forster. The confusion of identities would have been impossible, even if Carol Reed had not rightly objected to a rather far-fetched situation involving a great deal of explanation that increased the length of a film already far too long. Another minor point: in deference to American opinion a Rumanian was substituted for Cooler, since Mr. Orson Welles' engagement had already supplied us with one American villain. (Incidentally, the popular line of dialogue concerning Swiss cuckoo clocks was written into the script by Mr. Welles himself.)

One of the very few major disputes between Carol Reed and myself concerned the ending, and he has been proved triumphantly right. I held the view that an entertainment of this kind, which in England we call a thriller, was too light an affair to carry the weight of an unhappy ending. Reed on his side felt that my ending—indeterminate though it was, with no words spoken— would strike the audience, who had just seen Harry die, as unpleasantly cynical. I admit I was only half convinced; I was afraid few people would wait in their seats during the girl's long walk from the graveside and that they would leave the cinema under the impression that the ending was as conventional as mine and more drawn-out. I had not given enough consideration to the mastery of Reed's direction, and at that stage, of course, we neither of us could have anticipated Reed's brilliant discovery of Mr. Karas, the zither player.

The episode of the Russians kidnapping Anna (a perfectly possible incident in Vienna) was eliminated at a fairly late stage. It was not satisfactorily tied into the story, and it threatened to turn the film into a propagandist picture. We had no desire to move people's political emotions; we wanted to entertain them, to frighten them a little, to make them laugh.

Reality, in fact, was only a background to a fairy tale; nonetheless the story of the penicillin racket is based on a truth all the more grim because so many of the agents were more innocent than Joseph Harbin. The other day in London a surgeon took two friends to see the film. He was surprised to find them subdued and depressed by a picture he had enjoyed. They then told him that at the end of the war when they were with the Royal Air Force they had themselves sold penicillin in Vienna. The possible consequences of their act had never before occurred to them.

Boston, February 1950

One

One never knows when the blow may fall. When I saw Rollo Martins first I made this note on him for my security police files: "In normal circumstances a cheerful fool. Drinks too much and may cause a little trouble. Whenever a woman passes raises his eyes and makes some comment, but I get the impression that really he'd rather not be bothered. Has never really grown up and perhaps that accounts for the way he worshipped Lime." I wrote there that phrase "in normal circumstances" because I met him first at Harry Lime's funeral. It was February, and the gravediggers had been forced to use electric drills to open the frozen ground in Vienna's Central Cemetery. It was as if even nature were doing its best to reject Lime, but we got him in at last and laid the earth back on him like bricks. He was vaulted in, and Rollo Martins walked quickly away as though his long gangly legs wanted to break into a run, and the tears of a boy ran down his thirty-five-year-old cheeks. Rollo Martins believed in friendship, and that was why what happened later was a worse shock to him than it would have been to you or me (you because you would have put it down to an illusion and me because at once a rational explanation—however wrongly—would have come to my mind). If only he had come to tell me then, what a lot of trouble would have been saved.

If you are to understand this strange rather sad story you must have an impression at least of the background—the smashed dreary city of Vienna divided up in zones among the four powers; the Russian, the British, the American, the French zones, regions marked only by notice boards, and in the centre of the city, surrounded by the Ring with its heavy public buildings and its prancing statuary, the Inner Stadt under the control of all four powers. In this once fashionable Inner Stadt each power in turn, for a month at a time, takes, as we call it, "the chair," and becomes responsible for security; at night, if you were fool enough to waste your Austrian schillings on a night club, you would be fairly certain to see the International Patrol at work—four military police, one from each power, communicating with each other, if they communicated at all, in the common language of their enemy. I never knew Vienna between the wars, and I am too young to remember the old Vienna with its Strauss music and its bogus easy charm; to me it is simply a city of undignified ruins which turned that February into great glaciers of snow and ice. The Danube was a grey flat muddy river a long way off across the second bezirk, the Russian zone, where the Prater lay smashed and desolate and full of weeds, only the Great Wheel revolving slowly over the foundations of merry-go-rounds like abandoned millstones, the rusting iron of smashed tanks which nobody had cleared away, the frost-nipped weeds where the snow was thin. I haven't enough imagination to picture it as it had once been, any more than I can picture Sacher's Hotel as other than a transit hotel for English officers or see the Kärntnerstrasse as a fashionable shopping street instead of a street which exists, most of it, only at eye level, repaired up to the first story. A Russian soldier in a fur cap goes by with a rifle over his shoulder, and men in overcoats sip ersatz coffee in the windows of the Old Vienna. This was roughly the Vienna to which Rollo Martins came on February seventh last year. I have reconstructed the affair as best I can from my own files and from what Martins told me. It is as accurate as I can make it—I haven't invented a line of dialogue, though I can't vouch for Martins' memory; an ugly story if you leave out the girl: grim and sad and unrelieved if it were not for that absurd episode of the British Cultural Relations Society lecturer.

Two

A British subject can still travel if he is content to take with him only five English pounds which he is forbidden to spend abroad, but if Rollo Martins had not received an invitation from Lime he would not have been allowed to enter Austria, which counts still as occupied territory. Lime had suggested that Martins might write up the business of looking after the international refugees, and although it wasn't Martins' usual line, he had consented. It would give him a holiday, and he badly needed a holiday after the incident in Dublin and the other incident in Amsterdam; he always tried to dismiss women as "incidents," things that simply happen to him without any will of his own, acts of God in the eyes of insurance agents. He had a haggard look when he arrived in Vienna and a habit of looking over his shoulder that for a time made me suspicious of him until I realized that he went in fear that one of, say, six people might turn up unexpectedly. He told me vaguely that he had been mixing his drinks—that was another way of putting it.

Rollo Martins' usual line was the writing of cheap paper-covered Westerns under the name of Buck Dexter. His public was large but unremunerative. He couldn't have afforded Vienna if Lime had not offered to pay his expenses when he got there out of some vaguely described propaganda fund. Lime could also, he said, keep him supplied with paper bafs—the only currency in use from a penny upwards in British hotels and clubs. So it was with exactly five unusable pound notes that Martins arrived in Vienna.

An odd incident had occurred at Frankfurt, where the plane from London grounded for an hour. Martins was eating a hamburger in the American canteen (a kindly airline supplied the passengers with a voucher for sixty-five cents' worth of food) when a man he could recognize from twenty feet away as a journalist approached his table.

"You Mr. Dexter?" he asked.

"Yes," Martins said, taken off his guard.

"You look younger than your photographs," the man said. "Like to make a statement? I represent the local forces paper here. We'd like to know what you think of Frankfurt."

"I only touched down ten minutes ago."

"Fair enough," the man said. "What about views on the American novel?"

"I don't read them," Martins said.

"The well-known acid humour," the journalist said. He pointed at a small grey-haired man with two protruding teeth, nibbling a bit of bread. "Happen to know if that's Carey?"

"No. What Carey?"

"J. G. Carey of coursé."

"I've never heard of him."

"You novelists live out of the world. He's my real assignment," and Martins watched him make across the room for the great Carey, who greeted him with a false headline smile, laying down his crust. Dexter wasn't the man's assignment, but Martins couldn't help feeling a certain pride—nobody had ever before referred to him as a novelist; and that sense of pride and importance carried him over the disappointment when Lime was not there to meet him at the airport. We never get accustomed to being less important to other people than they are to us—Martins felt the little jab of dispensability, standing by the bus door, watching the snow come sifting down, so thinly and softly that the great drifts among the ruined buildings had an air of permanence, as though they were not the result of this meagre fall, but lay, forever, above the line of perpetual snow.

There was no Lime to meet him at the Hotel Astoria where the bus landed him, and no message—only a cryptic one for Mr. Dexter from someone he had never heard of called Crabbin. "We expected you on tomorrow's plane. Please stay where you are. On the way round. Hotel room booked," but Rollo Martins wasn't the kind of man who stayed around. If you stayed around in a hotel lounge sooner or later incidents occurred; one mixed one's drinks. I can hear Rollo Martins saying to me now, "I've done with incidents. No more incidents," before he plunged head first into the most serious incident of all. There was always a conflict in Rollo Martins—between the absurd Christian name and the sturdy Dutch (four generations back) surname. Rollo looked at every woman that passed, and Martins renounced them forever. I don't know which of them wrote the Westerns.

Martins had been given Lime's address and he felt no curiosity about the man called Crabbin; it was too obvious that a mistake had been made, though he didn't yet connect it with the conversation at Frankfurt. Lime had written that he could put Martins up in his own flat, a large apartment on the edge of Vienna that had been requisitioned from a Nazi owner. Lime could pay for the taxi when he arrived, so Martins drove straight away to the building lying in the third (British) zone. He kept the taxi waiting while he mounted to the third floor.

How quickly one becomes aware of silence even in so silent a city as Vienna with the snow steadily settling. Martins hadn't

reached the second floor before he was convinced that he would
not find Lime there, but the silence was deeper than just absence
—it was as if he would not find Harry Lime anywhere in Vienna,
and, as he reached the third floor and saw the big black bow over
the door handle, anywhere in the world at all. Of course it might
have been a cook who had died, a housekeeper, anybody but
Harry Lime, but he knew—he felt he had known twenty stairs
down—that Lime, the Lime he had hero-worshipped now for
twenty years, since the first meeting in a grim school corridor with
a cracked bell ringing for prayers, was gone. Martins wasn't
wrong, not entirely wrong. After he had rung the bell half a dozen
times a small man with a sullen expression put his head out from
another flat and told him in a tone of vexation, "It's no use ringing like that. There's nobody there. He's dead."

"Herr Lime?"

"Herr Lime of course."

Martins said to me later, "At first it didn't mean a thing. It was
just a bit of information, like those paragraphs in *The Times* they
call 'News in Brief.' I said to him, 'When did it happen? How?' "

"He was run over by a car," the man said. "Last Thursday."
He added sullenly, as if really this were none of his business,
"They are burying him this afternoon. You've only just missed
them."

"Them?"

"Oh, a couple of friends and the coffin."

"Wasn't he in hospital?"

"There was no sense in taking him to hospital. He was killed
here on his own doorstep—instantaneously. The right-hand mud-
guard struck him on his shoulder and bowled him over in front
like a rabbit."

It was only then, Martins told me, when the man used the word
"rabbit," that the dead Harry Lime came alive, became the boy
with the gun which he had shown Martins the means of "borrow-
ing"; a boy starting up among the long sandy barrows of Brickworth Common saying, "Shoot, you fool, shoot! There," and the
rabbit limped to cover, wounded by Martins' shot.

"Where are they burying him?" he asked the stranger on the
landing.

"In the Central Cemetery. They'll have a hard time of it in this
frost."

He had no idea how to pay for his taxi, or indeed where in

Vienna he could find a room in which he could live for five English pounds, but that problem had to be postponed until he had seen the last of Harry Lime. He drove straight out of town into the suburb (British zone) where the Central Cemetery lay. One passed through the Russian zone to reach it, and took a short cut through the American zone, which you couldn't mistake because of the ice-cream parlours in every street. The trams ran along the high wall of the Central Cemetery, and for a mile on the other side of the rails stretched the monumental masons and the market gardeners—an apparently endless chain of gravestones waiting for owners and wreaths waiting for mourners.

Martins had not realized the size of this huge snowbound park where he was making his last rendezvous with Lime. It was as if Harry had left a message to him, "Meet me in Hyde Park," without specifying a spot between the Achilles statue and Lancaster Gate; the avenues of graves, each avenue numbered and lettered, stretched out like the spokes of an enormous wheel; they drove for a half-mile towards the west, then turned and drove a half-mile north, turned south. . . . The snow gave the great pompous family headstones an air of grotesque comedy; a toupee of snow slipped sideways over an angelic face, a saint wore a heavy white moustache, and a shako of snow tipped at a drunken angle over the bust of a superior civil servant called Wolfgang Gottman. Even this cemetery was zoned between the powers: the Russian zone was marked by huge statues of armed men, the French by rows of anonymous wooden crosses and a torn tired tricolour flag. Then Martins remembered that Lime was a Catholic and was unlikely to be buried in the British one for which they had been vainly searching. So back they drove through the heart of a forest where the graves lay like wolves under the trees, winking white eyes under the gloom of the evergreens. Once from under the trees emerged a group of three men in strange eighteenth-century black and silver uniforms with three-cornered hats, pushing a kind of barrow: they crossed a ride in the forest of graves and disappeared again.

It was just chance that they found the funeral in time—one patch in the enormous park where the snow had been shovelled aside and a tiny group was gathered, apparently bent on some very private business. A priest was speaking, his words coming secretively through the thin patient snow, and a coffin was on the point of being lowered into the ground. Two men in lounge suits stood at the graveside; one carried a wreath that he obviously had forgotten to drop onto the coffin, for his companion nudged his elbow so that he came to with a start and dropped the flowers. A girl stood a little way away with her hands over her face, and I stood twenty yards away by another grave, watching with relief the last of Lime and noticing carefully who was there—just a man in a mackintosh I was to Martins. He came up to me and said, "Could you tell me who they are burying?"

"A fellow called Lime," I said, and was astonished to see the tears start to this stranger's eyes: he didn't look like a man who wept, nor was Lime the kind of man whom I thought likely to have mourners—genuine mourners with genuine tears. There was the girl of course, but one excepts women from all such generalizations.

Martins stood there, till the end, close beside me. He said to me later that as an old friend he didn't want to intrude on these newer ones—Lime's death belonged to them, let them have it. He was under the sentimental illusion that Lime's life—twenty years of it anyway—belonged to him. As soon as the affair was over—I am not a religious man and always feel a little impatient with the fuss that surrounds death—Martins strode away on his long gangly legs that always seemed likely to get entangled together, back to his taxi. He made no attempt to speak to anyone, and the tears now were really running, at any rate the few meagre drops that any of us can squeeze out at our age.

One's file, you know, is never quite complete; a case is never really closed, even after a century, when all the participants are dead. So I followed Martins: I knew the other three: I wanted to know the stranger. I caught him up by his taxi and said, "I haven't any transport. Would you give me a lift into town?"

"Of course," he said. I knew the driver of my jeep would spot me as we came out and follow us unobtrusively. As we drove away I noticed he never looked behind—it's nearly always the fake mourners and the fake lovers who take that last look, who wait waving on platforms, instead of clearing quickly out, not looking back. Is it perhaps that they love themselves so much and want to keep themselves in the sight of others, even of the dead?

I said, "My name's Calloway."

"Martins," he said.

"You were a friend of Lime?"

"Yes." Most people in the last week would have hesitated before they admitted quite so much.

"Been here long?"

"I only came this afternoon from England. Harry had asked me to stay with him. I hadn't heard."

"Bit of a shock?"

"Look here," he said, "I badly want a drink, but I haven't any cash—except five pounds sterling. I'd be awfully grateful if you'd stand me one."

It was my turn to say "Of course." I thought for a moment and told the driver the name of a small bar in the Kärtnerstrasse. I didn't think he'd want to be seen for a while in a busy British bar full of transit officers and their wives. This bar—perhaps because it was exorbitant in its prices—seldom had more than one self-occupied couple in it at a time. The trouble was too that it really only had one drink—a sweet chocolate liqueur that the waiter improved at a price with cognac—but I got the impression that Martins had no objection to any drink so long as it cast a veil over the present, and the past. On the door was the usual notice saying the bar opened at six till ten, but one just pushed the door and walked through the front rooms. We had a whole small room to ourselves; the only couple were next door, and the waiter, who knew me, left us alone with some caviar sandwiches. It was lucky that we both knew that I had an expense account.

Martins said over his second quick drink, "I'm sorry, but he was the best friend I ever had."

I couldn't resist saying, knowing what I knew, and because I was anxious to vex him—one learns a lot that way—"That sounds like a cheap novelette."

He said quickly, "I write cheap novelettes."

I had learned something anyway. Until he had had a third drink I was under the impression that he wasn't an easy talker, but I felt fairly certain that he was one of those who turn unpleasant after their fourth glass.

I said, "Tell me about yourself—and Lime."

"Look here," he said, "I badly need another drink, but I can't keep on scrounging on a stranger. Could you change me a pound or two into Austrian money?"

"Don't bother about that," I said and called the waiter. "You can treat me when I come to London on leave. You were going to tell me how you met Lime?"

The glass of chocolate liqueur might have been a crystal, the way he looked at it and turned it this way and that. He said, "It was a long time ago. I don't suppose anyone knows Harry the way I do," and I thought of the thick file of agents' reports in my office, each claiming the same thing. I believe in my agents; I've sifted them all very thoroughly.

"How long?"

"Twenty years—or a bit more. I met him my first term at school. I can see the place. I can see the notice board and what was on it. I can hear the bell ringing. He was a year older and knew the ropes. He put me wise to a lot of things." He took a quick dab at his drink and then turned the crystal again as if to see more clearly what there was to see. He said, "It's funny. I can't remember meeting any woman quite as well."

"Was he clever at school?"

"Not the way they wanted him to be. But what things he did think up! He was a wonderful planner. I was far better at subjects like History and English than Harry, but I was a hopeless mug when it came to carrying out his plans." He laughed: he was already beginning, with the help of drink and talk, to throw off the shock of the death. He said, "I was always the one who got caught."

"That was convenient for Lime."

"What the hell do you mean?" he asked. Alcoholic irritation was setting in.

"Well, wasn't it?"

"That was my fault, not his. He could have found someone cleverer if he'd chosen, but he liked me. He was endlessly patient with me." Certainly, I thought, the child is father to the man, for I too had found him patient.

"When did you see him last?"

"Oh, he was over in London six months ago for a medical congress. You know he qualified as a doctor, though he never practised. That was typical of Harry. He just wanted to see if he could do a thing and then he lost interest. But he used to say that it often came in handy." And that too was true. It was odd how like the Lime he knew was to the Lime I knew: it was only that he looked at Lime's image from a different angle or in a different light. He said, "One of the things I liked about Harry was his humour." He gave a grin which took five years off his age. "I'm a buffoon, I like playing the silly fool, but Harry had real wit. You know, he could have been a first-class light composer if he had worked at it."

He whistled a tune—it was oddly familiar to me. "I always remember that. I saw Harry write it. Just in a couple of minutes on the back of an envelope. That was what he always whistled when he had something on his mind. It was his signature tune." He whistled the tune a second time, and I knew then who had written it—of course it wasn't Harry. I nearly told him so, but what was the point? The tune wavered and went out. He stared down into his glass, drained what was left, and said, "It's a damned shame to think of him dying the way he did."

"It was the best thing that ever happened to him," I said.

He didn't take in my meaning at once: he was a little hazy with the drinks. "The best thing?"

"Yes."

"You mean there wasn't any pain?"

"He was lucky in that way, too."

It was my tone of voice and not my words that caught Martins' attention. He asked gently and dangerously—I could see his right hand tighten—"Are you hinting at something?"

There is no point at all in showing physical courage in all situations: I eased my chair far enough back to be out of reach of his fist. I said, "I mean that I had his case completed at police headquarters. He would have served a long spell—a very long spell—if it hadn't been for the accident."

"What for?"

"He was about the worst racketeer who ever made a dirty living in this city."

I could see him measuring the distance between us and deciding that he couldn't reach me from where he sat. Rollo wanted to hit out, but Martins was steady, careful. Martins, I began to realize, was dangerous. I wondered whether after all I had made a complete mistake: I couldn't see Martins being quite the mug that Rollo had made out. "You're a policeman?" he asked.

"Yes."

"I've always hated policemen. They are always either crooked or stupid."

"Is that the kind of books you write?"

I could see him edging his chair round to block my way out. I caught the waiter's eye and he knew what I meant—there's an advantage in always using the same bar for interviews.

Martins brought out a surface smile and said gently, "I have to call them sheriffs."

"Been in America?" It was a silly conversation.

"No. Is this an interrogation?"

"Just interest."

"Because if Harry was that kind of racketeer, I must be one too. We always worked together."

"I daresay he meant to cut you in—somewhere in the organization. I wouldn't be surprised if he had meant to give you the baby to hold. That was his method at school—you told me, didn't you? And, you see, the headmaster was getting to know a thing or two."

"You are running true to form, aren't you? I suppose there was some petty racket going on with petrol and you couldn't pin it on anyone, so you've picked a dead man. That's just like a policeman. You're a real policeman, I suppose?"

"Yes, Scotland Yard, but they've put me into a colonel's uniform when I'm on duty."

He was between me and the door now. I couldn't get away from the table without coming into range, I'm no fighter, and he had six inches of advantage anyway. I said, "It wasn't petrol."

"Tires, saccharin—why don't you policemen catch a few murderers for a change?"

"Well, you could say that murder was part of his racket."

He pushed the table over with one hand and made a dive at me with the other; the drink confused his calculations. Before he could try again my driver had his arms round him. I said, "Don't treat him roughly. He's only a writer with too much drink in him."

"Be quiet, can't you, sir," my driver said. He had an exaggerated sense of officer-class. He would probably have called Lime "sir."

"Listen, Callaghan, or whatever your bloody name is . . ."

"Calloway. I'm English, not Irish."

"I'm going to make you look the biggest bloody fool in Vienna.

There's one dead man you aren't going to pin your unsolved crimes on."

"I see. You're going to find me the real criminal? It sounds like one of your stories."

"You can let me go, Callaghan. I'd rather make you look the fool you are than black your bloody eye. You'd only have to go to bed for a few days with a black eye. But when I've finished with you you'll leave Vienna."

I took out a couple of pounds' worth of bafs and stuck them in his breast pocket. "These will see you through tonight," I said, "and I'll make sure they keep a seat for you on tomorrow's London plane."

"You can't turn me out. My papers are in order."

"Yes, but this is like other cities: you need money here. If you change sterling on the black market I'll catch up on you inside twenty-four hours. Let him go."

Rollo Martins dusted himself down. He said, "Thanks for the drinks."

"That's all right."

"I'm glad I don't have to feel grateful. I suppose they were on expenses?"

"Yes."

"I'll be seeing you again in a week or two when I've got the dope." I knew he was angry; I didn't believe then that he was serious. I thought he was putting over an act to cheer up his self-esteem.

"I might come and see you off tomorrow."

"I shouldn't waste your time. I won't be there."

"Paine here will show you the way to Sacher's. You can get a bed and dinner there. I'll see to that."

He stepped to one side as though to make way for the waiter and slashed out at me. I just avoided him, but stumbled against the table. Before he could try again Paine had landed on him on the mouth. He went bang over in the alleyway between the tables and came up bleeding from a cut lip. I said, "I thought you promised not to fight."

He wiped some of the blood away with his sleeve and said, "Oh, no, I said I'd rather make you a bloody fool. I didn't say I wouldn't give you a black eye as well."

I had had a long day and I was tired of Rollo Martins. I said to Paine, "See him safely into Sacher's. Don't hit him again if he behaves," and, turning away from both of them towards the inner bar (I deserved one more drink), I heard Paine say respectfully to the man he had just knocked down, "This way, sir. It's only just around the corner."

Three

What happened next I didn't hear from Paine but from Martins a long time afterwards, reconstructing the chain of events that did indeed—though not quite in the way he had expected—prove me to be a fool. Paine simply saw him to the head porter's desk and explained there, "This gentleman came in on the plane from London. Colonel Calloway says he's to have a room." Having made that clear, he said, "Good evening, sir," and left. He was probably a bit embarrassed by Martins' bleeding lip.

"Had you already got a reservation, sir?" the porter asked.

"No. No, I don't think so," Martins said in a muffled voice holding his handkerchief to his mouth.

"I thought perhaps you might be Mr. Dexter. We had a room reserved for a week for Mr. Dexter."

Martins said, "Oh, I am Mr. Dexter." He told me later that it occurred to him that Lime might have engaged him a room in that name because perhaps it was Buck Dexter and not Rollo Martins who was to be used for propaganda purposes. A voice said at his elbow, "I'm so sorry you were not met at the plane, Mr. Dexter. My name's Crabbin."

The speaker was a stout middle-aged young man with a natural tonsure and one of the thickest pairs of horn-rimmed glasses that Martins had ever seen. He went apologetically on, "One of our chaps happened to ring up Frankfurt and heard you were on the plane. HQ made one of their usual foolish mistakes and wired you were not coming. Something about Sweden, but the cable was badly mutilated. Directly I heard from Frankfurt I tried to meet the plane, but I just missed you. You got my note?"

Martins held his handkerchief to his mouth and said obscurely, "Yes. Yes?"

"May I say at once, Mr. Dexter, how excited I am to meet you?"

"Good of you."

"Ever since I was a boy, I've thought you the greatest novelist of our century."

Martins winced. It was painful opening his mouth to protest. He took an angry look instead at Mr. Crabbin, but it was impossible to suspect that young man of a practical joke.

"You have a big Austrian public, Mr. Dexter, both for your originals and your translations. Especially for *The Curved Prow,* that's my own favourite."

Martins was thinking hard. "Did you say—room for a week?"

"Yes."

"Very kind of you."

"Mr. Schmidt here will give you tickets every day, to cover all meals. But I expect you'll need a little pocket money. We'll fix that. Tomorrow we thought you'd like a quiet day—to look about."

"Yes."

"Of course any of us are at your service if you need a guide. Then the day after tomorrow in the evening there's a little quiet discussion at the Institute—on the contemporary novel. We thought perhaps you'd say a few words just to set the ball rolling, and then answer questions."

Martins at that moment was prepared to agree to anything, to get rid of Mr. Crabbin and also to secure a week's free board and lodging; and Rollo, of course, as I was to discover later, had always been prepared to accept any suggestion—for a drink, for a girl, for a joke, for a new excitement. He said now, "Of course, of course," into his handkerchief.

"Excuse me, Mr. Dexter, have you got toothache? I know a very good dentist."

"No. Somebody hit me, that's all."

"Good God. Were they trying to rob you?"

"No, it was a soldier. I was trying to punch his bloody colonel in the eye." He removed the handkerchief and gave Crabbin a view of his cut mouth. He told me that Crabbin was at a complete loss for words. Martins couldn't understand why because he had never read the work of his great contemporary, Benjamin Dexter: he hadn't even heard of him. I am a great admirer of Dexter, so that I could understand Crabbin's bewilderment. Dexter has been ranked as a stylist with Henry James, but he has a wider feminine streak than his master—indeed his enemies have sometimes described his subtle, complex, wavering style as old-maidish. For a man still just on the right side of fifty his passionate interest in embroidery and his habit of calming a not very tumultuous mind with tatting—a trait beloved by his disciples—certainly to others seems a little affected.

"Have you ever read a book called *The Lone Rider of Santa Fe*?"

"No, I don't think so."

Martins said, "This lone rider had his best friend shot by the sheriff of a town called Lost Claim Gulch. The story is how he hunted that sheriff down—quite legally—until his revenge was completed."

"I never imagined you reading Westerns, Mr. Dexter," Crabbin said, and it needed all Martins' resolution to stop Rollo saying, "But I write them."

"Well, I'm gunning just the same way for Colonel Callaghan."

"Never heard of him."

"Heard of Harry Lime?"

"Yes," Crabbin said cautiously, "but I didn't really know him."

"I did. He was my best friend."

"I shouldn't have thought he was a very—literary character."

"None of my friends are."

Crabbin blinked nervously behind the horn-rims. He said with an air of appeasement, "He was interested in the theatre though. A friend of his—an actress, you know—is learning English at the Institute. He called once or twice to fetch her."

"Young or old?"

"Oh, young, very young. Not a good actress in my opinion."

Martins remembered the girl by the grave with her hands over her face. He said, "I'd like to meet any friend of Harry's."

"She'll probably be at your lecture."

"Austrian?"

"She claims to be Austrian, but I suspect she's Hungarian. She works at the Josefstadt. I wouldn't be surprised if Lime had helped her with her papers. She calls herself Schmidt. Anna Schmidt. You can't imagine a young English actress calling herself Smith, can you? And a pretty one, too. It always struck me as a bit too anonymous to be true."

Martins felt he had got all he could from Crabbin, so he pleaded tiredness, a long day, promised to ring up in the morning, accepted ten pounds' worth of bafs for immediate expenses, and went to his room. It seemed to him that he was earning money rapidly—twelve pounds in less than an hour.

He was tired: he realized that when he stretched himself out on his bed in his boots. Within a minute he had left Vienna far behind him and was walking through a dense wood, ankle deep in snow. An owl hooted, and he felt suddenly lonely and scared. He had an appointment to meet Harry under a particular tree, but in a wood so dense as this how could he recognize any one tree from the rest? Then he saw a figure and ran towards it: it whistled a familiar tune and his heart lifted with the relief and joy at not after all being alone. Then the figure turned and it was not Harry at all—just a stranger who grinned at him in a little circle of wet slushy melted snow, while the owl hooted again and again. He woke suddenly to hear the telephone ringing by his bed.

A voice with a trace of foreign accent—only a trace—said, "Is that Mr. Rollo Martins?"

"Yes." It was a change to be himself and not Dexter.

"You wouldn't know me," the voice said unnecessarily, "but I was a friend of Harry Lime."

It was a change too to hear anyone claim to be a friend of Harry's. Martins' heart warmed towards the stranger. He said, "I'd be glad to meet you."

"I'm just round the corner at the Old Vienna."

"Wouldn't you make it tomorow? I've had a pretty awful day with one thing and another."

"Harry asked me to see that you were all right. I was with him when he died."

"I thought—" Rollo Martins said and stopped. He had been going to say "I thought he died instantaneously," but something suggested caution. He said instead, "You haven't told me your name."

"Kurtz," the voice said. "I'd offer to come round to you, only, you know, Austrians aren't allowed in Sacher's."

"Perhaps we could meet at the Old Vienna in the morning."

"Certainly," the voice said, "if you are *quite* sure that you are all right till then."

"How do you mean?"

"Harry had it on his mind that you'd be penniless." Rollo Martins lay back on his bed with the receiver to his ear and thought:

Come to Vienna to make money. This was the third stranger to stake him in less than five hours. He said cautiously, "Oh, I can carry on till I see you." There seemed no point in turning down a good offer till he knew what the offer was.

"Shall we say eleven then at the Old Vienna in the Kärtnerstrasse? I'll be in a brown suit and I'll carry one of your books."

"That's fine. How did you get hold of one?"

"Harry gave it to me." The voice had enormous charm and reasonableness, but when Martins had said good night and rung off, he couldn't help wondering how it was that if Harry had been so conscious before he died he had not had a cable sent to stop him. Hadn't Callaghan too said that Lime had died instantaneously—or without pain, was it?—or had he himself put the words into Callaghan's mouth? It was then that the idea first lodged firmly in Martins' mind that there was something wrong about Lime's death, something the police had been too stupid to discover. He tried to discover it himself with the help of two cigarettes, but he fell asleep without his dinner and with the mystery still unsolved. It had been a long day, but not quite long enough for that.

Four

"What I disliked about him at first sight," Martins told me, "was his toupee. It was one of those obvious toupees—flat and yellow, with the hair cut straight at the back and not fitting close. There *must* be something phoney about a man who won't accept baldness gracefully. He had one of those faces too where the lines have been put in carefully, like a make-up, in the right places—to express charm, whimsicality, lines at the corners of the eyes. He was made up to appeal to romantic schoolgirls."

This conversation took place some days later—he brought out his whole story when the trail was nearly cold. When he made that remark about the romantic schoolgirls I saw his rather hunted eyes focus suddenly. It was a girl—just like any other girl, I thought—hurrying by outside my office in the driving snow.

"Something pretty?"

He brought his gaze back and said, "I'm off that forever. You know, Calloway, a time comes in a man's life when he gives up all that sort of thing . . ."

"I see. I thought you were looking at a girl."

"I was. But only because she reminded me for a moment of Anna—Anna Schmidt."

"Who's she? Isn't she a girl?"

"Oh, yes, in a way."

"What do you mean, in a way?"

"She was Harry's girl."

"Are you taking her over?"

"She's not that kind, Calloway. Didn't you see her at his funeral? I'm not mixing my drinks any more. I've got a hangover to last me a lifetime."

"You were telling me about Kurtz," I said.

It appeared that Kurtz was sitting there, making a great show of reading *The Lone Rider of Santa Fe*. When Martins sat down at his table he said with indescribably false enthusiasm, "It's wonderful how you keep the tension."

"Tension?"

"Suspense. You're a master at it. At the end of every chapter one's left guessing . . ."

"So you were a friend of Harry's," Martins said.

"I think his best," but Kurtz added with the smallest pause in which his brain must have registered the error, "except you of course."

"Tell me how he died."

"I was with him. We came out together from the door of his flat and Harry saw a friend he knew across the road—an American called Cooler. He waved to Cooler and started across the road to him when a jeep came tearing round the corner and bowled him over. It was Harry's fault really—not the driver's."

"Somebody told me he died instantaneously."

"I wish he had. He died before the ambulance could reach us though."

"He could speak then?"

"Yes. Even in his pain he worried about you."

"What did he say?"

"I can't remember the exact words, Rollo—I may call you Rollo, mayn't I? he always called you that to us. He was anxious that I should look after you when you arrived. See that you were looked after. Get your return ticket for you." In telling me, Martins said, "You see I was collecting return tickets as well as cash."

"But why didn't you cable to stop me?"

"We did, but the cable must have missed you. What with censorship and the zones, cables can take anything up to five days."

"There was an inquest?"

"Of course."

"Did you know that the police have a crazy notion that Harry was mixed up in some racket?"

"No. But everyone in Vienna is. We all sell cigarettes and exchange schillings for bafs and that kind of thing."

"The police meant something worse than that."

"They get rather absurd ideas sometimes," the man with the toupee said cautiously.

"I'm going to stay here till I prove them wrong."

Kurtz turned his head sharply and the toupee shifted very very slightly. He said, "What's the good? Nothing can bring Harry back."

"I'm going to have that police officer run out of Vienna."

"I don't see what you can do."

"I'm going to start working back from his death. You were there and this man Cooler and the chauffeur. You can give me their addresses."

"I don't know the chauffeur's."

"I can get it from the coroner's records. And then there's Harry's girl . . ."

Kurtz said, "It will be painful for her."

"I'm not concerned about her. I'm concerned about Harry."

"Do you know what it is that the police suspect?"

"No. I lost my temper too soon."

"Has it occurred to you," Kurtz said gently, "that you might dig up something—well, discreditable to Harry?"

"I'll risk that."

"It will take a bit of time—and money."

"I've got time and you were going to lend me some money, weren't you?"

"I'm not a rich man," Kurtz said. "I promised Harry to see you were all right and that you got your plane back . . ."

"You needn't worry about the money—or the plane," Martins said. "But I'll make a bet with you—in pounds sterling—five pounds against two hundred schillings—that there's something queer about Harry's death."

It was a shot in the dark, but already he had this firm instinctive sense that there was something wrong, though he hadn't yet attached the word "murder" to the instinct. Kurtz had a cup of coffee halfway to his lips and Martins watched him. The shot apparently went wide; an unaffected hand held the cup to the mouth and Kurtz drank, a little noisily, in long sips. Then he put down the cup and said, "How do you mean—queer?"

"It was convenient for the police to have a corpse, but wouldn't it have been equally convenient, perhaps, for the real racketeers?" When he had spoken he realized that after all Kurtz had not been unaffected by his wild statement: hadn't he been frozen into caution and calm? The hands of the guilty don't necessarily tremble; only in stories does a dropped glass betray agitation. Tension is more often shown in the studied action. Kurtz had drunk his coffee as though nothing had been said.

"Well—" he took another sip—"of course I wish you luck, though I don't believe there's anything to find. Just ask me for any help you want."

"I want Cooler's address."

"Certainly. I'll write it down for you. Here it is. In the American zone."

"And yours?"

"I've already put it—underneath—in the Russian zone."

He rose, giving one of his studied Viennese smiles, the charm carefully painted in with a fine brush in the little lines about the mouth and eyes. "Keep in touch," he said, "and if you need help . . . but I still think you are very unwise." He picked up *The Lone Rider*. "I'm so proud to have met you. A master of suspense," and one hand smoothed the toupee, while another, passing softly over the mouth, brushed out the smile as though it had never been.

Five

Martins sat on a hard chair just inside the stage door of the Josefstadt Theatre. He had sent up his card to Anna Schmidt after the matinée, marking it "a friend of Harry's." An arcade of little windows, with lace curtains and the lights going out one after another, showed where the artists were packing up for home, for the cup of coffee without sugar, the roll without butter to sustain them for the evening performance. It was like a little street built indoors for a film set, but even indoors it was cold, even cold to a man in a heavy overcoat, so that Martins rose and walked up and down, underneath the little windows. He felt, he said, a little like a Romeo who wasn't sure of Juliet's balcony.

He had had time to think: he was calm now, Martins not Rollo was in the ascendant. When a light went out in one of the windows and an actress descended into the passage where he walked, he didn't even turn to take a look. He was done with all that. He thought, Kurtz is right. They are all right. I'm behaving like a romantic fool. I'll just have a word with Anna Schmidt, a word of commiseration, and then I'll pack and go. He had quite forgotten, he told me, the complication of Mr. Crabbin.

A voice over his head called "Mr. Martins," and he looked up at the face that watched him from between the curtains a few feet above his head. It wasn't beautiful, he firmly explained to me, when I accused him of once again mixing his drinks. Just an honest face; dark hair and eyes which in that light looked brown; a wide forehead, a large mouth which didn't try to charm. No danger anywhere, it seemed to Rollo Martins, of that sudden reckless moment when the scent of hair or a hand against the side alters life. She said, "Will you come up, please? The second door on the right."

There are some people, he explained to me carefully, whom one recognizes instantaneously as friends. You can be at ease with them because you know that never, never will you be in danger. "That was Anna," he said, and I wasn't sure whether the past tense was deliberate or not.

Unlike most actresses' rooms this one was almost bare; no wardrobe packed with clothes, no clutter of cosmetics and grease paints: a dressing gown on the door, one sweater he recognized from Act II on the only easy chair, a tin of half-used paints and grease. A kettle hummed softly on a gas ring. She said, "Would you like a cup of tea? Someone sent me a packet last week— sometimes the Americans do, instead of flowers, you know, on the first night."

"I'd like a cup," he said, but if there was one thing he hated it was tea. He watched her while she made it, made it, of course, all wrong: the water not on the boil, the teapot unheated, too few leaves. She said, "I never quite understand why English people like tea so."

He drank his cupful quickly like a medicine and watched her gingerly and delicately sip at hers. He said, "I wanted very much to see you. About Harry."

It was the dreadful moment; he could see her mouth stiffen to meet it.

"Yes?"

"I had known him twenty years. I was his friend. We were at school together, you know, and after that—there weren't many months running when we didn't meet . . ."

She said, "When I got your card, I couldn't say no. But there's nothing really for us to talk about, is there?—nothing."

"I wanted to hear—"

"He's dead. That's the end. Everything's over, finished. What's the good of talking?"

"We both loved him."

"I don't know. You can't know a thing like that—afterwards. I don't know anything any more except—"

"Except?"

"That I want to be dead too."

Martins told me, "Then I nearly went away. What was the good of tormenting her because of this wild idea of mine? But instead I asked her one question, 'Do you know a man called Cooler?' "

"An American?" she asked. "I think that was the man who brought me some money when Harry died. I didn't want to take it, but he said Harry had been anxious—at the last moment."

"So he didn't die instantaneously?"

"Oh, no."

Martins said to me, "I began to wonder why I had got that idea so firmly into my head, and then I thought it was only the man in the flat who told me so—no one else. I said to her, 'He must have been very clear in his head at the end—because he remembered about me too. That seems to show that there wasn't really any pain.' "

"That's what I tell myself all the time."

"Did you see the doctor?"

"Once. Harry sent me to him. He was Harry's own doctor. He lived nearby, you see."

Martins suddenly saw in that odd chamber of the mind that constructs such pictures, instantaneously, irrationally, a desert place, a body on the ground, a group of birds gathered. Perhaps it was a scene from one of his own books, not yet written, forming at the gate of consciousness. Immediately it faded, he thought how odd that they were all there, just at that moment, all Harry's friends—Kurtz, the doctor, this man Cooler; only the two people who loved him seemed to have been missing. He said, "And the driver? Did you hear his evidence?"

"He was upset, scared. But Cooler's evidence exonerated him. No, it wasn't his fault, poor man. I've often heard Harry say what a careful driver he was."

"He knew Harry too?" Another bird flapped down and joined the others round the silent figure on the sand who lay face down. Now he could tell that it was Harry, by the clothes, by the attitude like that of a boy asleep in the grass at a playing field's edge, on a hot summer afternoon.

Somebody called outside the window, "Fräulein Schmidt."

She said, "They don't like one to stay too long. It uses up *their* electricity."

He had given up the idea of sparing her anything. He told her, "The police say they were going to arrest Harry. They'd pinned some racket on him."

She took the news in much the same way as Kurtz. "Everybody's in a racket."

"I don't believe he was in anything serious."

"No."

"But he may have been framed. Do you know a man called Kurtz?"

"I don't think so."

"He wears a toupee."

"Oh." He could tell that that struck home. He said, "Don't you think it was odd they were all there—at the death. Everybody knew Harry. Even the driver, the doctor . . ."

She said with hopeless calm, "I've thought that too, though I didn't know about Kurtz. I wondered whether they'd murdered him, but what's the use of wondering?"

"I'm going to get those bastards," Rollo Martins said.

"It won't do any good. Perhaps the police are right. Perhaps poor Harry got mixed up—"

"Fräulein Schmidt," the voice called again.

"I must go."

"I'll walk with you a bit of the way."

The dark was almost down; the snow had ceased for a while to fall, and the great statues of the Ring, the prancing horses, the chariots and the eagles, were gunshot grey with the end of evening light. "It's better to give up and forget," Anna said. The moony snow lay ankle deep on the unswept pavements.

"Will you give me the doctor's address?"

They stood in the shelter of a wall while she wrote it down for him.

"And yours too?"

"Why do you want that?"

"I might have news for you."

"There isn't any news that would do any good now." He watched her from a distance board her tram, bowing her head against the wind, a little dark question mark on the snow.

Six

An amateur detective has this advantage over the professional, that he doesn't work set hours. Rollo Martins was not confined to the eight-hour day: his investigations didn't have to pause for meals. In his one day he covered as much ground as one of my men would have covered in two, and he had this initial advantage over us, that he was Harry's friend. He was, as it were, working from inside, while we pecked at the perimeter.

Dr. Winkler was at home. Perhaps he would not have been at home to a police officer. Again Martins had marked his card with the sesame phrase: "A friend of Harry Lime's."

Dr. Winkler's waiting room reminded Martins of an antique shop—an antique shop that specialized in religious objets d'art. There were more crucifixes than he could count, none of later date probably than the seventeenth century. There were statues in wood and ivory. There were a number of reliquaries: little bits of bone marked with saints' names and set in oval frames on a background of tinfoil. If they were genuine, what an odd fate it was, Martins thought, for a portion of Saint Susanna's knuckle to come to rest in Dr. Winkler's waiting room. Even the high-backed hideous chairs looked as if they had once been sat in by cardinals. The room was stuffy, and one expected the smell of incense. In a small gold casket was a splinter of the True Cross. A sneeze disturbed him.

Dr. Winkler was the cleanest doctor Martins had ever seen. He was very small and neat, in a black tail coat and a high stiff collar; his little black moustache was like an evening tie. He sneezed again: perhaps he was cold because he was so clean. He said, "Mr. Martins?"

An irresistible desire to sully Dr. Winkler assailed Rollo Martins. He said, "Dr. Winkle?"

"Dr. Winkler."

"You've got an interesting collection here."

"Yes."

"These saints' bones . . ."

"The bones of chickens and rabbits." Dr. Winkler took a large white handkerchief out of his sleeve rather as though he were a conjurer producing his country's flag, and blew his nose neatly and thoroughly twice, closing each nostril in turn. You expected him to throw away the handkerchief after one use. "Would you mind, Mr. Martins, telling me the purpose of your visit? I have a patient waiting."

"We were both friends of Harry Lime."

"I was his medical adviser," Dr. Winkler corrected him and waited obstinately between the crucifixes.

"I arrived too late for the inquest. Harry had invited me out here to help him in something. I don't quite know what. I didn't hear of his death till I arrived."

"Very sad," Dr. Winkler said.

"Naturally, under the circumstances, I want to hear all I can."

"There is nothing I can tell you that you don't know. He was knocked over by a car. He was dead when I arrived."

"Would he have been conscious at all?"

"I understand he was for a short time, while they carried him into the house."

"In great pain?"

"Not necessarily."

"You are quite certain that it was an accident?"

Dr. Winkler put out a hand and straightened a crucifix. "I was not there. My opinion is limited to the cause of death. Have you any reason to be dissatisfied?"

The amateur has another advantage over the professional: he can be reckless. He can tell unnecessary truths and propound wild theories. Martins said, "The police had implicated Harry in a very serious racket. It seemed to me that he might have been murdered —or even killed himself."

"I am not competent to pass an opinion," Dr. Winkler said.

"Do you know a man called Cooler?"

"I don't think so."

"He was there when Harry was killed."

"Then of course I have met him. He wears a toupee."

"That was Kurtz."

Dr. Winkler was not only the cleanest, he was also the most cautious doctor that Martins had ever met. His statements were so limited that you could not for a moment doubt their veracity. He said, "There was a second man there." If he had to diagnose a case of scarlet fever he would, you felt, have confined himself to a statement that a rash was visible, that the temperature was so and so. He would never find himself in error at an inquest.

"Had you been Harry's doctor for long?" He seemed an odd man for Harry to choose—Harry who liked men with a certain recklessness, men capable of making mistakes.

"For about a year."

"Well, it's good of you to have seen me." Dr. Winkler bowed. When he bowed there was a very slight creak as though his shirt were made of celluloid. "I mustn't keep you from your patients any longer." Turning away from Dr. Winkler, he confronted yet another crucifix, the figure hanging with arms above the head: a face of elongated El Greco agony. "That's a strange crucifix," he said.

"Jansenist," Dr. Winkler commented and closed his mouth sharply as though he had been guilty of giving away too much information.

"Never heard the word. Why are the arms above the head?"

Dr. Winkler said reluctantly, "Because He died, in their view, only for the elect."

Seven

As I see it, turning over my files, the notes of conversations, the statements of various characters, it would have been still possible, at this moment, for Rollo Martins to have left Vienna safely. He had shown an unhealthy curiosity, but the disease had been checked at every point. Nobody had given anything away. The smooth wall of deception had as yet shown no real crack to his roaming fingers. When Rollo Martins left Dr. Winkler's he was in no danger. He could have gone home to bed at Sacher's and slept with a quiet mind. He could even have visited Cooler at this stage without trouble. No one was seriously disturbed. Unfortunately for him—and there would always be periods of his life when he bitterly regretted it—he chose to go back to Harry's flat. He wanted to talk to the little vexed man who said he had seen the accident—or had he really not said so much? There was a moment in the dark frozen street when he was inclined to go straight to Cooler, to complete his picture of those sinister birds who sat around Harry's body, but Rollo, being Rollo, decided to toss a coin and the coin fell for the other action, and the deaths of two men.

Perhaps the little man—who bore the name of Koch—had drunk a glass too much of wine, perhaps he had simply spent a good day at the office, but this time, when Rollo Martins rang his bell, he was friendly and quite ready to talk. He had just finished dinner and had crumbs on his moustache. "Ah, I remember you. You are Herr Lime's friend."

He welcomed Martins in with great cordiality and introduced him to a mountainous wife whom he obviously kept under very strict control. "Ah, in the old days I would have offered you a cup of coffee, but now—"

Martins passed round his cigarette case and the atmosphere of cordiality deepened. "When you rang yesterday I was a little abrupt," Herr Koch said, "but I had a touch of migraine and my wife was out, so I had to answer the door myself."

"Did you tell me that you had actually seen the accident?"

Herr Koch exchanged glances with his wife. "The inquest is over, Ilse. There is no harm. You can trust my judgment. The gentleman is a friend. Yes, I saw the accident, but you are the only one who knows. When I say that I saw it, perhaps I should say that I heard it. I heard the brakes put on and the sound of the skid, and I got to the window in time to see them carry the body to the house."

"But didn't you give evidence?"

"It is better not to be mixed up in such things. My office cannot spare me. We are short of staff, and of course I did not actually see—"

"But you told me yesterday how it happened."

"That was how they described it in the papers."

"Was he in great pain?"

"He was dead. I looked right down from my window here and I saw his face. I know when a man is dead. You see, it is, in a way, my business. I am the head clerk at the mortuary."

"But the others say that he did not die at once."

"Perhaps they don't know death as well as I do."

"He was dead, of course, when the doctor arrived. He told me that."

"He was dead at once. You can take the word of a man who knows."

"I think, Herr Koch, that you should have given evidence."

"One must look after oneself, Herr Martins. I was not the only one who should have been there."

"How do you mean?"

"There were three people who helped to carry your friend to the house."

"I know—two men and the driver."

"The driver stayed where he was. He was very much shaken, poor man."

"Three men . . ." It was as though suddenly, fingering that bare wall, his fingers had encountered not so much a crack perhaps but at least a roughness that had not been smoothed away by the careful builders.

"Can you describe the men?"

But Herr Koch was not trained to observe the living: only the man with the toupee had attracted his eyes—the other two were just men, neither tall nor short, thick nor thin. He had seen them from far above, foreshortened, bent over their burden; they had not looked up, and he had quickly looked away and closed the window, realizing at once the wisdom of not being seen himself.

"There was no evidence I could really give, Herr Martins."

No evidence, Martins thought, no evidence! He no longer doubted that murder had been done. Why else had they lied about the moment of death? They wanted to quiet with their gifts of money and their plane ticket the only two friends Harry had in Vienna. And the third man? Who was he?

He said, "Did you see Herr Lime go out?"

"No."

"Did you hear a scream?"

"Only the brakes, Herr Martins."

It occurred to Martins that there was nothing—except the word of Kurtz and Cooler and the driver—to prove that in fact Harry had been killed at that precise moment. There was the medical evidence, but that could not prove more than that he had died, say, within a half-hour, and in any case the medical evidence was only as strong as Dr. Winkler's word: that clean controlled man creaking among his crucifixes.

"Herr Martins, it just occurs to me—you are staying in Vienna?"

"Yes."

"If you need accommodation and spoke to the authorities quickly, you might secure Herr Lime's flat. It is a requisitioned property."

"Who has the keys?"

"I have them."

"Could I see the flat?"

"Ilse, the keys."

Herr Koch led the way into the flat that had been Harry's. In the little dark hall there was still the smell of cigarette smoke— the Turkish cigarettes that Harry always smoked. It seemed odd that a man's smell should cling in the folds of curtains so long after the man himself had become dead matter, a gas, a decay. One light, in a heavily beaded shade, left them in semi-darkness, fumbling for door handles.

The living room was completely bare—it seemed to Martins too bare. The chairs had been pushed up against the walls; the desk at which Harry must have written was free from dust or any papers. The parquet reflected the light like a mirror. Herr Koch opened a door and showed the bedroom: the bed neatly made with clean sheets. In the bathroom not even a used razor blade indicated that a few days ago a living man had occupied it. Only the dark hall and the cigarette smell gave a sense of occupation.

"You see," Herr Koch said, "it is quite ready for a newcomer. Ilse has cleaned up."

That she certainly had done. After a death there should have been more litter left than this. A man can't go suddenly and unexpectedly on his longest journey without forgetting this or that, without leaving a bill unpaid, an official form unanswered, the photograph of a girl. "Were there no papers, Herr Koch?"

"Herr Lime was always a very tidy man. His wastepaper basket was full and his brief case, but his friend fetched that away."

"His friend?"

"The gentleman with the toupee."

It was possible, of course, that Lime had not taken the journey so unexpectedly, and it occurred to Martins that Lime had perhaps hoped he would arrive in time to help. He said to Herr Koch, "I believe my friend was murdered."

"Murdered?" Herr Koch's cordiality was snuffed out by the word. He said, "I would not have asked you in here if I had thought you would talk such nonsense."

"All the same your evidence may be very valuable."

"I have no evidence. I saw nothing. I am not concerned. You must leave here at once please. You have been very inconsiderate." He hustled Martins back through the hall; already the smell of the smoke was fading a little more. Herr Koch's last word before he slammed his own door was, "It's no concern of mine." Poor Herr Koch! We do not choose our concerns. Later, when I was questioning Martins closely, I said to him, "Did you see anybody at all on the stairs, or in the street outside?"

"Nobody." He had everything to gain by remembering some chance passer-by, and I believed him. He said, "I noticed myself how quiet and dead the whole street looked. Part of it had been bombed, you know, and the moon was shining on the snow slopes. It was so very silent. I could hear my own feet creaking in the snow."

"Of course it proves nothing. There is a basement where anybody who had followed you could have hidden."

"Yes."

"Or your whole story may be phoney."

"Yes."

"The trouble is I can see no motive for you to have done it. It's true you are already guilty of getting money on false pretences. You came out here to join Lime, perhaps to help him . . ."

Martins said to me, "What was this precious racket you keep on hinting at?"

"I'd have told you all the facts when I first saw you if you hadn't lost your temper so damned quickly. Now I don't think I shall be acting wisely to tell you. It would be disclosing official information, and your contacts, you know, don't inspire confidence. A girl with phoney papers supplied by Lime, this man Kurtz . . ."

"Dr. Winkler . . ."

"I've got nothing against Dr. Winkler. No, if you are phoney, you don't need the information, but it might help you to learn exactly what we know. You see, our facts are not complete."

"I bet they aren't. I could invent a better detective than you in my bath."

"Your literary style does not do your namesake justice." Whenever he was reminded of Mr. Crabbin, that poor harassed representative of the British Cultural Relations Society, Rollo Martins turned pink with annoyance, embarrassment, shame. That too inclined me to trust him.

He had certainly given Crabbin some uncomfortable hours. On returning to Sacher's Hotel after his interview with Herr Koch he had found a desperate note waiting for him from the representative.

"I have been trying to locate you all day," Crabbin wrote. "It is essential that we should get together and work out a proper programme for you. This morning by telephone I have arranged lectures at Innsbruck and Salzburg for next week, but I must have your consent to the subjects, so that proper programmes can be printed. I would suggest two lectures: 'The Crisis of Faith in the Western World' (you are very respected here as a Christian writer, but this lecture should be quite unpolitical) and 'The Technique of the Contemporary Novel.' The same lectures would be given in Vienna. Apart from this, there are a great many people here who would like to meet you, and I want to arrange a cocktail party for early next week. But for all this I must have a few words with you." The letter ended on a note of acute anxiety.

"You will be at the discussion tomorrow night, won't you? We all expect you at 8:30 and, needless to say, look forward to your coming. I will send transport to the hotel at 8:15 sharp."

Rollo Martins read the letter and, without bothering any further about Mr. Crabbin, went to bed.

Eight

After two drinks Rollo Martins' mind would always turn towards women—in a vague, sentimental, romantic way, as a Sex, in general. After three drinks, like a pilot who dives to find direction, he would begin to focus on one available girl. If he had not been offered a third drink by Cooler, he would probably not have gone quite so soon to Anna Schmidt's house, and if—but there are too many "ifs" in my style of writing, for it is my profession to balance possibilities, human possibilities, and the drive of destiny can never find a place in my files.

Martins had spent his lunchtime reading up the reports of the inquest, thus again demonstrating the superiority of the amateur to the professional, and making him more vulnerable to Cooler's liquor (which the professional in duty bound would have refused). It was nearly five o'clock when he reached Cooler's flat, which was over an ice-cream parlour in the American zone: the bar below was full of G.I.'s with their girls, and the clatter of the long spoons and the curious free uniformed laughter followed him up the stairs.

The Englishman who objects to Americans in general usually carries in his mind's eye just such an exception as Cooler: a man with tousled grey hair and a worried kindly face and long-sighted eyes, the kind of humanitarian who turns up in a typhus epidemic or a world war or a Chinese famine long before his countrymen have discovered the place in an atlas. Again the card marked "Harry's friend" was like an entrance ticket. The warm frank handclasp was the most friendly act that Martins had encountered in Vienna.

"Any friend of Harry is all right with me," Cooler said. "I've heard of you, of course."

"From Harry?"

"I'm a great reader of Westerns," Cooler said, and Martins believed him as he did not believe Kurtz.

"I wondered—you were there, weren't you?—if you'd tell me about Harry's death."

"It was a terrible thing," Cooler said. "I was just crossing the road to go to Harry. He and Mr. Kurtz were on the sidewalk. Maybe if I hadn't started across the road, he'd have stayed where he was. But he saw me and stepped straight off to meet me and this jeep—it was terrible, terrible. The driver braked, but he didn't stand a chance. Have a Scotch, Mr. Martins. It's silly of me, but I get shaken up when I think of it." He said as he splashed in the soda, "I'd never seen a man killed before."

"Was the other man in the car?"

Cooler took a long pull and then measured what was left with his tired kindly eyes. "What man would you be referring to, Mr. Martins?"

"I was told there was another man there."

"I don't know how you got that idea. You'll find all about it in the inquest reports." He poured out two more generous drinks. "There were just the three of us—me and Mr. Kurtz and the driver. The doctor, of course. I expect you were thinking of the doctor."

"This man I was talking to happened to look out of a window —he has the next flat to Harry's—and he said he saw three men and the driver. That's before the doctor arrived."

"He didn't say that in court."

"He didn't want to get involved."

"You'll never teach these Europeans to be good citizens. It was his duty." Cooler brooded sadly over his glass. "It's an odd thing, Mr. Martins, with accidents. You'll never get two reports that coincide. Why, even I and Mr. Kurtz disagreed about details. The thing happens so suddenly, you aren't concerned to notice things, until bang crash, and then you have to reconstruct, remember. I expect he got too tangled up trying to sort out what happened before and what after, to distinguish the four of us."

"The four?"

"I was counting Harry. What else did he see, Mr. Martins?"

"Nothing of interest—except he says Harry was dead when he was carried to the house."

"Well, he was dying—not much difference there. Have another drink, Mr. Martins?"

"No, I don't think I will."

"Well, I'd like another spot. I was very fond of your friend, Mr. Martins, and I don't like talking about it."

"Perhaps one more—to keep you company.

"Do you know Anna Schmidt?" Martins asked, while the whisky still tingled on his tongue.

"Harry's girl? I met her once, that's all. As a matter of fact, I helped Harry fix her papers. Not the sort of thing I should confess to a stranger, I suppose, but you have to break the rules sometimes. Humanity's a duty too."

"What was wrong?"

"She was Hungarian and her father had been a Nazi, so they said. She was scared the Russians would pick her up."

"Why should they want to?"

"Well, her papers weren't in order."

"You took her some money from Harry, didn't you?"

"Yes, but I wouldn't have mentioned that. Did she tell you?"

The telephone rang, and Cooler drained his glass. "Hullo," he said. "Why, yes. This is Cooler." Then he sat with the receiver at his ear and an expression of sad patience, while some voice a long way off drained into the room. "Yes," he said once. "Yes." His eyes dwelt on Martins' face, but they seemed to be looking a long way beyond him: flat and tired and kind, they might have been gazing out across the sea. He said, "You did quite right," in a tone of commendation, and then, with a touch of asperity, "Of course they will be delivered. I gave my word. Good-bye."

He put the receiver down and passed a hand across his forehead wearily. It was as though he were trying to remember something he had to do. Martins said, "Had you heard anything of this racket the police talk about?"

"I'm sorry. What's that?"

"They say Harry was mixed up in some racket."

"Oh, no," Cooler said. "No. That's quite impossible. He had a great sense of duty."

"Kurtz seemed to think it was possible."

"Kurtz doesn't understand how an Anglo-Saxon feels," Cooler replied.

Nine

It was nearly dark when Martins made his way along the banks of the canal: across the water lay the half-destroyed Diana baths and in the distance the great black circle of the Prater Wheel, stationary above the ruined houses. Over there across the grey water was the second bezirk, in Russian ownership. St. Stefanskirche shot its enormous wounded spire into the sky above the Inner City, and, coming up the Kärtnerstrasse, Martins passed the lit door of the Military Police station. The four men of the International Patrol were climbing into their jeep; the Russian M.P. sat beside the driver (for the Russians had that day taken over the chair for the next four weeks) and the Englishman, the Frenchman, and the American mounted behind. The third stiff whisky fumed into Martins' brain, and he remembered the girl in Amsterdam, the girl in Paris; loneliness moved along the crowded pavement at his side. He passed the corner of the street where Sacher's lay and went on. Rollo was in control and moved towards the only girl he knew in Vienna.

I asked him how he knew where she lived. Oh, he said, he'd looked up the address she had given him the night before, in bed, studying a map. He wanted to know his way about, and he was good with maps. He could memorize turnings and street names easily because he always went one way on foot.

"One way?"

"I mean when I'm calling on a girl—or someone."

He hadn't, of course, known that she would be in, that her play was not on that night in the Josefstadt, or perhaps he had memorized that too from the posters. In at any rate she was, if you could really call it being in, sitting alone in an unheated room, with the bed disguised as a divan, and a typewritten script lying open at the first page on the inadequate too-fancy topply table—because her thoughts were so far from being "in." He said awkwardly (and nobody could have said, not even Rollo, how much his awkwardness was part of his technique), "I thought I'd just look in and look you up. You see, I was passing . . ."

"Passing? Where to?" It had been a good half an hour's walk from the Inner City to the rim of the English zone, but he always had a reply. "I had too much whisky with Cooler. I needed a walk and I just happened to find myself this way."

"I can't give you a drink here. Except tea. There's some of that packet left."

"No, no thank you." He said, "You are busy," looking at the script.

"I didn't get beyond the first line."

He picked it up and read: *"Enter Louise.* LOUISE: I heard a child crying."

"Can I stay a little?" he asked with a gentleness that was more Martins than Rollo.

"I wish you would." He slumped down on the divan, and he told me a long time later (for lovers talk and reconstruct the smallest details if they can find a listener) that there it was he took his second real look at her. She stood there as awkward as himself in a pair of old flannel trousers which had been patched badly in the seat; she stood with her legs firmly straddled as though she were opposing someone and was determined to hold her ground—a small rather stocky figure with any grace she had folded and put away for use professionally.

"One of those bad days?" he asked.

"It's always bad about this time." She explained, "He used to look in, and when I heard your ring, just for a moment, I thought . . ." She sat down on a hard chair opposite him and said, "Please talk. You knew him. Just tell me anything."

And so he talked. The sky blackened outside the window while he talked. He noticed after a while that their hands had met. He said to me, "I never meant to fall in love, not with Harry's girl."

"When did it happen?" I asked him.

"It was very cold and I got up to close the window curtains. I only noticed my hand was on hers when I took it away. As I stood up I looked down at her face and she was looking up. It wasn't a beautiful face—that was the trouble. It was a face to live with, day in, day out. A face for wear. I felt as though I'd come into a new country where I couldn't speak the language. I had always thought it was beauty one loved in a woman. I stood there at the curtains, waiting to pull them, looking out. I couldn't see anything but my own face, looking back into the room, looking for her. She said, 'And what did Harry do that time?' and I wanted to say, 'Damn Harry. He's dead. We both loved him, but he's dead. The dead are made to be forgotten.' Instead of course all I said was,

'What do you think? He just whistled his old tune as if nothing was the matter,' and I whistled it to her as well as I could. I heard her catch her breath, and I looked round and before I could think, is this the right way, the right card, the right gambit?—I'd already said, 'He's dead. You can't go on remembering him forever.' "

She said, "I know, but perhaps something will happen first."

"What do you mean—something happen?"

"Oh, I mean, perhaps there'll be another way, or I'll die, or something."

"You'll forget him in time. You'll fall in love again."

"I know, but I don't want to. Don't you see I don't want to."

So Rollo Martins came back from the window and sat down on the divan again. When he had risen half a minute before he had been the friend of Harry, comforting Harry's girl; now he was a man in love with Anna Schmidt who had been in love with a man they had both once known called Harry Lime. He didn't speak again that evening about the past. Instead he began to tell her of the people he had seen. "I can believe anything of Winkler," he told her, "but Cooler—I liked Cooler. He was the only one of his friends who stood up for Harry. The trouble is, if Cooler's right, then Koch is wrong, and I really thought I had something there."

"Who's Koch?"

He explained how he had returned to Harry's flat and he described his interview with Koch, the story of the third man.

"If it's true," she said, "it's very important."

"It doesn't prove anything. After all, Koch backed out of the inquest; so might this stranger."

"That's not the point," she said. "It means that *they* lied. Kurtz and Cooler."

"They might have lied so as not to inconvenience this fellow—if he was a friend."

"Yet another friend—on the spot. And where's your Cooler's honesty then?"

"What do we do? He clamped down like an oyster and turned me out of his flat."

"He won't turn me out," she said, "or his Ilse won't."

They walked up the long road to the flat together; the snow clogged on their shoes and made them move slowly like convicts weighed down by irons. Anna Schmidt said, "Is it far?"

"Not very far now. Do you see that knot of people up the road? It's somewhere about there." The group of people up the road was like a splash of ink on the whiteness that flowed, changed shape, spread out. When they came a little nearer Martins said, "I think that is his block. What do you suppose this is, a political demonstration?"

Anna Schmidt stopped. She said, "Who else have you told about Koch?"

"Only you and Cooler. Why?"

"I'm frightened. It reminds me . . ." She had her eyes fixed on the crowd and he never knew what memory out of her confused past had risen to warn her. "Let's go away," she implored him.

"You're crazy. We're on to something here, something big . . ."

"I'll wait for you."

"But you're going to talk to him."

"Find out first what all those people . . ." She said strangely for one who worked behind the footlights, "I hate crowds."

He walked slowly on alone, the snow caking on his heels. It wasn't a political meeting, for no one was making a speech. He had the impression of heads turning to watch him come, as though he were somebody who was expected. When he reached the fringe of the little crowd, he knew for certain that it was the house. A man looked hard at him and said, "Are you another of them?"

"What do you mean?"

"The police."

"No. What are they doing?"

"They've been in and out all day."

"What's everybody waiting for?"

"They want to see him brought out."

"Who?"

"Herr Koch." It occurred vaguely to Martins that somebody besides himself had discovered Herr Koch's failure to give evidence, though that was hardly a police matter. He said, "What's he done?"

"Nobody knows that yet. They can't make their minds up in there—it might be suicide, you see, and it might be murder."

"Herr Koch?"

"Of course."

A small child came up to his informant and pulled at his hand.

"Papa, Papa." He wore a wool cap on his head, like a gnome; his face was pinched and blue with cold.

"Yes, my dear, what is it?"

"I heard them talking through the grating, Papa."

"Oh, you cunning little one. Tell us what you heard, Hansel."

"I heard Frau Koch crying, Papa."

"Was that all, Hansel?"

"No. I heard the big man talking, Papa."

"Ah, you cunning little Hansel. Tell Papa what he said."

"He said, 'Can you tell me, Frau Koch, what the foreigner looked like?' "

"Ha, ha, you see, they think it's murder. And who's to say they are wrong? Why should Herr Koch cut his own throat in the basement?"

"Papa, Papa."

"Yes, little Hansel?"

"When I looked through the grating, I could see some blood on the coke."

"What a child you are. How could you tell it was blood? The snow leaks everywhere." The man turned to Martins and said, "The child has such an imagination. Maybe he will be a writer when he grows up."

The pinched face stared solemnly up at Martins. The child said, "Papa."

"Yes, Hansel?"

"He's a foreigner too."

The man gave a big laugh that caused a dozen heads to turn. "Listen to him, sir, listen," he said proudly. "He thinks you did it just because you are a foreigner. As though there weren't more foreigners here these days than Viennese."

"Papa, Papa."

"Yes, Hansel?"

"They are coming out."

A knot of police surrounded the covered stretcher which they lowered carefully down the steps for fear of sliding on the trodden snow. The man said, "They can't get an ambulance into this street because of the ruins. They have to carry it round the corner." Frau Koch came out at the tail of the procession; she had a shawl over her head and an old sackcloth coat. Her thick shape looked like a snowman as she sank in a drift at the pavement's edge.

Someone gave her a hand and she looked round with a lost hopeless gaze at this crowd of strangers. If there were friends there she did not recognize them, looking from face to face. Martins bent as she passed, fumbling at his shoelace, but looking up from the ground he saw at his own eyes' level the scrutinizing cold-blooded gnome gaze of little Hansel.

Walking back down the street towards Anna, he looked back once. The child was pulling at his father's hand and he could see the lips forming round those syllables like the refrain of a grim ballad, "Papa, Papa."

He said to Anna, "Koch has been murdered. Come away from here." He walked as rapidly as the snow would let him, turning this corner and that. The child's suspicion and alertness seemed to spread like a cloud over the city—they could not walk fast enough to evade its shadow. He paid no attention when Anna said to him, "Then what Koch said was true. There *was* a third man," nor a little later when she said, "It must have been murder. You don't kill a man to hide anything less."

The tramcars flashed like icicles at the end of the street: they were back at the Ring. Martins said, "You had better go home alone. I'll keep away from you awhile till things have sorted out."

"But nobody can suspect you."

"They are asking about the foreigner who called on Koch yesterday. There may be some unpleasantness for a while."

"Why don't you go to the police?"

"They are so stupid. I don't trust them. See what they've pinned on Harry. And then I tried to hit this man Callaghan. They'll have it in for me. The least they'll do is send me away from Vienna. But if I stay quiet—there's only one person who can give me away. Cooler."

"And he won't want to."

"Not if he's guilty. But then I can't believe he's guilty."

Before she left him, she said, "Be careful. Koch knew so very little and they murdered him. You know as much as Koch."

The warning stayed in his brain all the way to Sacher's: after nine o'clock the streets are very empty, and he would turn his head at every padding step coming up the street behind him, as though that third man whom they had protected so ruthlessly were following him like an executioner. The Russian sentry outside the Grand Hotel looked rigid with the cold, but he was human, he had a face, an honest peasant face with Mongol eyes.

The third man had no face: only the top of a head seen from a window. At Sacher's Mr. Schmidt said, "Colonel Calloway has been in, asking after you, sir. I think you'll find him in the bar."

"Back in a moment," Martins said and walked straight out of the hotel again: he wanted time to think. But immediately he stepped outside a man came forward, touched his cap, and said firmly, "Please, sir." He flung open the door of a khaki-painted truck with a Union Jack on the windscreen and firmly urged Martins within. He surrendered without protest; sooner or later, he felt sure, inquiries would be made; he had only pretended optimism to Anna Schmidt.

The driver drove too fast for safety on the frozen road, and Martins protested. All he got in reply was a sullen grunt and a muttered sentence containing the word "orders." "Gave you orders to kill me?" Martins said and got no reply at all. He caught sight of the Titans on the Hofburg balancing great globes of snow above their heads, and then they plunged into ill-lit streets beyond where he lost all sense of direction.

"Is it far?" But the driver paid him no attention at all. At least, Martins thought, I am not under arrest: they have not sent a guard; I am being invited—wasn't that the word they used?—to visit the station to make a statement.

The car drew up and the driver led the way up two flights of stairs; he rang the bell of a great double door, and Martins was aware of many voices beyond it. He turned sharply to the driver and said, "Where the hell . . . ?" but the driver was already halfway down the stairs, and already the door was opening. His eyes were dazzled from the darkness by the lights inside; he heard but he could hardly see the advance of Crabbin. "Oh, Mr. Dexter, we have been so anxious, but better late than never. Let me introduce you to Miss Wilbraham and the Gräfin von Meyersdorf."

A buffet laden with coffee cups; an urn steamed; a woman's face shiny with exertion; two young men with the happy intelligent faces of sixth formers; and, huddled in the background, like faces in a family album, a multitude of the old-fashioned, the dingy, the earnest and cheery features of constant readers. Martins looked behind him, but the door had closed.

He said desperately to Mr. Crabbin, "I'm sorry, but—"

"Don't think any more about it," Mr. Crabbin said. "One cup of coffee and then let's go on to the discussion. We have a very good gathering tonight. They'll put you on your mettle, Mr. Dexter." One of the young men placed a cup in his hand, the other shovelled in sugar before he could say he preferred his coffee unsweetened. The youngest man breathed into his ear, "Afterwards would you mind signing one of your books, Mr. Dexter?" A large woman in black silk bore down upon him and said, "I don't mind if the Gräfin does hear me, Mr. Dexter, but I don't like your books, I don't approve of them. I think a novel should tell a good story."

"So do I," Martins said hopelessly.

"Now, Mrs. Bannock, wait for question time."

"I know I'm downright, but I'm sure Mr. Dexter values *honest* criticism."

An old lady, whom he supposed was the Gräfin, said, "I do not read many English books, Mr. Dexter, but I am told that yours . . ."

"Do you mind drinking up?" Crabbin said and hustled him through into an inner room where a number of elderly people were sitting on a semicircle of chairs with an air of sad patience.

Martins was not able to tell me very much about the meeting; his mind was still dazed with the death; when he looked up he expected to see at any moment the child Hansel and hear that persistent informative refrain, "Papa, Papa." Apparently Crabbin opened the proceedings, and, knowing Crabbin, I am sure that it was a very lucid, very fair and unbiased picture of the contemporary English novel. I have heard him give that talk so often, varied only by the emphasis given to the work of the particular English visitor. He would have touched lightly on various problems of technique—the point of view, the passage of time—and then he would have declared the meeting open for questions and discussions.

Martins missed the first question altogether, but luckily Crabbin filled the gap and answered it satisfactorily. A woman wearing a brown hat and a piece of fur round her throat said with passionate interest, "May I ask Mr. Dexter if he is engaged on a new work?"

"Oh, yes—yes."

"May I ask the title?"

" 'The Third Man,' " Martins said and gained a spurious confidence as the result of taking that hurdle.

"Mr. Dexter, could you tell us what author has chiefly influenced you?"

Martins, without thinking, said, "Grey." He meant of course the author of *Riders of the Purple Sage,* and he was pleased to find his reply gave general satisfaction—to all save an elderly Austrian who asked, "Grey. What Grey? I do not know the name."

Martins felt he was safe now and said, "Zane Grey—I don't know any other," and was mystified at the low subservient laughter from the English colony.

Crabbin interposed quickly for the sake of the Austrians. "That is a little joke of Mr. Dexter's. He meant the poet Gray—a gentle, mild, subtle genius—one can see the affinity."

"And he is called Zane Grey?"

"That was Mr. Dexter's joke. Zane Grey wrote what we call Westerns—cheap popular novelettes about bandits and cowboys."

"He is not a great writer?"

"No, no. Far from it," Mr. Crabbin said. "In the strict sense I would not call him a writer at all." Martins told me that he felt the first stirrings of revolt at that statement. He had never regarded himself before as a writer, but Crabbin's self-confidence irritated him—even the way the light flashed back from Crabbin's spectacles seemed an added cause of vexation. Crabbin said, "He was just a popular entertainer."

"Why the hell not?" Martins said fiercely.

"Oh, well, I merely meant—"

"What was Shakespeare?"

Somebody with great daring said, "A poet."

"Have you ever read Zane Grey?"

"No, I can't say—"

"Then you don't know what you are talking about."

One of the young men tried to come to Crabbin's rescue. "And James Joyce, where would you put James Joyce, Mr. Dexter?"

"What do you mean put? I don't want to put anybody anywhere," Martins said. It had been a very full day: he had drunk too much with Cooler; he had fallen in love; a man had been murdered—and now he had the quite unjust feeling that he was being got at. Zane Grey was one of his heroes: he was damned if he was going to stand any nonsense.

"I mean would you put him among the really great?"

"If you want to know, I've never heard of him. What did he write?"

He didn't realize it, but he was making an enormous impression. Only a great writer could have taken so arrogant, so original a line. Several people wrote Zane Grey's name on the backs of envelopes and the Gräfin whispered hoarsely to Crabbin, "How do you spell Zane?"

"To tell you the truth, I'm not quite sure."

A number of names were simultaneously flung at Martins—little sharp pointed names like Stein, round pebbles like Woolf. A young Austrian with an ardent intellectual black forelock called out, "Daphne du Maurier," and Mr. Crabbin winced and looked sideways at Martins. He said in an undertone, "Be kind to them."

A gentle kind-faced woman in a hand-knitted jumper said wistfully, "Don't you agree, Mr. Dexter, that no one, no one has written about *feelings* so poetically as Virginia Woolf? In prose, I mean."

Crabbin whispered, "You might say something about the stream of consciousness."

"Stream of what?"

A note of despair came into Crabbin's voice. "Please, Mr. Dexter, these people are your genuine admirers. They want to hear your views. If you knew how they have besieged the Society."

An elderly Austrian said, "Is there any writer in England today of the stature of the late John Galsworthy?"

There was an outburst of angry twittering in which the names of Du Maurier, Priestley, and somebody called Layman were flung to and fro. Martins sat gloomily back and saw again the snow, the stretcher, the desperate face of Frau Koch. He thought: if I had never returned, if I had never asked questions, would that little man still be alive? How had he benefited Harry by supplying another victim—a victim to assuage the fear of whom—Herr Kurtz, Cooler (he could not believe that), Dr. Winkler? Not one of them seemed adequate to the drab gruesome crime in the basement; he could hear the child saying, "I saw the blood on the coke," and somebody turned towards him a blank face without features, a grey plasticine egg, the third man.

Martins could not have said how he got through the rest of the discussion: perhaps Crabbin took the brunt; perhaps he was helped by some of the audience who got into an animated discussion about the film version of a popular American novel. He remembered very little more before Crabbin was making a final speech in his honour. Then one of the young men led him to a table stacked with books and asked him to sign them. "We have only allowed each member one book."

"What have I got to do?"

"Just a signature. That's all they expect. This is my copy of *The Curved Prow*. I would be so grateful if you'd just write a little something . . ."

Martins took his pen and wrote: "From B. Dexter, author of *The Lone Rider of Santa Fe*," and the young man read the sentence and blotted it with a puzzled expression. As Martins sat down and started signing Benjamin Dexter's title pages, he could see in a mirror the young man showing the inscription to Crabbin. Crabbin smiled weakly and stroked his chin, up and down, up and down. "B. Dexter, B. Dexter, B. Dexter." Martins wrote rapidly —it was not, after all, a lie. One by one the books were collected by their owners; little half-sentences of delight and compliment were dropped like curtsies—was this what it was to be a writer? Martins began to feel distinct irritation towards Benjamin Dexter. The complacent, tiring, pompous ass, he thought, signing the twenty-seventh copy of *The Curved Prow*. Every time he looked up and took another book he saw Crabbin's worried speculative gaze. The members of the Institute were beginning to go home with their spoils: the room was emptying. Suddenly in the mirror Martins saw a military policeman. He seemed to be having an argument with one of Crabbin's young henchmen. Martins thought he caught the sound of his own name. It was then he lost his nerve and with it any relic of common sense. There was only one book left to sign; he dashed off a last "B. Dexter" and made for the door. The young man, Crabbin, and the policeman stood together at the entrance.

"And this gentleman?" the policeman asked.

"It's Mr. Benjamin Dexter," the young man said.

"Lavatory. Is there a lavatory?" Martins said.

"I understood a Mr. Rollo Martins came here in one of your cars."

"A mistake. An obvious mistake."

"Second door on the left," the young man said.

Martins grabbed his coat from the cloakroom as he went and made down the stairs. On the first-floor landing he heard someone mounting the stairs and, looking over, saw Paine, whom I had sent to identify him. He opened a door at random and shut it behind him. He could hear Paine going by. The room where he stood was in darkness; a curious moaning sound made him turn and face whatever room it was.

He could see nothing and the sound had stopped. He made a tiny movement and once more it started, like an impeded breath. He remained still and the sound died away. Outside somebody called, "Mr. Dexter, Mr. Dexter." Then a new sound started. It was like somebody whispering—a long continuous monologue in the darkness. Martins said, "Is anybody there?" and the sound stopped again. He could stand no more of it. He took out his lighter. Footsteps went by and down the stairs. He scraped and scraped at the little wheel and no light came. Somebody shifted in the dark, and something rattled in mid-air like a chain. He asked once more with the anger of fear, "Is anybody there?" and only the click-click of metal answered him.

Martins felt desperately for a light switch, first to his right hand and then to his left. He did not dare go farther because he could no longer locate his fellow occupant; the whisper, the moaning, the click had all stopped. Then he was afraid that he had lost the door and felt wildly for the knob. He was far less afraid of the police than he was of the darkness, and he had no idea of the noise he was making.

Paine heard it from the bottom of the stairs and came back. He switched on the landing light, and the glow under the door gave Martins his direction. He opened the door and, smiling weakly at Paine, turned back to take a second look at the room. The eyes of a parrot chained to a perch stared beadily back at him. Paine said respectfully, "We were looking for you, sir. Colonel Calloway wants a word with you."

"I lost my way," Martins said.

"Yes, sir. We thought that was what had happened."

Ten

I had kept a very careful record of Martins' movements from the moment I knew that he had not caught the plane home. He had been seen with Kurtz, and at the Josefstadt Theatre; I knew about his visit to Dr. Winkler and to Cooler, his first return to the block where Harry had lived. For some reason my man lost him between Cooler's and Anna Schmidt's flats; he reported that Martins had wandered widely, and the impression we both got was that he had deliberately thrown off his shadower. I tried to pick him up at the hotel and just missed him.

Events had taken a disquieting turn, and it seemed to me that the time had come for another interview. He had a lot to explain.

I put a good wide desk between us and gave him a cigarette. I found him sullen but ready to talk, within strict limits. I asked him about Kurtz and he seemed to me to answer satisfactorily. I then asked him about Anna Schmidt and I gathered from his reply that he must have been with her after visiting Cooler; that filled in one of the missing points. I tried him with Dr. Winkler, and he answered readily enough. "You've been getting around," I said, "quite a bit. And have you found out anything about your friend?"

"Oh yes," he said. "It was under your nose but you didn't see it."

"What?"

"That he was murdered." That took me by surprise: I had at one time played with the idea of suicide, but I had ruled even that out.

"Go on," I said. He tried to eliminate from his story all mention of Koch, talking about an informant who had seen the accident. This made his story rather confusing, and I couldn't grasp at first why he attached so much importance to the third man.

"He didn't turn up at the inquest, and the others lied to keep him out."

"Nor did your man turn up—I don't see much importance in that. If it was a genuine accident, all the evidence needed was there. Why get the other chap in trouble? Perhaps his wife thought he was out of town; perhaps he was an official absent without leave—people sometimes take unauthorized trips to Vienna from places like Klagenfurt. The delights of the great city, for what they are worth."

"There was more to it than that. The little chap who told me about—they've murdered him. You see they obviously didn't know what else he had seen."

"Now we have it," I said. "You mean Koch."

"Yes."

"As far as we know you were the last person to see him alive."

I questioned him then, as I've written, to find out if he had been followed to Koch's by somebody who was sharper than my man and had kept out of sight. I said, "The Austrian police are anxious to pin this on you. Frau Koch told them how disturbed her husband was by your visit. Who else knew about it?"

"I told Cooler." He said excitedly, "Suppose immediately I left he telephoned the story to someone—to the third man. They had to stop Koch's mouth."

"When you told Cooler about Koch, the man was already dead. That night he got out of bed, hearing someone, and went downstairs—"

"Well, that rules me out. I was in Sacher's."

"But he went to bed very early. Your visit brought back the migraine. It was soon after nine that he got up. You returned to Sacher's at nine-thirty. Where were you before that?"

He said gloomily, "Wandering round and trying to sort things out."

"Any evidence of your movements?"

"No."

I wanted to frighten him, so there was no point in telling him that he had been followed all the time. I knew that he hadn't cut Koch's throat, but I wasn't sure that he was quite so innocent as he made out. The man who owns the knife is not always the real murderer.

"Can I have a cigarette?"

"Yes."

He said, "How did you know that I went to Koch's? That was why you pulled me here, wasn't it?"

"The Austrian police—"

"They hadn't identified me."

"Immediately you left Cooler's, he telephoned to me."

"Then that lets him out. If he had been concerned, he wouldn't have wanted to tell you my story—to tell Koch's story, I mean."

"He might assume that you were a sensible man and would come to me with your story as soon as you learned of Koch's death. By the way, how did you learn of it?"

He told me promptly and I believed him. It was then I began to believe him altogether. He said, "I still can't believe Cooler's concerned. I'd stake anything on his honesty. He's one of those Americans with a real sense of duty."

"Yes," I said, "he told me about that when he phoned. He apologized for it. He said it was the worst of having been brought up to believe in citizenship. He said it made him feel a prig. To tell you the truth, Cooler irritates me. Of course he doesn't know that I know about his tire deals."

"Is he in a racket, too, then?"

"Not a very serious one. I daresay he's salted away twenty-five thousand dollars. But I'm not a good citizen. Let the Americans look after their own people."

"I'm damned." He said thoughtfully, "Is that the kind of thing Harry was up to?"

"No. It was not so harmless."

He said, "You know this business—Koch's death—has shaken me. Perhaps Harry did get mixed up in something pretty bad. Perhaps he was trying to clear out again, and that's why they murdered him."

"Or perhaps," I said, "they wanted a bigger cut off the spoils. Thieves fall out."

He took it this time without any anger at all. He said, "We won't agree about motives, but I think you check your facts pretty well. I'm sorry about the other day."

"That's all right." There are times when one has to make a flash decision—this was one of them. I owed him something in return for the information he had given me. I said, "I'll show you enough of the facts in Lime's case for you to understand. But don't fly off the handle. It's going to be a shock."

It couldn't help being a shock. The war and the peace (if you can call it peace) let loose a great number of rackets, but none more vile than this one. The black marketeers in food did at least supply food, and the same applied to all the other racketeers who provided articles in short supply at extravagant prices. But the penicillin racket was a different affair altogether. Penicillin in Austria was supplied only to the military hospitals: no civilian doctor, not even a civilian hospital, could obtain it by legal means. As the racket started, it was relatively harmless. Penicillin would be stolen and sold to Austrian doctors for very high sums—a phial would fetch anything up to seventy pounds. You might say that this was a form of distribution—unfair distribution because it benefited only the rich patient, but the original distribution could hardly have a claim to greater fairness.

This racket went on quite happily for a while. Occasionally someone was caught and punished, but the danger simply raised the price of penicillin. Then the racket began to get organized: the big men saw big money in it, and while the original thief got less for his spoils, he received instead a certain security. If anything happened to him he would be looked after. Human nature too has curious twisted reasons that the heart certainly knows nothing of. It eased the conscience of many small men to feel that they were working for an employer: they were almost as respectable soon in their own eyes as wage-earners; they were one of a group, and if there was guilt, the leaders bore the guilt. A racket works very like a totalitarian party.

This I have sometimes called stage two. Stage three was when the organizers decided that the profits were not large enough. Penicillin would not always be impossible to obtain legitimately; they wanted more money and quicker money while the going was good. They began to dilute the penicillin with coloured water, and, in the case of penicillin dust, with sand. I keep a small museum in one drawer in my desk, and I showed Martins examples. He wasn't enjoying the talk, but he hadn't yet grasped the point. He said, "I suppose that makes the stuff useless."

I said, "We wouldn't worry so much if that was all, but just consider. You can be immunized from the effects of penicillin. At the best you can say that the use of this stuff makes a penicillin treatment for the particular patient ineffective in the future. That isn't so funny, of course, if you are suffering from V.D. Then the use of sand on a wound that requires penicillin—well, it's not healthy. Men have lost their legs and arms that way—and their lives. But perhaps what horrified me most was visiting the children's hospital here. They had bought some of this penicillin for use against meningitis. A number of children simply died, and a number went off their heads. You can see them now in the mental ward."

He sat on the other side of the desk, scowling into his hands. I said, "It doesn't bear thinking about very closely, does it?"

"You haven't showed me any evidence yet that Harry—"

"We are coming to that now," I said. "Just sit still and listen." I opened Lime's file and began to read. At the beginning the evidence was purely circumstantial, and Martins fidgeted. So much consisted of coincidence—reports of agents that Lime had been at a certain place at a certain time; the accumulation of opportunities; his acquaintance with certain people. He protested once, "But the same evidence would apply against me—now."

"Just wait," I said. For some reason Harry Lime had grown

careless: he may have realized that we suspected him and got rattled. He held a quite distinguished position, and a man like that is the more easily rattled. We put one of our agents as an orderly in the British Military Hospital: we knew by this time the name of our go-between, but we had never succeeded in getting the line right back to the source. Anyway, I am not going to bother the reader now, as I bothered Martins then, with all the stages—the long tussle to win the confidence of the go-between, a man called Harbin. At last we had the screws on Harbin, and we twisted them until he squealed. This kind of police work is very similar to secret service work: you look for a double agent whom you can really control, and Harbin was the man for us. But even he only led us as far as Kurtz.

"Kurtz!" Martins exclaimed. "But why haven't you pulled him in?"

"Zero hour is almost here," I said.

Kurtz was a great step forward, for Kurtz was in direct communication with Lime—he had a small outside job in connection with relief work. With Kurtz, Lime sometimes put things on paper —if he was pressed. I showed Martins the photostat of a note. "Can you identify that?"

"It's Harry's hand." He read it through. "I don't see anything wrong."

"No, but now read this note from Harbin to Kurtz—which we dictated. Look at the date. This is the result."

He read them both through twice.

"You see what I mean?" If one watched a world come to an end, a plane dive from its course, I don't suppose one would chatter, and a world for Martins had certainly come to an end, a world of easy friendship, hero-worship, confidence that had begun twenty years before—in a school corridor. Every memory—afternoons in the long grass, the illegitimate shoots on Brickworth Common, the dreams, the walks, every shared experience was simultaneously tainted, like the soil of an atomized town. One could not walk there with safety for a long while. While he sat there, looking at his hands and saying nothing, I fetched a precious bottle of whisky out of a cupboard and poured out two large doubles. "Go on," I said, "drink that," and he obeyed me as though I were his doctor. I poured him out another.

He said slowly, "Are you certain that he was the real boss?"

"It's as far back as we have got so far."

"You see he was always apt to jump before he looked."

I didn't contradict him, though that wasn't the impression he had before given of Lime. He was searching round for some comfort.

"Suppose," he said, "someone had got a line on him, forced him into this racket, as you forced Harbin to double cross . . ."

"It's possible."

"And they murdered him in case he talked when he was arrested."

"It's not impossible."

"I'm glad they did," he said. "I wouldn't have liked to hear Harry squeal." He made a curious little dusting movement with his hand on his knee as much as to say, "That's that." He said, "I'll be getting back to England."

"I'd rather you didn't just yet. The Austrian police would make an issue if you tried to leave Vienna at the moment. You see, Cooler's sense of duty made him call them up too."

"I see," he said hopelessly.

"When we've found the third man . . ." I said.

"I'd like to hear him squeal," he said. "The bastard. The bloody bastard."

Eleven

After he left me, Martins went straight off to drink himself silly. He chose the Oriental to do it in, the dreary smoky little night club that stands behind a sham Eastern façade. The same seminude photographs on the stairs, the same half-drunk Americans at the bar, the same bad wine and extraordinary gins—he might have been in any third-rate night haunt in any other shabby capital of a shabby Europe. At one point of the hopeless early hours the International Patrol took a look at the scene. Martins had drink after drink; he would probably have had a woman too, but the cabaret performers had all gone home, and there were practically no women left in the place, except for one beautiful shrewd-looking French journalist who made one remark to her companion and fell contemptuously asleep.

Martins moved on: at Maxim's a few couples were dancing rather gloomily, and at a place called Chez Victor the heating had failed and people sat in overcoats drinking cocktails. By this time the spots were swimming in front of Martins' eyes, and he was oppressed by a sense of loneliness. His mind reverted to the girl in Dublin, and the one in Amsterdam. That was one thing that didn't fool you—the straight drink, the simple physical act: one didn't expect fidelity from a woman. His mind revolved in circles—from sentiment to lust and back again from belief to cynicism.

The trams had stopped, and he set out obstinately on foot to find Harry's girl. He wanted to make love to her—just like that: no nonsense, no sentiment. He was in the mood for violence, and the snowy road heaved like a lake and set his mind on a new course towards sorrow, eternal love, renunciation.

It must have been about three in the morning when he climbed the stairs to Anna's room. He was nearly sober by that time and had only one idea in his head, that she must know about Harry too. He felt that somehow this knowledge would pay the mortmain that memory levies on human beings, and he would stand a chance with Harry's girl. If one is in love oneself, it never occurs to one that the girl doesn't know: one believes one has told it plainly in a tone of voice, the touch of a hand. When Anna opened the door to him, with astonishment at the sight of him tousled on the threshold, he never imagined that she was opening the door to a stranger.

He said, "Anna, I've found out everything."

"Come in," she said, "you don't want to wake the house." She was in a dressing gown; the divan had become a bed, the kind of tumbled bed that showed how sleepless the occupant had been.

"Now," she said, while he stood there, fumbling for words, "what is it? I thought you were going to keep away. Are the police after you?"

"No."

"You didn't really kill that man, did you?"

"Of course not."

"You're drunk, aren't you?"

"I am a bit," he said sulkily. The meeting seemed to be going on the wrong lines. He said angrily, "I'm sorry."

"Why? I could do with a bit of drink myself."

He said, "I've been with the British police. They are satisfied I didn't do it. But I've learned everything from them. Harry was in a racket—a bad racket." He said hopelessly, "He was no good at all. We were both wrong."

"You'd better tell me," Anna said. She sat down on the bed and he told her, swaying slightly beside the table where her type-script part still lay open at the first page. I imagine he told it to her pretty confusedly, dwelling chiefly on what had stuck most in his mind, the children dead with meningitis and the children in the mental ward. He stopped and they were silent. She said, "Is that all?"

"Yes."

"You were sober when they told you? They really proved it?"

"Yes." He added drearily, "So that, you see, was Harry."

"I'm glad he's dead now," she said. "I wouldn't have wanted him to rot for years in prison."

"But can you understand how Harry—your Harry, my Harry —could have got mixed up . . . ?" He said hopelessly, "I feel as though he had never really existed, that we'd dreamed him. Was he laughing at fools like us all the time?"

"He may have been. What does it matter?" she said. "Sit down. Don't worry." He had pictured himself comforting *her*—not this other way about. She said, "If he was alive now, he might be able to explain, but we've got to remember him as he was to us. There are always so many things one doesn't know about a person, even a person one loves—good things, bad things. We have to leave plenty of room for them."

"Those children—"

She said angrily, "For God's sake stop making people in *your* image. Harry was real. He wasn't just your hero and my lover. He was Harry. He was in a racket. He did bad things. What about it? He was the man we knew."

He said, "Don't talk such bloody wisdom. Don't you see that I love you?"

She looked at him in astonishment. "You?"

"Yes, me. I don't kill people with fake drugs. I'm not a hypo-crite who persuades people that I'm the greatest—I'm just a bad writer who drinks too much and falls in love with girls . . ."

She said, "But I don't even know what colour your eyes are. If you'd rung me up just now and asked me whether you were dark or fair or wore a moustache, I wouldn't have known."

"Can't you get him out of your mind?"

"No."

He said, "As soon as they've cleared up this Koch murder, I'm leaving Vienna. I can't feel interested any longer in whether Kurtz killed Harry—or the third man. Whoever killed him it was a kind of justice. Maybe I'd kill him myself under these circumstances. But you still love him. You love a cheat, a murderer."

"I loved a man," she said. "I told you—a man doesn't alter because you find out more about him. He's still the same man."

"I hate the way you talk. I've got a splitting headache, and you talk and talk . . ."

"I didn't ask you to come."

"You make me cross."

Suddenly she laughed. She said, "You are so comic. You come here at three in the morning—a stranger—and say you loved me. Then you get angry and pick a quarrel. What do you expect me to do—or say?"

"I haven't seen you laugh before. Do it again. I like it."

"There isn't enough for two laughs," she said.

He took her by the shoulders and shook her gently. He said, "I'd make comic faces all day long. I'd stand on my head and grin at you between my legs. I'd learn a lot of jokes from the books on after-dinner speaking."

"Come away from the window. There are no curtains."

"There's nobody to see." But automatically checking his statement, he wasn't quite so sure: a long shadow that had moved, perhaps with the movement of clouds over the moon, was motionless again. He said, "You still love Harry, don't you?"

"Yes."

"Perhaps I do. I don't know." He dropped his hands and said, "I'll be pushing off."

He walked rapidly away. He didn't bother to see whether he was being followed, to check up on the shadow. But, passing by the end of the street, he happened to turn and there just around the corner, pressed against a wall to escape notice, was a thick stocky figure. Martins stopped and stared. There was something familiar about that figure. Perhaps, he thought, I have grown unconsciously used to him during these last twenty-four hours; perhaps he is one of those who have so assiduously checked my movements. Martins stood there, twenty yards away, staring at the silent motionless figure in the dark side street who stared back at him. A police spy, perhaps, or an agent of those other men,

those men who had corrupted Harry first and then killed him—
even possibly the third man?

It was not the face that was familiar, for he could not make out
so much as the angle of the jaw; nor a movement, for the body
was so still that he began to believe that the whole thing was an
illusion caused by shadow. He called sharply, "Do you want anything?" and there was no reply. He called again with the irascibil-
ity of drink, "Answer, can't you," and an answer came, for a
window curtain was drawn petulantly back by some sleeper he
had awakened, and the light fell straight across the narrow street
and lit up the features of Harry Lime.

Twelve

"Do you believe in ghosts?" Martins said to me.

"Do you?"

"I do now."

"I also believe that drunk men see things—sometimes rats,
sometimes worse."

He hadn't come to me at once with his story—only the danger
to Anna Schmidt tossed him back into my office, like something
the sea had washed up, tousled, unshaven, haunted by an experience he couldn't understand. He said, "If it had been just the face,
I wouldn't have worried. I'd been thinking about Harry, and I
might easily have mistaken a stranger. The light was turned off
again at once, you see. I only got one glimpse, and the man made
off down the street—if he was a man. There was no turning for a
long way, but I was so startled I gave him another thirty yards'
start. He came to one of those newspaper kiosks and for a moment moved out of sight. I ran after him. It only took me ten
seconds to reach the kiosk, and he must have heard me running,
but the strange thing was he never appeared again. I reached the
kiosk. There wasn't anybody there. The street was empty. He
couldn't have reached a doorway without my meeting him. He'd
simply vanished."

"A natural thing for ghosts—or illusions."

"But I can't believe I was as drunk as all that!"

"What did you do then?"

"I had to have another drink. My nerves were all to pieces."

"Didn't that bring him back?"

"No, but it sent me back to Anna's."

I think he would have been ashamed to come to me with his absurd story if it had not been for the attempt on Anna Schmidt. My theory when he did tell me his story was that there had been a watcher—though it was drink and hysteria that had pasted on the man's face the features of Harry Lime. That watcher had noted his visit to Anna and the member of the ring—the penicillin ring —had been warned by telephone. Events that night moved fast. You remember that Kurtz lived in the Russian zone—in the second bezirk to be exact, in a wide empty desolate street that runs down to the Prater Platz. A man like that had probably obtained his influential contacts.

The original police agreement in Vienna between the Allies confined the military police (who had to deal with crimes involving Allied personnel) to their particular zones, unless permission was given to them to enter the zone of another power. I had to get on the phone to my opposite number in the American or French zone before I sent in my men to make an arrest or pursue an investigation. Perhaps forty-eight hours would pass before I received permission from the Russians, but in practice there are few occasions when it is necessary to work quicker than that. Even at home it is not always possible to obtain a search warrant or permission from one's superiors to detain a suspect with any greater speed.

This meant that if I wanted to pick up Kurtz it would be as well to catch him in the British zone.

When Rollo Martins went drunkenly back at four o'clock in the morning to tell Anna that he had seen the ghost of Harry, he was told by a frightened porter who had not yet gone back to sleep that she had been taken away by the International Patrol.

What happened was this. Russia, you remember, was in the chair as far as the Inner Stadt was concerned, and the Russians had information that Anna Schmidt was one of their nationals living with false papers. On this occasion, halfway through the patrol, the Russian policeman directed the car to the street where Anna Schmidt lived.

Outside Anna Schmidt's block the American took a hand in the game and demanded in German what it was all about. The Frenchman leaned against the bonnet and lit a stinking Caporal.

France wasn't concerned, and anything that didn't concern France had no genuine importance to him. The Russian dug out a few words of German and flourished some papers. As far as they could tell, a Russian national wanted by the Russian police was living there without proper papers. They went upstairs and found Anna in bed, though I don't suppose, after Martins' visit, that she was asleep.

There is a lot of comedy in these situations if you are not directly concerned. You need a background of general European terror, of a father who belonged to a losing side, of house searches and disappearances before the fear outweighs the comedy. The Russian, you see, refused to leave the room; the American wouldn't leave a girl unprotected, and the Frenchman—well, I think the Frenchman must have thought it was fun. Can't you imagine the scene? The Russian was just doing his duty and watched the girl all the time, without a flicker of sexual interest; the American stood with his back chivalrously turned; the Frenchman smoked his cigarette and watched with detached amusement the reflection of the girl dressing in the mirror of the wardrobe; and the Englishman stood in the passage wondering what to do next.

I don't want you to think the English policeman came too badly out of the affair. In the passage, undistracted by chivalry, he had time to think, and his thoughts led him to the telephone in the next flat. He got straight through to me at my flat and woke me out of that deepest middle sleep. That was why when Martins rang up an hour later I already knew what was exciting him; it gave him an undeserved but very useful belief in my efficiency. I never had another crack from him about policemen or sheriffs after that night.

When the M.P. went back to Anna's room a dispute was raging. Anna had told the American that she had Austrian papers (which was true) and that they were quite in order (which was rather stretching the truth). The American told the Russian in bad German that they had no right to arrest an Austrian citizen. He asked Anna for her papers and when she produced them, the Russian took them.

"Hungarian," he said, pointing at Anna. "Hungarian," and then, flourishing the papers, "bad, bad."

The American, whose name was O'Brien, said, "Give the goil back her papers," which the Russian naturally didn't understand.

The American put his hand on his gun, and Corporal Starling said gently, "Let it go, Pat."

"If those papers ain't in order we got a right to look."

"Just let it go. We'll see the papers at HQ."

"The trouble about you British is you never know when to make a stand."

"Oh, well," Starling said; he had been at Dunkirk, but he knew when to be quiet.

The driver put on his brakes suddenly: there was a road block. You see, I knew they would have to pass this military post. I put my head in at the window and said to the Russian, haltingly, in his own tongue, "What are you doing in the British zone?"

He grumbled that it was "orders."

"Whose orders? Let me see them." I noted the signature—it was useful information. I said, "This tells you to pick up a certain Hungarian national and war criminal who is living with faulty papers in the British zone. Let me see the papers."

He started on a long explanation. I said, "These papers look to me quite in order, but I'll investigate them and send a report of the result to your colonel. He can, of course, ask for the extradition of this lady at any time. All we want is proof of her criminal activities."

I said to Anna, "Get out of the car." I put a packet of cigarettes in the Russian's hand, said, "Have a good smoke," waved my hand to the others, gave a sigh of relief, and that incident was closed.

Thirteen

While Martins told me how he went back to Anna's and found her gone, I did some hard thinking. I wasn't satisfied with the ghost story or the idea that the man with Harry Lime's features had been a drunken illusion. I took out two maps of Vienna and compared them. I rang up my assistant and, keeping Martins silent with a glass of whisky, asked him if he had located Harbin yet. He said no; he understood he'd left Klagenfurt a week ago to visit his family in the adjoining zone. One always wants to do everything oneself; one has to guard against blaming one's juniors. I am convinced that I would never have let Harbin out of our clutches, but then I would probably have made all kinds of mistakes that my junior would have avoided. "All right," I said. "Go on trying to get hold of him."

"I'm sorry, sir."

"Forget it. It's just one of those things."

His young enthusiastic voice—if only one could still feel that enthusiasm for a routine job; how many opportunities, flashes of insight one misses simply because a job has become just a job— his voice tingled up the wire. "You know, sir, I can't help feeling that we ruled out the possibility of murder too easily. There are one or two points—"

"Put them on paper, Carter."

"Yes, sir. I think, sir, if you don't mind my saying so" (Carter is a very young man) "we ought to have him dug up. There's no real evidence that he died just when the others said."

"I agree, Carter. Get on to the authorities."

Martins was right! I had made a complete fool of myself, but remember that police work in an occupied city is not like police work at home. Everything is unfamiliar: the methods of one's foreign colleagues, the rules of evidence, even the procedure at inquests. I suppose I had got into the state of mind when one trusts too much to one's personal judgment. I had been immensely relieved by Lime's death. I was satisfied with the accident.

I said to Martins, "Did you look inside the newspaper kiosk or was it locked?"

"Oh, it wasn't exactly a newspaper kiosk," he said. "It was one of those solid iron kiosks you see everywhere plastered with posters."

"You'd better show me the place."

"But is Anna all right?"

"The police are watching the flat. They won't try anything else yet."

I didn't want to make a fuss and stir in the neighbourhood with a police car, so we took trams—several trams—changing here and there, and came into the district on foot. I didn't wear my uniform, and I doubted anyway, after the failure of the attempt on Anna, whether they would risk a watcher. "This is the turning," Martins said and led me down a side street. We stopped at the kiosk. "You see he passed behind here and simply vanished—into the ground."

"That was exactly where he did vanish to," I said.

"How do you mean?"

An ordinary passer-by would never have noticed that the kiosk had a door, and of course it had been dark when the man disappeared. I pulled the door open and showed to Martins the little curling iron staircase that disappeared into the ground. He said, "Good God, then I didn't imagine him."

"It's one of the entrances to the main sewer."

"And anyone can go down?"

"Anyone."

"How far can one go?"

"Right across Vienna. People used them in air raids; some of our prisoners hid for two years down there. Deserters have used them—and burglars. If you know your way about you can emerge again almost anywhere in the city through a manhole or a kiosk like this one. The Austrians have to have special police for patrolling these sewers." I closed the door of the kiosk again. I said, "So that's how your friend Harry disappeared."

"You really believe it was Harry?"

"The evidence points that way."

"Then whom did they bury?"

"I don't know yet, but we soon shall, because we are digging him up again. I've got a shrewd idea, though, that Koch wasn't the only inconvenient man they murdered."

Martins said, "It's a bit of a shock."

"Yes."

"What are you going to do about it?"

"I don't know. You can bet he's hiding out now in another zone. We have no line now on Kurtz, for Harbin's blown—he must have been blown or they wouldn't have staged that mock death and funeral."

"But it's odd, isn't it, that Koch didn't recognize the dead man's face from the window."

"The window was a long way up and I expect the face had been damaged before they took the body out of the car."

He said thoughtfully, "I wish I could speak to him. You see, there's so much I simply can't believe."

"Perhaps you are the only one who could speak to him. It's risky though, because you do know too much."

"I still can't believe—I only saw the face for a moment." He said, "What shall I do?"

"He won't leave his zone now. The only person who could persuade him to come over would be you—or her, if he still believes you are his friend. But first you've got to speak to him. I can't see the line."

"I could go and see Kurtz. I have the address."

I said, "Remember. Lime may not want you to leave the Russian zone when once you are there, and I can't protect you there."

"I want to clear the whole damned thing up," Martins said, "but I'm not going to act as a decoy. I'll talk to him. That's all."

Fourteen

Sunday had laid its false peace over Vienna; the wind had dropped and no snow had fallen for twenty-four hours. All the morning trams had been full, going out to Grinzing where the young wine was drunk and to the slopes of snow on the hills outside. Walking over the canal by the make-shift military bridge, Martins was aware of the emptiness of the afternoon: the young were out with their toboggans and their skis, and all around him was the after-dinner sleep of age. A notice board told him that he was entering the Russian zone, but there were no signs of occupation. You saw more Russian soldiers in the Inner City than here.

Deliberately he had given Mr. Kurtz no warning of his visit. Better to find him out than a reception prepared for him. He was careful to carry with him all his papers, including the laissez-passer of the four powers that on the face of it allowed him to move freely through all the zones of Vienna. It was extraordinarily quiet over here on the other side of the canal, and a melodramatic journalist had painted a picture of silent terror; but the truth was simply the wide streets, the greater shell damage, the fewer people—and Sunday afternoon. There was nothing to fear, but all the same, in this huge empty street where all the time you heard your own feet moving, it was difficult not to look behind.

He had no difficulty in finding Mr. Kurtz's block, and when he rang the bell the door was opened quickly, as though Mr. Kurtz expected a visitor, by Mr. Kurtz himself.

"Oh," Mr. Kurtz said, "it's you, Rollo," and made a perplexed motion with his hand to the back of his head. Martins had been wondering why he looked so different, and now he knew. Mr. Kurtz was not wearing the toupee, and yet his head was not bald. He had a perfectly normal head of hair cut close. He said, "It would have been better to have telephoned to me. You nearly missed me; I was going out."

"May I come in a moment?"

"Of course."

In the hall a cupboard door stood open, and Martins saw Mr. Kurtz's overcoat, his raincoat, a couple of soft hats, and, hanging sedately on a peg like a wrap, Mr. Kurtz's toupee. He said, "I'm glad to see your hair has grown," and was astonished to see, in the mirror on the cupboard door, the hatred flame and blush on Mr. Kurtz's face. When he turned Mr. Kurtz smiled at him like a conspirator and said vaguely, "It keeps the head warm."

"Whose head?" Martins asked, for it had suddenly occurred to him how useful that toupee might have been on the day of the accident. "Never mind," he went quickly on, for his errand was not with Mr. Kurtz. "I'm here to see Harry."

"Harry?"

"I want to talk to him."

"Are you mad?"

"I'm in a hurry, so let's assume that I am. Just make a note of my madness. If you should see Harry—or his ghost—let him know that I want to talk to him. A ghost isn't afraid of a man, is it? Surely it's the other way round. I'll be waiting in the Prater by the Big Wheel for the next two hours—if you can get in touch with the dead, hurry." He added, "Remember, I was Harry's friend."

Kurtz said nothing, but somewhere, in a room off the hall, somebody cleared his throat. Martins threw open a door: he had half expected to see the dead rise yet again, but it was only Dr. Winkler who rose from a kitchen stove, and bowed very stiffly and correctly with the same celluloid squeak.

"Dr. Winkle," Martins said. Dr. Winkler looked extraordinarily out of place in a kitchen. The debris of a snack lunch littered the kitchen table, and the unwashed dishes consorted very ill with Dr. Winkler's cleanness.

"Winkler," the doctor corrected him with stony patience.

Martins said to Kurtz, "Tell the doctor about my madness. He might be able to make a diagnosis. And remember the place—by the Great Wheel. Or do ghosts only rise by night?" He left the flat.

For an hour he waited, walking up and down to keep warm, inside the enclosure of the Great Wheel; the smashed Prater with its bones sticking crudely through the snow was nearly empty. One stall sold thin flat cakes like cartwheels, and the children queued with their coupons. A few courting couples would be packed together in a single car of the Wheel and revolve slowly above the city, surrounded by empty cars. As the car reached the highest point of the Wheel, the revolutions would stop for a couple of minutes and far overhead the tiny faces would press against the glass. Martins wondered who would come for him. Was there enough friendship left in Harry for him to come alone, or would a squad of police arrive? It was obvious from the raid on Anna Schmidt's flat that he had a certain pull. And then as his watch hand passed the hour, he wondered: was it all an invention of my mind? are they digging up Harry's body now in the Central Cemetery?

Somewhere behind the cake stall a man was whistling, and Martins knew the tune. He turned and waited. Was it fear or excitement that made his heart beat—or just the memories that tune ushered in, for life had always quickened when Harry came, came just as he came now, as though nothing much had happened, nobody had been lowered into a grave or found with cut throat in a basement, came with his amused deprecating take-it-or-leave-it manner—and of course one always took it.

"Harry."

"Hullo, Rollo."

Don't picture Harry Lime as a smooth scoundrel. He wasn't that. The picture I have of him on my files is an excellent one: he is caught by a street photographer with his stocky legs apart, big shoulders a little hunched, a belly that has known too much good food too long, on his face a look of cheerful rascality, a geniality, a recognition that his happiness will make the world's day. Now he didn't make the mistake of putting out a hand that might have been rejected, but instead just patted Martins on the elbow and said, "How are things?"

"We've got to talk, Harry."

"Of course."

"Alone."

"We couldn't be more alone than here."

He had always known the ropes, and even in the smashed pleasure park he knew them, tipping the woman in charge of the Wheel, so that they might have a car to themselves. He said, "Lovers used to do this in the old days, but they haven't the money to spare, poor devils, now," and he looked out of the window of the swaying, rising car at the figures diminishing below with what looked like genuine commiseration.

Very slowly on one side of them the city sank; very slowly on the other the great cross girders of the Wheel rose into sight. As the horizon slid away the Danube became visible, and the piers of the Kaiser Friedrich Brücke lifted above the houses. "Well," Harry said, "it's good to see you, Rollo."

"I was at your funeral."

"That was pretty smart of me, wasn't it?"

"Not so smart for your girl. She was there too—in tears."

"She's a good little thing," Harry said. "I'm very fond of her."

"I didn't believe the police when they told me about you."

Harry said, "I wouldn't have asked you to come if I'd known what was going to happen, but I didn't think the police were on to me."

"Were you going to cut me in on the spoils?"

"I've never kept you out of anything, old man, yet." He stood with his back to the door as the car swung upwards, and smiled back at Rollo Martins, who could remember him in just such an attitude in a secluded corner of the school quad, saying, "I've learned a way to get out at night. It's absolutely safe. You are the only one I'm letting in on it." For the first time Rollo Martins looked back through the years without admiration, as he thought, He's never grown up. Marlowe's devils wore squibs attached to their tails: evil was like Peter Pan—it carried with it the horrifying and horrible gift of eternal youth.

Martins said, "Have you ever visited the children's hospital? Have you seen any of your victims?"

Harry took a look at the toy landscape below and came away from the door. "I never feel quite safe in these things," he said. He felt the back of the door with his hand, as though he were afraid that it might fly open and launch him into that iron-ribbed space. "Victims?" he asked. "Don't be melodramatic, Rollo. Look down there," he went on, pointing through the window at the people moving like black flies at the base of the Wheel.

"Would you really feel any pity if one of those dots stopped moving—forever? If I said you can have twenty thousand pounds for every dot that stops, would you really, old man, tell me to keep my money—without hesitation? Or would you calculate how many dots you could afford to spare? Free of income tax, old man. Free of income tax." He gave his boyish conspiratorial smile. "It's the only way to save nowadays."

"Couldn't you have stuck to tires?"

"Like Cooler? No, I've always been ambitious.

"But they can't catch me, Rollo, you'll see. I'll pop up again. You can't keep a good man down." The car swung to a standstill at the highest point of the curve and Harry turned his back and gazed out of the window. Martins thought: one good shove and I could break the glass, and he pictured the body dropping among the flies. He said, "You know the police are planning to dig up your body. What will they find?"

"Harbin," Harry replied with simplicity. He turned away from the window and said, "Look at the sky."

The car had reached the top of the Wheel and hung there motionless, while the stain of the sunset ran in streaks over the wrinkled papery sky beyond the black girders.

"Why did the Russians try to take Anna Schmidt?"

"She had false papers, old man."

"I thought perhaps you were just trying to get her here—because she was your girl? Because you wanted her?"

Harry smiled. "I haven't all that influence."

"What would have happened to her?"

"Nothing very serious. She'd have been sent back to Hungary. There's nothing against her really. She'd be infinitely better off in her own country than being pushed around by the British police."

"She hasn't told them anything about you."

"She's a good little thing," Harry repeated with complacent pride.

"She loves you."

"Well, I gave her a good time while it lasted."

"And I love her."

"That's fine, old man. Be kind to her. She's worth it. I'm glad." He gave the impression of having arranged everything to everybody's satisfaction. "And you can help to keep her mouth shut. Not that she knows anything that matters."

"I'd like to knock you through the window."

"But you won't, old man. Our quarrels never last long. You remember that fearful one in the Monaco, when we swore we were through. I'd trust you anywhere, Rollo. Kurtz tried to persuade me not to come but I know you. Then he tried to persuade me to, well, arrange an accident. He told me it would be quite easy in this car."

"Except that I'm the stronger man."

"But I've got the gun. You don't think a bullet wound would show when you hit *that* ground?" Again the car began to move, sailing slowly down, until the flies were midgets, were recognizable human beings. "What fools we are, Rollo, talking like this, as if I'd do that to you—or you to me." He turned his back and leaned his face against the glass. One thrust . . . "How much do you earn a year with your Westerns, old man?"

"A thousand."

"Taxed. I earn thirty thousand free. It's the fashion. In these days, old man, nobody thinks in terms of human beings. Governments don't, so why should we? They talk of the people and the proletariat, and I talk of the mugs. It's the same thing. They have their five-year plans and so have I."

"You used to be a Catholic."

"Oh, I still *believe,* old man. In God and mercy and all that. I'm not hurting anybody's soul by what I do. The dead are happier dead. They don't miss much here, poor devils," he added with that odd touch of genuine pity, as the car reached the platform and the faces of the doomed-to-be-victims, the tired pleasure-hoping Sunday faces, peered in at them. "I could cut you in, you know. It would be useful. I have no one left in the Inner City."

"Except Cooler? And Winkler?"

"You really mustn't turn policeman, old man." They passed out of the car and he put his hand again on Martins' elbow. "That was a joke, I know you won't. Have you heard anything of old Bracer recently?"

"I had a card at Christmas."

"Those were the days, old man. Those were the days. I've got to leave you here. We'll see each other—sometime. If you are in a jam, you can always get me at Kurtz's." He moved away and, turning, waved the hand he had had the tact not to offer: it was like the whole past moving off under a cloud. Martins suddenly called after him, "Don't trust me, Harry," but there was too great a distance now between them for the words to carry.

Fifteen

"Anna was at the theatre," Martins told me, "for the Sunday matinée. I had to see the whole thing through a second time. About a middle-aged pianist and an infatuated girl and an under-standing—a terribly understanding—wife. Anna acted very badly —she wasn't much of an actress at the best of times. I saw her afterwards in her dressing room, but she was badly fussed. I think she thought I was going to make a serious pass at her all the time, and she didn't want a pass. I told her Harry was alive—I thought she'd be glad and that I would hate to see how glad she was, but she sat in front of her make-up mirror and let the tears streak the grease paint and I wished after that she had been glad. She looked awful and I loved her. Then I told her about my interview with Harry, but she wasn't really paying much attention because when I'd finished she said, "I wish he was dead.""

"He deserves to be."

"I mean he would be safe then—from everybody."

I asked Martins, "Did you show her the photographs I gave you—of the children?"

"Yes. I thought, it's got to be kill or cure this time. She's got to get Harry out of her system. I propped the pictures up among the pots of grease. She couldn't avoid seeing them. I said, 'The police can't arrest Harry unless they get him into this zone, and we've got to help!'

"She said, 'I thought he was your friend.' I said, 'He *was* my friend.' She said, 'I'll never help you to get Harry. I don't want to see him again, I don't want to hear his voice. I don't want to be touched by him, but I won't do a thing to harm him.'

"I felt bitter—I don't know why, because after all I had done nothing for her. Even Harry had done more for her than I had. I said, 'You want him still,' as though I were accusing her of a crime. She said, 'I don't want him, but he's in me. That's a fact—not like friendship. Why, when I have a love dream, he's always the man.'"

I prodded Martins on when he hesitated. "Yes?"

"Oh, I just got up and left her then. Now it's your turn to work on me. What do you want me to do?"

"I want to act quickly. You see it was Harbin's body in the coffin, so we can pick up Winkler and Cooler right away. Kurtz is out of our reach for the time being, and so is the driver. We'll put in a formal request to the Russians for permission to arrest Kurtz and Lime: it makes our files tidy. If we are going to use you as our decoy, your message must go to Lime straight away—not after you've hung around in this zone for twenty-four hours. As I see it you were brought here for a grilling almost as soon as you got back into the Inner City; you heard then from me about Harbin; you put two and two together and you go and warn Cooler. We'll let Cooler slip for the sake of the bigger game—we have no evidence he was in on the penicillin racket. He'll escape into the second bezirk to Kurtz, and Lime will know you've played the game. Three hours later you send a message that the police are after you: you are in hiding and must see him."

"He won't come."

"I'm not so sure. We'll choose our hiding place carefully—where he'll think there's a minimum of risk. It's worth trying. It would appeal to his pride and his sense of humour if he could scoop you out. And it would stop your mouth."

Martins said, "He never used to scoop me out—at school." It was obvious that he had been reviewing the past with care and coming to conclusions.

"That wasn't such serious trouble and there was no danger of your squealing."

He said, "I told Harry not to trust me, but he didn't hear."

"Do you agree?"

He had given me back the photographs of the children and they lay on my desk. I could see him take a long look at them. "Yes," he said, "I agree."

Sixteen

All the first arrangements went according to plan. We delayed arresting Winkler, who had returned from the second bezirk, until after Cooler had been warned. Martins enjoyed his short interview with Cooler. Cooler greeted him with patronage. "Why, Mr. Martins, it's good to see you. Sit down. I'm glad everything went off all right between you and Colonel Calloway. A very straight chap, Calloway."

"It didn't," Martins said.

"You don't bear any ill will, I'm sure, about my letting him know about you seeing Koch. The way I figured it was this—if you were innocent you'd clear yourself right away and if you were guilty, well, the fact that I liked you oughtn't to stand in the way. A citizen has his duties."

"Like giving false evidence at an inquest."

Cooler said, "Oh, that old story. I'm afraid you are riled at me, Mr. Martins. Look at it this way—you as a citizen, owing allegiance—"

"The police have dug up the body. They'll be after you and Winkler. I want you to warn Harry . . ."

"I don't understand."

"Oh, yes, you do." And it was obvious that he did. Martins left him abruptly. He wanted no more of that kindly tired humanitarian face.

It only remained then to bait the trap. After studying the map of the sewer system I came to the conclusion that a café anywhere near the main entrance of the great sewer, which was placed in what Martins had mistakenly called a newspaper kiosk—would be the most likely spot to tempt Lime. He had only to rise once again through the ground, walk fifty yards, bring Martins back with him, and sink again into the obscurity of the sewers. He had no idea that this method of evasion was known to us: he probably knew that one patrol of the sewer police ended before midnight, and the next did not start till two, and so at midnight Martins sat in the little cold café in sight of the kiosk, drinking coffee after coffee. I had lent him a revolver; I had men posted as close to the kiosk as I could, and the sewer police were ready when zero hour struck to close the manholes and start sweeping the sewers inwards from the edge of the city. But I intended if I could to catch him before he went underground again. It would save trouble—and risk to Martins. So there, as I say, in the café Martins sat.

The wind had risen again, but it had brought no snow; it came icily off the Danube and in the little grassy square by the café it whipped up the snow like the surf on top of a wave. There was no heating in the café, and Martins sat warming each hand in turn on a cup of ersatz coffee—innumerable cups. There was usually one of my men in the café with him, but I changed them every twenty minutes or so irregularly. More than an hour passed. Martins had long given up hope and so had I, where I waited at the end of a phone several streets away, with a party of the sewer police ready to go down if it became necessary. We were luckier than Martins because we were warm in our great boots up to the thighs and our reefer jackets. One man had a small searchlight about half as big again as a car headlight strapped to his breast, and another man carried a brace of Roman candles. The telephone rang. It was Martins. He said, "I'm perishing with cold. It's a quarter past one. Is there any point in going on with this?"

"You shouldn't telephone. You must stay in sight."

"I've drunk seven cups of this filthy coffee. My stomach won't stand much more."

"He can't delay much longer if he's coming. He won't want to run into the two o'clock patrol. Stick it another quarter of an hour, but keep away from the telephone."

Martins' voice said suddenly, "Christ, he's here. He's—" and then the telephone went dead. I said to my assistant, "Give the signal to guard all manholes," and to my sewer police, "We are going down."

What had happened was this. Martins was still on the telephone to me when Harry Lime came into the café. I don't know what he heard, if he heard anything. The mere sight of a man wanted by the police and without friends in Vienna speaking on the telephone would have been enough to warn him. He was out of the café again before Martins had put down the receiver. It was one of those rare moments when none of my men was in the café. One had just left and another was on the pavement about to come in. Harry Lime brushed by him and made for the kiosk. Martins came out of the café and saw my men. If he had called out then it would have been an easy shot, but it was not, I suppose, Lime the penicillin racketeer who was escaping down the street; it was Harry. He hesitated just long enough for Lime to put the kiosk between them; then he called out, "That's him," but Lime had already gone to ground.

What a strange world unknown to most of us lies under our feet: we live above a cavernous land of waterfalls and rushing rivers, where tides ebb and flow as in the world above. If you have ever read the adventures of Allan Quartermain and the account of his voyage along the underground river to the city of Molosis, you will be able to picture the scene of Lime's last stand. The main sewer, half as wide as the Thames, rushes by under a huge arch, fed by tributary streams: these streams have fallen in waterfalls from higher levels and have been purified in their fall, so that only in these side channels is the air foul. The main stream smells sweet and fresh with a faint tang of ozone, and everywhere in the darkness is the sound of falling and rushing water. It was just past high tide when Martins and the policeman reached the river: first the curving iron staircase, then a short passage so low they had to stoop, and then the shallow edge of the water lapped at their feet. My man shone his torch along the edge of the current and said, "He's gone that way," for just as a deep stream when it shallows at the rim leaves an accumulation of debris, so the sewer left in the quiet water against the wall a scum of orange peel, old cigarette cartons, and the like, and in this scum Lime had left his trail as unmistakably as if he had walked in mud. My policeman shone his torch ahead with his left hand, and carried his gun in his right. He said to Martins, "Keep behind me, sir, the bastard may shoot."

"Then why the hell should you be in front?"

"It's my job, sir." The water came halfway up their legs as they walked; the policeman kept his torch pointing down and ahead at the disturbed trail at the sewer's edge. He said, "The silly thing is the bastard doesn't stand a chance. The manholes are all guarded and we've cordoned off the way into the Russian zone. All our chaps have to do now is to sweep inwards down the side passes from the manholes." He took a whistle out of his pocket and blew, and very far away here and again there came the notes of the reply. He said, "They are all down here now. The sewer police, I mean. They know this place just as I know the Tottenham Court Road. I wish my old woman could see me now," he said, lifting his torch for a moment to shine it ahead, and at that moment the shot came. The torch flew out of his hand and fell in the stream. He said, "God blast the bastard."

"Are you hurt?"

"Scraped my hand, that's all. Here, take this other torch, sir, while I tie my hand up. Don't shine it. He's in one of the side passages." For a long time the sound of the shot went on reverberating: when the last echo died a whistle blew ahead of them, and Martins' companion blew an answer.

Martins said, "It's an odd thing—I don't even know your name."

"Bates, sir." He gave a low laugh in the darkness. "This isn't my usual beat. Do you know the Horseshoe, sir?"

"Yes."

"And the Duke of Grafton?"

"Yes."

"Well, it takes a lot to make a world."

Martins said, "Let me come in front. I don't think he'll shoot at me, and I want to talk to him."

"I had orders to look after you, sir, careful."

"That's all right." He edged round Bates, plunging a foot deeper in the stream as he went. When he was in front he called out, "Harry," and the name set up an echo, "Harry, Harry, Harry!" that travelled down the stream and woke a whole chorus of whistles in the darkness. He called again, "Harry. Come out. It's no use."

A voice startlingly close made them hug the wall. "Is that you, old man?" it called. "What do you want me to do?"

"Come out. And put your hands above your head."

"I haven't a torch, old man. I can't see a thing."

"Be careful, sir," Bates said.

"Get flat against the wall. He won't shoot at me," Martins said. He called, "Harry, I'm going to shine the torch. Play fair and come out. You haven't got a chance." He flashed the torch on, and twenty feet away, at the edge of the light and the water, Harry stepped into view. "Hands above the head, Harry." Harry raised his hand and fired. The shot ricocheted against the wall a foot from Martins' head, and he heard Bates cry out. At the same moment a searchlight from fifty yards away lit the whole channel, caught Harry in its beams, Martins, the staring eyes of Bates slumped at the water's edge with the sewage washing to his waist. An empty cigarette carton wedged into his armpit and stayed. My party had reached the scene.

Martins stood dithering there above Bates's body, with Harry Lime halfway between us. We couldn't shoot for fear of hitting Martins, and the light of the searchlight dazzled Lime. We moved slowly on, our revolvers trained for a chance, and Lime turned this way and that way like a rabbit dazzled by headlights; then suddenly he took a flying jump into the deep central rushing stream. When we turned the searchlight after him he was submerged, and the current of the sewer carried him rapidly on, past the body of Bates, out of the range of the searchlight into the dark. What makes a man, without hope, cling to a few more minutes of existence? Is it a good quality or a bad one? I have no idea.

Martins stood at the outer edge of the searchlight beam, staring downstream. He had his gun in his hand now, and he was the only one of us who could fire with safety. I thought I saw a movement and called out to him, "There. There. Shoot." He lifted his gun and fired, just as he had fired at the same command all those years ago on Brickworth Common, fired, as he did then, inaccurately. A cry of pain came tearing back like calico down the cavern: a reproach, an entreaty. "Well done," I called and halted by Bates's body. He was dead. His eyes remained blankly open as we turned the searchlight on him; somebody stooped and dislodged the carton and threw it in the river, which whirled it on—a scrap of yellow Gold Flake: he was certainly a long way from the Tottenham Court Road.

I looked up and Martins was out of sight in the darkness. I called his name and it was lost in a confusion of echoes, in the rush and the roar of the underground river. Then I heard a third shot.

Martins told me later, "I walked upstream to find Harry, but I must have missed him in the dark. I was afraid to lift the torch: I didn't want to tempt him to shoot again. He must have been struck by my bullet just at the entrance of a side passage. Then I suppose he crawled up the passage to the foot of the iron stairs. Thirty feet above his head was the manhole, but he wouldn't have had the strength to lift it, and even if he had succeeded the police were waiting above. He must have known all that, but he was in great pain, and just as an animal creeps into the dark to die, so I suppose a man makes for the light. He wants to die at home, and the darkness is never home to *us*. He began to pull himself up the stairs, but then the pain took him and he couldn't go on. What made him whistle that absurd scrap of a tune I'd been fool enough to believe he had written himself? Was he trying to attract attention, did he want a friend with him, even the friend who had trapped him, or was he delirious and had he no purpose at all? Anyway I heard his whistle and came back along the edge of the stream, and felt the wall end and found my way up the passage where he lay. I said, 'Harry,' and the whistling stopped, just above my head. I put my hand on an iron handrail and climbed. I was still afraid he might shoot. Then, only three steps up, my foot stamped down on his hand, and he was there. I shone my torch on him: he hadn't got a gun; he must have dropped it when my bullet hit him. For a moment I thought he was dead, but then he whimpered with pain. I said, 'Harry,' and he swivelled his eyes with a great effort to my face. He was trying to speak, and I bent down to listen. 'Bloody fool,' he said—that was all. I don't know whether he meant that for himself—some sort of act of contrition, however inadequate (he was a Catholic)—or was it for me—with my thousand a year taxed and my imaginary cattle rustlers who couldn't even shoot a rabbit clean? Then he began to whimper again. I couldn't bear it any more and I put a bullet through him."

"We'll forget that bit," I said.

Martins said, "I never shall."

Seventeen

A thaw set in that night, and all over Vienna the snow melted, and the ugly ruins came to light again: steel rods hanging like stalactites, and rusty girders thrusting like bones through the grey slush Burials were much simpler than they had been a week before when electric drills had been needed to break the frozen ground. It was almost as warm as a spring day when Harry Lime had his second funeral. I was glad to get him under earth again, but it had taken two men's deaths. The group by the grave was smaller now: Kurtz wasn't there, nor Winkler—only the girl and Rollo Martins and myself. And there weren't any tears.

After it was over the girl walked away without a word to either of us down the long avenue of trees that led to the main entrance and the tram stop, splashing through the melted snow. I said to Martins, "I've got transport. Can I give you a lift?"

"No," he said, "I'll take a tram back."

"You win, you've proved me a bloody fool."

"I haven't won," he said. "I've lost." I watched him striding off on his overgrown legs after the girl. He caught her up and they walked side by side. I don't think he said a word to her: it was like the end of a story. He was a very bad shot and a very bad judge of character, but he had a way with Westerns (a trick of tension) and with girls (I wouldn't know what). And Crabbin?

Oh, Crabbin is still arguing with the British Cultural Relations Society about Dexter's expenses. They say they can't pass simultaneous payments in Stockholm and Vienna. Poor Crabbin. Poor all of us when you come to think of it.

Our
Man
in Havana

"And the sad man is cock of all his jests."
—GEORGE HERBERT

In a fairy story like this set at some indeterminate date in the future it seems unnecessary to disclaim any connection between my characters and any living people. However I would like to state that not one character is drawn from a living person, that there is no police officer like Captain Segura in Cuba today and certainly no British Ambassador of the kind I have drawn. Nor, I should imagine, is the Chief of the Secret Service anything like my mythical character.

GRAHAM GREENE

PART I

One

1

"That nigger going down the street," said Dr. Hasselbacher, standing in the Wonder Bar, "he reminds me of you, Mr. Wormold." It was typical of Dr. Hasselbacher that after fifteen years of friendship he still used the prefix Mr.—friendship proceeded with the slowness and assurance of a careful diagnosis. On Wormold's deathbed, when Dr. Hasselbacher came to feel his failing pulse, he would perhaps become Jim.

The Negro was blind in one eye and one leg was shorter than the other; he wore an ancient felt hat and his ribs showed through his torn shirt like a ship's under demolition. He walked at the edge of the pavement, beyond the yellow and pink pillars of a colonnade, in the hot January sun, and he counted every step as he went. As he passed the Wonder Bar, going up Virdudes, he had reached 1369. He had to move slowly to give time for so long a numeral. "One thousand three hundred and seventy." He was a familiar figure near the National Square where he would sometimes linger and stop his counting long enough to sell a packet of pornographic photographs to a tourist. Then he would take up his count where he had left it. At the end of the day, like an energetic passenger on a trans-Atlantic liner, he must have known to a yard how far he had walked.

"Joe?" Wormold asked. "I don't see any resemblance. Except the limp, of course," but instinctively he took a quick look at himself in the mirror marked Cerveza Tropical, as though he might really have been so broken down and darkened during his walk from the store in the old town. But the face which looked back at him was only a little discoloured by the dust from the harbour works; it was still the same, anxious and criss-crossed and fortyish: much younger than Dr. Hasselbacher's, yet a stranger might have felt certain it would be extinguished sooner—the shadow was there already, the anxieties which are beyond the reach of a tranquilizer. The Negro limped out of sight, round the corner of the Paseo. The day was full of bootblacks.

"I didn't mean the limp. You don't see the likeness?"

"No."

"He's got two ideas in his head," Dr. Hasselbacher explained. "To do his job and to keep count. And, of course, he's British."

"I still don't see . . ." Wormold cooled his mouth with his morning daiquiri. Seven minutes to get to the Wonder Bar: seven minutes back to the store: six minutes for companionship. He looked at his watch. He remembered that it was one minute slow.

"He's reliable, you can depend on him, that's all I meant," said Dr. Hasselbacher with impatience. "How's Milly?"

"Wonderful," Wormold said. It was his invariable answer but he meant it.

"Seventeen on the seventeenth, eh?"

"That's right." He looked quickly over his shoulder as though somebody were hunting him and then at his watch again. "You'll be coming to split a bottle with us?"

"I've never failed yet, Mr. Wormold. Who else will be there?"

"Well, I thought just the three of us. You see, Cooper's gone home, and poor Marlowe's in hospital still, and Milly doesn't seem to care for any of this new crowd at the Consulate. So I thought we'd keep it quiet, in the family."

"I'm honoured to be one of the family, Mr. Wormold."

"Perhaps a table at the Nacional, or would you say that wasn't quite—well, suitable?"

"This isn't England or Germany, Mr. Wormold. Girls grow up quickly in the tropics."

A shutter across the way creaked open and then regularly blew to in the slight breeze from the sea, click clack like an ancient clock. Wormold said, "I must be off."

"Phastkleaners will get on without you, Mr. Wormold." It was a day of uncomfortable truths. "Like my patients," Dr. Hasselbacher added with kindliness.

"People have to get ill, they don't have to buy vacuum cleaners."

"But you charge them more."

"And get only twenty per cent for myself. One can't save much on twenty per cent."

"This is not an age for saving, Mr. Wormold."

"I must—for Milly. If something happened to me . . ."

"We none of us have a great expectation of life nowadays, so why worry?"

"All these disturbances are very bad for trade. What's the good of a vacuum cleaner if the power's cut off?"

"I could manage a small loan, Mr. Wormold."

"No, no. It's not like that. My worry isn't this year's or even next year's, it's a long-term worry."

"Then it's not worth calling a worry. We live in an atomic age, Mr. Wormold. Push a button—piff bang—where are we? Another Scotch please."

"And that's another thing. You know what the firm has done now? They've sent me an Atomic Pile Cleaner."

"Really? I didn't know science had got that far."

"Oh, of course, there's nothing atomic about it—it's only a name. Last year there was the Turbo Jet; this year it's the Atomic. It works off the light plug just the same as the other."

"Then why worry?" Dr. Hasselbacher repeated like a theme tune, leaning into his whisky.

"They don't realize that sort of name may go down in the States, but not here, where the clergy are preaching all the time against the misuse of science. Milly and I went to the cathedral last Sunday—you know how she is about Mass, thinks she'll convert me, I wouldn't wonder. Well, Father Mendez spent half an hour describing the effect of a hydrogen bomb. Those who believe in heaven on earth, he said, are creating a hell; he made it sound that way too—it was very lucid. How do you think I liked it on Monday morning when I had to make a window display of the new Atomic Pile Suction Cleaner? It wouldn't have surprised me if one of the wild boys around here had broken the window. Catholic Action, Christ the King, all that stuff. I don't know what to do about it, Hasselbacher."

"Sell one to Father Mendez for the Bishop's palace."

"But he's satisfied with the Turbo. It was a good machine. Of course this one is too. Improved suction for bookcases. You know I wouldn't sell anyone a machine that wasn't good."

"I know, Mr. Wormold. Can't you just change the name?"

"They won't let me. They are proud of it. They think it's the best phrase anyone has thought up since 'It beats as it sweeps as it cleans.' You know they had something called an air-purifying pad with the Turbo. Nobody minded—it was a good gadget, but yesterday a woman came in and looked at the Atomic Pile and she asked whether a pad that size could really absorb all the radioactivity. And what about strontium 90, she asked."

"I could give you a medical certificate," said Dr. Hasselbacher.

"Do you never worry about anything?"

"I have a secret defence, Mr. Wormold. I am interested in life."

"So am I, but . . ."

"You are interested in a person, not in life, and people die or leave us—I'm sorry. I wasn't referring to your wife. But if you are interested in life it never lets you down. I am interested in the blueness of the cheese. You don't do crosswords, do you, Mr. Wormold? I do, and they are like people: one reaches an end. I can finish any crossword within an hour, but I have a discovery concerned with the blueness of cheese that will never come to a conclusion—although of course one dreams that perhaps a time might come. . . . One day I must show you my laboratory."

"I must be going, Hasselbacher."

"You should dream more, Mr. Wormold. Reality in our century is not something to be faced."

2

When Wormold arrived at his store in Lamparilla Street, Milly had not yet returned from her American convent school, and in spite of the two figures he could see through the door, the shop seemed to him empty. How empty! And so it would remain until Milly came back. He was aware, whenever he entered the shop, of a vacuum that had nothing to do with his cleaners. No customer could fill it, particularly not the one who stood there now looking too spruce for Havana and reading a leaflet in English on the Atomic Pile, pointedly neglecting Wormold's assistant. Lopez was an impatient man who did not like to waste his time away from the Spanish edition of *Confidential*. He was glaring at the stranger and making no attempt to win him over.

"Buenos días," Wormold said. He looked at all strangers in the shop with an habitual suspicion. Ten years ago a man had entered the shop, posing as a customer, and he had guilelessly sold him a sheep's wool for the high-gloss finishing on his car. He had been a plausible impostor, but no one could be a less likely purchaser of a vacuum cleaner than this man. Tall and elegant, in his stone-coloured tropical suit, and wearing an exclusive tie, he carried with him the breath of beaches and the leathery smell of a good club: you expected him to say, "The Ambassador will see you in a minute." His cleaning would always be arranged for him —by an ocean or a valet.

"Don't speak the lingo, I'm afraid," the stranger answered. The slang word was a blemish on his suit, like an egg stain after breakfast. "You are British, aren't you?"

"Yes."

"I mean—really British. British passport and all that."

"Yes. Why?"

"One likes to do business with a British firm. One knows where one is, if you see what I mean."

"What can I do for you?"

"Well, first, I just wanted to look around." He spoke as though he were in a bookshop. "I couldn't make your chap understand that."

"You are looking for a vacuum cleaner?"

"Well, not exactly looking."

"I mean, you are thinking of buying one?"

"That's it, old man, you've hit it on the nail." Wormold had the impression that the man had chosen his tone because he felt it matched the store—a protective colouring in Lamparilla Street, for the breeziness certainly didn't match his clothes. One can't successfully follow St. Paul's technique of being all things to all men without a change of suit.

Wormold said briskly, "You couldn't do better than the Atomic Pile."

"I notice one here called the Turbo."

"That too is a very good cleaner. Have you a big apartment?"

"Well, not exactly big."

"Here, you see, you get two sets of brushes—this one for waxing and this for polishing—oh no, I think it's the other way round. The Turbo is air-powered."

"What does that mean?"

"Well, of course, it's . . . well, it's what it says, air-powered."

"This funny little bit here—what's that for?"

"That's a two-way carpet nozzle."

"You don't say so? Isn't that interesting? Why two-way?"

"You push and you pull."

"The things they think up," the stranger said. "I suppose you sell a lot of these?"

"I'm the only agent here."

"All the important people, I suppose, have to have an Atomic Pile?"

"Or a Turbo Jet."

"Government offices?"

"Of course. Why?"

"What's good enough for a government office should be good enough for me."

"You might prefer our Midget Make-Easy."

"Make what easy?"

"The full title is Midget Make-Easy Air-Powered Suction Small Home Cleaner."

"That word air-powered again."

"I'm not responsible for it."

"Don't get riled, old man."

"Personally I hate the words Atomic Pile," Wormold said with sudden passion. He was deeply disturbed. It occurred to him that this stranger might be an inspector sent from the head office in London or New York. In that case they should hear nothing but the truth.

"I see what you mean. It's not a happy choice. Tell me, do you service these things?"

"Quarterly. Free of charge during the period of guarantee."

"I meant yourself."

"I send Lopez."

"The sullen chap?"

"I'm not much of a mechanic. When I touch one of these things it somehow seems to give up working."

"Don't you drive a car?"

"Yes, but if there's anything wrong, my daughter sees to it."

"Oh yes, your daughter. Where's she?"

"At school. Now let me show you this snap-action coupling." But of course, when he tried to demonstrate, it wouldn't couple. He pushed and screwed. "Faulty part," he said desperately.

"Let me try," the stranger said, and in the coupling went as smooth as you could wish.

"How old is your daughter?"

"Sixteen," he said and was angry with himself for answering.

"Well," the stranger said, "I must be getting along. Enjoyed our chat."

"Wouldn't you like to watch a cleaner at work? Lopez here would give you a demonstration."

"Not at the moment. I'll be seeing you again—here or there," the man said with a vague and insolent confidence, and was gone out of the door before Wormold thought to give him a trade-card. In the square at the top of Lamparilla Street he was swallowed up among the pimps and lottery sellers of the Havana noon.

Lopez said, "He never intended to buy."

"What did he want then?"

"Who knows? He looked a long time through the window at me. I think perhaps if you had not come in, he would have asked me to find him a girl."

"A girl?"

He thought of the day ten years ago and then with uneasiness of Milly, and he wished he had not answered so many questions. He also wished that the snap-action coupling had coupled for once with a snap.

Two

He could distinguish the approach of Milly like that of a police car from a long way off. Whistles instead of sirens warned him of her coming. She was accustomed to walk from the bus stop in the Avenida de Belgica, but today the wolves seemed to be operating from the direction of Compostella. They were not dangerous wolves, he had reluctantly to admit that. The salute which had begun about her thirteenth birthday was really one of respect, for even by the high Havana standard Milly was beautiful. She had hair the colour of pale honey, dark eyebrows, and her pony trim was shaped by the best barber in town. She paid no open attention to the whistles, they only made her step the higher—seeing her walk, you could almost believe in levitation. Silence would have seemed like an insult to her now.

Unlike Wormold, who believed in nothing, Milly was a Catholic: he had been made to promise her mother that before they married. Now her mother, he supposed, was of no faith at all, but she had left a Catholic on his hands. It brought Milly closer to Cuba than he could come himself. He believed that in the rich families the custom of keeping a duenna lingered still, and sometimes it seemed to him that Milly too carried a duenna about with her, invisible to all eyes but her own. In church, where she looked more lovely than in any other place, wearing her featherweight mantilla embroidered with leaves transparent as winter, the duenna was always seated by her side, to observe that her back was straight, her face covered at the suitable moment, the sign of the cross correctly performed. Small boys might suck sweets with impunity around her or giggle from behind the pillars; she sat with the rigidity of a nun, following the Mass in a small gilt-edged missal bound in a morocco the colour of her hair (she had chosen it herself). The same invisible duenna saw to it that she ate fish on Friday, fasted on Ember Days and attended Mass not only on Sundays and the special feasts of the church, but also on her saint's day. Milly was her home name: her given name was Seraphina—in Cuba "a double of the second class," a mysterious phrase which reminded Wormold of the race track.

It had been a long time before Wormold realized that the duenna was not always by her side. Milly was meticulous in her behaviour at meals and had never neglected her night prayers, as he had good reason to know since, even as a child, she had kept him waiting, to mark him out as the non-Catholic he was, before her bedroom door until she had finished. A light burnt continually in front of the image of Our Lady of Guadalupe. He remembered how he had overheard her at the age of four praying, "Hail Mary, quite contrary."

One day, however, when Milly was thirteen, he had been summoned to the convent school of the American Sisters of Clare in the white rich suburb of Vedado. There he learnt for the first time how the duenna left Milly under the religious plaque by the grilled gateway of the school. The complaint was of a serious nature: she had set fire to a small boy called Thomas Earl Parkman, Junior. It was true, the Reverend Mother admitted, that Earl, as he was known in the school, had pulled Milly's hair first, but this she considered in no way justified Milly's action, which might well have had serious results if another girl had not pushed Earl into a fountain. Milly's only defense of her conduct had been that Earl was a Protestant and if there was going to be a persecution Catholics could always beat Protestants at that game.

"But how did she set Earl on fire?"

"She put petrol on the tail of his shirt."

"Petrol!"

"Lighter fluid, and then she struck a match. We think she must have been smoking in secret."

"It's a most extraordinary story."

"I guess you don't know Milly then. I must tell you, Mr. Wormold, our patience has been sadly strained."

Apparently, six months before setting fire to Earl, Milly had circulated round her art class a set of postcards of the world's great pictures.

"I don't see what's wrong in that."

"At the age of twelve, Mr. Wormold, a child shouldn't confine her appreciation to the nude, however classical the paintings."

"They were all nude?"

"All except Goya's Draped Maja. But she had her in the nude version too."

Wormold had been forced to fling himself on Reverend Mother's mercy: he was a poor non-believing father with a Catholic child, the American convent was the only Catholic school in Havana which was not Spanish, and he couldn't afford a governess. They wouldn't want him to send her to the Hiram C. Truman School, would they? And it would be breaking the promise he had made to his wife. He wondered in private whether it was his duty to find a new wife, but the nuns might not put up with that and in any case he still loved Milly's mother.

Of course he spoke to Milly and her explanation had the virtue of simplicity.

"Why did you set fire to Earl?"

"I was tempted by the devil," she said.

"Milly, please be sensible."

"Saints have been tempted by the devil."

"You are not a saint."

"Exactly. That's why I fell." The chapter was closed—at any rate it would be closed that afternoon between four and six in the confessional. Her duenna was back at her side and would see to that. If only, he thought, I could know for certain when the duenna takes her day off.

There had been also the question of smoking in secret.

"Are you smoking cigarettes?" he asked her.

"No."

Something in her manner made him rephrase the question. "Have you ever smoked at all, Milly?"

"Only cheroots," she said.

Now that he heard the whistles warning him of her approach he wondered why Milly was coming up Lamparilla Street from the direction of the harbour instead of from the Avenida de Belgica. But when he saw her he saw the reason too. She was followed by a young shop assistant who carried a parcel so large that it obscured his face. Wormold realized sadly that she had been shopping again. He went upstairs to their apartment above the store and presently he could hear her superintending in another room the disposal of her purchases. There was a thump, a rattle, and a clang of metal. "Put it there," she said, and "No, there." Drawers opened and closed. She began to drive nails into the wall. A piece of plaster on his side shot out and fell into the salad; the daily maid had laid a cold lunch.

Milly came in strictly on time. It was always hard for him to disguise his sense of her beauty, but the invisible duenna looked coldly through him as though he were an undesirable suitor. It had been a long time now since the duenna had taken a holiday; he almost regretted her assiduity, and sometimes he would have been glad to see Earl burn again. Milly said grace and crossed herself and he sat respectfully with his head lowered until she had finished—it was one of her longer graces, which probably meant that she was not very hungry, or that she was stalling for time.

"Had a good day, Father?" she asked politely. It was the kind of remark a wife might have made after many years.

"Not so bad, and you?" He became a coward when he watched her; he hated to oppose her in anything, and he tried to avoid for as long as possible the subject of her purchases. He knew that her monthly allowance had gone two weeks ago on some earrings she had fancied and a small statue of St. Seraphina.

"I got top marks today in Dogma and Morals."

"Fine, fine. What were the questions?"

"I did best on Venial Sin."

"I saw Dr. Hasselbacher this morning," he said with apparent irrelevance.

She replied politely, "I hope he was well." The duenna, he considered, was overdoing it: people praised Catholic schools for teaching deportment, but surely deportment was intended only to impress strangers. He thought sadly: But I *am* a stranger. He was unable to follow her into her strange world of candles and lace and holy water and genuflections. Sometimes he felt that he had no child.

"He's coming in for a drink on your birthday. I thought we might go afterwards to a nightclub."

"A nightclub!" The duenna must have momentarily looked elsewhere as Milly exclaimed, "O Gloria Patri."

"You always used to say Alleluia."

"That was in Lower Four. Which nightclub?"

"I thought perhaps the Nacional."

"Not the Shanghai Theatre?"

"Certainly not the Shanghai Theatre. I can't think how you've even heard of the place."

"In a school things get around."

Wormold said, "We haven't discussed your present. A seventeenth birthday is no ordinary one. I was wondering . . ."

"Really and truly," Milly said, "there's nothing in the world I want."

Wormold remembered with apprehension that enormous package. If she had really gone out and got everything she wanted . . . He pleaded with her. "Surely there must be something you still want."

"Nothing. Really nothing."

"A new swim suit," he suggested desperately.

"Well, there is one thing. . . . But I thought we might count it as a Christmas present too, and next year's and the year after that. . . ."

"Good heavens, what is it?"

"You wouldn't have to worry about presents any more for a long time."

"Don't tell me you want a Jaguar."

"Oh, no, this is quite a small present. Not a car. This would last for years. It's an awfully economical idea. It might even, in a way, save petrol."

"Save petrol?"

"And today I got all the etceteras—with my own money."

"You haven't got any money—I had to lend you three pesos for Saint Seraphina."

"But my credit's good."

"Milly, I've told you over and over again I won't have you buying on credit. Anyway it's my credit, not yours, and my credit's going down all the time."

"Poor Father. Are we on the edge of ruin?"

"Oh, I expect things will pick up again when the disturbances are over."

"I thought there were always disturbances in Cuba. If the worst came to the worst I could go out and work, couldn't I?"

"What at?"

"Like Jane Eyre I could be a governess."

"Who would take you?"

"Señor Perez."

"Milly, what on earth are you talking about? He's living with his fourth wife, you're a Catholic. . . ."

"I might have a special vocation to sinners," Milly said.

"Milly, what nonsense you talk. Anyway, I'm not ruined. Not yet. As far as I know. Milly, what have you been buying?"

"Come and see." He followed her into her bedroom. A saddle lay on her bed; a bridle and bit were hanging on the wall from the nails she had driven in (she had knocked off a heel from her best evening shoes in doing it); reins were draped between the light brackets; a whip was propped up on the dressing table. He said hopelessly, "Where's the horse?" and half expected it to appear from the bathroom.

"In a stable near the Country Club. Guess what's she called."

"How can I?"

"Seraphina. Isn't it just like the hand of God?"

"But, Milly, I can't possibly afford . . ."

"You needn't pay for her all at once. She's a chestnut."

"What difference does the colour make?"

"She's in the stud book. Out of Santa Teresa by Ferdinand of Castile. She would have cost twice as much, but she fouled a fet-lock jumping wire. There's nothing wrong, only a kind of lump, so they can't show her."

"I don't mind if it's a quarter the price. Business is too bad, Milly."

"But I've explained to you, you needn't pay all at once. You can pay over the years."

"And I'll still be paying for it when it's dead."

"She's not an it, she's a she, and Seraphina will last much longer than a car. She'll probably last longer than you will."

"But, Milly, your trips out to the stables, and the stabling alone . . ."

"I've talked about all that with Captain Segura. He's offering me a rock-bottom price. He wanted to give me free stabling, but I knew you wouldn't like me to take favours."

"Who's Captain Segura, Milly?"

"The head police officer in Vedado."

"Where on earth did you meet him?"

"Oh, he often gives me a lift to Lamparilla in his car."

"Does Reverend Mother know about this?"

Milly said stiffly, "One must have one's private life."

"Listen, Milly, I can't afford a horse, you can't afford all this— stuff. You'll have to take it back." He added with fury, "And I won't have you taking lifts from Captain Segura."

"Don't worry. He never touches me," Milly said. "He only sings sad Mexican songs while he drives. About flowers and death. And one about a bull."

"I won't have it, Milly. I shall speak to Reverend Mother, you've got to promise . . ." He could see under the dark brows how the green and amber eyes contained the coming tears. Wormold felt the approach of panic; just so his wife had looked at him one blistering October afternoon when six years of life suddenly ended. He said, "You aren't in love, are you, with this Captain Segura?"

Two tears chased each other with a kind of elegance round the curve of a cheek-bone and glittered like the harness on the wall— they were part of her equipment too. "I don't care a damn about Captain Segura," Milly said. "It's just Seraphina I care about. She's fifteen hands and she's got a mouth like velvet, everybody says so."

"Milly dear, you know that if I could manage it . . ."

"Oh I knew you'd take it like this," Milly said. "I knew it in my heart of hearts. I said two novenas to make it come right, but they haven't worked. I was so careful too. I was in a state of grace all the time I said them. I'll never believe in a novena again. Never. Never." Her voice had the lingering resonance of Poe's Raven. He had no faith himself, but he never wanted by any action of his own to weaken hers. Now he felt a fearful responsibility: at any moment she would be denying the existence of God. Ancient promises he had made came up out of the past to weaken him.

He said, "Milly, I'm sorry. . . ."

"I've done two extra Massès as well." She shovelled on to his shoulders all her disappointment in the old familiar magic. It was all very well talking about the easy tears of a child, but if you are a father you can't take risks as a schoolteacher can, or a governess. Who knows whether there may not be a moment in childhood when the world changes forever, like making a face when the clock strikes?

"Milly, I promise if it's possible next year . . . Listen, Milly, you can keep the saddle till then, and all the rest of the stuff."

"What's the good of a saddle without a horse? And I told Captain Segura—"

"Damn Captain Segura—what did you tell him?"

"I told him I had only to ask you for Seraphina and you'd give her to me. I said you were wonderful. I didn't tell him about the novenas."

"How much is she?"

"Three hundred pesos."

"Oh, Milly, Milly." There was nothing he could do but surrender. "You'll have to pay out of your allowance towards the stabling."

"Of course I will." She kissed his ear. "I'll start next month." They both knew very well that she would never start. She said, "You see, they did work after all, the novenas, I mean. I'll begin another tomorrow, to make business good. I wonder which saint is best for that."

"I've heard that Saint Jude is the saint of lost causes," Wormold said.

Three

1

It was Wormold's daydream that he would wake some day and find that he had amassed savings, bearer bonds and share certificates, and that he was receiving a steady flow of dividends like the rich inhabitants of the Vedado suburb; then he would retire with Milly to England, where there would be no Captain Seguras and no wolf whistles. But the dream faded whenever he entered the big American bank in Obispo. Passing through the great stone portals which were decorated with four-leaved clovers, he became again the small dealer he really was, whose pension would never be sufficient to take Milly to the region of safety.

Drawing a cheque is not nearly so simple an operation in an American bank as in an English one. American bankers believe in the personal touch; the teller conveys a sense that he happens to be there accidentally and he is overjoyed at the lucky chance of the encounter. "Well," he seems to express in the sunny warmth of his smile, "who would have believed that I'd meet you here, you of all people, in a bank of all places?" After exchanging with him news of your health and of his health, and after finding a common interest in the fineness of the winter weather, you shyly, apologetically, slide the cheque towards him (how tiresome and incidental all such business is), but he barely has time to glance at it when the telephone rings at his elbow. "Why, Henry," he exclaims in astonishment over the telephone, as though Henry too were the last person he expected to speak to on such a day, "what's the news of you?" The news takes a long time to absorb; the teller smiles whimsically at you: business is business.

"I must say Edith was looking swell last night," the teller said.

Wormold shifted restlessly.

"It was a swell evening, it certainly was. Me? Oh, I'm fine. Well now, what can we do for you today?"

". . ."

"Why, anything to oblige, Henry, you know that. . . . A hundred and fifty thousand dollars for three years . . . no, of course there won't be any difficulty for a business like yours. We have to get the O.K. from New York, but that's a formality. Just step in any time and talk to the manager. Monthly payments? That's not necessary with an American firm. I'd say we could arrange five per cent. Make it two hundred thousand for four years? Of course, Henry."

"Wormold's cheque shrank to insignificance in his fingers. "Three hundred and fifty dollars"—the writing seemed to him almost as thin as his resources.

"See you at Mrs. Slater's tomorrow? I expect there'll be a rubber. Don't bring any aces up your sleeve, Henry. How long for the O.K.? Oh, a couple of days if we cable. Eleven tomorrow? Any time you say, Henry. Just walk in. I'll tell the manager. He'll be tickled to death to see you."

"Sorry to keep you waiting, Mr. Wormold." Surname again.

Perhaps, Wormold thought, I am not worth cultivating or perhaps it is our nationalities that keep us apart. "Three hundred and fifty dollars?" The teller took an unobtrusive glance in a file before counting out the notes. He had hardly begun when the telephone rang a second time.

"Why, Mrs. Ashworth, where have you been hiding yourself? Over at Miami? No kidding?" It was several minutes before he had finished with Mrs. Ashworth. As he passed the notes to Wormold, he handed over a slip of paper as well. "You don't mind, do you, Mr. Wormold? You asked me to keep you informed." The slip showed an overdraft of fifty dollars.

"Not at all. It's very kind of you," Wormold said. "But there's nothing to worry about."

"Oh, the bank's not worrying, Mr. Wormold. You just asked, that's all."

Wormold thought: If the overdraft had been 50,000 dollars, he would have called me Jim.

2

For some reason that morning he had no wish to meet Dr. Hasselbacher for his morning daiquiri—there were times when Dr. Hasselbacher was a little too carefree—so he looked in at Sloppy Joe's instead of at the Wonder Bar. No Havana resident ever went to Sloppy Joe's, because it was the rendezvous of tourists, but tourists were sadly reduced nowadays in number, for the President's regime was creaking dangerously towards its end. There had always been unpleasant doings out of sight, in the inner rooms of the Jefatura, which had not disturbed the tourists in the Nacional and the Seville-Biltmore, but one tourist had recently been killed by a stray bullet while he was taking a photograph of a picturesque beggar under a balcony near the palace, and the death had sounded the knell of the all-in tour "including a trip to Varadero beach and the night-life of Havana." The victim's Leica had been smashed as well, and that had impressed his companions more than anything with the destructive power of a bullet. Wormold had heard them talking afterwards in the bar of the Nacional. "Ripped right through the camera," one of them said. "Five hundred dollars gone just like that."

"Was he killed at once?"

"Sure. And the lens—you could pick up bits for fifty yards around. Look—I'm taking a piece home to show Mr. Humpelnicker."

The long bar that morning was empty except for the elegant stranger at one end and a stout member of the Tourist police who was smoking a cigar at the other. The Englishman was absorbed in the sight of so many bottles and it was quite a while before he spotted Wormold. "Well I never," he said, "Mr. Wormold, isn't it?" Wormold wondered how he knew his name, for he had forgotten to give him a trade-card. "Eighteen different kinds of Scotch," the stranger said, "including Black Label. And I haven't counted the Bourbons. It's a wonderful sight. Wonderful," he repeated, lowering his voice with respect. "Have you ever seen so many whiskies?"

"As a matter of fact I have. I collect miniatures and I have ninety-nine at home."

"Interesting. And what's your choice today? A Dimpled Haig?"

"Thanks, I've just ordered a daiquiri."

"Can't take those things. They relax me."

"Have you decided on a cleaner yet?" Wormold asked for the sake of conversation.

"Cleaner?"

"Vacuum cleaner. The things I sell."

"Oh, cleaner. Ha-ha. Throw away that stuff and have a Scotch."

"I never drink Scotch before the evening."

"You Southerners!"

"I don't see the connection."

"Makes the blood thin. Sun, I mean. You were born in Nice, weren't you?"

"How do you know that?"

"Oh well, one picks things up. Here and there. Talking to this chap and that. I've been meaning to have a word with you as a matter of fact."

"Well, here I am."

"I'd like it more on the quiet, you know. Chaps keep on coming in and out."

No description could have been less accurate. No one even passed the door in the hard straight sunlight outside. The officer of the Tourist police had fallen contentedly asleep after propping his cigar over an ash-tray; there were no tourists at this hour to protect or to supervise. Wormold said, "If it's about a cleaner, come down to the shop."

"I'd rather not, you know. Don't want to be seen hanging about there. Bar's not a bad place after all. You run into a fellow countryman, have a get-together, what more natural?"

"I don't understand."

"Well, you know how it is."

"I don't."

"Well, wouldn't you say it was natural enough?"

Wormold gave up. He left eighty cents on the counter and said, "I must be getting back to the shop."

"Why?"

"I don't like to leave Lopez for long."

"Ah, Lopez. I want to talk to you about Lopez." Again the explanation that seemed most probable to Wormold was that the stranger was an eccentric inspector from headquarters, but surely he had reached the limit of eccentricity when he added in a low voice, "You go to the Gents and I'll follow you."

"The Gents? Why should I?"

"Because I don't know the way."

In a mad world it always seems simpler to obey. Wormold led the stranger through a door at the back, down a short passage, and indicated the toilet. "It's in there."

"After you, old man."

"But I don't need it."

"Don't be difficult," the stranger said. He put a hand on Wormold's shoulder and pushed him through the door. Inside there were two wash basins, a chair with a broken back, and the usual cabinets and pissoirs. "Take a pew, old man," the stranger said, "while I turn on a tap." But when the water ran he made no attempt to wash. "Looks more natural," he explained (the word "natural" seemed a favourite adjective of his), "if someone barges in. And of course it confuses a mike."

"A mike?"

"You're quite right to question that. Quite right. There probably wouldn't be a mike in a place like this, but it's the drill, you know, that counts. You'll find it always pays in the end to follow the drill. It's lucky they don't run to waste-plugs in Havana. We can just keep the water running."

"Please will you explain?"

"Can't be too careful even in a Gents, when I come to think of it. A chap of ours in Denmark in 1940 saw from his own window the German fleet coming down the Kattegat."

"What gut?"

"Kattegat. Of course he knew then the balloon had gone up. Started burning his papers. Put the ashes down the lav and pulled the chain. Trouble was—late frost. Pipes frozen. All the ashes floated up into the bath down below. Flat belonged to an old maiden lady—Baronin someone or other. She was just going to have a bath. Most embarrassing for our chap."

"It sounds like the Secret Service."

"It *is* the Secret Service, old man, or so the novelists call it. That's why I wanted to talk to you about your chap Lopez. Is he reliable or ought you to fire him?"

"Are you in the Secret Service?"

"If you like to put it that way."

"Why on earth should I fire Lopez? He's been with me ten years."

"We could find you a chap who knew all about vacuum cleaners. But of course—naturally—we'll leave that decision to you."

"But I'm not in your Service."

"We'll come to that in a moment, old man. Anyway we've traced Lopez—he seems clear. But your friend Hasselbacher, I'd be a bit careful of him."

"How do you know about Hasselbacher?"

"I've been around a day or two, picking things up. One has to on these occasions."

"What occasions?"

"Where was Hasselbacher born?"

"Berlin, I think."

"Sympathies East or West?"

"We never talk politics."

"Not that it matters—East or West they play the German game. Remember the Ribbentrop Pact. We won't be caught that way again."

"Hasselbacher's not a politician. He's an old doctor and he's lived here for thirty years."

"All the same, you'd be surprised. . . . But I agree with you, it would be conspicuous if you dropped him. Just play him carefully, that's all. He might even be useful if you handle him right."

"I've no intention of handling him."

"You'll find it necessary for the job."

"I don't want any job. Why do you pick on me?"

"Patriotic Englishman. Been here for years. Respected member of the European Traders' Association. We must have our man in Havana, you know. Submarines need fuel. Dictators drift together. Big ones draw in the little ones."

"Atomic submarines don't need fuel."

"Quite right, old man, quite right. But wars always start a little behind the times. Have to be prepared for conventional weapons too. Then there's economic intelligence—sugar, coffee, tobacco."

"You can find all that in the government yearbooks."

"We don't trust them, old man. Then political intelligence. With your cleaners you've got the entrée everywhere."

"Do you expect me to analyse the fluff?"

"It may seem a joke to you, old man, but the main source of the French intelligence at the time of Dreyfus was a charwoman who collected the scraps out of the wastepaper baskets at the German Embassy."

"I don't even know your name."

"Hawthorne."

"But who are you?"

"Well, you might say I'm setting up the Caribbean network. One moment. Someone's coming. I'll wash. You slip into a closet. Mustn't be seen together."

"We *have* been seen together."

"Passing encounter. Fellow countrymen." He thrust Wormold into the compartment as he had thrust him into the lavatory—"It's the drill, you know"—and then there was silence except for the running tap. Wormold sat down. There was nothing else to do. When he was seated his legs still showed under the half door. A handle turned. Feet crossed the tiled floor towards the pissoir. Water went on running. Wormold felt an enormous bewilderment. He wondered why he had not stopped all this nonsense at the beginning. No wonder Mary had left him. He remembered one of their quarrels. "Why don't you do something, act some way, any way at all? You just stand there. . . ." At least, he thought, this time I'm not standing, I'm sitting. But in any case what could he have said? He hadn't been given time to get a word in. Minutes passed. What enormous bladders Cubans had, and how clean Hawthorne's hands must be getting by this time. The water stopped running. Presumably he was drying his hands, but Wor-

mold remembered there were no towels. That was another problem
for Hawthorne, but he would be up to it. All part of the drill. At
last the feet passed towards the door. The door closed.

"Can I come out?" Wormold asked. It was like a surrender. He
was under orders now.

He heard Hawthorne tip-toeing near. "Give me a few minutes
to get away, old man. Do you know who that was? The policeman. A bit suspicious, eh?"

"He may have recognized my legs under the door. Do you
think we ought to change trousers?"

"Wouldn't look natural," Hawthorne said, "but you are getting
the idea. I'm leaving the key of my room in the basin. Fifth floor
Seville-Biltmore. Just walk up. Ten tonight. Things to discuss.
Money and so on. Sordid issues. Don't ask for me at the desk."

"Don't you need your key?"

"Got a pass key. I'll be seeing you."

Wormold stood up in time to see the door close behind the
elegant figure and the appalling slang. The key was there in the
wash basin—Room 510.

3

At half past nine Wormold went to Milly's room to say good
night. Here, where the duenna was in charge, everything was in
order—the candle had been lit before the statue of St. Seraphina,
the honey-coloured missal lay beside the bed, the clothes were
eliminated as though they had never existed, and a faint smell of
eau de Cologne blew about like incense.

"You've got something on your mind," Milly said. "You aren't
still worrying, are you, about Captain Segura?"

"You never pull my leg, do you, Milly?"

"No. Why?"

"Everybody else seems to."

"Did Mother?"

"I suppose so. In the early days."

"Does Dr. Hasselbacher?"

He remembered the Negro limping slowly by. He said, "Perhaps. Sometimes."

"It's a sign of affection, isn't it?"

"Not always. I remember at school—" He stopped.

"What do you remember, Father?"

"Oh, a lot of things."

Childhood was the germ of all mistrust. You were cruelly joked upon and then you cruelly joked. You lost the remembrance of pain through inflicting it. But somehow, through no virtue of his own, he had never taken that course. Lack of character perhaps. Schools were said to construct character by chipping off the edges. His edges had been chipped, but the result had not, he thought, been character—only shapelessness, like an exhibit in the Museum of Modern Art.

"Are you happy, Milly?" he asked.

"Oh yes."

"At school too?"

"Yes. Why?"

"Nobody pulls your hair now?"

"Of course not."

"And you don't set anyone on fire?"

"That was when I was thirteen," she said with scorn. "What's worrying you, Father?"

She sat up in bed, wearing a white nylon dressing gown. He loved her when the duenna was there, and he loved her even more when the duenna was absent: he couldn't afford the time not to love. It was as if he had come with her a little way on a journey that she would finish alone. The separating years approached them both, like a station down the line, all gain for her and all loss for him. That evening hour was real—but not Hawthorne, mysterious and absurd, not the cruelties of police stations and governments, the scientists who tested the new H-bomb on Christmas Island, Khrushchev who wrote notes: these seemed less real to him than the inefficient tortures of a school dormitory. The small boy with the damp towel whom he had just remembered—where was he now? The cruel come and go like cities and thrones and powers, leaving their ruins behind them. They had no permanence. But the clown whom he had seen last year with Milly at the circus—that clown was permanent, for his act never changed. That was the way to live: the clown was unaffected by the vagaries of public men and the enormous discoveries of the great.

Wormold began to make faces in the glass.

"What on earth are you doing, Father?"

"I wanted to make myself laugh."

Milly giggled. "I thought you were being sad and serious."

"That's why I wanted to laugh. Do you remember the clown last year, Milly?"

"He walked off the end of a ladder and fell in a bucket of whitewash."

"He falls in it every night at ten o'clock. We should all be clowns, Milly. Don't ever learn from experience."

"Reverend Mother says . . ."

"Don't pay any attention to her. God doesn't learn from experience, does He, or how could He hope anything of man? It's the scientists who add the digits and make the same sum who cause the trouble. Newton discovering gravity—he learned from experience and after that . . ."

"I thought it was from an apple."

"It's the same thing. It was only a matter of time before Lord Rutherford went and split the atom. He had learned from experience too, and so did the men of Hiroshima. If only we had been born clowns, nothing bad would happen to us except a few bruises and a smear of whitewash. Don't learn from experience, Milly. It ruins our peace and our lives."

"What are you doing now?"

"I'm trying to waggle my ears. I used to be able to do it. But the trick doesn't work any longer."

"Are you still unhappy about Mother?"

"Sometimes."

"Are you still in love with her?"

"Perhaps. Now and then."

"I suppose she was very beautiful when she was young."

"She can't be old now. Thirty-six."

"That's pretty old."

"Don't you remember her at all?"

"Not very well. She was away a lot, wasn't she?"

"A good deal."

"Of course I pray for her."

"What do you pray? That she'll come back?"

"Oh no, not *that*. We can do without her. I pray that she'll be a good Catholic again."

"I'm not a good Catholic."

"Oh, that's different. You are invincibly ignorant."

"Yes, I expect I am."

"I'm not insulting you, Father. It's only theology. You'll be saved like the good pagans. Socrates, you know, and Cetewayo."

"Who was Cetewayo?"

"He was king of the Zulus."

"What else do you pray?"

"Well, of course, lately I've been concentrating on the horse."
He kissed her good night. She asked, "Where are you going?"

"There are things I've got to arrange about the horse."

"I give you a lot of trouble," she said meaninglessly. Then she
sighed with content, pulling the sheet up to her neck. "It's wonderful, isn't it, how you always get what you pray for?"

Four

1

At every corner there were men who called "Taxi" at him as
though he were a stranger, and all down the Paseo, at intervals of
a few yards, the pimps accosted him automatically without any
real hope. "Can I be of service, sir?" "I know all the pretty girls."
"You desire a beautiful woman." "Postcards?" "You want to see
a dirty movie." They had been mere children when he first came
to Havana, they had watched his car for a nickel, and though they
had aged alongside him they had never got used to him. In their
eyes he never became a resident: he remained a permanent tourist, and so they went pegging along—sooner or later, like all the
others, they were certain that he would want to see Superman
performing at the San Francisco brothel. At least, like the clown,
they had the comfort of not learning from experience.

By the corner of Virdudes Dr. Hasselbacher hailed him from
the Wonder Bar. "Mr. Wormold, where are you off to in such a
hurry?"

"An appointment."

"There is always time for a Scotch." It was obvious from the
way he pronounced Scotch that Dr. Hasselbacher had already had
time for a great many.

"I'm late as it is."

"There's no such thing as late in this city, Mr. Wormold. And I
have a present for you."

Wormold turned in to the bar from the Paseo. He smiled unhappily at one of his own thoughts. "Are your sympathies with the East or the West, Hasselbacher?"

"East or West of what? Oh, you mean *that*. A plague on both."

"What present have you got for me?"

"I asked one of my patients to bring them from Miami," Hasselbacher said. He took from his pocket two miniature bottles of whisky: one was Lord Calvert, the other Old Taylor. "Have you got them?" he asked with anxiety.

"I've got the Calvert, but not the Taylor. It was kind of you to remember my collection, Hasselbacher." It always seemed strange to Wormold that he continued to exist for others when he was not there.

"How many have you got now?"

"A hundred with the Bourbon and the Irish. Seventy-six Scotch."

"When are you going to drink them?"

"Perhaps when they reach two hundred."

"Do you know what I'd do with them if I were you?" Hasselbacher said. "Play checkers. When you take a piece you drink it."

"That's quite an idea."

"A natural handicap," Hasselbacher said. "That's the beauty of it. The better player has to drink more. Think of the finesse. Have another Scotch."

"Perhaps I will."

"I need your help. I was stung by a wasp this morning."

"You are the doctor, not me."

"That's not the point. One hour later, going out on a sick call beyond the airport, I ran over a chicken."

"I still don't understand."

"Mr. Wormold, Mr. Wormold, your thoughts are far away. Come back to earth. We have to find a lottery ticket at once, before the draw. Twenty-seven means a wasp. Thirty-seven a chicken."

"But I have an appointment."

"Appointments can wait. Drink down that Scotch. We've got to hunt for the ticket in the market." Wormold followed him to his car. Like Milly, Dr. Hasselbacher had faith. He was controlled by numbers as she was by saints.

All round the market hung the important numbers in blue and

red. What were called the ugly numbers lay under the counter; they were left for the small fry and the street sellers to dispose of. They were without importance—they contained no significant figure, no number that represented a nun or a cat, a wasp or a chicken. "Look. There's 2 7 4 8 3," Wormold pointed out.

"A wasp is no good without a chicken," said Dr. Hasselbacher. They parked the car and walked. There were no pimps around this market: the lottery was a serious trade uncorrupted by tourists. Once a week the numbers were distributed by a government department, and a politician would be allotted tickets according to the value of his support. He paid eighteen dollars a ticket to the department and he resold to the big merchants for twenty-one dollars. Even if his share were a mere twenty tickets he could depend on a profit of sixty dollars a week. A beautiful number containing omens of a popular kind could be sold by the merchants for anything up to thirty dollars. No such profits, of course, were possible for the little man in the street. With only ugly numbers, for which he had paid as much as twenty-three dollars, he really had to work for a living. He would divide a ticket up into a hundred parts at twenty-five cents a part; he would haunt car parks until he found a car with the same number as one of his tickets (no owner could resist a coincidence like that); he would even search for his numbers in the telephone book and risk a nickel on a call. "Señora, I have a lottery ticket for sale which is the same number as your telephone."

Wormold said, "Look, there's a 37 with a 72."

"Not good enough," Dr. Hasselbacher flatly replied.

Dr. Hasselbacher thumbed through the sheets of numbers which were not considered beautiful enough to be displayed. One never knew; beauty was not beauty to all men; there might be some to whom a wasp was insignificant. A police siren came shrieking through the dark round three sides of the market; a car rocked by. A man sat on the curb with a single number displayed on his shirt like a convict. He said, "The Red Vulture."

"Who's the Red Vulture?"

"Captain Segura, of course," Dr. Hasselbacher said. "What a sheltered life you lead."

"Why do they call him that?"

"He specializes in torture and mutilation."

"Torture?"

"There's nothing here," Dr. Hasselbacher said. "We'd better try Obispo."

"Why not wait till the morning?"

"Last day before the draw. Besides, what kind of cold blood runs in your veins, Mr. Wormold? When fate gives you a lead like this one—a wasp and a chicken—you have to follow it without delay. One must deserve one's good fortune."

They climbed back into the car and made for Obispo. "This Captain Segura," Wormold began.

"Yes?"

"Nothing."

It was eleven o'clock before they found a ticket that satisfied Dr. Hasselbacher's requirements, and then, as the shop which displayed it was closed until the morning, there was nothing to do but have another drink. "Where is your appointment?"

Wormold said, "The Seville-Biltmore."

"One place is as good as another," Dr. Hasselbacher said.

"Don't you think the Wonder Bar . . . ?"

"No, no. A change will be good. When you feel unable to change your bar you have become old."

They groped their way through the darkness of the Seville-Biltmore bar. They were only dimly aware of their fellow guests, who sat crouched in silence and shadow like parachutists gloomily waiting the signal to leap. Only the high proof of Dr. Hasselbacher's spirits could not be quenched.

"You haven't won yet," Wormold whispered, trying to check him, but even a whisper caused a reproachful head to turn towards them in the darkness.

"Tonight I have won," Dr. Hasselbacher said in a loud firm voice. "Tomorrow I may have lost, but nothing can rob me of my victory tonight. A hundred and forty thousand dollars, Mr. Wormold. It is a pity that I am too old for women—I could have made a beautiful woman very happy with a necklace of rubies. Now I am at a loss. How shall I spend my money, Mr. Wormold? Endow a hospital?"

"Pardon me," a voice whispered out of the shadows. "Has this guy really won a hundred and forty thousand bucks?"

"Yes, sir, I have won them," Dr. Hasselbacher said firmly before Wormold could reply. "I have won them as certainly as you exist, my almost unseen friend. You would not exist if I didn't believe you existed—nor would those dollars. I believe, therefore you are."

"What do you mean I wouldn't exist?"

"You exist only in my thoughts, my friend. If I left this room . . ."

"You're nuts."

"Prove you exist, then."

"What do you mean, prove? Of course I exist. I've got a first-class business in real estate; a wife and a couple of kids in Miami. I flew here this morning by Delta. I'm drinking this Scotch, aren't I?" The voice contained a hint of tears.

"Poor fellow," Dr. Hasselbacher said, "you deserve a more imaginative creator than I have been. Why didn't I do better for you than Miami and real estate? Something of imagination. A name to be remembered."

"What's wrong with my name?"

The parachutists at both ends of the bar were tense with disapproval—one shouldn't show nerves before the jump.

"Nothing that I cannot remedy by taking a little thought."

"You ask anyone in Miami about Harry Morgan . . ."

"I really should have done better than that. But I'll tell you what I'll do," Dr. Hasselbacher said, "I'll go out of the bar for a minute and eliminate you. Then I'll come back with an improved version."

"What do you mean, an improved version?"

"Now if my friend, Mr. Wormold here, had invented you, you would have been a happier man. He would have given you an Oxford education, a name like Pennyfeather . . ."

"What do you mean, Pennyfeather? You've been drinking."

"Of course I've been drinking. Drink blurs the imagination. That's why I thought you up in so banal a way: Miami and real estate, flying Delta. Pennyfeather would have come from Europe by K.L.M., he would be drinking his national drink, a pink gin."

"I'm drinking Scotch and I like it."

"You think you're drinking Scotch. Or rather, to be accurate, I have imagined you drinking Scotch. But we're going to change all that," Dr. Hasselbacher said cheerily. "I'll just go out in the hall for a minute and think up some real improvements."

"You can't monkey around with me," the man said with anxiety.

Dr. Hasselbacher drained his drink, laid a dollar on the bar, and rose with uncertain dignity. "You'll thank me for this," he said. "What shall it be? Trust me and Mr. Wormold here. A painter, a poet, or would you prefer a life of adventure—a gun-runner, a secret service agent?"

He bowed from the doorway to the agitated shadow. "I apologize for the real estate."

The voice said nervously, seeking reassurance, "He's drunk or nuts," but the parachutists made no reply.

Wormold said, "Well, I'll be saying good night, Hasselbacher. I'm late."

"The least I can do, Mr. Wormold, is to accompany you and explain how I came to delay you. I'm sure when I tell your friend ·of my good fortune he will understand."

"It's not necessary. It's really not necessary," Wormold said. Hawthorne, he knew, would jump to conclusions. A reasonable Hawthorne, if such existed, was bad enough, but a suspicious Hawthorne . . . his mind boggled at the thought.

He made towards the lift with Dr. Hasselbacher trailing behind. Ignoring a red signal light and a warning *Mind the Step,* Dr. Hasselbacher stumbled. "Oh dear," he said, "my ankle."

"Go home, Hasselbacher," Wormold said with desperation. He stepped into the lift, but Dr. Hasselbacher, putting on a turn of speed, entered too. He said, "There's no pain that money won't cure. It's a long time since I've had such a good evening."

"Sixth floor," Wormold said. "I want to be alone, Hasselbacher."

"Why? Excuse me. I have the hiccups."

"This is a private meeting."

"A lovely woman, Mr. Wormold? You shall have some of my winnings to help you stoop to folly."

"Of course it isn't a woman. It's business, that's all."

"Private business?"

"I told you so."

"What can be so private about a vacuum cleaner, Mr. Wormold?"

"A new agency," Wormold said, and the liftman announced, "Sixth floor."

Wormold was a length ahead and his brain was clearer than Hasselbacher's. The rooms were built like prison cells round a rectangular balcony; on the ground floor two bald heads gleamed upwards like traffic globes. He limped to the corner of the balcony where the stairs were, and Dr. Hasselbacher limped after him, but Wormold was practised in limping. "Mr. Wormold," Dr. Hasselbacher called, "Mr. Wormold, I'd be happy to invest a hundred thousand of my dollars. . . ."

Wormold got to the bottom of the stairs while Dr. Hasselbacher was still manoeuvring the first step; 510 was close by. He unlocked the door. A small table lamp showed him an empty sitting room. He closed the door very softly—Dr. Hasselbacher had not yet reached the bottom of the stairs. He stood listening and heard Dr. Hasselbacher's hop, skip, and hiccup pass the door and recede. Wormold thought: I feel like a spy, I behave like a spy. This is absurd. What am I going to say to Hasselbacher in the morning?

The bedroom door was closed and he began to move towards it. Then he stopped. Let sleeping dogs lie. If Hawthorne wanted him, let Hawthorne find him without his stir; but a curiosity about Hawthorne induced him to make a parting examination of the room.

On the writing desk were two books—identical copies of Lamb's *Tales from Shakespeare*. A memo pad—on which perhaps Hawthorne had made notes for their meeting—read, "1. Salary. 2. Expenses. 3. Transmission. 4. Charles Lamb. 5. Ink." He was just about to open the Lamb when a voice said, "Put up your hands. *Arriba los manos."*

"Las manos," Wormold corrected him. He was relieved to see that it was Hawthorne.

"Oh, it's only you," Hawthorne said.

"I'm a bit late. I'm sorry. I was out with Hasselbacher."

Hawthorne was wearing mauve silk pyjamas with a monogram H. R. H. on the pocket. This gave him a royal air. He said, "I fell asleep and then I heard you moving around." It was as though he had been caught without his slang; he hadn't yet had time to put it on with his clothes. He said, "You've moved the Lamb," accusingly, as though he were in charge of a Salvation Army chapel.

"I'm sorry. I was just looking round."

"Never mind. It shows you have the right instinct."

"You seem fond of that particular book."

"One copy is for you."

"But I've read it," Wormold said, "years ago, and I don't like Lamb."

"It's not meant for reading. Have you never heard of a book-code?"

"As a matter of fact, no."

"In a minute I'll show you how to work it. I keep one copy. All you have to do when you communicate with me is to indicate the page and line where you begin the coding. Of course it's not so hard to break as a machine code, but it's hard enough for the mere Hasselbachers."

"I wish you'd get Dr. Hasselbacher out of your head."

"When we have your office here properly organized, with sufficient security—a combination safe, radio, trained staff, all the gimmicks—then of course we can abandon a primitive code like this, but except for an expert cryptologist it's damned hard to break without knowing the name and edition of the book."

"Why did you choose Lamb?"

"It was the only book I could find in duplicate except *Uncle Tom's Cabin*. I was in a hurry and had to get something at the C.T.S. bookshop in Kingston before I left. Oh, there was something too called *The Lit Lamp: A Manual of Evening Devotion*, but I thought somehow it might look conspicuous on your shelves if you weren't a religious man."

"I am not."

"I brought you some ink as well. Have you got an electric kettle?"

"Yes. Why?"

"For opening letters. We like our men to be equipped against an emergency."

"What's the ink for? I've got plenty of ink at home."

"Secret ink of course. In case you have to send anything by the ordinary mail. Your daughter has a knitting needle, I suppose?"

"She doesn't knit."

"Then you'll have to buy one. Plastic is best. Steel sometimes leaves a mark."

"Mark where?"

"On the envelopes you open."

"Why on earth should I want to open envelopes?"

"It might be necessary for you to examine Dr. Hasselbacher's mail. Of course, you'll have to find a sub-agent in the post office."

"I absolutely refuse . . ."

"Don't be difficult. I'm having traces of him sent out from London. We'll decide about his mail after we've read them. A good tip—if you run short of ink use bird shit, or am I going too fast?"

"I haven't even said I was willing . . ."

"London agrees to $150 a month, with another hundred and fifty as expenses; you'll have to justify those, of course. Payment of sub-agents, et cetera. Anything above that will have to be specially authorized."

"You are going much too fast."

"Free of income tax, you know," Hawthorne said and winked slyly. The wink somehow didn't go with the royal monogram.

"You must give me time. . . ."

"Your code number is 59200 stroke 5." He added with pride, "Of course I am 59200. You'll number your sub-agents 59200 stroke 5 stroke 1 and so on. Got the idea?"

"I don't see how I can possibly be of use to you."

"You are English, aren't you?" Hawthorne said briskly.

"Of course I'm English."

"And you refuse to serve your country?"

"I didn't say that. But the vacuum cleaners take up a great deal of time."

"They are an excellent cover," Hawthorne said. "Very well thought out. Your profession has quite a natural air."

"But it *is* natural."

"Now if you don't mind," Hawthorne said firmly, "we must get down to our Lamb."

2

"Milly," Wormold said, "you haven't taken any cereals."

"I've given up cereals."

"You only took one lump of sugar in your coffee. You aren't going on a diet, are you?"

"No."

"Or doing a penance?"

"No."

"You'll be awfully hungry by lunchtime."

"I've thought of that. I'm going to eat a terrible lot of potatoes."

"Milly, what's going on?"

"I'm going to economize. Suddenly in the watches of the night I realized what an expense I was to you. It was like a voice speaking. I nearly said, 'Who are you?' but I was afraid it would say, 'Your Lord and your God.' I'm about the age, you know."

"Age for what?"

"Voices. I'm older than Saint Thérèse was when she went into the convent."

"Now, Milly, don't tell me you're contemplating . . ."

"No, I'm not. I think Captain Segura's right. He said I wasn't the right material for a convent."

"Milly, do you know what they call your Captain Segura?"

"Yes. The Red Vulture. He tortures prisoners."

"Does he admit that?"

"Oh, of course with me he's on his best behaviour, but he has a cigarette case made out of human skin. He pretends it's calf—as if I didn't know calf when I see it."

"You must drop him, Milly."

"I shall—slowly, but I have to arrange my stabling first. And that reminds me of the voice."

"What did the voice say?"

"It said—only it sounded much more apocalyptic in the middle of the night—'You've bitten off more than you can chew, my girl. What about the Country Club?' "

"What about the Country Club?"

"It's the only place where I can get any real riding, and we aren't members. What's the good of a horse in a stable? Of course Captain Segura is a member, but I knew you wouldn't want me to depend on him. So I thought perhaps if I could help you to cut the housekeeping by fasting . . ."

"What good . . . ?"

"Well, then, you might be able to afford to take a family membership. You ought to enter me as Seraphina. It somehow sounds more suitable than Milly."

It seemed to Wormold that all she said had a quality of sense; it was Hawthorne who belonged to the cruel and inexplicable world of childhood.

INTERLUDE IN LONDON

In the basement of the big steel and concrete building near Maida
Vale a light over a door changed from red to green, and Hawthorne entered. He had left his elegance behind in the Caribbean
and wore a grey flannel suit which had seen better days. At home
he didn't have to keep up appearances; he was part of grey January London.

The Chief sat behind a desk on which an enormous green marble paper weight held down a single sheet of paper. A half-drunk
glass of milk, a bottle of grey pills, and a packet of Kleenex stood
by the black telephone. (The red one was for scrambling.) His
black morning coat, black tie, and black monocle hiding the left
eye gave him the appearance of an undertaker, just as the basement room had the effect of a vault, a mausoleum, a grave.

"You wanted me, sir?"

"Just a gossip, Hawthorne. Just a gossip." It was as though a
mute were gloomily giving tongue after the day's burials were
over. "When did you get back, Hawthorne?"

"A week ago, sir. I'll be returning to Jamaica on Friday."

"All going well?"

"I think we've got the Caribbean sewn up now, sir," Hawthorne said.

"Martinique?"

"No difficulties there, sir. You remember at Fort de France we
are working with the Deuxième Bureau."

"Only up to a point?"

"Oh yes, of course, only up to a point. Haiti was more of a
problem, but 59200 stroke 2 is proving energetic. I was more
uncertain at first about 59200 stroke 5."

"Stroke 5?"

"Our man in Havana, sir. I didn't have much choice there, and at first he didn't seem very keen on the job. A bit stubborn."

"That kind sometimes develops best."

"Yes, sir. I was a little worried too by his contacts. (There's a German called Hasselbacher, but we haven't found any traces of him yet.) However he seems to be going ahead. We got a request for extra expenses just as I was leaving Kingston."

"Always a good sign."

"Yes, sir."

"Shows the imagination is working."

"Yes. He wanted to become a member of the Country Club. Haunt of the millionaires, you know. Best source for political and economic information. The subscription's very high, about ten times the size of White's, but I've allowed it."

"You did right. How are his reports?"

"Well, as a matter of fact, we haven't had any yet, but of course it will take time for him to organize his contacts. Perhaps I rather over-emphasized the need of security."

"You can't. No use having a live wire if it fuses."

"As it happens, he's rather advantageously placed. Very good business contacts—a lot of them with government officials and leading ministers."

"Ah," the Chief said. He took off the black monocle and began to polish it with a piece of Kleenex. The eye that he disclosed was made of glass; pale blue and unconvincing, it might have come out of a doll which said "Mama."

"What's his business?"

"Oh, he imports, you know. Machinery, that sort of thing." It was always important to one's own career to employ agents who were men of good social standing. The petty details on the secret file dealing with the store in Lamparilla Street would never, in ordinary circumstances, reach this basement room.

"Why isn't he already a member of the Country Club?"

"Well, I think he's been rather a recluse of recent years. Bit of domestic trouble."

"Doesn't run after women, I hope?"

"Oh, nothing of that sort, sir. His wife left him. Went off with an American."

"I suppose he's not anti-American? Havana's not the place for any prejudice like that. We have to work with them—only up to a point of course."

"Oh, he's not at all that way, sir. He's a very fair-minded man, very balanced. Took his divorce well and keeps his child in a Catholic school according to his wife's wishes. I'm told he sends her greeting telegrams at Christmas. I think we'll find his reports when they do come in are a hundred per cent reliable."

"Rather touching, that about the child, Hawthorne. Well, give him a prod, so that we can judge his usefulness. If he's all you say he is, we might consider enlarging his staff. Havana could be a key spot. The Communists always go where there's trouble. How does he communicate?"

"I've arranged for him to send reports by the weekly bag to Kingston in duplicate. I keep one and send one to London. I've given him the book code for cables. He sends them through the Consulate."

"They won't like that."

"I've told them it's temporary."

"I would be in favour of establishing a radio unit if he proves to be a good man. He could expand his office staff, I suppose?"

"Oh, of course. At least—you understand it's not a big office, sir. Old-fashioned. You know how these merchant adventurers make do."

"I know the type, Hawthorne. Small scrubby desk. Half a dozen men in an outer office meant to hold two. Out-of-date accounting machines. Woman secretary who is completing forty years with the firm."

Hawthorne now felt able to relax; the Chief had taken charge. Even if one day he read the secret file, the words would convey nothing to him. The small shop for vacuum cleaners had been drowned beyond recovery in the tide of the Chief's literary imagination. Agent 59200/5 was established.

"It's all part of the man's character," the Chief explained to Hawthorne, as though he and not Hawthorne had pushed open the door in Lamparilla Street. "A man who has always learnt to count the pennies and to risk the pounds. That's why he's not a member of the Country Club—nothing to do with the broken marriage. You're a romantic, Hawthorne. Women have come and gone in his life; I suspect they never meant as much to him as his work. The secret of successfully using an agent is to understand him. Our man in Havana belongs—you might say—to the Kipling age. Walking with kings—how does it go?—and keeping your virtue, crowds and the common touch. I expect somewhere in that ink-stained desk of his there's an old penny notebook of black wash leather in which he kept his first accounts—a quarter gross of indiarubbers, six boxes of steel nibs . . ."

"I don't think he goes quite as far back as steel nibs, sir."

The Chief sighed and replaced the black lens. The innocent eye had gone back into hiding at the hint of opposition.

"Details don't matter, Hawthorne," the Chief said with irritation. "But if you are to handle him successfully you'll have to find that penny notebook. I speak metaphorically."

"Yes, sir."

"This business about being a recluse because he lost his wife—it's a wrong appreciation, Hawthorne. A man like that reacts quite differently. He doesn't show his loss, he doesn't wear his heart on his sleeve. If your appreciation were correct why wasn't he a member of the Club before his wife died?"

"She left him."

"Left him? Are you sure?"

"Quite sure, sir."

"Ah, she never found that penny notebook. Find it, Hawthorne, and he's yours for life. What were we talking about?"

"The size of his office, sir. It won't be very easy for him to absorb many in the way of new staff."

"We'll weed out the old ones gradually. Pension off that old secretary of his . . ."

"As a matter of fact . . ."

"Of course this is just speculation, Hawthorne. He may not be the right man after all. Sterling stuff, these old merchant kings, but sometimes they can't see far enough beyond the counting house to be of use to people like ourselves. We'll judge by his first reports, but it's always well to plan a step ahead. Have a word with Miss Jenkinson and see if she has a Spanish-speaker in her pool."

Hawthorne rose in the elevator floor by floor from the basement: a rocket's-eye view of the world. Western Europe sank below him: the Near East: Latin America. The filing cabinets stood around Miss Jenkinson like the pillars of a temple round an ageing oracle. She alone was known by her surname. For some inscrutable reason of security every other inhabitant in the building went by a Christian name. She was dictating to a secretary when Hawthorne entered: "Memo to A.O. Angelica has been transfered to C 5 with an increase of salary to £8 a week. Please see that this increase goes through at once. To anticipate your objections I would point out that Angelica is now approaching the financial level of a bus conductress."

"Yes?" Miss Jenkinson asked sharply. "Yes?"

"The Chief told me to see you."

"I have nobody to spare."

"We don't want anybody at the moment. We're just discussing possibilities."

"Ethel, dear, telephone to D 2 and say I will not have my secretaries kept after seven P.M. except in a national emergency. If a war has broken out or is likely to break out say that the secretaries' pool should have been informed."

"We may be needing a Spanish-speaking secretary in the Caribbean."

"There's no one I can spare," Miss Jenkinson said mechanically.

"Havana—a small station, agreeable climate."

"How big is the staff?"

"At present one man."

"I'm not a marriage bureau," Miss Jenkinson said.

"A middle-aged man with a child of sixteen."

"Married?"

"You could call him that," Hawthorne said vaguely.

"Is he stable?"

"Stable?"

"Reliable, safe, emotionally secure?"

"Oh yes, yes, you may be certain of that. He's one of those old-fashioned merchant types," Hawthorne said, picking up where the Chief had left off. "Built up the business from nothing. Uninterested in women. You might say he'd gone beyond sex."

"No one goes beyond sex," Miss Jenkinson said. "I'm responsible for the girls I send abroad."

"I thought you had nobody available."

"Well," Miss Jenkinson said, "I might possibly, under certain circumstances, let you have Beatrice."

"Beatrice, Miss Jenkinson!" a voice exclaimed from behind the filing cabinets.

"I said Beatrice, Ethel, and I mean Beatrice."

"But, Miss Jenkinson . . ."

"Beatrice needs some practical experience—that is really all that is amiss. The post would suit her. She is not too young. She is fond of children."

"What this station will need," Hawthorne said, "is someone who speaks Spanish. The love of children is not essential."

"Beatrice is half French. She speaks French really better than she does English."

"I said Spanish."

"It's much the same. They're both Latin tongues."

"Perhaps I could see her, have a word with her. Is she fully trained?"

"She's a very good encoder and she's finished a course in microphotography at Ashley Park. Her shorthand is weak, but her typewriting is excellent. She has a good knowledge of electro-dynamics."

"What's that?"

"I'm not sure, but a fuse box holds no terrors for her."

"She'd be good with vacuum cleaners then?"

"She's a secretary, not a domestic help."

A file drawer slammed shut. "Take her or leave her," Miss Jenkinson said. Hawthorne had the impression that she would willingly have referred to Beatrice as "it."

"She's the only one you can suggest?"

"The only one."

Again a file drawer was noisily closed. "Ethel," Miss Jenkinson said, "unless you can relieve your feelings more silently, I shall return you to D 3."

Hawthorne went thoughtfully away; he had the impression that Miss Jenkinson with considerable agility had sold him something she didn't herself believe in—a gold brick or a small dog—bitch, rather.

PART II

One

1

Wormold came away from the Consulate Department carrying a cable in his breast-pocket. It had been shovelled rudely at him, and when he tried to speak he had been checked. "We don't want to know anything about it. A temporary arrangement. The sooner it's over the better we shall be pleased."

"Mr. Hawthorne said . . ."

"We don't know any Mr. Hawthorne. Please bear that in mind. Nobody of the name is employed here. Good morning."

He walked home. The long city lay spread along the open Atlantic; waves broke over the Avenida de Maceo and misted the windscreens of cars. The pink, grey, yellow pillars of what had once been the aristocratic quarter were eroded like rocks; an ancient coat of arms, smudged and featureless, was set over the doorway of a shabby hotel, and the shutters of a night club were varnished in bright crude colors to protect them from the wet and salt of the sea. In the west the steel skyscrapers of the new town rose higher than lighthouses into the clear February sky. It was a city to visit, not a city to live in, but it was the city where Wormold had first fallen in love and he was held to it as though to the scene of a disaster. Time gives poetry to a battlefield, and perhaps Milly resembled a little the flower on an old rampart where an attack had been repulsed with heavy loss many years ago. Women passed him in the street marked on the forehead with ashes as though they had come up into the sunlight from underground. He remembered that it was Ash Wednesday.

In spite of the school holiday Milly was not at home when he reached the house—perhaps she was still at Mass or perhaps she was out riding at the Country Club. Lopez was demonstrating the Turbo Jet Cleaner to a priest's housekeeper who had rejected the Atomic Pile. Wormold's worst fears about the new model had been justified, for he had not succeeded in selling a single specimen. He went upstairs and opened the telegram; it was addressed to a department at the British Consulate, and the figures which followed had an ugly look like the lottery tickets that remained unsold on the last day of a draw. There was 2674 and then a string of five-figure numerals: 42811 79145 72312 59200 80947 62533 10605 and so on. It was his first telegram and he noticed that it was addressed from London. He was not even certain (so long ago his lesson seemed) that he could decode it, but he recognized a single group—59200—which had an abrupt and monitory appearance as though Hawthorne that moment had come accusingly up the stairs. Gloomily he took down Lamb's *Tales from Shakespeare*—how he had always detested Elia and the essay on roast pork. The first group of figures, he remembered, indicated the page, the line, and the word with which the coding began. "Dionysia, the wicked wife of Cleon," he read, "met with an end proportionable to her deserts." He began to decode from "deserts." To his surprise something really did emerge. It was rather as though some strange inherited parrot had begun to speak. "Number 1 of January 24. Following from 59200 begin paragraph A."

After working for three quarters of an hour at adding and subtracting he had decoded the whole message, apart from the final paragraph, where something had gone wrong either with himself or 59200, or perhaps with Charles Lamb. "Following from 59200 begin paragraph A nearly a month since membership Country Club approved and no repeat no information concerning proposed sub agents yet received stop trust you are not repeat not recruiting any sub agents before having them properly traced stop begin paragraph B economic and political report on lines of questionnaire left with you should be despatched forthwith to 59200 stop begin paragraph C cursed galloon must be forwarded kingston primary tubercular message ends."

The last paragraph had an effect of angry incoherence which worried Wormold. For the first time it occurred to him that in their eyes—whoever *they* were—he had taken money and given nothing in return. This troubled him. It had seemed to him till then that he had been the recipient of an eccentric gift which had enabled Milly to ride at the Country Club and himself to order from England a few books he had coveted. The rest of the money was now on deposit in the bank; he half believed that some day he might be in a position to return it to Hawthorne.

He thought: I must do something—give them some names to trace, recruit an agent, keep them happy. He remembered how Milly used to play at shops and give him her pocket money for imaginary purchases. One had to play the child's game, but sooner or later Milly always required her money back.

He wondered how one recruited an agent. It was difficult for him to remember exactly how Hawthorne had recruited *him*—except that the whole affair had begun in a lavatory, but surely that was not an essential feature. He decided to begin with a reasonably easy case.

"You called me, Señor Vormell." For some reason the name Wormold was quite beyond Lopez' power of pronunciation, and, as he seemed unable to settle on a satisfactory substitute, it was seldom that Wormold went by the same name twice.

"I want to talk to you, Lopez."

"Si, Señor Vomell."

Wormold said, "You've been with me a great many years now. We trust each other."

Lopez expressed the completeness of his trust with a gesture towards the heart.

"How would you like to earn a little more money each month?"

"Why naturally . . . I was going to speak to you myself, Señor Ommel. I have a child coming. Perhaps twenty pesos?"

"This has nothing to do with the firm. Trade is too bad, Lopez. This will be confidential work, for me personally, you understand."

"Ah yes, señor. Personal services I understand. You can trust me. I am discreet. Of course I will say nothing to the señorita."

"I think perhaps you *don't* understand."

"When a man reaches a certain age," Lopez said, "he no longer wishes to search for a woman himself, he wishes to rest from trouble. He wishes to command, 'Tonight yes, tomorrow night no.' To give his directions to someone he trusts . . ."

"I don't mean anything of the kind. What I was trying to say— well, it had nothing to do . . ."

"You do not need to be embarrassed in speaking to me, Señor Vormole. I have been with you many years."

"You are making a mistake," Wormold said. "I had no intention . . ."

"I understand that for an Englishman in your position places like the San Francisco are unsuitable. Even the Mamba Club."

Wormold knew that nothing he could say would check the eloquence of his assistant now that he had embarked on the great Havana subject; the sexual exchange was not only the chief commerce of the city, but the whole *raison d'être* of a man's life. One sold sex or one bought it—immaterial which, but it was never given away.

"A youth needs variety," Lopez said, "but so too does a man of a certain age. For the youth it is the curiosity of ignorance, for the old it is the appetite which needs to be refreshed. No one can serve you better than I can, because I have studied you, Señor Venell. You are not a Cuban; for you the shape of a girl's bottom is less important than a certain gentleness of behaviour. . . ."

"You have misunderstood me completely," Wormold said.

"The señorita this evening goes to a concert."

"How do you know?"

Lopez ignored the question. "While she is out, I will bring you a young lady to see. If you don't like her, I will bring another."

"You'll do nothing of the sort. Those are not the kind of services I want, Lopez. I want . . . well, I want you to keep your eyes and ears open and report to me . . ."

"On the señorita?"

"Good heavens no."

"Report on what then, Señor Vommold?"

Wormold said, "Well, things like . . ." But he hadn't the faintest idea on what subjects Lopez was capable of reporting. He remembered only a few points in the long questionnaire and none of them seemed suitable: "Possible Communist infiltration in the armed forces. Actual figures of coffee and tobacco production last year." Of course there were the contents of waste-paper baskets in the offices where Lopez serviced the cleaners, but surely even Hawthorne was joking when he spoke of the Dreyfus case—if those men ever joked.

"Like what, señor?"

Wormold said, "I'll let you know later. Go back to the shop now."

2

It was the hour of the daiquiri, and in the Wonder Bar Dr. Hasselbacher was happy with his second Scotch. "You are worrying still, Mr. Wormold?" he said.

"Yes, I am worrying."

"Still the cleaner—the Atomic cleaner?"

"Not the cleaner." He drained his daiquiri and ordered another.

"Today you are drinking very fast."

"Hasselbacher, you've never felt the need of money, have you? But then you have no child."

"Before long you will have no child either."

"I suppose not." The comfort was as cold as the daiquiri. "When that time comes, Hasselbacher, I want us both to be away from here. I don't want Milly woken up by any Captain Segura."

"That I can understand."

"The other day I was offered money."

"Yes?"

"To get information."

"What sort of information?"

"Secret information."

Dr. Hasselbacher sighed. He said, "You are a lucky man, Mr. Wormold. That information is always easy to give."

"Easy?"

"If it is secret enough, you alone know it. All you need is a little imagination, Mr. Wormold."

"They want me to recruit agents. How does one recruit an agent, Hasselbacher?"

"You could invent them too, Mr. Wormold."

"You sound as though you had experience."

"Medicine is my experience, Mr. Wormold. Have you never read the advertisement for secret remedies? A hair tonic confided by the dying chief of a Red Indian tribe. With a secret remedy you don't have to print the formula. And there is something about a secret which makes people believe . . . perhaps a relic of magic. Have you read Sir James Frazer?"

"Have you heard of a book code?"

"Don't tell me too much, Mr. Wormold, all the same. Secrecy

is not my business—I have no child. Please don't invent me as your agent."

"No, I can't do that. These people don't like our friendship, Hasselbacher. They want me to stay away from you. They are tracing you. How do you suppose they trace a man?"

"I don't know. Be careful, Mr. Wormold. Take their money, but don't give them anything in return. You are vulnerable to the Seguras. Just lie and keep your freedom. They don't deserve truth."

"Whom do you mean by they?"

"Kingdoms, republics, powers." He drained his glass. "I must go and look at my culture, Mr. Wormold."

"Is anything happening yet?"

"Thank goodness, no. As long as nothing happens anything is possible, you agree? It is a pity that a lottery is ever drawn. I lose 140,000 dollars a week, and I am a poor man."

"You won't forget Milly's birthday?"

"Perhaps the traces will be bad, and you will not want me to come. But remember, as long as you lie you do no harm."

"I take their money."

"They have no money except what they take from men like you and me."

He pushed open the half-door and was gone. Dr. Hasselbacher never talked in terms of morality; it was outside the province of a doctor.

3

Wormold found a list of Country Club members in Milly's room. He knew where to look for it, between the latest volume of the *Horsewoman's Year Book* and a novel called *White Mare* by Miss "Pony" Traggers. He had joined the Country Club to find suitable agents, and here they all were in double column, over twenty pages of them. His eye caught an Anglo-Saxon name— Vincent C. Parkman; perhaps this was Earl's father. It seemed to Wormold that it was only right to keep the Parkmans in the family.

By the time he sat down to encode he had chosen two other names—an Engineer Cifuentes and a Professor Luis Sanchez. The professor, whoever he was, seemed a reasonable candidate for economic intelligence, the engineer could provide technical information, and Mr. Parkman political. With the *Tales from Shakespeare* open before him (he had chosen, for his key passage, "May that which follows be happy") he encoded "Number 1 of January 25 paragraph A begins I have recruited my assistant and assigned him the symbol 59200/5/1 stop proposed payment fifteen pesos a month stop paragraph B begins please trace the following . . ."

All this paragraphing seemed to Wormold extravagant of time and money, but Hawthorne had told him it was part of the drill, just as Milly had insisted that all purchases from her shop should be wrapped in paper, even a single glass bead. "Paragraph C begins economic report as requested will follow shortly by bag."

There was nothing to do now but wait for the replies and to prepare the economic report. This troubled him. He had sent Lopez out to buy all the Government papers he could obtain on the sugar and tobacco industries—it was Lopez' first mission, and each day now he spent hours reading the local papers in order to mark any passages which could suitably be used by the professor or the engineer; it was unlikely that anyone in Kingston or London studied the daily papers of Havana. Even he found a new world in those badly printed pages; perhaps in the past he had depended too much on the *New York Times* or *Herald Tribune* for his picture of the world. Round the corner from the Wonder Bar a girl had been stabbed to death, "A martyr for love." Havana was full of martyrs of one kind or another. A man lost a fortune in one night at the Tropicana, climbed on the stage, embraced a coloured singer, then ran his car into the harbour and was drowned. Another man elaborately strangled himself with a pair of braces. There were miracles too; a virgin wept salt tears and a candle lit before Our Lady of Guadalupe burnt inexplicably for one week, from a Friday to a Friday. From this picture of violence and passion and love the victims of Captain Segura were alone excluded—they suffered and died without benefit of press.

The economic report proved to be a tedious chore, for Wormold had never learnt to type with more than two fingers or to use the tabulator on his machine. It was necessary to alter the official statistics in case someone in the head office thought to compare the two reports, and sometimes Wormold forgot he had altered a figure. Addition and subtraction were never his strong points. A decimal point got shifted and had to be chased up and down a dozen columns. It was rather like steering a miniature car in a slot machine.

After a week he began to worry about the absence of replies. Had Hawthorne smelt a rat? But he was temporarily encouraged by a summons to the Consulate, where the sour clerk handed him a sealed envelope addressed for no reason he could understand to "Mr. Luke Penny." Inside the outer envelope was another envelope marked "Henry Leadbetter. Civilian Research Services"; a third envelope was inscribed "59200/5" and contained three months' wages and expenses in Cuban notes. He took them to the bank in Obispo.

"Office account, Mr. Wormold?"

"No. Personal." But he had a sense of guilt as the teller counted; he felt as though he had embezzled his own company's money.

Two

1

Ten days passed and no word reached him. He couldn't even send his economic report until the notional agent who supplied it had been traced and approved. The time had arrived for his annual visit to retailers outside Havana, at Matanzas, Cienfuegos, Santa Clara, and Santiago. Those towns he was in the habit of visiting by road in his ancient Hillman. Before leaving he sent a cable to Hawthorne. "On pretext of visiting sub-agents for vacuums propose to investigate possibilities for recruitment port of Matanzas, industrial centre Santa Clara, naval headquarters Cienfuegos, and dissident centre Santiago. Calculate expenses of journey fifty dollars a day." He kissed Milly, made her promise to take no lifts in his absence from Captain Segura, and rattled off for a stirrup-cup in the Wonder Bar with Dr. Hasselbacher.

2

Once a year, and always on his tour, Wormold wrote to his younger sister who lived in Northampton. (Perhaps writing to

Mary momentarily healed the loneliness he felt at being away from Milly.) Invariably too he included the latest Cuban postage stamps for his nephew. The boy had begun to collect at the age of six and somehow, with the quick jog trot of time, it slipped Wormold's memory that his nephew was now long past seventeen and had probably given up his collection years ago. In any case he must have been too old for the kind of note Wormold folded around the stamps—it was too juvenile even for Milly and his nephew was her senior by several years.

"Dear Mark," Wormold wrote, "here are some stamps for your collection. It must be quite a big collection by now. I'm afraid these ones are not very interesting. I wish we had birds or beasts or butterflies in Cuba like the nice ones you showed me from Guatemala. Your affectionate uncle. P.S. I am sitting looking at the sea and it is very hot."

To his sister he wrote more explicitly, "I am sitting by the bay in Cienfuegos and the temperature is over 90, though the sun has been down for an hour. They are showing Marilyn Monroe at the cinema, and there is one boat in the harbour called, oddly enough, the *Juan Belmonte*. (Do you remember that winter in Madrid when we went to the bullfight?) The Chief—I think he's the Chief —is sitting at the next table drinking Spanish brandy. There's nothing else for him to do except go to the cinema. This must be one of the quietest ports in the world. Just the pink and yellow street and a few cantinas and the big chimney of a sugar refinery and at the end of a weed-grown path the *Juan Belmonte*. Somehow I wish I could be sailing in it with Milly, but I don't know. Vacuum cleaners are not selling well—electric current is too uncertain in these troubled days. Last night at Matanzas the lights all went out three times—the first time I was in my bath. These are silly things to write all the way to Northampton.

"Don't think I am unhappy. There is a lot to be said for where we are. Sometimes I fear going home to Boots and Woolworths and cafeterias, and I'd be a stranger now even in the White Horse. The Chief has got a girl with him—I expect he has a girl in Matanzas too; he's pouring brandy down her throat as you give a cat medicine. The light here is wonderful just before the sun goes down: a long trickle of gold and the sea-birds are bright patches on the pewter swell. The big white statue in the Paseo which looks in daytime like Queen Victoria is a lump of ectoplasm now. The bootblacks have all packed up their boxes under the armchairs in the pink colonnade: you sit high above the pavement as though on library steps and rest your feet on the back of two little sea horses in bronze that might have been brought here by a Phoenician. Why am I so nostalgic? I suppose because I have a little money saved and soon I must decide to go away forever. I wonder if Milly will be able to settle down in a secretarial-training college in a grey street in north London.

"How is Aunt Alice and the famous wax in her ears? And how is Uncle Edward? Or is he dead now? I've reached the time of life when relatives die unnoticed."

He paid his bill and asked for the name of the Chief Engineer—it had struck him that he must have a few names checked when he got home, to justify his expenses.

3

In Santa Clara his old Hillman lay down beneath him like a tired mule. Something was seriously wrong with its innards—only Milly would have known what. The man at the garage said that the repairs would take several days, and Wormold decided to go on to Santiago by coach. Perhaps in any case it was quicker and safer that way, for in the Oriente Province, where the usual rebels held the mountains and government troops the roads and cities, blocks were frequent and buses were less liable to delay than private cars.

He arrived at Santiago in the evening, the empty, dangerous hours of the unofficial curfew. All the shops in the piazza built against the cathedral façade were closed. A single couple hurried across in front of the hotel; the night was hot and humid, and the greenery hung dark and heavy in the pallid light of half-strength lamps. In the reception office they greeted him with suspicion as though they assumed him to be a spy of one kind or another. He felt like an impostor, for this was a hotel of real spies, real police informers, and real rebel agents. A drunk man talked endlessly in the drab bar—as though he were saying in the style of Gertrude Stein, "Cuba is Cuba is Cuba."

Wormold had for his dinner a dry, flat omelette, stained and dog-eared like an old manuscript, and drank some sour wine. While he ate he wrote on a picture postcard a few lines to Dr. Hasselbacher. Whenever he left Havana he despatched to Milly and Dr. Hasselbacher, and sometimes even to Lopez, bad pictures of bad hotels with a cross against one window, like the cross in a detective story which indicates where the crime has been committed. "Car broken down. Everything very quiet. Hope to be back Thursday." A picture postcard is a symptom of loneliness.

At nine o'clock Wormold set out to find his retailer. He had forgotten how abandoned the streets of Santiago were after dark. Shutters were closed behind the iron grills, and as in an occupied city the houses turned their backs on the passerby. A cinema cast a little light but no customer went in; by law it had to remain open, but no one except a soldier or a policeman was likely to visit it after dark. Down a side street Wormold saw a military patrol go by.

Wormold sat with the retailer in a small hot room; an open door gave onto a patio, a palm tree, and a well-head of wrought iron, but the air outside was as hot as the air within. They sat opposite each other in rocking chairs, rocking towards each other and rocking away, making little currents of air.

Trade was bad—rock rock—nobody was buying electrical goods in Santiago—rock rock—what was the good? rock rock. As though to illustrate the point the electric light went out and they rocked in darkness. Losing the rhythm, their heads came into gentle collision.

"I'm sorry."

"My fault."

Rock rock rock.

Somebody scraped a chair in the patio.

"Your wife?" asked Wormold.

"No. Nobody at all. We are quite alone."

Wormold rocked forward, rocked back, rocked forward again, listening to the furtive movements in the patio.

"Of course." This was Santiago. Any house might contain a man on the run. It was best to hear nothing, and to see nothing was no problem, even when the light came half-heartedly back with a tiny yellow glow on the filament.

On his way to the hotel he was stopped by two policemen. They wanted to know what he was doing out so late.

"It's only ten o'clock," he said.

"What are you doing in the street at ten o'clock?"

"There's no curfew, is there?"

Suddenly, without warning, one of the policemen slapped his face. He felt shock rather than anger. He belonged to the law-abiding class: the police were his natural protectors. He put his hand to his cheek and said, "What in God's name do you think . . . ?" The other policeman with a blow in the back sent him stumbling along the pavement. His hat fell off into the filth of the gutter. He said, "Give me my hat," and felt himself pushed again. He began to say something about the British Consul and they swung him sideways across the road and sent him reeling. This time he landed inside a doorway in front of a desk where a man slept with his head on his arms. He woke up and shouted at Wormold; his mildest expression was "pig."

Wormold said, "I am a British subject, my name is Wormold, my address Havana—Lamparilla 37. My age 45, divorced, and I want to ring up the Consul."

The man who had called him a pig and who carried on his arm the badge of a sergeant told him to show his passport.

"I can't. It's in my brief-case at the hotel."

One of his captors said with satisfaction, "Found on the street without papers."

"Empty his pockets," the sergeant said. They took out his wallet and the picture postcard to Dr. Hasselbacher, which he had forgotten to post, and a miniature whisky bottle, Old Granddad, that he had bought in the hotel bar. The sergeant studied the bottle and the postcard.

He said, "Why do you carry this bottle? What does it contain?"

"What do you suppose?"

"The rebels make grenades out of bottles."

"Surely not such small bottles." The sergeant drew the cork, sniffed, and poured a little on the palm of his hand. "It appears to be whisky," he said and turned to the postcard. He said, "Why have you made a cross on this picture?"

"It's the window of my room."

"Why show the window of your room?"

"Why shouldn't I? It's just—well, it's one of the things one does when travelling."

"Were you expecting a visitor by the window?"

"Of course not."

"Who is Dr. Hasselbacher?"

"An old friend."

"Is he coming to Santiago?"

"No."

"Then why do you want to show him where your room is?"

He began to realize what the criminal class knows so well—the impossibility of explaining anything to a man with power.

He said flippantly, "Dr. Hasselbacher is a woman."

"A woman doctor!" the sergeant exclaimed with disapproval.

"A doctor of philosophy. A very beautiful woman." He made two curves in the air.

"And she is joining you in Santiago?"

"No, no. But you know how it is with a woman, sergeant. They like to know where their man is sleeping."

"You are her lover?" The atmosphere had changed for the better. "That still does not explain your wandering about the streets at night."

"There's no law . . ."

"No law, but prudent people stay at home. Only mischief-makers go out."

"I couldn't sleep for thinking of Emma."

"Who is Emma?"

"Dr. Hasselbacher."

The sergeant said slowly, "There is something wrong here. I can smell it. You are not telling me the truth. If you are in love with Emma, why are you in Santiago?"

"Her husband suspects."

"She has a husband? *No es muy agreable.* Are you a Catholic?"

"No."

The sergeant picked up the postcard and studied it again. "The cross at a bedroom window—that is not very nice, either. How will she explain that to her husband?"

Wormold thought rapidly. "Her husband is blind."

"And that too is not nice. Not nice at all."

"Shall I hit him again?" one of the policemen asked.

"There is no hurry. I must interrogate him first. How long have you known this woman, Emma Hasselbacher?"

"A week."

"A week? Nothing that you say is nice. You are a Protestant and an admirer. When did you meet this woman?"

"I was introduced by Captain Segura."

The sergeant held the postcard suspended in midair. Wormold heard one of the policemen behind him swallow. Nobody said anything for a long while.

"Captain Segura?"

"Yes."

"You know Captain Segura?"

"He is a friend of my daughter."

"So you have a daughter. You are married." He began to say again, "That is not n—" when one of the policemen interrupted him. "He knows Captain Segura."

"How can I tell that you are speaking the truth?"

"You could telephone to him and find out."

"It would take several hours to reach Havana on the telephone."

"I can't leave Santiago at night. I will wait for you at the hotel."

"Or in a cell at the station here."

"I don't think Captain Segura would be pleased."

The sergeant considered the matter for a long time, going through the contents of the wallet while he thought. Then he told one of the men to accompany Wormold back to the hotel and there to examine his passport (in this way the sergeant obviously thought that he was saving face). The two walked back in an embarrassed silence, and it was only when Wormold had lain down that he remembered the postcard to Dr. Hasselbacher was still on the sergeant's desk. It seemed to him to have no importance; he could always send another in the morning. How long it takes to realize in one's life the intricate patterns of which everything—even a picture postcard—can form a part, and the rashness of dismissing anything as unimportant. Three days later Wormold took the bus back to Santa Clara; his Hillman was ready; the road to Havana offered him no problems.

Three

A great many telegrams were waiting for him when he arrived in Havana in the late afternoon. There was also a note from Milly. "What have you been up to? You-know-who" (but he didn't) "very pressing—not in any bad way. Dr. Hasselbacher wants to speak to you urgently. Love. P.S. Riding at Country Club. Seraphina's picture taken by press photographer. Is this fame? Go, bid the soldiers shoot."

Dr. Hasselbacher could wait. Two of the telegrams were marked urgent.

"Number 2 of March 5 paragraph A begins trace of Hasselbacher ambiguous stop use utmost caution in any contact and keep these to minimum message ends."

Vincent C. Parkman was rejected as an agent out of hand. "You are not repeat not to contact him stop probability that he is already employed by American service."

The next telegram—Number 1 of March 4—read coldly: "Please in future as instructed confine each telegram to one subject."

Number 1 of March 5 was more encouraging: "No traces Professor Sanchez and Engineer Cifuentes stop you may recruit them stop presumably men of their standing will require no more than out-of-pocket expenses."

The last telegram was rather an anti-climax. "Following from A.O. recruitment of 59200/5/1"—that was Lopez—"recorded but please note proposed payments below recognized European scale and you should revise to 25 repeat 25 pesos monthly message ends."

Lopez was shouting up the stairs, "It is Dr. Hasselbacher."

"Tell him I'm busy. I'll call him later."

"He says will you come quick. He sounds strange."

Wormold went down to the telephone. Before he could speak he heard an agitated and an old voice—it had never occurred to him before that Dr. Hasselbacher was old. "Please, Mr. Wormold . . ."

"Yes. What is it?"

"Please come to me. Something has happened."

"Where are you?"

"In my apartment."

"What's wrong, Hasselbacher?"

"I can't tell you over the telephone."

"Are you sick . . . hurt?"

"If only that were all," Hasselbacher said. "Please come." In all the years they had known each other, Wormold had never visited Hasselbacher's home. They had met at the Wonder Bar, and on Milly's birthdays in a restaurant, and once Dr. Hasselbacher had visited him in Lamparilla Street when he had a high fever. There had been an occasion too when he had wept in front of

Hasselbacher, sitting on a seat in the Paseo, telling him that Milly's mother had flown away on the morning plane to Miami, but their friendship was safely founded on distance—it was always the closest friendships that were most liable to break. Now he even had to ask Hasselbacher how to find his home.

"You don't know?" Hasselbacher asked in bewilderment.

"No."

"Please come quickly," Hasselbacher said. "I do not wish to be alone."

But speed was impossible at this evening hour. Obispo was a solid block of traffic, and it was half an hour before Wormold reached the undistinguished block in which Hasselbacher lived—twelve storeys high of livid stone. Twenty years ago it had been modern, but the new steel architecture to the west outsoared and outshone it. It belonged to the age of tubular chairs, and a tubular chair was what Wormold saw first when Dr. Hasselbacher let him in. That and an old colour print of some castle on the Rhine.

Dr. Hasselbacher, like his voice, had grown suddenly old. It was not a question of colour; that seamed and sanguine skin could change no more than a tortoise's, and nothing could bleach his hair whiter than the years had already done. It was the expression which had altered; a whole mood of life had suffered violence: Dr. Hasselbacher was no longer an optimist. He said humbly, "It is good of you to come, Mr. Wormold." Wormold remembered the day when the old man had led him away from the Paseo and filled him with drink in the Wonder Bar, talking all the time, cauterizing the pain with alcohol and laughter and irresistible hope. He asked, "What has happened, Hasselbacher?"

"Come inside," Hasselbacher said.

The sitting room was in confusion; it was as though a malevolent child had been at work among the tubular chairs, opening this, upsetting that, smashing and sparing at the dictation of some irrational impulse. A photograph of a group of young men holding beer mugs had been taken from the frame and torn apart; a coloured reproduction of "The Laughing Cavalier" hung still on the wall over the sofa, where one cushion out of three had been ripped open. The contents of a cupboard—old letters and bills—were scattered over the floor and a strand of very fair hair tied with black ribbon lay like a washed-up fish among the debris.

"Why?" Wormold asked.

"This does not matter so much," Hasselbacher said, "but come here."

A small room, which had been converted into a laboratory, was now reconverted into chaos. A gas jet burnt yet among the ruins. Dr. Hasselbacher turned it off. He held up a test tube; the contents were smeared over the sink. He said, "You won't understand. I was trying to make a culture from—never mind. I knew nothing would come of it. It was a dream only." He sat heavily down on a tall tubular adjustable chair, which shortened suddenly under his weight and spilt him on the floor. Somebody always leaves a banana skin on the scene of a tragedy. Hasselbacher got up and dusted his trousers.

"When did it happen?"

"Somebody telephoned to me—a sick call. I felt there was something wrong, but I had to go. I could not risk not going. When I came back there was *this*."

"Who did it?"

"I don't know. A week ago somebody called on me. A stranger. He wanted me to help him. It was not a doctor's job. I said no. He asked me whether my sympathies were with the East or the West. I tried to joke with him. I said they were in the middle." Dr. Hasselbacher said accusingly, "Once a few weeks ago you asked me the same question."

"I was only joking, Hasselbacher."

"I know. Forgive me. The worst thing they do is making all this suspicion." He stared into the sink. "An infantile dream. Of course I know that. Fleming discovered penicillin by an inspired accident. But an accident has to be inspired. An old second-rate doctor would never have an accident like that, but it was no business of theirs—was it?—if I wanted to dream."

"I don't understand. What's behind it? Something political? What nationality was this man?"

"He spoke English like I do, with an accent. Nowadays, all the world over, people speak with accents."

"Have you rung up the police?"

"For all I know," Dr. Hasselbacher said, "he *was* the police."

"Have they taken anything?"

"Yes. Some papers."

"Important?"

"I should never have kept them. They were more than thirty

years old. When one is young one gets involved. No one's life is quite clean, Mr. Wormold. But I thought the past was the past. I was too optimistic. You and I are not like the people here—we have no confessional box where we can bury the bad past."

"You must have some idea. . . . What will they do next?"

"Put me on a card index perhaps," Dr. Hasselbacher said. "They have to make themselves important. Perhaps on the card I will be promoted to atomic scientist."

"Can't you start your experiment again?"

"Oh, yes. Yes, I suppose so. But, you see, I never believed in it and now it has gone down the drain." He let a tap run to clear the sink. "I would only remember all this dirt. That was a dream, this is reality." Something that looked like a fragment of toadstool stuck in the exit pipe. He poked it down with his finger. "Thank you for coming, Mr. Wormold. You are a real friend."

"There is so little I can do."

"You let me talk. I am better already. Only I have this fear because of the papers. Perhaps it was an accident that they have gone. Perhaps I have overlooked them in all this mess."

"Let me help you search."

"No, Mr. Wormold. I wouldn't want you to see something of which I am ashamed."

They had two drinks together in the ruins of the sitting room and then Wormold left. Dr. Hasselbacher was on his knees under the Laughing Cavalier, sweeping below the sofa. Shut in his car Wormold felt guilt nibbling around him like a mouse in a prison cell. Perhaps soon the two of them would grow accustomed to each other and guilt would come to eat out of his hand. People similar to himself had done this—men who allowed themselves to be recruited while sitting in lavatories, who opened hotel doors with other men's keys and received instructions in secret ink and in novel uses for Lamb's *Tales from Shakespeare*. There was always another side to a joke, the side of the victim.

The bells were ringing in Santo Christo, and the doves rose from the roof in the golden evening and circled away over the lottery shops of O'Reilly Street and the banks of Obispo; little boys and girls, almost as indistinguishable in sex as birds, streamed out from the School of the Holy Innocents in their black and white uniforms, carrying their little black satchels. Their age divided them from the adult world of 59200 and their credulity was of a different quality. He thought with tenderness, Milly will

be home soon. He was glad that she could still accept fairy stories
—a virgin who bore a child, pictures that wept or spoke words of
love in the dark. Hawthorne and his kind were equally credulous,
but what they swallowed were nightmares—grotesque stories out
of science fiction.

What was the good of playing a game with half a heart? At
least let him give them something they would enjoy for their
money, something to put on their files better than an economic
report. He wrote a rapid draft: "Number 1 of February 8 paragraph A begins in my recent trip to Santiago I heard reports from
several sources of big military installations under construction in
mountains of Oriente Province stop these constructions too extensive to be aimed at small rebel bands holding out there stop
stories of widespread forest clearance under cover of forest fires
stop peasants from several villages impressed to carry loads of
stone paragraph B begins in bar of Santiago hotel met Spanish
pilot of Cubana air line in advanced stage drunkenness stop he
spoke of observing on flight Havana Santiago large concrete platform too extensive for any building paragraph C 59200/5/3 who
accompanied me to Santiago undertook dangerous mission near
military HQ at Bayamo and made drawings of strange machinery
in transport to forest stop these drawings will follow by bag paragraph D have I your permission to pay him bonus in view of
serious risks of his mission and to suspend work for a time on
economic report in view disquieting and vital nature of these reports from Oriente paragraph E have you any traces Raul Dominguez Cubana pilot whom I propose to recruit as 59200/5/4."

Wormold joyfully encoded. He thought, I never believed I had
it in me. He thought with pride: 59200 stroke 5 knows his job.
His good humour even embraced Charles Lamb. He chose for his
passage page 217, line 12: "But I will draw the curtain and show
the picture. Is it not well done?"

Wormold called Lopez from the shop. He handed him 25 pesos. He said, "This is your first month's pay in advance." He
knew Lopez too well to expect any gratitude for the extra five
pesos, but all the same he was a little taken aback when Lopez
said, "Thirty pesos would be a living wage."

"What do you mean, a living wage? The agency pays you very
well as it is."

"This will mean a great deal of work," Lopez said.

"It will, will it? What work?"

"Personal service."

"What personal service?"

"It must obviously be a great deal of work or you wouldn't pay me twenty-five pesos."

He had never been able to get the better of Lopez in a financial argument.

"I want you to bring me an Atomic Pile from the shop," Wormold said.

"We have only one in the store."

"I want it up here."

Lopez sighed. "Is that a personal service?"

"Yes."

When he was alone Wormold unscrewed the cleaner into its various parts. Then he sat down at his desk and began to make a series of careful drawings. As he sat back and contemplated his sketch of the sprayer detached from the hose-handle of the cleaner—the needle jet, the nozzle, and the telescopic tube, he wondered. Am I perhaps going too far? He realized he had forgotten to indicate the scale. He ruled a line and numbered it off: one inch representing three feet. Then for better measure he drew a little man two inches high below the nozzle. He dressed him neatly in a dark suit, and gave him a bowler hat and an umbrella.

When Milly came home that evening he was still busy, writing his first report with a large map of Cuba spread over his desk.

"What are you doing, Father?"

"I am taking the first step in a new career."

She looked over his shoulder. "Are you becoming a writer?"

"Yes—an imaginative writer."

"Will that earn you a lot of money?"

"A moderate income, Milly, if I set my mind to it and write regularly. I plan to compose an essay like this every Saturday evening."

"Will you be famous?"

"I doubt it. Unlike most writers I shall give all the credit to my ghosts."

"Ghosts?"

"That's what they call those who do the real work while the author takes the pay. In my case I shall do the real work and it will be the ghosts who take the credit."

"But you'll have the pay?"

"Oh, yes."

"Then can I buy a pair of spurs?"

"Certainly."

"Are you feeling all right, Father?"

"I never felt better. What a great sense of release you must have experienced when you set fire to Thomas Earl Parkman, Junior."

"Why do you go on bringing that up, Father? It was years ago."

"Because I admire you for it. Can't you do it again?"

"Of course not. I'm too old. Besides, there are no boys in the senior school. Father, one other thing. Could I buy a hunting flask?"

"Anything you like. Oh, wait. What are you going to put in it?"

"Lemonade."

"Be a good girl and fetch me a new sheet of paper. Engineer Cifuentes is a man of many words."

"Had a good flight?" the Chief asked.

"A bit bumpy over the Azores," Hawthorne said. On this occasion he had not had time to change from his pale-grey tropical suit—the summons had come to him urgently in Kingston and a car had met him at London Airport. He sat as close to the steam radiator as he could, but sometimes he couldn't help a shiver.

"What's that odd flower you're wearing?"

Hawthorne had quite forgotten it. He put his hand up to his lapel.

"It looks as though it had once been an orchid," the Chief said with disapproval.

"Pan American gave it us with our dinner last night," Hawthorne explained. He took out the limp mauve rag and put it in the ash-tray.

"With your dinner? What an odd thing to do," the Chief said. "It can hardly have improved the meal. Personally, I detest orchids. Decadent things. There was someone, wasn't there, who wore green ones?"

"I only put it in my buttonhole so as to clear the dinner tray. There was so little room, what with the champagne and the sweet salad and the tomato soup and the chicken Maryland and ice cream . . ."

"What a terrible mixture. You should travel B.O.A.C."

"You didn't give me enough time, sir, to get a booking."

"Well, the matter is rather urgent. You know our man in Havana has been turning out some pretty disquieting stuff lately."

"He's a good man," Hawthorne said.

"I don't deny it. I wish we had more like him. What I can't

understand is how the Americans have not tumbled to anything there."

"Have you asked them, sir?"

"Of course not. I don't trust their discretion."

"Perhaps they don't trust ours."

The Chief said, "Those drawings—did you examine them?"

"I'm not very knowledgeable that way, sir. I sent them straight on."

"Well, take a good look at them now."

The Chief spread the drawings over his desk. Hawthorne reluctantly left the radiator and was immediately shaken by a shiver.

"Anything the matter?"

"The temperature was ninety-two yesterday in Kingston."

"Your blood's getting thin. A spell of cold will do you good. What do you think of them?"

Hawthorne stared at the drawings. They reminded him of something. He was touched—he didn't know why—by an odd uneasiness.

"You remember the reports that came with them?" the Chief said. "The source was stroke 3. Who is he?"

"I think that would be Engineer Cifuentes, sir."

"Well, even he was mystified. With all his technical knowledge. These machines were being transported by lorry from the army headquarters at Bayamo to the edge of the forest. Then mules took over. General direction those unexplained concrete platforms."

"What does the Air Ministry say, sir?"

"They are worried, very worried. Interested too, of course."

"What about the atomic research people?"

"We haven't shown them the drawings yet. You know what those fellows are like. They'll criticize points of detail, say the whole thing is unreliable, that the tube is out of proportion or points the wrong way. You can't expect an agent working from memory to get every detail right. I want photographs, Hawthorne."

"That's asking a lot, sir."

"We have got to have them. At any risk. Do you know what Savage said to me? I can tell you, it gave me a very nasty nightmare. He said that one of the drawings reminded him of a giant vacuum cleaner."

"A vacuum cleaner!" Hawthorne bent down and examined the drawings again, and the cold struck him.

"Makes you shiver, doesn't?"

"But that's impossible, sir." He felt as though he were pleading for his own career. "It couldn't be a vacuum cleaner, sir. Not a vacuum cleaner."

"Fiendish, isn't it?" the Chief said. "The ingenuity, the simplicity, the devilish imagination of the thing." He removed his black monocle and his baby-blue eye caught the light and made it jig on the wall over the radiator. "See this one here—six times the height of a man. Like a gigantic spray. And this—what does this remind you of?"

Hawthorne said unhappily, "A two-way nozzle."

"What's a two-way nozzle?"

"You sometimes find them with a vacuum cleaner."

"Vacuum cleaner again. Hawthorne, I believe we may be on to something so big that the H-bomb will become a conventional weapon."

"Is that desirable, sir?"

"Of course it's desirable. Nobody worries about conventional weapons."

"What have you in mind, sir?"

"I'm no scientist," the Chief said, "but look at this great tank. It must stand nearly as high as the forest trees. A huge gaping mouth at the top, and this pipe-line—the man's only indicated it. For all we know it may extend for miles—from the mountains to the sea, perhaps. You know the Russians are said to be working on some idea—something to do with the power of the sun, sea evaporation—I don't know what it's all about, but I do know this thing is Big. Tell our man we must have photographs."

"I don't quite see how he can get near enough. . . ."

"Let him charter a plane and lose his way over the area. Not himself personally, of course, but stroke 3 or stroke 2. Who is stroke 2?"

"Professor Sanchez, sir. But he'd be shot down. They have Air Force planes patrolling all that section."

"They have, have they?"

"To spot for rebels."

"So they say. Do you know, I've got a hunch, Hawthorne."

"Yes, sir?"

"That the rebels don't exist. They're purely notional. It gives the government all the excuse it needs to shut down a censorship over the area."

"I hope you are right, sir."

"It would be better for all of us," the Chief said with exhilaration, "if I were wrong. I fear these things—I fear them, Hawthorne." He put back his monocle and the light left the wall. "Hawthorne, when you were here last did you speak to Miss Jenkinson about a secretary for 59200 stroke 5?"

"Yes, sir. She had no obvious candidate, but she thought a girl called Beatrice would do."

"Beatrice? How I hate all these Christian names. Fully trained?"

"Yes."

"The time has come to give our man in Havana some help. This is altogether too big for an untrained agent with no assistance. Better send a radio operator with her."

"Wouldn't it be a good thing if I went over first and saw him? I could take a look at things and have a talk with him."

"Bad security, Hawthorne. We can't risk blowing him now. With a radio he can communicate direct with London. I don't like this tie-up with the Consulate nor do they."

"What about his reports, sir?"

"He'll have to organize some kind of courier service to Kingston. One of his travelling salesmen. Send out instructions with the secretary. Have you seen her?"

"No, sir."

"See her at once. Make sure she's the right type. Capable of taking charge on the technical side. You'll have to put her *au fait* with his establishment. His old secretary will have to go. Speak to the A.O. about a reasonable pension until her natural date for retirement."

"Yes, sir," Hawthorne said. "Could I take one more look at those drawings?"

"That one seems to interest you. What's your idea of it?"

"It looks," Hawthorne said miserably, "like a snap-action coupling."

When he was at the door the Chief spoke again. "You know, Hawthorne, we owe a great deal of this to you. I was told once that you were no judge of men, but I backed my private judgment. Well done, Hawthorne."

"Thank you, sir." He had his hand on the door knob.

"Hawthorne."

"Yes, sir?"

"Did you find that penny notebook?"

"No, sir."

"Perhaps Beatrice will."

PART III

One

It was not a night Wormold was ever likely to forget. He had chosen on Milly's seventeenth birthday to take her to the Tropicana. It was a more innocent establishment than the Nacional in spite of the roulette rooms through which visitors passed before they reached the cabaret. Stage and dance floor were open to the sky. Chorus girls paraded twenty feet up among the great palm trees, while pink and mauve searchlights swept the floor. A man in bright blue evening clothes sang in Anglo-American about Paree. Then the piano was wheeled away into the undergrowth, and the dancers stepped down like awkward birds from among the branches.

"It's like the Forest of Arden," Milly said ecstatically. The duenna wasn't there; she had left after the first glass of champagne.

"I don't think there were palms in the Forest of Arden. Or dancing girls."

"You are so literal, Father."

"You like Shakespeare?" Dr. Hasselbacher asked.

"Oh, not Shakespeare—there's far too much poetry. You know the kind of thing—enter a messenger. 'My Lord, the Duke advances on the right.' 'Thus make we with glad heart toward the fight.' "

"Is that Shakespeare?"

"It's like Shakespeare."

"What nonsense you talk, Milly."

"All the same the Forest of Arden is Shakespeare too, I think," Dr. Hasselbacher said.

"Yes, but I only read him in Lamb's *Tales from Shakespeare.*

He cuts out all the messengers and the sub-Dukes and the poetry."

"They give you that at school?"

"Oh no, I found a copy in Father's room."

"You read Shakespeare in that form, Mr. Wormold?" Dr. Hasselbacher asked with some surprise.

"Oh no, no. Of course not. I really bought it for Milly."

"Then why were you so cross the other day when I borrowed it?" Milly said.

"I wasn't cross. It was just that I don't like you poking about . . . among things that don't concern you."

"You talk as though I were a spy."

"Dear Milly, please don't quarrel on your birthday. You are neglecting Dr. Hasselbacher."

"Why are you so silent, Dr. Hasselbacher?" Milly asked, pouring out her second glass of champagne.

"One day you must lend me Lamb's *Tales,* Milly. I too find Shakespeare difficult."

A very small man in a very tight uniform waved his hand towards their table.

"You aren't worried, are you, Dr. Hasselbacher?"

"What should I be worried about, dear Milly, on your birthday? Except about the years, of course."

"Is seventeen so old?"

"For me they have gone too quickly."

The man in the tight uniform stood by their table and bowed. His face had been pocked and eroded like the pillars on the sea front. He carried a chair which was almost as big as himself.

"This is Captain Segura, Father."

"May I sit down?" He inserted himself between Milly and Dr. Hasselbacher without waiting for Wormold's reply. He said, "I am so glad to meet Milly's father." He had an easy rapid insolence you had no time to resent before he had given fresh cause for annoyance. "Introduce me to your friend, Milly."

"This is Dr. Hasselbacher."

Captain Segura ignored Dr. Hasselbacher and filled Milly's glass. He called a waiter. "Bring me another bottle."

"We are just going, Captain Segura," Wormold said.

"Nonsense. You are my guest. It is only just after midnight."

Wormold's sleeve caught a glass. It fell and smashed like the birthday party. "Waiter, another glass." Segura began to sing softly, "The rose I plucked in the garden," leaning towards Milly, turning his back on Dr. Hasselbacher.

Milly said, "You are behaving very badly."

"Badly? To you?"

"To all of us. This is my seventeenth-birthday party, and it's my father's party—not yours."

"Your seventeenth birthday? Then you must certainly be my guests. I'll invite some of the dancers to our table."

"We don't want any dancers," Milly said.

"I am in disgrace?"

"Yes."

"Ah," he said with pleasure, "it was because today I was not outside the school to pick you up. But, Milly, sometimes I have to put police work first. Waiter, tell the conductor to play 'Happy Birthday to You.' "

"Do no such thing," Milly said. "How can you be so—so vulgar?"

"Me? Vulgar?" Captain Segura laughed happily. "She is such a little jester," he said to Wormold. "I like to joke too. That is why we get on so well together."

"She tells me you have a cigarette case made out of human skin."

"How she teases me about that. I tell her that her skin would make a lovely . . ."

Dr. Hasselbacher got up abruptly. He said, "I am going to watch the roulette."

"He doesn't like me?" Captain Segura asked. "Perhaps he is an old admirer, Milly? A very old admirer, ha-ha!"

"He's an old friend," Wormold said.

"But you and I, Mr. Wormold, know that there is no such thing as friendship between a man and a woman."

"Milly is not a woman."

"You speak like a father, Mr. Wormold. No father knows his daughter."

Wormold looked at the champagne bottle and at Captain Segura's head. He was sorely tempted to bring them together. At a table immediately behind the Captain, a young woman whom he had never seen before gave Wormold a grave encouraging nod; he touched the champagne bottle and she nodded again. She must, he thought, be as clever as she was pretty to have read his thoughts so accurately. He was envious of her companions—two pilots from K.L.M. and an air hostess.

"Come and dance, Milly," Captain Segura said, "and show that I am forgiven."

"I don't want to dance."

"Tomorrow I swear I will be waiting at the convent gates."

Wormold made a little gesture, as much as to say, "I haven't the nerve. Help me." The girl watched him seriously; it seemed to him that she was considering the whole of the situation and any decision she reached would be final and call for immediate action. She syphoned some soda into her whisky.

"Come, Milly. You must not spoil my party."

"It's not your party. It's Father's."

"You stay angry so long. You must understand that sometimes I have to put work even before my dear little Milly."

The girl behind Captain Segura altered the angle of the syphon.

"No," Wormold said instinctively, "no." The spout of the syphon was aimed upwards at Captain Segura's neck. The girl's finger was ready for action. He was hurt that anyone so pretty should look at him with such contempt. He said, "Yes. Please. Yes," and she triggered the syphon. The stream of soda hissed off Captain Segura's neck and ran down the back of his collar. Dr. Hasselbacher's voice called "Bravo" from among the tables. Captain Segura exclaimed, "Coño!"

"I'm so sorry," the young woman said. "I meant it for my whisky."

"Your whisky!"

"Dimpled Haig," the girl said. Milly giggled.

Captain Segura bowed stiffly. You could not estimate his danger from his size any more than that of a hard drink.

Dr. Hasselbacher said, "You have finished your syphon, madam, let me find you another." The Dutchmen at the table whispered together uncomfortably.

"I don't think I'm to be trusted with another," the girl said.

Captain Segura squeezed out a smile. It seemed to come from the wrong place, like toothpaste when the tube splits. He said, "For the first time I have been shot in the back. I am glad that it was by a woman." He had made an admirable recovery; the water still dripped from his hair and his collar was limp with it. He said,

"Another time I would have offered you a return match, but I am late at the barracks. I hope I may see you again?"

"I am staying here," she said.

"On holiday?"

"No. Work."

"If you have any trouble with your permit," he said ambiguously, "you must come to me. Good night, Milly. Good night, Mr. Wormold. I will tell the waiter that you are my guests. Order what you wish."

"He made a creditable exit," the girl said.

"It was a creditable shot."

"To have hit him with a champagne bottle might have been a bit exaggerated. Who is he?"

"A lot of people call him the Red Vulture."

"He tortures prisoners," Milly said.

"I seem to have made quite a friend of him."

"I wouldn't be too sure of that," Dr. Hasselbacher said.

They joined their tables together. The two pilots bowed and gave unpronounceable names. Dr. Hasselbacher said with horror to the Dutchmen, "You are drinking Coca-Cola."

"It is the regulation. We take off at three-thirty for Montreal."

Wormold said, "If Captain Segura is going to pay, let's have more champagne. And Coca-Cola."

"I don't think I can drink any more Coca-Cola, can you, Hans?"

"I could drink a Bols," the younger pilot said.

"You can have no Bols," the air hostess told him firmly, "before Amsterdam."

The young pilot whispered to Wormold, "I wish to marry her."

"Who?"

"Miss Pfunk—" or so it sounded.

"Won't she?"

"No."

The elder Dutchman said, "I have a wife and three children." He unbuttoned his breast pocket. "I have their photographs here."

He handed Wormold a coloured card showing a girl in a tight yellow sweater and bathing drawers adjusting her skates. The sweater was marked Mamba Club, and below the picture Wormold read, "We guarantee you a lot of fun. Fifty beautiful girls. You won't be alone."

"I don't think this is the right picture," Wormold said.

The young woman, who had chestnut hair and, as far as he could tell in the confusing Tropicana lights, hazel eyes, said, "Let's dance."

"I'm not very good at dancing."

"It doesn't matter, does it?"

He shuffled her around. She said, "I see what you mean. This is meant to be a rumba. Is that your daughter?"

"Yes."

"She's very pretty."

"Have you just arrived?"

"Yes. The crew were making a night of it, so I joined up with them. I don't know anybody here." Her head reached his chin and he could smell her hair; it touched his mouth as they moved. He was vaguely disappointed that she wore a wedding ring. She said, "My name's Severn. Beatrice Severn."

"Mine's Wormold."

"Then I'm your secretary," she said.

"What do you mean? I have no secretary."

"Oh yes you have. Didn't they tell you I was coming?"

"No." He didn't need to ask who "they" were.

"But I sent the telegram myself."

"There was one last week—but I couldn't make head or tail of it."

"What's your edition of Lamb's *Tales?*"

"Everyman."

"Damn. They gave me the wrong edition. I suppose the telegram *was* rather a mess. Anyway, I'm glad I found you."

"I'm glad too. A bit taken aback of course. Where are you staying?"

"The Inglaterra tonight, and then I thought I'd move in."

"Move in where?"

"To your office, of course. I don't mind where I sleep. I'll just doss down in one of your staff rooms."

"There aren't any. It's a very small office."

"Well, there's a secretary's room anyway."

"But I've never had a secretary, Mrs. Severn."

"Call me Beatrice. It's supposed to be good for security."

"Security?"

"It *is* rather a problem if there isn't even a secretary's room. Let's sit down."

A man—wearing a conventional black dinner jacket among the jungle trees like an English district officer—was singing:

"Sane men surround
 You, old family friends.
 They say the earth is round—
 My madness offends.
 An orange has pips, they say,
 And an apple has rind.
 I say that night is day
 And I've no axe to grind.

 "Please don't believe . . ."

They sat at an empty table at the back of the roulette room. They could hear the hiccup of the little balls. She wore her grave look again, a little self-consciously, like a girl in her first long gown. She said, "If I had known I was your secretary I would never have syphoned that policeman without your telling me."

"You don't have to worry."

"I was really sent here to make things easier for you. Not more difficult."

"Captain Segura doesn't matter."

"You see, I've had a very full training. I've passed in codes and microphotography. I can take over contact with your agents."

"Oh."

"You've done so well they're anxious you should take no risk of being blown. It doesn't matter so much if I'm blown."

"I'd hate to see you blown. Half-blown would be all right."

"I don't understand."

"I was thinking of roses."

She said, "Of course, as that telegram was mutilated, you don't even know about the radio operator."

"I don't."

"He's at the Inglaterra too. Air-sick. We have to find room for him as well."

"If he's air-sick perhaps . . ."

"You can make him assistant accountant. He's been trained for that."

"But I don't need one. I haven't even got a chief accountant."

"Don't worry. I'll get things straight in the morning. That's what I'm here for."

"There's something about you," Wormold said, "that reminds me of my daughter. Do you say novenas?"

"What are they?"

"You don't know? Thank God for that."

The man in the dinner jacket was finishing his song:

"I say that winter's May
And I've no axe to grind."

The lights changed from blue to rose and the dancers went back to perch among the palm trees. The dice rattled at the crap tables, and Milly and Dr. Hasselbacher made their way happily towards the dance floor. It was as though her birthday had been constructed again out of its broken pieces.

Two

1

Next morning Wormold was up early. He had a slight hangover from the champagne, and the unreality of the Tropicana night extended into the office day. Beatrice had told him he was doing well—she was the mouthpiece of Hawthorne and "those people." He had a sense of disappointment at the thought that she, like Hawthorne, belonged to the notional world of his agents. His agents . . .

He sat down before his card index. He had to make his cards look as plausible as possible before she came. Some of the agents seemed to him now to verge on the improbable. Professor Sanchez and Engineer Cifuentes were already deeply committed; he couldn't get rid of them; they had drawn nearly 200 pesos in expenses. Lopez was a fixture too. The drunken pilot of the Cubana Air Line had received a handsome bonus of 500 pesos for the story of the construction in the mountains, but perhaps he could be jettisoned as insecure. There was the Chief Engineer of the *Juan Belmonte* whom he had seen drinking in Cienfuegos; he seemed a probable enough character and he was only drawing 75 pesos a month. But there were other characters who he feared might not bear close inspection: Rodriguez, for example, described on his card as a night-club king, and Teresa, a dancer at the Shanghai Theatre whom he had listed as the mistress simultaneously of the Minister of Defence and of the Director of Posts and Telegraphs (it was not surprising that London had found no trace of either Rodriguez or Teresa). He was ready to jettison Rodriguez, for anyone who came to know Havana well would certainly question his existence sooner or later. But he could not bear to relinquish Teresa. She was his only woman spy—his Mata Hari. It was unlikely that his new secretary would visit the Shanghai, where three pornographic films were shown nightly between nude dances.

Milly sat down beside him. "What are all these cards?" she asked.

"Customers."

"Who was that girl last night?"

"She's going to be my secretary."

"How grand you are getting."

"Do you like her?"

"I don't know. You didn't give me a chance to talk to her. You were too busy dancing and spooning."

"I wasn't spooning."

"Does she want to marry you?"

"Good heavens, no."

"Do you want to marry her?"

"Milly, do be sensible. I only met her last night."

"Marie, a French girl at the convent, says that all true love is a *coup de foudre.*"

"Is that the kind of thing you talk about at the convent?"

"Naturally. It's the future, isn't it? We haven't got a past to talk about, though Sister Agnes has."

"Who is Sister Agnes?"

"I've told you about her. She's the sad and lovely one. Marie says she had an unhappy *coup de foudre* when she was young."

"Did she tell Marie that?"

"No, of course not. But Marie knows. She's had two unhappy *coups de foudre* herself. They came quite suddenly—out of a clear sky."

"I'm old enough to be safe."

"Oh no. There was an old man—he was nearly fifty—who had a *coup de foudre* for Marie's mother. He was married—like you."

"Well, my secretary's married too, so that should be all right."

"Is she really married or a lovely widow?"

"I don't know. I haven't asked her. Do you think she's lovely?"

"Rather lovely. In a way."

Lopez called up the stairs, "There is a lady here. She says you expect her."

"Tell her to come up."

"I'm going to stay," Milly warned him.

"Beatrice, this is Milly."

Her eyes, he noticed, were the same colour as the night before, and so was her hair; it had not, after all, been the effect of the champagne and the palm trees. He thought, She looks real.

"Good morning. I hope you had a good night," Milly said in the voice of the duenna.

"I had terrible dreams." She looked at Wormold and the card index and Milly. She said, "I enjoyed last night."

"You were wonderful with the soda-water syphon," Milly said generously, "Miss . . ."

"Mrs. Severn. But please call me Beatrice."

"Oh, are you married?" Milly asked with phoney curiosity.

"I *was* married."

"Is he dead?"

"Not that I know of. He sort of faded away."

"Oh."

"It does happen with his type."

"What was his type?"

"Milly, it's time you were off. You've no business asking Mrs. Severn—Beatrice . . ."

"At my age," Milly said, "one has to learn from other people's experiences."

"You are quite right. I suppose you'd call his type intellectual and sensitive. I thought he was very beautiful—he had a face like a young fledgling looking out of a nest in one of those nature films, and flufflike feathers round his Adam's apple—a rather large Adam's apple. The trouble was when he got to forty he still looked like a fledgling. Girls loved him. He used to go to UNESCO conferences in Venice and Vienna and places like that. Have you a safe, Mr. Wormold?"

"No."

"What happened?" Milly asked.

"Oh, I got to see through him. I mean literally, not in a nasty

way. He was very thin and concave and he got sort of transparent.
When I looked at him I could see all the delegates sitting there
between his ribs and the chief speaker rising and saying, 'Freedom
is of importance to creative writers.' It was very uncanny at
breakfast."

"And don't you know if he's alive?"

"He was alive last year, because I saw in the papers that he
read a paper on 'The Intellectual and the Hydrogen Bomb' at
Taormina. You ought to have a safe, Mr. Wormold."

"Why?"

"You can't leave things just lying about. Besides, it's expected
of an old-fashioned merchant king like you."

"Who called me an old-fashioned merchant king?"

"It's the impression they have in London. I'll go out and find
you a safe right away."

"I'll be off," Milly said. "You'll be sensible, won't you, Father?
You know what I mean."

2

It proved an exhausting day. First Beatrice went out and pro-
cured a large combination safe, which required a lorry and six
men to transport it. They broke the banisters and a picture while
getting it up the stairs. A crowd collected outside, including several truants from the school next door, two beautiful Negresses,
and a policeman. When Wormold complained that the affair was
making him conspicuous, Beatrice retorted that the way to become really conspicuous was to try to escape notice.

"For example—that syphon," she said. "Everybody will remember me as the woman who syphoned the policeman. Nobody
will ask questions any more about who I am. They have the answer."

While they were still struggling with the safe, a taxi drove up
and a young man got out and unloaded the largest suitcase Wormold had ever seen.

"This is Rudy," Beatrice said.

"Who is Rudy?"

"Your assistant accountant. I told you last night."

"Thank God," Wormold said, "there seems to be something
I've forgotten about last night."

"Come along in, Rudy, and relax."

"It's no earthly use telling him to come in," Wormold said. "Come in where? There's no room for him."

"He can sleep in the office," Beatrice said.

"There isn't enough room for a bed and that safe and my desk."

"I'll get you a smaller desk. How's the air-sickness, Rudy? This is Mr. Wormold, the boss."

Rudy was very young and very pale and his fingers were stained yellow with nicotine or acid. He said, "I vomited twice in the night, Beatrice. They've broken a Roentgen tube."

"Never mind that now. We'll just get the preliminaries fixed. Go off and buy a camp bed."

"Righto," Rudy said and disappeared. One of the Negresses sidled up to Beatrice and said, "I'm British."

"So am I," Beatrice said. "Glad to meet you."

"You the gel who poured water on Captain Segura?"

"Well, more or less. Actually I squirted."

The Negress turned and explained to the crowd in Spanish. Several people clapped. The policeman moved away looking embarrassed. The Negress said, "You very lovely gel, miss."

"You're pretty lovely yourself," Beatrice said. "Give me a hand with this case." They struggled with Rudy's suitcase, pushing and pulling.

"Excuse me," a man said, elbowing through the crowd, "excuse me, please."

"What do you want?" Beatrice asked. "Can't you see we are busy? Make an appointment."

"I only want to buy a vacuum cleaner."

"Oh, a vacuum cleaner. I suppose you'd better go inside. Can you climb over the suitcase?"

Wormold called to Lopez, "Look after him. For goodness' sake, try and sell him an Atomic Pile. We haven't sold one yet."

"Are you going to live here?" the Negress asked.

"I'm going to work here. Thanks a lot for your help."

"We Britishers have to stick together," the Negress said.

The men who had been setting up the safe came downstairs spitting on their hands and rubbing them on their jeans to show how hard it had all been. Wormold tipped them. He went upstairs and looked gloomily at his office. The chief trouble was that there was just room for a camp bed, which robbed him of any excuse. He said, "There's nowhere for Rudy to keep his clothes."

"Rudy's used to roughing it. Anyway there's your desk. You can empty what's in the drawers into your safe and Rudy can keep his things in them."

"I've never used a combination."

"It's perfectly simple. You choose three sets of numbers you can keep in your head. What's your street number?"

"I don't know."

"Well, your telephone number—no, that's not secure. It's the kind of thing a burglar might try. What's the date of your birth?"

"1914."

"And your birthday?"

"December 6."

"Well then let's make it 19–6–14."

"I won't remember that."

"Oh yes, you will. You can't forget your own birthday. Now watch me. You turn the knob anti-clockwise four times, then forward to 19, clockwise three times, then to 6, anti-clockwise twice, forward to 14, whirl it round and it's locked. Now you unlock it the same way—19–6–14—and hey presto, it opens." In the safe was a dead mouse. Beatrice said, "Shop-soiled. I should have got a reduction."

She began to open Rudy's case, pulling out bits and pieces of a radio set, batteries, camera equipment, mysterious tubes wrapped up in Rudy's soiled socks.

Wormold said, "How on earth did you bring all that stuff through the customs?"

"We didn't; 59200 stroke 4 stroke 5 brought it for us from Kingston."

"Who's he?"

"A Creole smuggler. He smuggles in cocaine, opium, and marijuana. Of course he has the customs all lined up. This time they assumed it was his usual cargo."

"It would need a lot of drugs to fill that case."

"Yes. We had to pay rather heavily."

She stowed everything quickly and neatly away after emptying his drawers into the safe. She said, "Rudy's shirts are going to get a bit crushed, but never mind."

"I don't."

"What are these?" she asked, picking up the cards he had been examining.

"My agents."

"You mean you keep them lying about on your desk?"

"Oh, I lock them away at night."

"You haven't got much idea of security, have you?" She looked at a card. "Who is Teresa?"

"She dances naked."

"Quite naked?"

"Yes."

"How interesting for you. London wants me to take over contact with your agents. Will you introduce me to Teresa some time when she's got her clothes on?"

Wormold said, "I don't think she'd work for a woman. You know how it is with these girls."

"I don't. You do. Ah, Engineer Cifuentes. London thinks a lot of him. You can't say he would mind working for a woman."

"He doesn't speak English."

"Perhaps I could learn Spanish. That wouldn't be a bad cover, taking Spanish lessons. Is he as good-looking as Teresa?"

"He's got a very jealous wife."

"Oh, I think I could deal with her."

"It's absurd, of course, because of his age."

"What's his age?"

"Sixty-five. Besides, there's no other woman who would look at him because of his paunch. I'll ask him about the Spanish lessons if you like."

"No hurry. We'll leave it for the moment. I could start with this other one. Professor Sanchez. I got used to intellectuals with my husband."

"He doesn't speak English either."

"I expect he speaks French. My mother was French. I'm bilingual."

"I don't know whether he does or not. I'll find out."

"You know, you oughtn't to have all these names written like this *en clair* on the cards. Suppose Captain Segura investigated you. I'd hate to think of Engineer Cifuentes's paunch being skinned to make a cigarette case. Just put enough details under their symbol to remember them by—59200 stroke 5 stroke 3— jealous wife and paunch. I will write them for you and burn the old ones. Damn. Where are those celluloid sheets?"

"Celluloid sheets?"

"To help burn papers in a hurry. Oh, I expect Rudy put them in his shirts."

"What a lot of knick-knacks you carry around."

"Now we've got to arrange the darkroom."

"I haven't got a darkroom."

"Nobody has, nowadays. I've come prepared. Blackout curtains and a red globe. And a microscope, of course."

"What do we want a microscope for?"

"Microphotography. You see, if there's anything really urgent that you can't put in a telegram, London wants us to communicate direct and save all the time it takes via Kingston. We can send a microphotograph in an ordinary letter. You stick it on as a full stop and they float the letter in water until the dot comes unstuck. I suppose you do write letters home sometimes. Business letters . . . ?"

"I send those to New York."

"Friends and relations?"

"I've lost touch in the last ten years. Except with my sister. Of course I send Christmas cards."

"We mightn't be able to wait till Christmas."

"Sometimes I send postage stamps to a small nephew."

"The very thing. We could put a microphotograph on the back of one of the stamps."

Rudy came heavily up the stairs carrying his camp bed, and the picture frame was broken all over again. Beatrice and Wormold retired into the next room to give him space and sat on Wormold's bed. There was a lot of banging and clanking, and something broke.

"Rudy isn't very good with his hands," Beatrice said. Her gaze wandered. She said, "Not a single photograph. Have you no private life?"

"I don't think I have much. Except for Milly. And Dr. Hasselbacher."

"London doesn't like Dr. Hasselbacher."

"London can go to hell," Wormold said. He suddenly wanted to describe to her the ruin of Dr. Hasselbacher's flat and the destruction of his futile experiments. He said, "It's people like your folk in London . . . I'm sorry. You are one of them."

"So are you."

"Yes, of course. So am I."

Rudy called from the other room, "I've got it fixed."

"I wish you weren't one of them," Wormold said.

"It's a living," she said.

"It's not a real living. All this spying. Spying on what? Secret agents discovering what everybody knows already . . ."

"Or just making it up," she said. He stopped short, and she went on without a change of voice, "There are lots of other jobs that aren't real. Designing a new plastic soapbox, making poker-work jokes for public houses, writing advertising slogans, being an M.P., talking to UNESCO conferences. But the money's real. What happens after work is real. I mean your daughter is real and her seventeenth birthday is real."

"What do you do after work?"

"Nothing much now, but when I was in love . . . we went to cinemas and drank coffee in Espresso bars and sat on summer evenings in the Park."

"What happened?"

"It takes two to keep something real. He was acting all the time. He thought he was the great lover. Sometimes I almost wished he would turn impotent for a while just so that he'd lose his confidence. You can't love and be as confident as he was. If you love you are afraid of losing it, aren't you?" She said, "Oh hell, why am I telling you all this? Let's go and make microphotographs and code cables." She looked through the door. "Rudy's lying on his bed. I suppose he's feeling air-sick again. Can you be air-sick all this while? Haven't you got a room where there isn't a bed? Beds always make one talk." She opened another door. "Table laid for lunch. Cold meat and salad. Two places. Who does all this? A little fairy?"

"A woman comes in for two hours in the morning."

"And the room beyond?"

"That's Milly's. It's got a bed in it too."

Three

1

The situation, whichever way he looked at it, was uncomfortable. Wormold was in the habit now of drawing occasional expenses for Engineer Cifuentes and the professor, and monthly salaries for himself, the chief engineer of the *Juan Belmonte,* and Teresa, the nude dancer. The drunken air pilot was usually paid in whisky. The money Wormold accumulated he put into his deposit account—one day it would make a dowry for Milly. Naturally to justify these payments he had to compose a regular supply of reports. With the help of a large map, the weekly number of *Time* which gave generous space to Cuba in its section on the Western Hemisphere, various economic publications issued by the government, above all with the help of his imagination, he had been able to arrange at least one report a week, and until the arrival of Beatrice he had kept his Saturday evenings free for homework. The professor was the economic authority, and Engineer Cifuentes dealt with the mysterious constructions in the mountains of Oriente (his reports were sometimes confirmed and sometimes contradicted by the Cubana pilot—a contradiction had a flavour of authenticity). The chief engineer supplied descriptions of labour conditions in Santiago, Matanzas, and Cienfuegos and reported on the growth of unrest in the Navy. As for the nude dancer, she supplied spicy details of the private lives and sexual eccentricities of the Defence Minister and the Director of Posts and Telegraphs. Her reports closely resembled articles about film stars in *Confidential,* for Wormold's imagination in this direction was not very strong.

Now that Beatrice was here, Wormold had a great deal more to worry about than his Saturday evening exercises. There was not only the basic training which Beatrice insisted on giving him in microphotography, there were also the cables he had to think up in order to keep Rudy happy, and the more cables Wormold sent the more he received. Every week now London bothered him for photographs of the installations in Oriente, and every week Beatrice became more impatient to take over the contact with his agents. It was against all the rules, she told him, for the head of a station to meet his own sources. Once he took her to dinner at the Country Club and, as bad luck would have it, Engineer Cifuentes was paged. A very tall lean man with a squint rose from a table near by.

"Is that Cifuentes?" Beatrice asked sharply.

"Yes."

"But you told me he was sixty-five."

"He looks young for his age."

"And you said he had a paunch?"

"Not paunch—ponch. It's the local dialect for squint." It was a very narrow squeak.

After that she began to interest herself in a more romantic figure of Wormold's imagination—the pilot of Cubana. She worked enthusiastically to make his entry in the index complete and wanted the most personal details. Raul Dominguez certainly had pathos. He had lost his wife in a massacre during the Spanish civil war and had become disillusioned with both sides, with his Communist friends in particular. The more Beatrice asked Wormold about him, the more his character developed, and the more anxious she became to contact him. Sometimes Wormold felt a twinge of jealousy towards Raul and he tried to blacken the picture. "He gets through a bottle of whisky a day," he said.

"It's his escape from loneliness and memory," Beatrice said. "Don't *you* ever want to escape?"

"I suppose we all do sometimes."

"I know what that kind of loneliness is like," she said with sympathy. "Does he drink all day?"

"No. The worst hour is two in the morning. When he wakes then he can't sleep for thinking, so he drinks instead." It astonished Wormold how quickly he could reply to any questions about his characters; they seemed to live on the dark threshold of consciousness—he had only to turn a light on and there they were, frozen in some characteristic action. Soon after Beatrice arrived, Raul had a birthday and she suggested they should give him a case of champagne.

"He won't touch it," Wormold said—he didn't know why. "He suffers from acidity. If he drinks champagne he comes out in spots. Now the professor on the other hand won't drink anything else."

"An expensive taste."

"A depraved taste," Wormold said without taking any thought. "He prefers Spanish champagne." Sometimes he was scared at the way these people grew in the dark without his knowledge. What was Teresa doing down there, out of sight? He didn't care to think. Her unabashed description of what life was like with her two lovers sometimes shocked him. But the immediate problem was Raul. There were moments when Wormold thought that it might have been easier if he had recruited real agents.

Wormold always thought best in his bath. He was aware one

morning, when he was concentrating hard, of indignant noises; a fist beat on the door a number of times, somebody stamped on the stairs, but a creative moment had arrived and he paid no attention to the world beyond the steam. Raul had been dismissed by the Cubana Air Line for drunkenness. He was desperate; he was without a job; there had been an unpleasant interview between him and Captain Segura, who threatened . . . "Are you all right?" Beatrice called from outside. "Are you dying? Shall I break down the door?"

He wrapped a towel round his middle and emerged into his bedroom, which was now his office.

"Milly went off in a rage," Beatrice said. "She missed her bath."

"This is one of those moments," Wormold said, "which might change the course of history. Where is Rudy?"

"You know you gave him weekend leave."

"Never mind. We'll have to send the cable through the Consulate. Get out the code book."

"It's in the safe. What's the combination? Your birthday—that was it, wasn't it? December 6?"

"I changed it."

"Your birthday?"

"No, no. The combination, of course." He added sententiously, "The fewer who know the combination the better for all of us. Rudy and I are quite sufficient. It's the drill, you know, that counts." He went into Rudy's room and began to twist the knob —four times to the left, three times thoughtfully to the right. His towel kept slipping. "Besides, anyone can find out the date of my birth from my registration card. Most unsafe. The sort of number they'd try at once."

"Go on," Beatrice said, "one more turn."

"This is one nobody could find out. Absolutely secure."

"What are you waiting for?"

"I must have made a mistake. I shall have to start again."

"This combination certainly seems secure."

"Please don't watch. You're fussing me."

Beatrice went and stood with her face to the wall. She said, "Tell me when I can turn round again."

"It's very odd. The damn thing must have broken. Get Rudy on the phone."

"I can't. I don't know where he's staying. He's gone to Veradero Beach."

"Damn!"

"Perhaps if you told me how you remembered the number, if you can call it remembering . . ."

"It was my great-aunt's telephone number."

"Where does she live?"

"Ninety-five Woodstock Road, Oxford."

"Why your great-aunt?"

"Why not my great-aunt?"

"I suppose we could put through a directory inquiry to Oxford."

"I doubt whether they could help."

"What's her name?"

"I've forgotten that too."

"The combination really is secure, isn't it?"

"We always just knew her as Great-Aunt Kate. Anyway she's been dead for fifteen years and the number may have been changed."

"I don't see why you chose her number."

"Don't you have a few numbers that stick in your head all your life for no reason at all?"

"This doesn't seem to have stuck very well."

"I'll remember it in a moment. It's something like 7,7,5,3,9."

"O dear, they would have five numbers in Oxford."

"We could try all the combinations of 77539."

"Do you know how many there are? Somewhere around six hundred, I'd guess. I hope your cable's not urgent."

"I'm certain of everything except the seven."

"That's fine. Which seven? I suppose now we might have to work through about six thousand arrangements. I'm no mathematician."

"Rudy must have it written down somewhere."

"Probably on waterproof paper so that he can take it in with him bathing. We're an efficient office."

"Perhaps," Wormold said, "we had better use the old code."

"It's not very secure. However . . ." They found Charles Lamb at last by Milly's bed; a leaf turned down showed that she was in the middle of *Two Gentlemen of Verona*.

Wormold said, "Take down this cable. Blank of March blank."

"Don't you even know the day of the month?"

"Following from 59200 stroke 5 paragraph A begins 59200 stroke 5 stroke 4 sacked for drunkenness on duty stop fears deportation to Spain where his life is in danger stop."

"Poor old Raul."

"Paragraph B begins 59200 stroke 5 stroke 4 . . ."

"Couldn't I just say 'he'?"

"All right. He. He might be prepared under these circumstances and for reasonable bonus with assured refuge in Jamaica to pilot private plane over secret constructions to obtain photographs stop paragraph C begins he would have to fly on from Santiago and land at Kingston if 59200 can make arrangements for reception stop."

"We really are doing something at last, aren't we?" Beatrice said.

"Paragraph D begins will you authorize five hundred dollars for hire of plane for 59200 stroke 5 stroke 4 stop further two hundred dollars may be required to bribe airport staff Havana stop paragraph E begins bonus to 59200 stroke 5 stroke 4 should be generous as considerable risk of interception by patrolling planes over Oriente mountains stop I suggest one thousand dollars stop."

"What a lot of lovely money," Beatrice said.

"Message ends. Go on. What are you waiting for?"

"I'm just trying to find a suitable phrase. I don't much care for Lamb's *Tales*, do you?"

"Seventeen hundred dollars," Wormold said thoughtfully.

"You should have made it two thousand. The A.O. likes round figures."

"I don't want to seem extravagant," Wormold said. Seventeen hundred dollars would surely cover one year at a finishing school in Switzerland.

"You're looking pleased with yourself," Beatrice said. "Doesn't it occur to you that you may be sending a man to his death?" He thought: That is exactly what I plan to do.

He said, "Tell them at the Consulate that the cable has to have top priority."

"It's a long cable," Beatrice said. "Do you think this sentence will do? 'He presented Polydore and Cadwal to the king, telling him they were his two lost sons, Guiderius and Arviragus.' There are times, aren't there, when Shakespeare is a little dull."

2

A week later he took Beatrice out to supper at a fish restaurant near the harbour. The authorization had come, though they had cut him down by two hundred dollars so that the A.O. got his round figure after all. Wormold thought of Raul driving out to the airport to embark on his dangerous flight. The story was not yet complete. Just as in real life, accidents could happen; a character might take control. Perhaps Raul would be intercepted before embarking; perhaps he would be stopped by a police car on his way. He might disappear into the torture chambers of Captain Segura. No reference would appear in the press. Wormold would warn London that he was going off the air in case Raul was forced to talk. The radio set would be dismantled and hidden after the last message had been sent, the celluloid sheets would be kept ready for a final conflagration. . . . Or perhaps Raul would take off in safety and they would never know what exactly happened to him over the Oriente mountains. Only one thing in the story was certain: he would not arrive in Jamaica and there would be no photographs.

"What are you thinking?" Beatrice asked. He hadn't touched his stuffed langouste.

"I was thinking of Raul." The wind blew up from the Atlantic. Morro Castle lay like a liner gale-bound across the harbour.

"Anxious?"

"Of course I'm anxious." If Raul had taken off at midnight, he would refuel just before dawn in Santiago, where the ground staff were friendly, everyone within the Oriente Province being rebels at heart. Then when it was just light enough for photography and too early for the patrol planes to be up, he would begin his reconnaissance over the mountains and the forest.

"He hasn't been drinking?"

"He promised me he wouldn't. One can't tell."

"Poor Raul."

"Poor Raul."

"He's never had much fun, has he? You should have introduced him to Teresa."

He looked sharply up at her, but she seemed deeply engaged over her langouste.

"That wouldn't have been very secure, would it?"

"Oh, damn security," she said.

After supper they walked back along the landward side of the Avenida de Maceo. There were few people about in the wet windy night and little traffic. The rollers came in from the Atlantic and smashed over the sea wall. The spray drove across the road, over the four traffic lanes, and beat like rain under the pock-marked pillars where they walked. The clouds came racing from the east, and he felt himself to be part of the slow erosion of Havana. Fifteen years was a long time. He said, "One of those lights up there may be him. How solitary he must feel."

"You talk like a novelist," she said.

He stopped under a pillar and watched her with anxiety and suspicion.

"What do you mean?"

"Oh, nothing in particular. Sometimes I think you treat your agents like lay figures, people in a book. It's a real man up there —isn't it?"

"That's not a very nice thing to say about me."

"Oh, forget it. Tell me about someone you really care about. Your wife. Tell me about her."

"She was pretty."

"Do you miss her?"

"Of course. When I think of her."

"I don't miss Peter."

"Peter?"

"My husband. The UNESCO man."

"You're lucky then. You're free." He looked at his watch and the sky. "He should be over Matanzas by now. Unless he's been delayed."

"Have you sent him that way?"

"Oh, of course he decides his own route."

"And his own end?"

Something in her voice—a kind of enmity—startled him again. Was it possible she had begun to suspect him already? He walked quickly on. They passed the Carmen Bar and the Cha Cha Club —bright signs painted on the old shutters of the 18th-century façade. Lovely faces looked out of dim interiors, brown eyes, dark hair, Spanish and high yellow; beautiful buttocks leant against the bars, waiting for any life to come along the sea-wet street. To live in Havana was to live in a factory that turned out human beauty on a conveyor belt. He didn't want beauty. He stopped under a lamp and looked directly back at the direct eyes. He wanted honesty. "Where are we going?"

"Don't you know? Isn't it all planned like Raul's flight?"

"I was just walking."

"Don't you want to sit beside the radio? Rudy's on duty."

"We won't have any news before the early morning."

"You haven't planned a late message then—the crash at Santiago?"

His lips were dry with salt and apprehension. It seemed to him that she must have guessed everything. Would she report him to Hawthorne? What would be "their" next move? They had no legal remedy, but he supposed they could stop his ever returning to England. He thought, She will go back by the next plane—life will be the same as before, and, of course, it was better that way: his life belonged to Milly. He said, "I don't understand what you mean." A great wave had broken against the sea wall of the Avenida, and now it rose like a Christmas tree covered with plastic frost. Then it sank out of sight, and another tree rose farther down the driveway towards the Nacional. He said, "You've been strange all the evening." There was no point in delay: if the game were coming to an end, it was better to close it quickly. He said, "What are you hinting at?"

"You mean there isn't to be a crash at the airport—or on the way?"

"How do you expect me to know?"

"You've been behaving all the evening as if you did. You haven't spoken about him as though he were a living man. You've been writing his elegy like a bad novelist preparing an effect."

The wind knocked them together. She said, "Aren't you ever tired of other people taking risks? For what? For a *Boys' Own Paper* game?"

"You play the game."

"I don't believe in it like Hawthorne does." She said furiously, "I'd rather be a crook than a simpleton or an adolescent. Don't you earn enough with your vacuum cleaners to keep out of all this?"

"No. There's Milly."

"Suppose Hawthorne hadn't walked in on you?"

He joked miserably, "Perhaps I'd have married again for money."

"Would you ever marry again?" She seemed determined to be serious.

"Well," he said, "I don't know that I would. Milly wouldn't consider it a marriage, and one can't shock one's own child. Shall we go home and listen to the radio?"

"But you don't expect a message, do you? You said so."

He said evasively, "Not for another three hours. But I expect he'll radio before he lands." The odd thing was he began to feel the tension. He almost hoped for some message to reach him out of the windy sky.

She said, "Will you promise me that you haven't arranged—anything?"

He avoided answering, turning back towards the President's palace with the dark windows where the President had never slept since the last attempt on his life, and there, coming down the pavement with head bent to avoid the spray, was Dr. Hasselbacher. He was probably on his way home from the Wonder Bar.

"Dr. Hasselbacher," Wormold called to him.

The old man looked up. For a moment Wormold thought he was going to turn tail without a word. "What's the matter, Hasselbacher?"

"Oh, it's you, Mr. Wormold. I was just thinking of you. Talk of the devil—" he said, making a joke of it, but Wormold could have sworn that the devil had scared him.

"You remember Mrs. Severn, my secretary."

"The birthday party, yes, and the syphon. What are you doing up so late, Mr. Wormold?"

"We've been out to supper . . . a walk . . . and you?"

"The same thing."

Out of the vast tossing sky the sound of an engine came spasmodically down, increased, faded again, died out in the noise of wind and sea. Dr. Hasselbacher said, "The plane from Santiago, but it's very late. The weather must be bad in Oriente."

"Are you expecting anyone?" Wormold asked.

"No. No. Not expecting. Would you and Mrs. Severn care to have a drink at my apartment?"

Violence had come and gone. The pictures were back in place, the tubular chairs stood around like awkward guests. The apartment had been reconstructed like a man for burial. Dr. Hasselbacher poured out the whisky.

"It is nice for Mr. Wormold to have a secretary," he said. "Such a short time ago you were worried, I remember. Business was not so good. That new cleaner . . ."

"Things change for no reason."

He noticed for the first time the photograph of a young Dr. Hasselbacher in the dated uniform of an officer in the First World War; perhaps it had been one of the pictures the intruders had taken off the wall. "I never knew you had been in the Army, Hasselbacher."

"I had not finished my medical training, Mr. Wormold, when the war came. It struck me as a very silly business—curing men so that they could be killed sooner. One wanted to cure people so that they could live longer."

"When did you leave Germany, Dr. Hasselbacher?" Beatrice asked.

"In 1934. So I can plead not guilty, young lady. to what you are wondering."

"That was not what I meant."

"You must forgive me then. Ask Mr. Wormold—there was a time when I was not so suspicious. Shall we have some music?"

He put on a record of *Tristan*. Wormold thought of his wife: she was even less real than Raul. She had nothing to do with love and death—only with the *Women's Home Journal*, a diamond engagement ring, twilight sleep. He looked across the room at Beatrice Severn, and she seemed to him to belong to the same world as the fatal drink, the hopeless journey from Ireland, the surrender in the forest. Abruptly Dr. Hasselbacher stood up and pulled the plug from the wall. He said, "Forgive me. I am expecting a call. The music is too loud."

"A sick call?"

"Not exactly." He poured out more whisky.

"Have you started your experiments again, Hasselbacher?"

"No." He looked despairingly around. "I am sorry. There is no more soda water."

"I like it straight," Beatrice said. She went to the bookshelf. "Do you read anything but medical books, Dr. Hasselbacher?"

"Very little. Heine, Goethe. All German. Do you read German, Mrs. Severn?"

"No. But you have a few English books."

"They were given me by a patient instead of a fee. I'm afraid I haven't read them. Here is your whisky, Mrs. Severn."

She came away from the bookcase and took the whisky. "Is that your home, Dr. Hasselbacher?" She was looking at a Victorian coloured lithograph hanging beside young Captain Hasselbacher's portrait.

"I was born there. Yes. It is a very small town, some old walls, a castle in ruins . . ."

"I've been there," Beatrice said, "before the war. My father took us. It's near Leipzig, isn't it?"

"Yes, Mrs. Severn," Dr. Hasselbacher said, watching her bleakly, "it is near Leipzig."

"I hope the Russians left it undisturbed."

The telephone in Dr. Hasselbacher's hall began to ring. He hesitated a moment. "Excuse me, Mrs. Severn," he said. When he went into the hall he shut the door behind him. "East or west," Beatrice said, "home's best."

"I suppose you want to report that to London? But I've known him for fifteen years, he's lived here for more than twenty. He's a good old man, the best friend . . ." The door opened and Dr. Hasselbacher returned. He said, "I'm sorry. I don't feel very well. Perhaps you will come and hear music some other evening." He sat heavily down, picked up his whisky, put it back again. There was sweat on his forehead, but after all it was a humid night.

"Bad news?" Wormold asked.

"Yes."

"Can I help?"

"You!" Dr. Hasselbacher said. "No. *You* can't help. Or Mrs. Severn."

"A patient?"

Dr. Hasselbacher shook his head. He took out his handkerchief and dried his forehead. He said, "Who is not a patient?"

"We'd better go."

"Yes, go. It is like I said. One ought to be able to cure people so that they can live longer."

"I don't understand."

"Was there never such a thing as peace?" Dr. Hasselbacher asked. "I am sorry. A doctor is always supposed to get used to death. But I am not a good doctor."

"Who has died?"

"There has been an accident," Dr. Hasselbacher said. "Just an accident. Of course an accident. A car has crashed on the road near the airport. A young man . . ." He said furiously, "There are always accidents, aren't there, everywhere. And this must surely have been an accident. He was too fond of the glass."

Beatrice said, "Was his name by any chance Raul?"

"Yes," Dr. Hasselbacher said. "That was his name."

PART IV

One

1

Wormold unlocked the door. The street lamp over the way vaguely disclosed the vacuum cleaners standing around like tombs. He started for the stairs. Beatrice whispered, "Stop, stop. I thought I heard . . ." They were the first words either of them had spoken since he had shut the door of Dr. Hasselbacher's apartment.

"What's the matter?"

She put out a hand and clutched some metallic part from the counter; she held it like a club and said, "I'm frightened."

Not half as much as I am, he thought. Can we write human beings into existence? And what sort of existence? Had Shakespeare listened to the news of Duncan's death in a tavern or heard the knocking on his own bedroom door after he had finished the writing of *Macbeth*? He stood in the shop and hummed a tune to keep his courage up.

> *"They say the earth is round—*
> *My madness offends."*

"Quiet," Beatrice said. "Somebody's moving upstairs."

He thought he was afraid only of his own imaginary characters, not of a living person who could creak a board. He ran up and was stopped abruptly by a shadow; he was tempted to call out to all his creations at once and have done with the lot of them—Teresa, the chief, the professor, the engineer.

"How late you are," Milly's voice said. It was only Milly standing there in the passage between the lavatory and her room.

"We went for a walk."

"You brought her back?" Milly asked. "Why?"

Beatrice cautiously climbed the stairs, holding her improvised club on guard.

"Is Rudy awake?"

"I don't think so."

Beatrice said, "If there'd been a message, he would have sat up for you."

If one's characters were alive enough to die, they were surely real enough to send messages. He opened the door of the office. Rudy stirred.

"Any message, Rudy?"

"No."

Milly said, "You've missed all the excitement."

"What excitement?"

"The police were dashing everywhere. You should have heard the sirens. I thought it was a revolution, so I rang up Captain Segura."

"Yes?"

"Someone tried to assassinate someone as he came out of the Ministry of the Interior. He must have thought it was the Minister, only it wasn't. He shot out of a car window and got clean away."

"Who was it?"

"They haven't caught him yet."

"I mean the—the assassinee."

"Nobody important. But he looked like the Minister. Where did you have supper?"

"The Victoria."

"Did you have stuffed langouste?"

"Yes."

"I'm so glad you don't look like the President. Captain Segura said poor Dr. Cifuentes was so scared he went and wet his trousers and then got drunk at the Country Club."

"Dr. Cifuentes?"

"You know—the engineer."

"They shot at him?"

"I told you it was a mistake."

"Let's sit down," Beatrice said. She spoke for both of them.

He said, "The dining room . . ."

"I don't want a hard chair. I want something soft. I may want to cry."

"Well, if you don't mind the bedroom," he said doubtfully, looking at Milly.

"Did you know Dr. Cifuentes?" Milly asked Beatrice sympathetically.

"No. I only know he has a ponch."

"What's a ponch?"

"Your father said it was a dialect word for a squint."

"He told you that? Poor Father," Milly said, "you are in deep waters."

"Look, Milly, will you please go to bed? Beatrice and I have work to do."

"Work?"

"Yes, work."

"It's awfully late for work."

"He's paying me overtime," Beatrice said.

"Are you learning all about vacuum cleaners?" Milly asked. "That thing you are holding is a sprayer."

"Is it? I just picked it up in case I had to hit someone."

"It's not well suited for that," Milly said. "It has a telescopic tube."

"What if it has?"

"It might telescope at the wrong moment."

"Milly, please . . ." Wormold said. "It's nearly two."

"Don't worry. I'm off. And I shall pray for Dr. Cifuentes. It's no joke to be shot at. The bullet went right through a brick wall. Think of what it could have done to Dr. Cifuentes."

"Pray for someone called Raul too," Beatrice said. "They got *him.*"

Wormold lay down flat on the bed and shut his eyes. "I don't understand a thing," he said. "Not a thing. It's a coincidence. It must be."

"They're getting rough—whoever they are."

"But why?"

"Spying is a dangerous profession."

"But Cifuentes hadn't really . . . I mean he wasn't important."

"Those constructions in Oriente are important. Your agents seem to have a habit of getting blown. I wonder how. I think you'll have to warn Professor Sanchez and the girl."

"The girl?"

"The nude dancer."

"But how?" He couldn't explain to her he had no agents, that he had never met Cifuentes or Dr. Sanchez, that neither Teresa nor Raul even existed; Raul had come alive only in order to be killed.

"What did Milly call this?"

"A sprayer."

"I've seen something like it before somewhere."

"I expect you have. Most vacuum cleaners have them." He took it away from her. He couldn't remember whether he had included it in the drawings he had sent to Hawthorne.

"What do I do now, Beatrice?"

"I think your people should go into hiding for a while. Not here, of course. It would be too crowded and anyway not safe. What about that chief engineer of yours—could he smuggle them on board?"

"He's away at sea on the way to Cienfuegos."

"Anyway he's probably blown too," she said thoughtfully. "I wonder why they've let you and me get back here."

"What do you mean?"

"They could easily have shot us down on the front. Or perhaps they're using us for bait. Of course you throw away the bait if it's no good."

"What a macabre woman you are."

"Oh, no. We're back into the *Boy's Own Paper* world, that's all. You can count yourself lucky."

"Why?"

"It might have been the *Sunday Mirror*. The world is modelled after the popular magazines nowadays. My husband came out of *Encounter*. The question we have to consider is to which paper *they* belong."

"They?"

"Let's assume they belong to the *Boy's Own Paper* too. Are they Russian agents, German agents, American, what? Cuban very likely. Those concrete platforms must be official, mustn't they? Poor Raul. I hope he died quickly."

He was tempted to tell her everything, but what was "everything"? He no longer knew. Raul had been killed. Hasselbacher said so.

"First the Shanghai Theatre," she said. "Will it be open?"

"The second performance won't be over."

"If the police are not there before us. Of course they didn't use the police against Cifuentes. He was probably too important. In murdering anyone you have to avoid scandal."

"I hadn't thought of it in that light before."

Beatrice turned out the bedside light and went to the window. She said, "Don't you have a back door?"

"No."

"We'll have to change all that," she said airily, as though she were an architect too. "Do you know a nigger with a limp?"

"That will be Joe."

"He's going slowly by."

"He sells dirty postcards. He's going home, that's all."

"He couldn't be expected to follow you with that limp, of course. He may be their tictac man. Anyway, we'll have to risk it. They are obviously making a sweep tonight. Women and children first. The professor can wait."

"But I've never seen Teresa at the theatre. She probably has a different name there."

"You can pick her out, can't you, even without her clothes? Though I suppose we do look a bit the same naked, like the Japanese."

"I don't think you ought to come."

"I must. If one is stopped the other can make a dash for it."

"I meant to the Shanghai. It's not exactly *Boy's Own Paper.*"

"Nor is marriage," she said, "even in UNESCO."

2

The Shanghai was in a narrow street off Zanja surrounded by cheap bars. A board advertised *Posiciones,* and the tickets for some reason were sold on the pavement outside. Perhaps because there was no room for a box office, as the foyer was occupied by a pornographic bookshop for the benefit of those who wanted entertainment during the entr'acte. The black pimps in the street watched them with curiosity. They were not used to European women here.

"It feels far from home," Beatrice said.

The seats all cost one peso twenty-five and there were very few empty ones left in the large hall. The man who showed them the way offered Wormold a packet of pornographic postcards for a peso. When Wormold refused them, he drew a second selection from his pocket.

"Buy them if you want to," Beatrice said. "If it embarrasses you I'll keep my eye on the show."

"There's not much difference," Wormold said, "between the show and the postcards."

The attendant asked if the lady would like a marijuana cigarette.

"*Nein, danke,*" Beatrice said, getting her languages confused.

On both sides of the stage posters advertised clubs in the neighbourhood where the girls were said to be beautiful. A notice in Spanish and bad English forbade the audience to molest the dancers.

"Which is Teresa?" Beatrice asked.

"I think it must be the fat one in the mask," Wormold said at random.

She was just leaving the stage with a heave of her great naked buttocks, and the audience clapped and whistled. Then the lights went down and a screen was lowered. A film began—quite mildly at first. It showed a bicyclist, some woodland scenery, a punctured tire, a chance encounter, a gentleman raising a straw hat; there was a great deal of flicker and fog.

Beatrice sat silent. There was an odd intimacy between them as they watched together this blueprint of love. Similar movements of the body had once meant more to them than anything else the world had to offer. The act of lust and the act of love are the same; it cannot be falsified like a sentiment.

The lights went on. They sat in silence. "My lips are dry," Wormold said.

"I haven't any spit left. Can't we go behind and see Teresa now?"

"There's another film after this and then the dancers come on again."

"I'm not tough enough for another film," Beatrice said.

"They won't let us go behind until the show's over."

"We can wait in the street, can't we? At least we'll know then if we've been followed."

They left as the second film started. They were the only ones to rise, so if somebody had tailed them he was waiting for them in the street, but there was no obvious candidate among the taxi-drivers and the pimps. One man slept against the lamp-post with a lottery number slung askew round his neck. Wormold remembered the night with Dr. Hasselbacher. That was when he had learnt the new use for Lamb's *Tales from Shakespeare*. Poor Hasselbacher had been very drunk. Wormold remembered how he had sat slumped in the lounge when he came down from Hawthorne's room. He said to Beatrice, "How easy is it to break a book-code if once you've got the right book?"

"Not hard for an expert," she said. "Only a question of patience." She went across to the lottery seller and straightened the number. The man didn't wake. She said, "It was difficult to read it sideways."

Had he carried Lamb under his arm, in his pocket, or in his brief-case? Had he laid the book down when he helped Dr. Hasselbacher to rise? He could remember nothing, and such suspicions were ungenerous.

"I thought of a funny coincidence," Beatrice said. "Dr. Hasselbacher reads Lamb's *Tales* in the right edition." It was as though her basic training had included telepathy.

"You saw it in his flat?"

"Yes."

"But he would have hidden it," he protested, "if it meant anything at all."

"Or he wanted to warn you. Remember he brought us back there. He told us about Raul."

"He couldn't have known that he would meet us."

"How do you know?"

He wanted to protest that nothing made sense, that Raul didn't exist, and Teresa didn't exist, and then he thought of how she would pack up and go away and it would be like a story without a purpose.

"People are coming out," Beatrice said.

They found a side door that led to the one big dressing room. The passage was lit by a bare globe that had burned far too many days and nights. The passage was nearly blocked by dustbins and a Negro with a broom was sweeping up scraps of cotton wool stained with face powder, lipstick, and ambiguous things; the place smelled of pear drops. Perhaps after all there would be no one here called Teresa, but he wished that he had not chosen so popular a saint. He pushed a door open and it was like a medieval inferno full of smoke and naked women.

He said to Beatrice, "Don't you think you'd better go home?"

"It's you who need protection here," she said.

Nobody even noticed them. The mask of the fat woman dangled from one ear and she was drinking a glass of wine with one leg up on a chair. A very thin girl with ribs like piano keys was pulling on her stockings. Breasts swayed, buttocks bent, cigarettes half finished fumed in saucers; the air was thick with burning paper. A man stood on a stepladder with a screwdriver, fixing something.

"Where is she?" Beatrice asked.

"I don't think she's here. Perhaps she's sick—or with her lover."

The air flapped warmly round them as someone put on a dress. Little grains of powder settled like ash.

"Try calling her name."

He shouted "Teresa" half-heartedly. Nobody paid any attention. He tried again and the man with the screwdriver looked down at him.

"Pasa algo?" he asked.

Wormold told him in Spanish that he was looking for a girl called Teresa. The man suggested that Maria would do just as well. He pointed his screwdriver at the fat woman.

"What's he saying?"

"He doesn't seem to know Teresa."

The man with the screwdriver sat down on top of the ladder and began to make a speech. He said that Maria was the best woman you could find in Havana. She weighed one hundred and ten kilos with nothing on.

"Obviously Teresa is not here," Wormold explained with relief.

"Teresa. Teresa. What do you want with Teresa?"

"Yes. What do you want with me?" the thin girl demanded, coming forward, holding out one stocking. Her little breasts were the size of pears.

"Who are you?"

"Soy Teresa."

Beatrice said, "Is that Teresa? You said she was fat—like that one with the mask."

"No, no," Wormold said. "That's not Teresa—she's Teresa's sister. *Soy* means sister." He said, "I'll send a message by her." He took the thin girl's arm and moved her a little away. He tried to explain to her in Spanish that she had to be careful.

"Who are you? I don't understand."

"There has been a mistake. It is too long a story. There are people who may try to do you an injury. Please stay at home for a few days. Don't come to the theatre."

"I have to. I meet my clients there."

Wormold took out a wad of money. He said, "Have you relations?"

"I have my mother."

"Go to her."

"But she is in Cienfuegos."

"There is plenty of money there to take you to Cienfuegos." Everybody was listening now. They pressed close around. The man with the screwdriver had come down from the ladder. Wormold saw Beatrice outside the circle; she was pushing closer, trying to make out what he was saying.

The man with the screwdriver said, "That girl belongs to Pedro. You can't take her away like that. You must talk to Pedro first."

"I do not want to go to Cienfuegos," the girl said.

"You will be safe there."

She appealed to the man. "He frightens me. I cannot understand what he wants." She exhibited the pesos. "This is too much money." She appealed to them. "I am a good girl."

"A lot of wheat does not make a bad year," the fat woman said with solemnity.

"Where is your Pedro?" the man asked.

"He is ill. Why does the man give me all this money? I am a good girl. You know that my price is fifteen pesos. I am not a hustler."

"A lean dog is full of fleas," said the fat woman. She seemed to have a proverb for every occasion.

"What's happening?" Beatrice asked.

A voice hissed "Psst, psst!" It was the Negro who had been sweeping the passage. He said *"Policia!"*

"Oh hell," Wormold said, "that tears it. I've got to get you out of here." No one seemed unduly disturbed. The fat woman drained her wine and put on a pair of knickers; the girl who was called Teresa pulled on her second stocking.

"It doesn't matter about me," Beatrice said. "You've got to get *her* away."

"What do the police want?" Wormold asked the man on the ladder.

"A girl," he said cynically.

"I want to get this girl out," Wormold said. "Isn't there some back way?"

"With the police there's always a back way."

"Where?"

"Got fifty pesos to spare?"

"Yes."

"Give them to him. Hi, Miguel," he called to the Negro. "Tell them to stay asleep for three minutes. Now who wants to be treated to freedom?"

"I prefer the police station," the fat woman said. "But one has to be properly clothed." She adjusted her bra.

"Come with me," Wormold said to Teresa.

"Why should I?"

"You don't realize—they want you."

"I doubt it," said the man with the screwdriver. "She's too thin. You had better hurry. Fifty pesos do not last for ever."

"Here, take my coat," Beatrice said. She wrapped it round the shoulders of the girl, who had now two stockings on but nothing else. The girl said, "But I want to stay."

The man slapped her bottom and gave her a push. "You have his money," he said. "Go with him." He herded them into a small and evil toilet and then through a window. They found themselves in the street. A policeman on guard outside the theatre ostentatiously looked elsewhere. A pimp whistled and pointed to Wormold's car. The girl said again, "I want to stay," but Beatrice pushed her into the rear seat and followed her in. "I shall scream," the girl told them and leant out of the window.

"Don't be a fool," Beatrice said, pulling her inside. Wormold got the car started.

The girl screamed but only in a tentative way. The policeman turned and looked in the opposite direction. The fifty pesos seemed to be still effective. They turned right and drove towards the seafront. No car followed them. It was as easy as all that. The girl, now that she had no choice, adjusted the coat for modesty and leant comfortably back. She said, *"Hay mucha corriente."*

"What's she saying?"

"She's complaining of the draught," Wormold said.

"She doesn't seem a very grateful girl. Where's her sister?"

"With the Director of Posts and Telegraphs in Cienfuegos. Of course I could drive her there—we'd arrive by breakfast time. But there's Milly."

"There's more than Milly. You've forgotten Professor Sanchez."

"Surely Professor Sanchez can wait."

"They seem to be acting fast, whoever they are."

"I don't know where he lives."

"I do. I looked him up in the Country Club list before we came."

"You take this girl home and wait there."

They came out onto the front. "You turn left here," Beatrice said.

"I'm taking you home."

"It's better to stay together."

"Milly . . ."

"You don't want to compromise *her,* do you?"

Reluctantly Wormold turned left. "Where to?"

"Vedado," Beatrice said.

3

The skyscrapers of the new town stood up ahead of them like icicles in the moonlight. A great H.H. was stamped on the sky, like the monogram on Hawthorne's pocket, but it wasn't royal either—it only advertised Mr. Hilton. The wind rocked the car, and the spray broke across the traffic lanes and misted the seaward window. The hot night tasted of salt. Wormold swung the car away from the sea. The girl said, *"Hace demasiado calor."*

"What's she saying now?"

"She says it's too hot."

"She's a difficult girl," Beatrice said.

"Better turn down the window again."

"Suppose she screams?"

"Slap her."

They were in the new quarter of Vedado: little cream and white houses owned by rich men. You could tell how rich a man was by the fewness of the floors. Only a millionaire could afford a bungalow on a site that might have held a skyscraper. When Beatrice lowered the window they could smell the flowers. She stopped him by a gate in a high white wall. She said, "I can see lights in the patio. Everything seems all right. I'll guard your precious bit of flesh while you go in."

"He seems to be very wealthy for a professor."

"He's not too rich to charge expenses, according to your accounts."

Wormold said, "Give me a few minutes. Don't go away."

"Am I likely to? You'd better hurry. So far they've only scored one out of three—and a near miss, of course."

He tried the grilled gate. It was not locked. The position was absurd. How was he to explain his presence? "You are an agent of mine without knowing it. You are in danger. You must hide." He didn't even know of what subject Sanchez was a professor.

A short path between two palm trees led to a second grilled gate, and beyond was the little patio where the lights were on. A gramophone was playing softly and two tall figures revolved in silence cheek to cheek. As he limped up the path a concealed alarm bell rang. The dancers stopped and one of them came out on to the path to meet him.

"Who is that?"

"Professor Sanchez?"

"Yes."

They both converged into the area of light. The professor wore a white dinner jacket, his hair was white, he had white morning stubble on his chin, and he carried a revolver in his hand, which he pointed at Wormold. Wormold saw that the woman behind him was very young and very pretty. She stooped and turned off the gramophone.

"Forgive me for calling on you at this hour," Wormold said. He had no idea how he should begin, and he was disquieted by the revolver. Professors ought not to carry revolvers.

"I am afraid I don't remember your face." The professor spoke politely and kept the revolver pointed at Wormold's stomach.

"There's no reason why you should. Unless you have a vacuum cleaner."

"Vacuum cleaner? I suppose I have. Why? My wife would know." The young woman came through from the patio and joined them. She had no shoes on. The discarded shoes stood beside the gramophone like mousetraps. "What does he want?" she asked disagreeably.

"I'm sorry to disturb you, Señora Sanchez."

"Tell him I'm not Señora Sanchez," the young woman said.

"He says he has something to do with vacuum cleaners," the professor said. "Do you think Maria, before she went away . . . ?"

"Why does he come here at one in the morning?"

"You must forgive me," the professor said with an air of embarrassment, "but this *is* an unusual time." He allowed his revolver to move a little off target. "One doesn't as a rule expect visitors . . ."

"You seem to expect them."

"Oh, this—one has to take precautions. You see, I have some very fine Renoirs."

"He's not after the pictures. Maria sent him. You are a spy, aren't you?" the young woman asked fiercely.

"Well, in a way."

The young woman began to wail, beating at her own long slim flanks. Her bracelets jangled and glinted.

"Don't, dear, don't. I'm sure there's an explanation."

"She envies our happiness," the young woman said. "First she sent the Cardinal, didn't she, and now this man . . . Are you a priest?" she asked.

"My dear, of course he's not a priest. Look at his clothes."

"You may be a professor of comparative education," the young woman said, "but you can be deceived by anyone. Are you a priest?" she repeated.

"No."

"What are you?"

"As a matter of fact I sell vacuum cleaners."

"You said you were a spy."

"Well, yes, I suppose in a sense . . ."

"What have you come here for?"

"To warn you."

The young woman gave an odd bitchlike howl. "You see," she said to the professor, "she's threatening us now. First the Cardinal and then . . ."

"The Cardinal was only doing his duty. After all, he's Maria's cousin."

"You're afraid of him. You want to leave me."

"My dear, you know that isn't true." He said to Wormold, "Where is Maria now?"

"I don't know."

"When did you see her last?"

"But I've never seen her."

"You do rather contradict yourself, don't you?"

"He's a lying hound," the young woman said.

"Not necessarily, dear. He's probably employed by some agency. We had better sit down quietly and hear what he has to say. Anger is always a mistake. He's doing his duty—which is more than can be said of us." The professor led the way back to the patio. He had put his revolver back in his pocket. The young woman waited until Wormold began to follow and then brought up the rear like a watchdog. He half expected her to bite his ankle. He thought, Unless I speak soon, I shall never speak.

"Take a chair," the professor said. What *was* comparative education?

"May I give you a drink?"

"Please don't bother."

"You don't drink on duty?"

"Duty!" the young woman said. "You treat him like a human being. What duty has he got except to his despicable employers?"

"I came here to warn you that the police . . ."

"Oh, come, come, adultery is not a crime," the professor said. "I think it has seldom been regarded as that except in the American colonies in the seventeenth century. And in the Mosaic Law, of course."

"Adultery has got nothing to do with it," the young woman said. "She didn't mind us sleeping together, she only minded our being together."

"You can hardly have one without the other—unless you are thinking of the New Testament," the professor said. "Adultery in the heart."

"You have no heart unless you turn this man out. We sit here talking as though we had been married for years. If all you want to do is to sit up all night and talk, why didn't you stick to Maria?"

"My dear, it was your idea to dance before bed."

"You call what you did dancing?"

"I told you that I would take lessons."

"Oh yes, so as to be with the girls at the school."

The conversation seemed to Wormold to be reeling out of sight. He said desperately, "They shot at Engineer Cifuentes. You are in the same danger."

"If I wanted girls, dear, there are plenty at the university. They come to my lectures. No doubt you are aware of that, as you came yourself."

"You taunt me with it?"

"We are straying from the subject, dear. The subject is what action Maria is likely to take next."

"She ought to have given up starchy foods two years ago," the young girl said rather cheaply, "knowing you. You only care for the body. You ought to be ashamed at your age."

"If you don't wish me to love you . . ."

"Love. Love." The young woman began to pace the patio. She made gestures in the air as though she were dismembering love. Wormold said, "It's not Maria you have to worry about."

"You lying hound," she screamed at him. "You said you'd never seen her."

"I haven't."

"Then why do you call her Maria?" she cried and began to do triumphant dance-steps with an imaginary partner.

"You said something about Cifuentes, young man?"

"He was shot at this evening."

"Who by?"

"I don't know exactly, but it's all part of the same round-up. It's a bit difficult to explain, but you really seem to be in great danger, Professor Sanchez. It's all a mistake, of course. The police have been to the Shanghai Theatre too."

"What have I to do with the Shanghai Theatre?"

"What indeed?" cried the young woman melodramatically. "Men," she said, "men! Poor Maria. She hasn't only one woman to deal with. She'll have to plan a massacre."

"I've never had anything to do with anybody at the Shanghai Theatre."

"Maria is better informed. I expect you walk in your sleep."

"You heard what he said—it's a mistake. After all, they shot at Cifuentes. You can't blame her for that."

"Cifuentes? Did he say Cifuentes? Oh, you Spanish oaf. Just because he talked to me one day at the Club while you were in the shower you go and hire desperados to kill him."

"Please, dear, be reasonable. I only heard of it just now when this gentleman . . ."

"He's not a gentleman. He's a lying hound." They had again come full circle in the conversation.

"If he's a liar we need pay no attention to what he says. He's probably slandering Maria too."

"Ah, you would stick up for her."

Wormold said with desperation—it was his last fling—"This has got nothing to do with Maria—with Señora Sanchez, I mean."

"What on earth has Señora Sanchez to do with it?" the professor asked.

"I thought you thought that Maria . . ."

"Young man, you aren't seriously telling me that Maria is planning to do something to my wife as well as to my . . . my friend here? It's too absurd."

Until now the mistake had seemed to Wormold fairly simple to deal with. But now it was as though he had tugged a stray piece of cotton and a whole suit had begun to unwind. Was this comparative education? He said, "I thought I was doing you a favour by coming to warn you, but it looks as if death for you might be the best solution."

"You are a very mystifying young man."

"Not young. It's you, professor, who are young by the look of things." In his anxiety he spoke aloud, "If only Beatrice were here."

The professor said quickly, "I absolutely assure you, dear, that I know nobody called Beatrice. Nobody."

The young woman gave a tigerish laugh.

"You seem to have come here," the professor said, "with the sole purpose of making trouble." It was his first complaint and it seemed a very mild one under the circumstances. "I cannot think what you have to gain by it," he said and walked into the house and closed the door.

"He's a monster," the girl said. "A monster. A sexual monster. A satyr."

"You don't understand."

"I know that tag—to know all is to forgive all. Not in this case it isn't." She seemed to have lost her hostility to Wormold. "Maria, me, Beatrice—I don't count his wife, poor woman. I've got nothing against his wife. Have you a gun?"

"Of course not. I only came here to save him," Wormold said.

"Let them shoot," the young woman said, "in the belly—low down." And she too went into the house with an air of purpose.

There was nothing left for Wormold to do but go. The invisible alarm gave another warning as he walked towards the gate, but no one stirred in the little white house. I've done my best, Wormold thought. The professor seemed well prepared for any danger and perhaps the arrival of the police might be a relief to him. They would be easier to cope with than the young woman.

4

Walking away through the smell of the night-flowering plants he had only one wish—to tell Beatrice everything: I am no secret agent, I'm a fraud, none of these people are my agents, and I don't know what's happening. I'm lost. I'm scared. Surely somehow she would take control of the situation; after all, she was a professional. But he knew that he would not appeal to her. It meant giving up security for Milly. He would rather be eliminated like Raul. Did they, in his service, give pensions to offspring? But who was Raul?

Before he had reached the second gate Beatrice called to him. "Jim. Look out. Keep away." Even at that urgent moment the thought occurred to him, My name is Wormold, Mr. Wormold. Señor Vomel, nobody calls me Jim. Then he ran—hop and skip —towards the voice and came out to the street, to a radio car, to three police officers, and another revolver pointing at his stomach. Beatrice stood on the sidewalk and the girl was beside her, trying to keep a coat closed which hadn't been designed that way.

"What's the matter?"

"I can't understand a word they say."

One of the officers told him to get into their car.

"What about my own?"

"It will be brought to the station." Before he obeyed they felt him down the breast and side for arms. He said to Beatrice, "I don't know what it's all about, but it looks like the end of a bright career." The officer spoke again. "He wants you to get in too."

"Tell him," Beatrice said, "I'm going to stay with Teresa's sister. I don't trust them."

The two cars drove softly away among the little houses of the millionaires, to avoid disturbing anyone, as though they were in a street of hospitals—the rich need sleep. They had not far to go: a courtyard, a gate closing behind them, and then the odour of a police station like the ammoniac smell of all zoos all the world over. Along the whitewashed passage the portraits of wanted men hung, with the spurious look of bearded old masters. In the room at the end Captain Segura sat playing checkers. "Huff," he said, and took two pieces. Then he looked up at them. "Mr. Wormold," he said with surprise, and rose like a small tight green snake from his seat when he saw Beatrice. He looked beyond her at Teresa—the coat had fallen open again, perhaps with intention. He said, "Who in God's name . . . ?" and then to the policeman with whom he had been playing, *"Anda!"*

"What's the meaning of all this, Captain Segura?"

"You are asking me that, Mr. Wormold?"

"Yes."

"I wish you would tell me the meaning. I had no idea I should see you—Milly's father. Mr. Wormold, we had a call from a Professor Sanchez about a man who had broken into his house with vague threats. He thought it had something to do with his pictures —he has very valuable pictures. I sent a radio car at once and it is you they pick up, with the señorita here (we have met before) and a naked tart." Like the police sergeant in Santiago he added, "That is not very nice, Mr. Wormold."

"We had been at the Shanghai."

"That is not very nice either."

"I'm tired of being told by the police that I am not nice."

"Why did you visit Professor Sanchez?"

"That was all a mistake."

"Why do you have a naked tart in your car?"

"We were giving her a lift."

"She has no right to be naked on the streets." The police officer leant across the desk and whispered. "Ah," Captain Segura said. "I begin to understand. There was a police inspection tonight at the Shanghai. I suppose the girl had forgotten her papers and wanted to avoid a night in the cells. She appealed to you . . ."

"It wasn't that way at all."

"It had better be that way, Mr. Wormold." He said to the girl in Spanish, "Your papers. You have no papers."

She said indignantly, *"Sí, yo tengo."* She bent down and pulled pieces of crumpled paper from the top of her stockings. Captain Segura took them and examined them. He gave a deep sigh. "Mr. Wormold, Mr. Wormold, her papers are in order. Why do you drive about the streets with a naked girl? Why do you break into the house of Professor Sanchez and talk to him about his wife and threaten him? What is his wife to you?" He said, "Go," sharply to the girl. She hesitated and began to take off the coat.

"Better let her keep it," Beatrice said.

Captain Segura sat wearily down in front of the draughts board. "Mr. Wormold, for your sake I tell you this: do not get mixed up with the wife of Professor Sanchez. She is not a woman you can treat lightly."

"I am not mixed up . . ."

"Do you play checkers, Mr. Wormold?"

"Yes. Not very well, I'm afraid."

"Better than these pigs in the station, I expect. We must play together sometime, you and I. But in checkers you must move very carefully, just as with the wife of Professor Sanchez." He moved a piece at random on the board and said, "Tonight you were with Dr. Hasselbacher."

"Yes."

"Was that wise, Mr. Wormold?" He didn't look up, moving the pieces here and there, playing against himself.

"Wise?"

"Dr. Hasselbacher has got into strange company."

"I know nothing about that."

"Why did you send him a postcard from Santiago marked with the position of your room?"

"What a lot of unimportant things you know, Captain Segura."

"I have a reason to be interested in you, Mr. Wormold. I don't want to see you involved. What was it that Dr. Hasselbacher wished to tell you tonight? His telephone, you understand, is tapped."

"He wanted to play us a record of *Tristan.*"

"And perhaps to speak of this?" Captain Segura reversed a photograph on his desk—a flashlight picture with the characteristic glare of white faces gathered round a heap of smashed metal which had once been a car. "And this?" A young man's face unflinching in the flashlight; an empty cigarette carton crumpled like his life; a man's foot touching his shoulders.

"Do you know him?"

"No."

Captain Segura depressed a lever and a voice spoke in English from a box on his desk. *"Hullo. Hullo. Hasselbacher speaking."*

"Is anyone with you. H-Hasselbacher?"

"Yes. Friends."

"What friends?"

"If you must know, Mr. Wormold is here."

"Tell him Raul's dead."

"Dead? But you promised . . ."

"You can't always control an accident, H-Hasselbacher." The voice had a slight hesitation before the aspirate.

"You gave me your word . . ."

"The car turned over too many times."

"You said it would be just a warning."

"It is still a warning. Go in and tell h-him that Raul is dead."

The hiss of the tape went on a moment; a door closed.

"Do you still say you know nothing of Raul?" Segura asked.

Wormold looked at Beatrice. She made a slight negative motion of her head. Wormold said, "I give you my word of honour, Segura, that I didn't even know he existed until tonight."

Segura moved a piece. "Your word of honour?"

"My word of honour."

"You are Milly's father. I have to accept it. But stay away from naked women and the professor's wife. Good night, Mr. Wormold."

"Good night."

They had reached the door when Segura spoke again. "And our game of checkers, Mr. Wormold. We won't forget that."

The old Hillman was waiting in the street. Wormold said, "I'll leave you with Milly."

"Aren't you going home?"

"It's too late to sleep now."

"Where are you going? Can't I come with you?"

"I want you to stay with Milly in case of accidents. Did you see that photograph?"

"No."

They didn't speak again before Lamparilla Street. Then Beatrice said, "I wish you hadn't given your word of honour. You needn't have gone as far as that."

"No?"

"Oh, it was professional of you, I can see that. I'm sorry. It's stupid of me. But you are more professional than I ever believed you were." He opened the street door for her and watched her move away among the vacuum cleaners like a mourner in a cemetery.

Two

At the door of Dr. Hasselbacher's apartment house he rang the bell of a stranger on the second floor whose light was on. There was a buzz and the door unlatched. The lift stood ready and he took it up to Dr. Hasselbacher's flat. Dr. Hasselbacher too had apparently not found sleep. A light shone under the crack of the door. Was he alone or was he in conference with the taped voice?

He was beginning to learn the caution and tricks of his unreal trade. There was a tall window on the landing which led to a purposeless balcony too narrow for use. From this balcony he could see a light in the doctor's flat and it was only a long stride from one balcony to another. He took it without looking at the ground below. The curtains were not quite drawn. He peered between.

Dr. Hasselbacher sat facing him wearing an old *pickelhauber* helmet, a breastplate, boots, white gloves—what could only be the ancient uniform of a Uhlan. His eyes were closed and he seemed to be asleep. He was wearing a sword, and he looked like an extra in a film studio. Wormold tapped on the window. Dr. Hasselbacher opened his eyes and stared straight at him.

"Hasselbacher."

The doctor gave a small movement that might have been panic. He tried to whip off his helmet, but the chinstrap prevented him.

"It's me, Wormold."

The doctor came reluctantly forward to the window. His breeches were far too tight. They had been made for a younger man.

"What are you doing there, Mr. Wormold?"

"What are you doing, Hasselbacher?"

The doctor opened the window and let Wormold in. He found that he was in the doctor's bedroom. A big wardrobe stood open and two white suits hung there like the last teeth in an old mouth. Hasselbacher began to take off his gloves. "Have you been to a fancy-dress dance, Hasselbacher?"

Dr. Hasselbacher said in a shamed voice, "You wouldn't understand." He began piece by piece to rid himself of his paraphernalia—first the gloves, then the helmet, then the breastplate, in which Wormold and the furnishings of the room were reflected and distorted like figures in a hall of mirrors. "Why did you come back? Why didn't you ring the bell?"

"I want to know who Raul is."

"You know already."

"I've no idea."

Dr. Hasselbacher sat down and pulled at his boots.

"Are you an admirer of Charles Lamb, Dr. Hasselbacher?"

"Milly lent it me. Don't you remember how she talked of it . . . ?" He sat forlornly in the bulging breeches. Wormold saw that they had been unstitched along a seam to allow room for the contemporary Hasselbacher. Yes, he remembered now the evening at the Tropicana.

"I suppose," Hasselbacher said, "this uniform seems to you to need an explanation."

"Other things need one more."

"I was a Uhlan officer—oh, forty-five years ago."

"I remember a photograph of you in the other room. You were not dressed like that. You looked more—practical."

"That was after the war started. Look over there by my dressing table—1913, the June manoeuvres, the Kaiser was inspecting us." The old brown photograph with the photographer's indented seal in the corner showed the long ranks of the cavalry, swords drawn, and a little Imperial figure with a withered arm on a white horse riding by. "It was all so peaceful," Dr. Hasselbacher said, "in those days."

"Peaceful?"

"Until the war came."

"But I thought you were a doctor."

"I deceived you about that. I became one later. When the war was over. After I'd killed a man. You kill a man—that is so easy," Dr. Hasselbacher said, "it needs no skill. You can be certain of what you've done, you can judge death, but to save a man —that takes more than six years of training, and in the end you can never be quite sure that it was you who saved him. Germs are killed by other germs. People just survive. There is not one patient whom I know for certain that I saved, but the man I killed— I know him. He was Russian and he was very thin. I scraped the bone when I pushed the steel in. It set my teeth on edge. There was nothing but marshes around, and they called it Tannenberg. I hate war, Mr. Wormold."

"Then why do you dress up like a soldier?"

"I was not dressed up in this way when I killed a man. This was peaceful. I loved this." He touched the breastplate beside him on the bed. "But there we had the mud of the marshes on us." He said, "Do you never have a desire, Mr. Wormold, to go back to peace? Oh no, I forget, you're young, you've never known it. This was the last peace for any of us. The trousers don't fit any more."

"What made you—tonight—want to dress up like this, Hasselbacher?"

"A man's death."

"Raul?"

"Yes."

"Did you know him?"

"Yes."

"Tell me about him."

"I don't want to talk."

"It would be better to talk."

"We were both responsible for his death, you and I," Hasselbacher said. "I don't know who trapped you into it or how, but if I had refused to help them they would have had me deported. What could I do out of Cuba now? I told you I had lost papers."

"What papers?"

"Never mind that. Don't we all have something in the past to worry about? I know why they broke up my flat now. Because I was a friend of yours. Please go away, Mr. Wormold. Who knows what they might expect me to do if they knew you were here?"

"Who are they?"

"You know that better than I do, Mr. Wormold. They don't introduce themselves." Something moved rapidly in the next room.

"Only a mouse, Mr. Wormold. I keep a little cheese for it at night."

"So Milly lent you Lamb's *Tales?*"

"I'm glad you have changed your code," Dr. Hasselbacher said. "Perhaps now they will leave me alone. I can't help them any longer. One begins with acrostics and crosswords and mathematical puzzles and then, before you know, you are employed. . . . Nowadays we have to be careful even of our hobbies."

"But Raul—he didn't even exist. You advised me to lie and I lied. They were nothing but inventions, Hasselbacher."

"And Cifuentes? Are you telling me he didn't exist either?"

"He was different. I invented Raul."

"Then you invented him too well, Mr. Wormold. There's a whole file on him now."

"He was no more real than a character in a novel."

"Are they always invented? I don't know how a novelist works, Mr. Wormold. I have never known one before you."

"There was no drunk pilot in the Cubana Air Line."

"Oh I agree, you must have invented that detail—I don't know why."

"If you were breaking my cables you must have realized there was no truth in them, you know the city. A pilot dismissed for drunkenness, a friend with a plane, they were all inventions."

"I don't know your motive, Mr. Wormold. Perhaps you wanted to disguise his identity in case we broke your code. Perhaps if your friends had known he had private means and a plane of his own, they wouldn't have paid him so much. How much of it all got into his pocket, I wonder, and how much into yours?"

"I don't understand a word you're saying."

"You read the papers, Mr. Wormold. You know he had his flying licence taken away a month ago when he landed drunk in a child's playground."

"I don't read the local papers."

"Never? Of course he denied working for you. They offered him a lot of money if he would work for them instead. They too want photographs, Mr. Wormold, of those platforms you discovered in the Oriente hills."

"There are no platforms."

"Don't expect me to believe too much, Mr. Wormold. You referred in one cable to plans you had sent to London. They needed photographs too."

"You must know who They are."

"Cui bono?"

"And what do they plan for me?"

"At first they promised me they were planning nothing. You have been useful to them. They knew about you from the very beginning, Mr. Wormold, but they didn't take you seriously. They even thought you might be inventing your reports. But then you changed your codes and your staff increased. The British Secret Service would not be so easily deceived as all that, would it?" A kind of loyalty to Hawthorne kept Wormold silent. "Mr. Wormold, Mr. Wormold, why did you ever begin?"

"You know why. I needed the money." He found himself taking to truth like a tranquilizer.

"I would have lent you money. I offered to."

"I needed more than you could lend me."

"For Milly?"

"Yes."

"Take good care of her, Mr. Wormold. You are in a trade where it is unsafe to love anybody or anything. They strike at that. You remember the culture I was making?"

"Yes."

"Perhaps if they hadn't destroyed my will to live, they wouldn't have persuaded me so easily."

"Do you really think . . . ?"

"I only ask you to be careful."

"Can I use your telephone?"

"Yes."

Wormold rang up his house. Did he only imagine that slight click which indicated that the tapper was at work? Beatrice answered. He said, "Is everything quiet?"

"Yes."

"Wait till I come. Is Milly all right?"

"Fast asleep."

"I'm coming back."

Dr. Hasselbacher said, "You shouldn't have shown love in your voice. Who knows who was listening?" He walked with difficulty to the door because of his tight breeches. "Good night, Mr. Wormold. Here is the Lamb."

"I won't need it any more."

"Milly may want it. Would you mind saying nothing to anyone about this—this—costume? I know that I am absurd, but I loved those days. Once the Kaiser spoke to me."

"What did he say?"

"He said, 'I remember you. You are Captain Müller.' "

INTERLUDE IN LONDON

When the chief had guests he dined at home and cooked his own dinner, for no restaurant satisfied his meticulous and romantic standard. There was a story that once when he was ill he refused to cancel an invitation to an old friend, but cooked the meal from his bed by telephone. With a watch before him on the bed-table he would interrupt the conversation at the correct interval, to give directions to his valet. "Hallo, hallo, Brewer, hallo, you should take that chicken out now and baste it again."

It was also said that once when he had been kept late at the office and had tried to cook the meal from there, dinner had been ruined because from force of habit he had used his red telephone —the scrambler—and only strange noises resembling rapid Japanese had reached the valet's ears.

The meal which he served to the Permanent Under-Secretary was simple and excellent: a roast with a touch of garlic. A Wensleydale cheese stood on the sideboard and the quiet of Albany lay deeply around them like snow. After his exertions in the kitchen the Chief himself smelt faintly of gravy.

"It's really excellent. Excellent."

"An old Norfolk recipe. Granny Brown's Ipswich Roast."

"And the meat itself . . . it really melts . . ."

"I've trained Brewer to do the marketing, but he'll never make a cook. He needs constant supervision."

They ate for a while reverently in silence; the clink of a woman's shoes along the Rope Walk was the only distraction.

"A good wine," the Permanent Under-Secretary said at last.

" 'Fifty-five is coming along nicely. Still a little young?"

"Hardly."

With the cheese the Chief spoke again. "The Russian note—what does the F.O. think?"

"We are a little puzzled by the reference to the Caribbean bases." There was a crackling of Romary biscuits. "They can hardly refer to the Bahamas. They are worth about what the Yankees paid us—a few old destroyers. Yet we've always assumed that those constructions in Cuba had a Communist origin. You don't think they could have an American origin after all?"

"Wouldn't we have been informed?"

"Not necessarily, I'm afraid. Since the Fuchs case. They say we keep a good deal under our own hat too. What does your man in Havana say?"

"I'll ask him for a full assessment. How's the Wensleydale?"

"Perfect."

"Help yourself to the port."

"Cockburn 'twenty-seven, isn't it?"

" 'Thirty-five."

"Do you believe they intend war eventually?" the Chief asked.

"Your guess is as good as mine."

"They've become very active in Cuba—apparently with the help of the police. Our man in Havana has had a difficult time. His best agent, as you know, was killed—accidentally of course—on his way to take aerial photographs of the constructions—a very great loss to us. But I would give much more than a man's life for those photographs. As it was we had given fifteen hundred dollars. They shot at another of our agents in the street and he's taken fright. A third's gone underground. There's a woman too, they interrogated her, in spite of her being the mistress of the Director of Posts and Telegraphs. They have left our man alone so far—perhaps to watch. . . . Anyway he's a canny bird."

"Surely he must have been a bit careless to lose all those agents?"

"At the beginning we have to expect casualties. They broke his book-code. I'm never happy with these book-codes. There's a German out there who seems to be their biggest operator and an expert at cryptography. Hawthorne warned our man, but you know what these old merchants are like—they have an obstinate loyalty. Perhaps it was worth a few casualties to open his eyes. Cigar?"

"Thanks. Will he be able to start again if he's blown?"

"He has a trick worth two of that. Struck right home into the enemy camp. Recruited a double agent in the police headquarters itself."

"Aren't double agents always a bit—tricky? You never know whether you're getting the fat or the lean."

"I trust our man to huff him every time," the Chief said. "I say huff because they are both great draughts players. Checkers they call it there. As a matter of fact, that's their excuse for contacting each other."

"I can't exaggerate how worried we are about the constructions, C. If only you had got the photographs before they killed your man. The P.M. is pressing us to inform the Yankees and ask their help."

"You musn't let him. You can't depend on their security."

PART V

One

"Huff," said Captain Segura. They had met at the Havana Club. At the Havana Club, which was not a club at all and was owned by Bacardi's rival, all rum drinks were free, and this enabled Wormold to increase his savings, for naturally he continued to charge for the drinks in his expenses—the fact that the drinks were free would have been tedious, if not impossible, to explain in London. The bar was on the first floor of a 17th-century house and the windows faced the cathedral where the body of Christopher Columbus had once lain. A grey stone statue of Columbus stood outside the cathedral and looked as though it had been formed through the centuries under water, like a coral reef, by the action of insects.

"You know," Captain Segura said, "there was a time when I thought you didn't like me."

"There are other motives for playing draughts than liking a man."

"Yes, for me too," Captain Segura said. "Look! I make a king."

"And I huff you three times."

"You think I did not see that, but you will find the move is in my favour. There, now I take your only king. Why did you go to Santiago, Santa Clara, and Cienfuegos two weeks ago?"

"I always go about this time to see the retailers."

"It really looked as though that *was* your reason. You stayed in the new hotel at Cienfuegos. You had dinner alone in a restaurant on the waterfront. You went to a cinema and you went home. Next morning . . ."

"Do you really believe I'm a secret agent?"

"I'm beginning to doubt it. I think our friends have made a mistake."

"Who are our friends?"

"Oh, let's say the friends of Dr. Hasselbacher."

"And who are they?"

"It's my job to know what goes on in Havana," said Captain Segura, "not to take sides or give information." He was moving his king unchecked up the board.

"Is there anything in Cuba important enough to interest a secret service?"

"Of course we are only a small country, but we lie very close to the American coast. And we point at your own Jamaica base. If a country is surrounded, as Russia is, it will try to punch a hole through from inside."

"What use would I be—or Dr. Hasselbacher—in global strategy? A man who sells vacuum cleaners. A retired doctor."

"There are unimportant pieces in any game," said Captain Segura. "Like this one here. I take it and you don't mind losing it. Dr. Hasselbacher, of course, is very good at crosswords."

"What have crosswords to do with it?"

"A man like that makes a good cryptographer. Somebody once showed me a cable of yours with its interpretation—or rather they let me discover it. Perhaps they thought I would run you out of Cuba." He laughed. "Milly's father. They little knew."

"What was it about?"

"You claimed to have recruited Engineer Cifuentes. Of course that was absurd. I know him well. Perhaps they shot at him to make the cable sound more convincing. Perhaps they wrote it because they wanted to get rid of you. Or perhaps they are more credulous than I am."

"What an extraordinary story." He moved a piece. "How are you so certain that Cifuentes is not my agent?"

"By the way you play checkers, Mr. Wormold, and because I interrogated Cifuentes."

"Did you torture him?"

Captain Segura laughed. "No. He doesn't belong to the torturable class."

"I didn't know there were class distinctions in torture."

"Dear Mr. Wormold, surely you realize there are people who expect to be tortured and others who would be outraged by the idea. One never tortures except by a kind of mutual agreement."

"There's torture and torture. When they broke up Dr. Hassel-bacher's laboratory they were torturing . . . ?"

"One can never tell what amateurs may do. The police had no concern in that. Dr. Hasselbacher does not belong to the tortur-able class."

"Who does?"

"The poor in my own country—in any Latin American coun-try. The poor of Central Europe and the Orient. Of course in your welfare states you have no poor, so you are untorturable. In Cuba the police can deal as harshly as they like with émigrés from Latin America and the Baltic States, but not with visitors from your country or Scandinavia. It is an instinctive matter on both sides. Catholics are more torturable than Protestants, just as they are more criminal. You see I was right to make that king, and now I shall huff you for the last time."

"You always win, don't you? That's an interesting theory of yours."

"One reason why the West hates the great Communist states is that they don't recognize class distinctions. Sometimes they tor-ture the wrong people. So too of course did Hitler and shocked the world. Nobody cares what goes on in our prisons or the pris-ons of Lisbon or Caracas, but Hitler was too promiscuous. It was rather as though in your country a chauffeur had slept with a peeress."

"We're not shocked by that any longer."

"It is a great danger for everyone when what is shocking changes."

They had another free daiquiri each, frozen so stiffly that it had to be drunk in tiny drops to avoid a sinus pain. "And how is Milly?" Captain Segura asked.

"Well."

"I'm very fond of the child. She has been properly brought up."

"I'm glad you think so."

"That is another reason why I would not wish you to get into any trouble, Mr. Wormold, which might mean the loss of your residence permit. Havana would be poorer without your daugh-ter."

"I don't suppose you really believe me, Captain, but Cifuentes was no agent of mine."

"I do believe you. I think perhaps someone wanted to use you as a stalking horse, or perhaps as one of those painted ducks which attract the real wild ducks to settle." He finished his daiquiri. "That of course suits my book. I too like to watch the wild duck come in, from Russia, America, England, even Germany once again. They despise the poor local dago marksman, but one day, when they are all settled, what a shoot I will have."

"It's a complicated world. I find it easier to sell vacuum cleaners."

"The business prospers, I hope?"

"Oh yes, yes."

"I was interested that you had enlarged your staff. That charming secretary with the syphon and the coat that wouldn't close. And the young man."

"I need someone to superintend accounts. Lopez is not reliable."

"Ah, Lopez. Another of your agents." Captain Segura laughed. "Or so it was reported to me."

"Yes. He supplies me with secret information about the police department."

"Be careful, Mr. Wormold. He is one of the torturable." They both laughed, drinking daiquiris. It is easy to laugh at the idea of torture on a sunny day. "I must be going, Mr. Wormold."

"I suppose the cells are full of my spies."

"We can always make room for another by having a few executions."

"One day, Captain, I am going to beat you at draughts."

"I doubt it, Mr. Wormold."

From the window he watched Captain Segura pass the grey pumice-like figure of Columbus on the way to his office. Then he had another free daiquiri. The Havana Club and Captain Segura seemed to have taken the place of the Wonder Bar and Dr. Hasselbacher—it was like a change of life and he had to make the best of it. There was no turning time back. Dr. Hasselbacher had been humiliated in front of him, and friendship cannot stand humiliation. He had not seen Dr. Hasselbacher again. In the club he felt himself, as in the Wonder Bar, a citizen of Havana; the elegant young man who brought him a drink made no attempt to sell him one of the assorted bottles of rum arranged on his table. A man with a grey beard read his morning paper as always at this hour; as usual a postman had interrupted his daily round for his free drink: all of them were citizens too. Four tourists left the bar carrying woven baskets, containing bottles of rum; they were flushed and cheerful and harboured the illusion that their drinks had cost them nothing. He thought: They are the foreigners, and of course untorturable.

Wormold drank his daiquiri too fast and left the Havana Club with his eyes aching. The tourists leant over the 17th-century well; they had flung into it enough coins to have paid for their drinks twice over: they were ensuring a happy return. A woman's voice called him and he saw Beatrice standing between the pillars of the colonnade among the gourds and rattles and Negro dolls of the curio shop.

"What are you doing here?"

She explained, "I'm always unhappy when you meet Segura. This time I wanted to be sure. . . ."

"Sure of what?" He wondered whether at last she had begun to suspect that he had no agents; perhaps she had received instructions to watch him, from London or from 59200 in Kingston. They began to walk home.

"Sure that it's not a trap, that the police aren't waiting for you. A double agent is tricky to handle."

"You worry too much."

"And you have so little experience. Look what happened to Raul and Cifuentes."

"Cifuentes has been interrogated by the police." He added with relief," He's blown, so he's no use to us now."

"Then aren't you blown too?"

"He gave nothing away. It was Captain Segura who chose the questions, and Segura is one of us. I think perhaps it's time we gave him a bonus. He's trying to compile a complete list for us of foreign agents here—American as well as Russian. Wild duck—that's what he calls them."

"It would be quite a coup. And the constructions?"

"We'll have to let those rest awhile. I can't make him act against his own country."

Passing the cathedral he gave his usual coin to the blind beggar who sat on the steps outside. Beatrice said, "It seems almost worth while being blind in this sun."

The creative instinct stirred in Wormold. He said, "You know, he's not really blind. He sees everything that goes on."

"He must be a good actor. I've been watching him all the time you were with Segura."

"And he's been watching you. As a matter of fact he's one of my best informers. I always have him stationed here when I meet Segura. An elementary precaution. I'm not as careless as you think."

"You've never told H.Q."

"There's no point. They could hardly have traces of a blind beggar, and I don't use him for information. All the same, if I had been arrested you'd have known of it in ten minutes. What would you have done?"

"Burnt all records and driven Milly to the Embassy."

"What about Rudy?"

"I'd have told him to radio London that we were breaking off and then to go underground."

"How does one go underground?" He didn't probe for an answer. He said slowly as the story grew of itself, "The beggar's name is Miguel. He really does all this for love. You see, I saved his life once."

"How?"

"Oh, it was nothing. An accident to the ferry. It just happened that I could swim and he couldn't."

"Did they give you a medal?"

He looked at her quickly, but in her face he could see only innocent interest.

"No. There was no glory. As a matter of fact, they fined me for bringing him to shore in a defence zone."

"What a very romantic story. And now of course he would give his life for you."

"Oh, I wouldn't go as far as that."

"Do tell me—have you somewhere a small penny account book in black wash leather?"

"I shouldn't think so. Why?"

"With your first purchases of pen nibs and indiarubbers?"

"Why on earth pen nibs?"

"I was just wondering, that's all."

"You can't buy account books for a penny. And pen nibs—nobody uses pen nibs nowadays."

"Forget it. Just something Henry said to me. A natural mistake."

"Who's Henry?" he asked.

"59200," she said. He felt an odd jealousy, for in spite of security rules she had only once called him Jim.

The house was empty as usual when they came in; he was aware that he no longer missed Milly, and he felt the sad relief of a man who realizes that there is one love at least that no longer hurts him.

"Rudy's out," Beatrice said. "Buying sweets, I suppose. He eats too many. He must consume an awful lot of energy, because he gets no fatter, but I don't see how."

"We'd better get down to work. There's a cable to send. Segura gave some valuable information about Communist infiltration in the police. You'd hardly believe . . ."

"I can believe almost anything. Look at this. I've just discovered something fascinating in the code book. Did you know there was a group for 'eunuch'? Do you think it crops up often in cables?"

"I expect they need it in the Istanbul office."

"I wish we could use it. Can't we?"

"Are you ever going to marry again?"

Beatrice said, "Your free associations are rather obvious sometimes. Do you think Rudy has a secret life? He can't consume all that energy in the office."

"What's the drill for a secret life? Do you have to ask permission from London before you start one?"

"Well, of course, you would have to get traces before going very far. London prefers to keep sex inside the department."

Two

1

"I must be getting important," Wormold said. "I've been invited to make a speech."

"Where?" Milly asked, looking politely up from the *Horsewoman's Year Book*. It was the evening hour when work was over and the last gold light lay flat across the roofs and touched the honey-coloured hair and the whisky in his glass.

"At the annual lunch of the European Traders' Association. Dr. Braun, the President, has asked me to make one—as the oldest member. The guest of honour is the American Consul-General," he added with pride. It seemed such a short time ago that he had come to Havana and met with her family in the Floridita bar the girl who was Milly's mother; now he was the oldest trader there. Many had retired: some had gone home to fight in the last war—English, German, French—but he had been rejected because of his bad leg. None of these had returned to Cuba.

"What will you talk about?"

He said sadly, "I shan't. I wouldn't know what to say."

"I bet you'd speak better than any of them."

"Oh no. I may be the oldest member, Milly, but I'm the smallest too. The rum exporters and the cigar men—they are the really important people."

"You are you."

"I wish you had chosen a cleverer father."

"Captain Segura says you are pretty good at checkers."

"But not as good as he is."

"Please accept, Father," she said. "I'd be so proud of you."

"I'd make a fool of myself."

"You wouldn't. For my sake."

"For your sake I'd turn cartwheels. All right. I'll accept."

Rudy knocked at the door. This was the hour when he listened in for the last time—it would be midnight in London. He said, "There's an urgent cable from Kingston. Shall I fetch Beatrice?"

"No, I can manage it myself. She's going to a movie."

"Business does seem brisk," Milly said.

"Yes."

"But you don't seem to *sell* any more cleaners."

"It's all long-term promotion," Wormold said.

He went into his bedroom and deciphered the cable. It was from Hawthorne. Wormold was to come by the first possible plane to Kingston and report. He thought: So they know at last.

2

The rendezvous was the Myrtle Bank Hotel. Wormold had not been to Jamaica for many years, and he was appalled by the dirt and the heat. What accounted for the squalor of British possessions? The Spanish, the French, and the Portuguese built cities where they settled, but the English just allowed cities to grow. The poorest street in Havana had dignity compared with the shanty life of Kingston—huts built out of old petrol tins roofed with scrap metal purloined from some cemetery of abandoned cars.

Hawthorne sat in a long chair on the veranda of Myrtle Bank drinking a planter's punch through a straw. His suit was just as immaculate as when Wormold had met him first; the only sign of the great heat was a little powder caked under his left ear. He said, "Take a pew." Even the slang was back.

"Thanks."

"Had a good trip?"

"Yes, thank you."

"I expect you're glad to be at home."

"Home?"

"I mean here—having a holiday from the dagoes. Back in British territory." Wormold thought of the huts he had seen along the harbour and a hopeless old man asleep in a patch of shade and a ragged child nursing a piece of driftwood. He said, "Havana's not so bad."

"Have a planter's punch. They are good here."

"Thanks."

Hawthorne said, "I asked you to come over because there's a spot of trouble."

"Yes?" He supposed that the truth was coming out. Could he be arrested now that he was on British territory? What would the charge be? Obtaining money on false pretences, perhaps, or some obscurer charge heard *in camera* under the Official Secrets Act.

"About these constructions."

He wanted to explain that Beatrice knew nothing of all this; he had no accomplice except the credulity of other men.

"What about them?" he asked.

"I wish you'd been able to get photographs."

"I tried. You know what happened."

"Yes. The drawings are a bit confusing."

"They are not by a skilled draughtsman."

"Don't get me wrong, old man. You've done wonders, but, you know, there was a time when I was—almost suspicious."

"What of?"

"Well, some of them sort of reminded me—to be frank, they reminded me of parts of a vacuum cleaner."

"Yes, that struck me too."

"And then you see I remembered all the thingummies in your shop."

"You thought I'd pulled the leg of the Secret Service?"

"Of course it sounds fantastic now, I know. All the same, in a way I was relieved when I found that the others have made up their minds to murder you."

"Murder me?"

"You see, that really proves the drawings are genuine."

"What others?"

"The other side. Of course I'd luckily kept those absurd suspicions to myself."

"How are they going to murder me?"

"Oh, we'll come to that—a matter of poisoning. What I mean is that next to having photographs one can't have a better confirmation of your reports. We had been rather sitting on them, but we've circulated them now to all the Service Departments. We sent them to Atomic Research as well—they weren't helpful. Said they had no connection with nuclear fission. The trouble is we've been bemused by the atom boys and have quite forgotten that there may be other forms of scientific warfare just as dangerous."

"How are they going to poison me?"

"First things first, old man. You see one mustn't forget the economics of warfare. Cuba can't afford to start making H-bombs, but have they found something equally effective at short range, and *cheap?* That's the important word—cheap."

"Please would you mind telling me how they are going to murder me? You see, it interests me personally."

"Of course I'm going to tell you. I just wanted to give you the background first and to tell you how pleased we all are—at the confirmation of your reports, I mean. They plan to poison you at some sort of business lunch."

"The European Traders' Association?"

"I think that's the name."

"How do you know?"

"We've penetrated their organization here. You'd be surprised how much we know of what goes on in your territory. I can tell you for instance that the death of stroke 4 was an accident—they just wanted to scare him as they scared stroke 3 by shooting at him. You are the first one they've really decided to murder."

"That's comforting."

"In a way, you know, it's a compliment. You are dangerous now." Hawthorne made a long sucking noise, draining up the last liquid between the layers of ice and orange and pineapple and the cherry on top.

"I suppose," Wormold said, "I'd better not go." He felt a surprising disappointment. "It will be the first lunch I've missed in ten years. They'd even asked me to speak. The firm always expects me to attend. Like showing the flag."

"But of course you've got to go."

"And be poisoned?"

"You needn't eat anything, need you?"

"Have you ever tried going to a public lunch and not eating anything? There's also the question of drink."

"They can't very well poison a bottle of wine. You could give the impression of being an alcoholic, somebody who doesn't eat but only drinks."

"Thank you. That would certainly be good for business."

"People have a soft spot in their hearts for alcoholics," Hawthorne said. "Besides, if you don't go they'll suspect something. It puts my source in danger. We have to protect our sources."

"That's the drill, I suppose."

"Exactly, old man. Another point—we know the plot, but we don't know the plotters—except their symbols. If we discover who they are, we can insist on having them locked up. We'll disrupt the organization."

"Yes—there aren't any perfect murders, are there? I daresay there'll be a clue at the post-mortem on which you can persuade Segura to act."

"You aren't afraid, are you? This is a dangerous job. You shouldn't have taken it unless you were prepared . . ."

"You're like a Spartan mother, Hawthorne. Come back victorious or stay beneath the table."

"That's quite an idea, you know. You could slip under the table at the right moment. The murderers would think you were dead and the others would just think you were drunk."

"This is not a meeting of the Big Four at Moscow. The European Traders don't fall under the table."

"Never?"

"Never. You think I'm unduly concerned, don't you?"

"I don't think there's any need for you to worry yet. They don't serve you, after all. You help yourself."

"Of course. Except that there's always a Morro crab to start with at the Nacional. That's prepared in advance."

"You mustn't eat that. Lots of people don't eat crab. When they serve the other courses never take the portion next to you. It's like a conjuror forcing a card on you. You just have to reject it."

"But the conjuror usually manages to force the card just the same."

"I tell you what—did you say the lunch was at the Nacional?"

"Yes."

"Then why can't you use stroke 7?"

"Who's stroke 7?"

"Don't you remember your own agents? Surely he's the head waiter at the Nacional? He can help to see your plate isn't tampered with. It's time he did something for his money. I don't remember you sending a single report from him."

"Can't you give me any idea who the man at the lunch will be? I mean the man who plans to . . ." he boggled at the word "kill" . . . "to do it."

"Not a clue, old man. Just be careful of everyone. Have another planter's punch."

3

The plane back to Cuba had few passengers; a Spanish woman with a pack of children—some of them screamed and some of them were air-sick as soon as they left the ground; a Negress with a live cock wrapped in her shawl; a Cuban cigar exporter with whom Wormold had a nodding acquaintance; and an Englishman in a tweed jacket who smoked a pipe until the air hostess told him to put it out. Then he sucked the empty pipe ostentatiously for the rest of the journey and sweated heavily into the tweed. He had the ill-humoured face of a man who is always in the right.

When lunch was served he moved back several places and sat down beside Wormold. He said, "Can't stand those screaming brats. Do you mind?" He looked at the papers on Wormold's knee. "You with Phastkleaners?" he said.

"Yes."

"I'm with Nucleaners. The name's Carter."

"Oh."

"This is only my second trip to Cuba. Gay spot, they tell me," he said, blowing down his pipe and laying it aside for lunch.

"It can be," Wormold said, "if you like roulette or brothels."

Carter patted his tobacco pouch as though it were a dog's head —*My faithful hound shall bear me company.* "I didn't exactly mean . . . though I'm not a Puritan, mind. I suppose it would be interesting. Do as the Romans do." He changed the subject— "Sell many of your machines?"

"Trade's not so bad."

"We've got a new model that's going to wipe the market." He took a large mouthful of sweet mauve cake and then cut himself a piece of chicken.

"Really."

"Runs on a motor like a lawn mower. No effort by the little woman. No tubes trailing all over the place."

"Noisy?"

"Special silencer. Less noise than your model. We are calling it the Whisper Wife." After taking a swig of turtle soup he began to eat his fruit salad, crunching the grape stones between his teeth. He said, "We are opening an agency in Cuba soon. Know Dr. Braun?"

"I've met him. At the European Traders' Association. He's our President. Imports precision instruments from Geneva."

"That's the man. He's given us very useful advice. In fact I'm going to your bean feast as his guest. Do they give you a good lunch?"

"You know what hotel lunches are like."

"Better than this, anyway," he said, spitting out a grape-skin. He had overlooked the asparagus in mayonnaise and now began on that. Afterwards he fumbled in his pocket. "Here's my card." The card read: "William Carter, B. Tech. (Nottwich)" and in the corner "Nucleaners Ltd." He said, "I'm staying at the Seville-Biltmore for a week."

"I'm afraid I haven't a card on me. My name's Wormold."

"Met a fellow called Davis?"

"I don't think so."

"Shared digs with him at college. He went into Gripfix and came out to this part of the world. It's funny—you find Nottwich men everywhere. You weren't there yourself, were you?"

"No."

"Reading?"

"I wasn't at a university."

"I couldn't have told it," Carter told him kindly. "I'd have gone to Oxford, you know, but they are very backward in technology.

All right for schoolmasters, I suppose." He began to suck again at his empty pipe like a child at a comforter till it whistled between his teeth. Suddenly he spoke again, as though some remains of tannin had touched his tongue with a bitter flavour. "Outdated," he said, "relics, living on the past. I'd abolish them."

"Abolish what?"

"Oxford and Cambridge." He took the only food that was left in the tray, a roll of bread, and crumbled it like age or ivy crumbling a stone.

At the Customs Wormold lost him. He was having trouble with his sample Nucleaner, and Wormold saw no reason why the representative of Phastkleaners should assist him to enter. Beatrice was there to meet him with the Hillman. It was many years since he had been met by a woman.

"Everything all right?" she asked.

"Yes. Oh, yes. They seem pleased with me." He watched her hands on the wheel; she wore no gloves in the hot afternoon. They were beautiful and competent hands. He said, "You aren't wearing your ring."

She said, "I didn't think anyone would notice. Milly did too. You are an observant family."

"You haven't lost it?"

"I took it off yesterday to wash and I forgot to put it back. There's no point—is there?—wearing a ring you forget."

It was then he told her about the lunch.

"You won't go?"

"Hawthorne expects me to. To protect his source."

"Damn his source."

"There's a better reason. Something that Dr. Hasselbacher said to me. They like to strike at what you love. If I don't go, they'll think up something else. Something worse. And we shan't know what. Next time it mightn't be me—I don't think I love myself enough to satisfy them—it might be Milly. Or you." He didn't realize the implication of what he had said until she had dropped him at his door and driven on.

Three

1

Milly said, "You've had a cup of coffee, and that's all. Not even a piece of toast."

"I'm just not in the mood."

"You'll go and over-eat at the Traders' lunch today, and you know perfectly well that Morro crab doesn't agree with your stomach."

"I promise you I'll be very careful."

"You'd do much better to have a proper breakfast. You need a cereal to mop up all the liquor you'll be drinking." It was one of her duenna days.

"I'm sorry, Milly, I just can't. I've got things on my mind. Please don't pester me. Not today."

"Have you prepared your speech?"

"I've done my best, but I'm no speaker, Milly. I don't know why they asked me." But he was uneasily conscious that perhaps he did know why. Somebody must have brought influence to bear on Dr. Braun, somebody who had to be identified at any cost. He thought: I am the cost.

"I bet you'll be a sensation."

"I'm trying hard not to be a sensation at this lunch."

Milly went to school and he sat on at the table. The cereal company which Milly patronized had printed on the carton of Wheatbrix the latest adventure of Little Dwarf Doodoo. Little Dwarf Doodoo in a rather brief instalment encountered a rat the size of a St. Bernard dog and he frightened the rat away by pretending to be a cat and saying miaou. It was a very simple story. You could hardly call it a preparation for life. The company also gave away an air-gun in return for twelve lids. As the packet was almost empty, Wormold began to cut off the lid, driving his knife carefully along the dotted line. He was turning the last corner when Beatrice entered. She said, "What are you doing?"

"I thought an air-gun might be useful in the office. We only need eleven more lids."

"I couldn't sleep last night."

"Too much coffee?"

"No. Something you told me Dr. Hasselbacher said. About Milly. Please don't go to the lunch."

"It's the least I can do."

"You do quite enough. They are pleased with you in London. I can tell that from the way they cable you. Whatever Henry may say, London wouldn't want you to run a silly risk."

"It's quite true what he said—that if I don't go they will try something else."

"Don't worry about Milly. I'll watch her like a lynx."

"And who's going to watch you?"

"I'm in this line of business—it's my own choice. You needn't feel responsible for me."

"Have you been in a spot like this before?"

"No, but I've never had a boss like you before. You seem to stir them up. You know, this job is usually just an office desk and files and dull cables—we don't go in for murder. And I don't want you murdered. You see, you are real. You aren't *Boys' Own Paper*. For God's sake put down that silly packet and listen to me."

"I was re-reading Little Dwarf Doodoo."

"Then stay at home with him this morning. I'll go out and buy you all the back cartons so that you can catch up."

"All Hawthorne said was sense. I only have to be careful what I eat. It *is* important to find out who they are. Then I'll have done something for my money."

"You've done plenty as it is. There's no point in going to this damned lunch."

"Yes, there is a point. Pride."

"Who are you showing off to?"

"You."

2

He made his way through the lounge of the Nacional Hotel between the show cases full of Italian shoes and Danish ashtrays and Swedish glass and mauve British woollies; the private dining room where the European Traders always met lay just beyond the chair where Dr. Hasselbacher now sat, conspicuously waiting. Wormold approached with slowing steps—it was the first time he had seen Dr. Hasselbacher since the night when he had sat on the bed in his Uhlan's uniform talking of the past. Members of the

Association, passing into the private dining room, stopped and spoke to Dr. Hasselbacher; he paid them no attention.

Wormold reached the chair where he sat. Dr. Hasselbacher said, "Don't go in there, Mr. Wormold." He spoke without lowering his voice, the words shivering among the show cases, attracting attention.

"How are you, Hasselbacher?"

"I said, don't go in."

"I heard you the first time."

"They are going to kill you, Mr. Wormold."

"How do you know that, Hasselbacher?"

"They are planning to poison you in there."

Several of the guests stopped and stared and smiled. One of them, an American, said, "Is the food that bad?" and everybody laughed.

Wormold said, "Don't stay here, Hasselbacher. You are too conspicuous."

"Are you going in?"

"Of course. I'm one of the speakers."

"There's Milly. Don't forget her."

"Don't worry about Milly. I'm going to come out on my feet, Hasselbacher. Please go home."

"All right, but I had to try," Dr. Hasselbacher said. "I'll be waiting at the telephone."

"I'll call you when I leave."

"Goodbye, Jim."

"Goodbye, Doctor." The use of his first name took Wormold unawares. It reminded him of what he had always jokingly thought: that Dr. Hasselbacher would use the name only at his bedside when he had given up hope. He felt suddenly frightened, alone, a long way from home.

"Wormold," a voice said, and turning he saw that it was Carter of Nucleaners, but it was also for Wormold at that moment the English midlands, English snobbery, English vulgarity, all the sense of kinship and security the word England implied to him.

"Carter!" he exclaimed, as though Carter were the one man in Havana he wanted most to meet, and at that instant he was.

"Damned glad to see you," Carter said. "Don't know a soul at this lunch. Not even my—not even Dr. Braun." His pocket bulged with his pipe and his pouch; he patted them as though for reassurance, as though he too felt far from home.

"Carter, this is Dr. Hasselbacher, an old friend of mine."

"Good day, Doctor." He said to Wormold, "I was looking all over the place for you last night. I don't seem able to find the right spots."

They moved in together to the private dining room. It was quite irrational, the confidence he had in a fellow countryman, but on the side where Carter walked he felt protected.

3

The dining room had been decorated with two big flags of the United States in honour of the Consul-General, and little paper flags as in an airport restaurant indicated where each national was to sit. There was a Swiss flag at the head of the table for Dr. Braun, the President; there was even the flag of Monaco for the Monegasque Consul, who was one of the largest exporters of cigars in Havana. He was to sit on the Consul-General's right hand in recognition of the Royal alliance. Cocktails were circulating when Wormold and Carter entered, and a waiter at once approached them. Was it Wormold's imagination or did the waiter shift the tray so that the last remaining daiquiri lay nearest to Wormold's hand?

"No. No thank you."

Carter put out his hand, but the waiter had already moved on towards the service door.

"Perhaps you would prefer a dry martini, sir?" a voice said. He turned; it was the head waiter.

"No, no, I don't like them."

"A Scotch, sir? A sherry? An old-fashioned? Anything you care to order."

"I'm not drinking," Wormold said, and the head waiter abandoned him for another guest. Presumably he was stroke 7: strange if by an ironic coincidence he was also the would-be assassin. Wormold looked around for Carter, but he had moved away in pursuit of his host.

"You'd do better to drink all you can," said a voice with a Scotch accent. "My name is MacDougall. It seems we're sitting together."

"I haven't seen you here before, have I?"

"I've taken over from McIntyre. You'd have known McIntyre surely?"

"Oh yes, yes." Dr. Braun, who had palmed off the unimportant Carter upon another Swiss who dealt in watches, was now leading the American Consul-General round the room, introducing him to the more exclusive members. The Germans formed a group apart —rather suitably against the west wall; they carried the superiority of the deutschmark on their features like duelling scars; national honour which had survived Belsen depended now on a rate of exchange. Wormold wondered whether it was one of them who had betrayed the secret of the lunch to Dr. Hasselbacher. Betrayed? Not necessarily. Perhaps the Doctor had been blackmailed to supply the poison. At any rate he would have chosen, for the sake of old friendship, something painless, if any poison were painless.

"I was telling you," Mr. MacDougall went energetically on like a Scottish reel, "that you would do better to drink now. It's all you'll be getting."

"There'll be wine, won't there?"

"Look at the table." Small individual milk bottles stood by every place. "Didn't you read your invitation? An American blue-plate lunch in honour of our great American allies."

"Blue plate?"

"Surely you know what a blue plate is, man? They shove the whole meal at you under your nose, already dished up on your plate—roast turkey, cranberry sauce, sausages and carrots and French fried. I can't bear French fried, but there's no pick and choose with a blue plate."

"No pick and choose?"

"You eat what you're given. That's democracy, man."

Dr. Braun was summoning them to the table. Wormold had a hope that fellow nationals would sit together and that Carter would be on his other side, but it was a strange Scandinavian who sat on his left, scowling at his milk bottle. Wormold thought, Someone has arranged this well. Nothing is safe, not even the milk. Already the waiters were bustling round the board with the Morro crabs. Then he saw with relief that Carter faced him across the table. There was something so secure in his vulgarity. You could appeal to him as you could appeal to an English policeman —because you knew his thoughts.

"No," he said to the waiter, "I won't take crab."

"You are wise not to take those things," Mr. MacDougall said. "I'm refusing them myself. They don't go with whisky. Now if you will drink a little of your iced water and hold it under the table, I've got a flask in my pocket with enough for the two of us."

Without thinking, Wormold stretched out his hand to his glass, and then the doubt came. Who was MacDougall? He had never seen him before, and he hadn't heard until now that McIntyre had gone away. Wasn't it possible that the water was poisoned, or even the whisky in the flask?

"Why did McIntyre leave?" he asked, his hand round the glass.

"Oh, it was just one of those things," Mr. MacDougall said, "you know the way it is. Toss down your water. You don't want to drown the Scotch. This is the best Highland malt."

"It's too early in the day for me. Thank you all the same."

"If you don't trust the water, you are right not to," Mr. Mac-Dougall said ambiguously. "I'm taking it neat myself. If you don't mind sharing the cap of the flask . . ."

"No, really. I don't drink at this hour."

"It was the English who made hours for drinking, not the Scotch. They'll be making hours for dying next."

Carter said across the table, "I don't mind if I do. The name's Carter," and Wormold saw with relief that Mr. MacDougall was pouring out the whisky; there was one suspicion less, for no one surely would want to poison Carter. All the same, he thought, there is something wrong with Mr. MacDougall's Scottishness. It smelt of fraud like Ossian.

"Svenson," the gloomy Scandinavian said sharply from behind his little Swedish flag—at least Wormold thought it was Swedish; he could never distinguish with certainty between the Scandinavian colours.

"Wormold," he said.

"What is all this nonsense of the milk?"

"I think," Wormold said, "that Dr. Braun is being a little too literal."

"Or funny," Carter said.

"I don't think Dr. Braun has much sense of humour."

"And what do you do, Mr. Wormold?" the Swede asked. "I don't think we have met before, although I know you by sight."

"Vacuum cleaners. And you?"

"Glass. As you know, Swedish glass is the best in the world. This bread is very good. Do you not eat bread?" He might have prepared his conversation beforehand from a phrase book.

"Given it up. Fattening, you know."

"I would have said you could have done with fattening." Mr. Svenson gave a dreary laugh like jollity in a long northern night. "Forgive me. I make you sound like a goose."

At the end of the table, where the Consul-General sat, they were beginning to serve the blue plates. Mr. MacDougall had been wrong about the turkey—the main course was Maryland chicken—but he was right about the carrots and the French fried and the sausages. Dr. Braun was a little behind the rest: he was still picking at his Morro crab. The Consul-General must have slowed him down by the earnestness of his conversation and the fixity of his convex lenses. Two waiters came round the table, one whisking away the remains of the crab, the other substituting the blue plates. Only the Consul-General had thought to open his milk. The word "Dulles" drifted dully down to where Wormold sat. The waiter approached, carrying two plates. He put one in front of the Scandinavian; the other was Wormold's. The thought that the whole threat to his life might be a nonsensical practical joke came to Wormold. Perhaps Hawthorne was a humorist, and Dr. Hasselbacher. . . . He remembered Milly asking whether Dr. Hasselbacher had ever pulled his leg. Sometimes it seems easier to run the risk of death than ridicule. He wanted to confide in Carter and hear his commonsense reply; then, looking at his plate, he noticed something odd. There were no carrots. He said quickly, "You prefer it without carrots," and slipped the plate along to Mr. MacDougall.

"It's the French fried I dislike," said Mr. MacDougall quickly and passed the plate on to the Luxemburg Consul. The Luxemburg Consul, who was deep in conversation with a German across the table, handed the plate with absent-minded politeness to his neighbor. Politeness infected all who had not yet been served, and the plate went whisking along towards Dr. Braun, who had just had the remains of his Morro crab removed. The head waiter saw what was happening and began to stalk the plate up the table, but it kept a pace ahead of him. The waiter, returning with more blue plates, was intercepted by Wormold, who took one. He looked confused. Wormold began to eat with appetite. "The carrots are excellent," he said.

The head waiter hovered by Dr. Braun. "Excuse me, Dr. Braun," he said, "they have given you no carrots."

"I don't like carrots," Dr. Braun said, cutting up a piece of chicken.

"I am so sorry," the head waiter said and seized Dr. Braun's plate. "A mistake in the kitchen." Plate in hand like a verger with the collection, he walked up the length of the room towards the service door. Mr. MacDougall was taking a sip of his own whisky.

"I think I might venture now," Wormold said. "As a celebration."

"Good man. Water or straight?"

"Could I take your water? Mine's got a fly in it."

"Of course." Wormold drank two-thirds of the water and held it out for the whisky from Mr. MacDougall's flask. Mr. MacDougall gave him a generous double. "Hold it out again—you are behind the two of us," he said, and Wormold was back in the territory of trust; he felt a kind of tenderness for the neighbour he had suspected. He said, "We must see each other again."

"An occasion like this would be useless if it didn't bring people together."

"I wouldn't have met you or Carter without it."

They all three had another whisky. "You must both meet my daughter," Wormold said, the whisky warming his cockles.

"How is business with you?"

"Not so bad. We are expanding the office."

Dr. Braun rapped the table for silence.

"Surely," Carter said in the loud irrepressible Nottwich voice as warming as the whisky, "they'll have to serve drinks with the toast."

"My lad," Mr. MacDougall said, "there'll be speeches, but no toasts. We have to listen to the bastards without alcoholic aid."

"I'm one of the bastards," Wormold said.

"You speaking?"

"As the oldest member."

"I'm glad you've survived long enough for that," Mr. MacDougall said.

The American Consul-General, called on by Dr. Braun, began to speak. He spoke of the spiritual links between the democracies —he seemed to number Cuba among the democracies. Trade was important because without trade there would be no spiritual links —or perhaps it was the other way round. He spoke of American aid to distressed countries which would enable them to buy more goods and by buying more goods strengthen the spiritual links.

. . . A dog was howling somewhere in the wastes of the hotel and the head waiter signalled for the door to be closed. It had been a great pleasure to the American Consul-General to be invited to this lunch today and to meet the leading representatives of European trade and so strengthen still further the spiritual links. . . . Wormold had two more whiskies.

"And now," Dr. Braun said, "I am going to call upon the oldest member of our Association—I am not of course referring to his years, but to the length of time he has served the cause of European trade in this beautiful city, where, Mr. Minister"—he bowed to his other neighbour, a dark man with a squint—"we have the privilege and happiness of being your guests. I am speaking, you all know, of Mr. Wormold." He took a quick look at his notes. "Mr. James Wormold, the Havana representative of Phast-kleaners."

Mr. MacDougall said, "We've finished the whisky. Fancy that now. Just when you need your Dutch courage most."

Carter said, "I came armed as well—but I drank most of it in the plane. There's only one glass left in the flask."

"Obviously our friend here must have it," Mr. MacDougall said. "His need is greater than ours."

Dr. Braun said, "We may take Mr. Wormold as a symbol for all that service means—modesty, quietness, perseverance, and efficiency. Our enemies picture the salesman often as a loud-mouthed braggart who is intent only on putting across some product which is useless, unnecessary, or even harmful. That is not a true picture . . ."

Wormold said, "It's kind of you, Carter, I could certainly do with a drink."

"Not used to speaking?"

"It's not only the speaking." He leant forward across the table towards that common-or-garden Nottwich face on which he felt he could rely for incredulity, reassurance, the easy humour based on inexperience; he was safe with Carter. He said, "I know you won't believe a word of what I'm telling you," but he didn't want Carter to believe. He wanted to learn from him how not to be-lieve. Something nudged his leg and looking down he saw a black dachshund face pleading with him between the drooping ringlet ears for a scrap—the dog must have slipped in through the service door unseen by the waiters and now it led a hunted life, half-hidden below the tablecloth.

Carter pushed a small flask across to Wormold. "There's not enough for two. Take it all."

"Very kind of you, Carter." He unscrewed the top and poured all that there was into his glass.

"Only a Johnnie Walker. Nothing fancy."

Dr. Braun said, "If anyone here can speak for all of us about the long years of patient service a trader gives to the public, I am sure it is Mr. Wormold, whom now I call upon . . ."

Carter winked and raised an imaginary glass.

"H-hurry," Carter said. "You've got to h-hurry."

Wormold lowered the whisky. "What did you say, Carter?"

"I said drink it up quick."

"Oh no, you didn't, Carter." Why hadn't he noticed that stammered aspirate before? Was Carter conscious of it and did he avoid an initial "h" except when he was preoccupied by fear or h-hope?

"What's the matter, Wormold?"

Wormold put his hand down to pat the dog's head and as though by accident he knocked the glass from the table.

"You pretended not to know the doctor."

"What doctor?"

"You would call him H-Hasselbacher."

"Mr. Wormold," Dr. Braun called down the table.

He rose uncertainly to his feet. The dog, for want of any better provender, was lapping at the whisky on the floor.

Wormold said, "I appreciate your asking me to speak, whatever your motives." A polite titter took him by surprise—he hadn't meant to say anything funny. He said, "This is my first, and it looked at one time as though it was going to be my last, public appearance." He caught Carter's eye. Carter was frowning. He felt guilty of a solecism by his survival as though he were drunk in public. Perhaps he was drunk. He said, "I don't know whether I've got any friends here—I've certainly got some enemies." Somebody said, "Shame" and several people laughed. If this went on he would get the reputation of being a witty speaker. He said, "We hear a lot nowadays about the cold war, but any trader will tell you that the war between two manufacturers of the same goods can be quite a hot war. Take Phastkleaners and Nucleaners—there's not much difference between the two machines any more than there is between two human beings—one Russian —or German—and one British. There would be no competition and no war if it wasn't for the ambition of a few men in both firms; just a few men dictate competition and invent needs and set Mr. Carter and myself at each other's throats."

Nobody laughed now. Dr. Braun whispered something into the ear of the Consul-General. Wormold lifted Carter's whisky flask and said, "I don't suppose Mr. Carter even knows the name of the man who sent him to poison me for the good of his firm." Laughter broke out again with a note of relief. Mr. MacDougall said, "We could do with more poison here," and suddenly the dog began to whimper. It broke cover and made for the service door. "Max!" the head waiter exclaimed. "Max!" There was silence, and then a few uneasy laughs. The dog was uncertain on its feet. It howled and tried to bite its own breast. The head waiter caught it by the door and picked it up, but it cried as though with pain, hunched itself, and broke from his arms. "It's had a couple," Mr. MacDougall said uneasily.

"You must excuse me, Dr. Braun," Wormold said. "The show is over." He followed the head waiter through the service door. "Stop."

"What do you want?"

"I want to find out what happened to my plate."

"What do you mean, sir? Your plate?"

"You were very anxious that my plate should not be given to anyone else."

"I don't understand."

"Did you know that it was poisoned?"

"You mean the food was bad, sir?"

"I mean it was poisoned and you were careful to save Dr. Braun's life—not mine."

"I'm afraid, sir, I don't understand you. I am busy. You must excuse me." The sound of a howling dog came up the long passage from the kitchen—a low dismal howl intercepted by a sharper burst of pain. The head waiter called, "Max!" and ran like a human being down the passage. He flung open the kitchen door. "Max!"

The dachshund lifted a melancholy head from where it crouched below the table, then began to drag its body painfully towards the head waiter. A man in a chef's cap said, "He ate nothing here. The plate was thrown away." The dog collapsed at the waiter's feet and lay there like a length of offal.

The waiter went down on his knees beside the dog. He said,

"Max, *mein Kind. Mein Kind.*" The black body was like an elongation of his own black suit; they were not one flesh, but they might well have been one piece of serge. The kitchen staff gathered around.

The black tube made a slight movement and a pink tongue came out like tooth paste and lay on the kitchen floor. The head waiter put his hand on the dog and then looked up at Wormold. The tear-filled eyes so accused him of standing there alive while the dog was dead that he nearly found it in his heart to apologize, but instead he turned and went. At the end of the passage he looked back; the black figure knelt beside the black dog and the white chef stood above them and the kitchen hands waited, like mourners round a grave, carrying their troughs and mops and dishes like wreaths. My death, he thought, would have been more unobtrusive than that.

4

"I have come back," he said to Beatrice, "I am not under the table. I have come back victorious. The dog it was that died."

Four

1

Captain Segura said, "I'm glad to find you alone. Are you alone?"

"Quite alone."

"I'm sure you don't mind. I have put two men at the door to see that we aren't disturbed."

"Am I under arrest?"

"Of course not."

"Milly and Beatrice are out at a cinema. They'll be surprised if they are not allowed in."

"I will not take up much of your time. There are two things I have come to see you about. One is important. The other is only routine. May I begin with what is important?"

"Please."

"I wish, Mr. Wormold, to ask for the hand of your daughter."

"Does that require two policemen at the door?"

"It's convenient not to be disturbed."

"Have you spoken to Milly?"

"I would not dream of it before speaking to you."

"I suppose even here you *would* need my consent by law."

"It is not a matter of law but of common courtesy. May I smoke?"

"Why not? Is that case really made from human skin?"

Captain Segura laughed. "Ah, Milly, Milly. What a tease she is!" He added ambiguously, "Do you really believe that story, Mr. Wormold?" Perhaps he had an objection to a direct lie—he might be a good Catholic.

"She's much too young to marry, Captain Segura."

"Not in this country."

"I'm sure she has no wish to marry yet."

"But you could influence her, Mr. Wormold."

"They call you the Red Vulture, don't they?"

"That, in Cuba, is a kind of compliment."

"Aren't you rather an uncertain life? You seem to have a lot of enemies."

"I have saved enough to take care of my widow. In that way, Mr. Wormold, I am a more reliable support than you are. This establishment—it can't bring you in much money and at any moment it is liable to be closed."

"Closed?"

"I am sure you do not intend to cause trouble, but a lot of trouble has been happening around you. If you had to leave this country, would you not feel happier if your daughter were well established here?"

"What kind of trouble, Captain Segura?"

"There was a car which crashed—never mind why. There was an attack on poor Engineer Cifuentes—a friend of the Minister of the Interior. Professor Sanchez complained that you broke into his house and threatened him. There is even a story that you poisoned a dog."

"That I poisoned a dog?"

"It sounds absurd, of course. But a head waiter at the Hotel Nacional said you gave his dog poisoned whisky. Why should you give a dog whisky at all? I don't understand. Nor does he. He thinks perhaps because it was a German dog. You don't say anything, Mr. Wormold."

"I am at a loss for words."

"He was in a terrible state, poor man. Otherwise I would have thrown him out of the office for talking nonsense. He said you came into the kitchen to gloat over what you had done. It sounded very unlike you, Mr. Wormold. I have always thought of you as a humane man. Just assure me there is no truth in this story . . ."

"The dog *was* poisoned. The whisky came from my glass. But it was intended for me, not the dog."

"Why should anyone try to poison you?"

"I don't know."

"Two strange stories—they cancel out. Probably there was no poison and the dog just died. I gather it was an old dog. But you must admit, Mr. Wormold, that a lot of trouble seems to go on around you. Perhaps you are like one of those innocent children I have read about in your country who set poltergeists to work."

"Perhaps I am. Do you know the names of the poltergeists?"

"Most of them. I think the time has come to exorcise them. I am drawing up a report for the President."

"Am I on it?"

"You needn't be. I ought to tell you, Mr. Wormold, that I have saved money—enough money to leave Milly in comfort if anything were ever to happen to me. And of course enough for us to settle in Miami if there were a revolution."

"There's no need for you to tell me all this. I'm not questioning your financial capacity."

"It is customary, Mr. Wormold. Now for my health—that is good. I can show you the certificates. Nor will there be any difficulty about children—that has been amply proved."

"I see."

"There is nothing in that which need worry your daughter. The children are provided for. My present encumbrance is not an important one. I know that Protestants are rather particular about these things."

"I'm not exactly a Protestant."

"And luckily your daughter is a Catholic. It would really be a most suitable marriage, Mr. Wormold."

"Milly is only seventeen."

"It is the best and easiest age to bear a child, Mr. Wormold. Have I your permission to speak to her?"

"Do you need it?"

"It's more correct."

"And if I said no . . ."

"I would of course try to persuade you."

"You said once that I was not of the torturable class."

Captain Segura laid his hand affectionately on Wormold's shoulder. "You have Milly's sense of humour. But seriously, there is always your residence permit to consider."

"You seem very determined. All right. You may as well speak to her. You have plenty of opportunity on her way from school. But Milly's got sense. I don't think you stand a chance."

"In that case I may ask you later to use a father's influence."

"How Victorian you are, Captain Segura. A father today has no influence. You said there was something important . . ."

Captain Segura said reproachfully, "This was the important subject. The other is a matter of routine only. Would you come with me to the Wonder Bar?"

"Why?"

"A police matter. Nothing for you to worry about. I am asking you a favour, that's all, Mr. Wormold."

They went in Captain Segura's scarlet sports car with a motorcycle policeman before and behind. All the bootblacks from the Paseo seemed to be gathered in Virdudes. There were policemen on either side of the swing doors of the Wonder Bar and the sun lay heavy overhead.

The motorcycle policemen leapt off their machines and began to shoo the bootblacks away. Policemen ran out from the bar and formed an escort for Captain Segura. Wormold followed him. As always at that time of day the jalousies above the colonnade were creaking in the small wind from the sea. The barman stood on the wrong side of the bar, the customers' side. He looked sick and afraid. Several broken bottles behind him were still dripping single drops, but they had spilt their main contents a long while ago. Someone on the floor was hidden by the bodies of the policemen, but the boots showed—the thick over-repaired boots of a not-rich old man. "It's just a formal identification," Captain Segura said. Wormold hardly needed to see the face, but they cleared a way before him so that he could look down at Dr. Hasselbacher.

"It's Dr. Hasselbacher," he said. "You know him as well as I do."

"There is a form to be observed in these matters," Segura said. "An independent identification."

"Who did it?"

Segura said, "Who knows? You had better have a glass of whisky. Barman!"

"No. Give me a daiquiri. It was always a daiquiri I used to drink with him."

"Someone came in here with a gun. Two shots missed. Of course we shall say it was the rebels from Oriente. It will be useful in influencing foreign opinion. Perhaps it was the rebels."

The face stared up from the floor without expression. You couldn't describe that impassivity in terms of peace or anguish. It was as though nothing at all had ever happened to it: an unborn face.

"When you bury him put his helmet on the coffin."

"Helmet?"

"You'll find an old uniform in his flat. He was a sentimental man." It was odd that Dr. Hasselbacher had survived two world wars and had died at the end of it in so-called peace much the same death as he might have died upon the Somme.

"You know very well it had nothing to do with the rebels," Wormold said.

"It is convenient to say so."

"The poltergeists again."

"You blame yourself too much."

"He warned me not to go to the lunch, Carter heard him, everybody heard him, so they killed him."

"Who are They?"

"You have the list."

"The name Carter wasn't on it."

"Ask the waiter with the dog, then. You can torture *him* surely. I won't complain."

"He is German and he has high political friends. Why should he want to poison you?"

"Because they think I'm dangerous. Me! They little know. Give me another daiquiri. I always had two before I went back to the shop. Will you show me your list, Segura?"

"I might to a father-in-law, because I could trust him."

They can print statistics and count the populations in hundreds of thousands, but to each man a city consists of no more than a few streets, a few houses, a few people. Remove those few and a city exists no longer except as a pain in the memory, like the pain of an amputated leg no longer there. It was time, Wormold thought, to pack up and go and leave the ruins of Havana.

"You know," Captain Segura said, "this only emphasizes what I meant. It might have been you. Milly should be safe from accidents like this."

"Yes," Wormold said. "I shall have to see to that."

2

The policemen were gone from the shop when he returned. Lopez was out—he had no idea where. He could hear Rudy fidgeting with his tubes and an occasional snatch of atmospherics beat around the apartment. He sat down on the bed. Three deaths: an unknown man called Raul, a black dachshund called Max, and an old doctor called Hasselbacher; he was the cause—and Carter. Carter had not planned the death of Raul nor the dog, but Dr. Hasselbacher had been given no chance. It had been a reprisal: one death for one life, a reversal of the Mosaic Code. He could hear Milly and Beatrice talking in the next room. Although the door was ajar he only half took in what they were saying. He stood on the frontier of violence, a strange land he had never visited before; he had his passport in his hand. "Profession: Spy." "Characteristic Features: Friendlessness." "Purpose of Visit: Murder." No visa was required. His papers were in order.

And on this side of the border he heard the voices talking in the language he knew.

Beatrice said, "No, I wouldn't advise deep carnation. Not at your age."

Milly said, "They ought to give lessons in make-up during the last term. I can just hear Sister Agnes saying, 'A drop of *Nuit d'Amour* behind the ears.' "

"Try this light carnation. No, don't smear the edge of your mouth. Let me show you."

Wormold thought, I have no arsenic or cyanide. Besides, I will have no opportunity to drink with him. I should have forced that whisky down his throat—easier said than done off the Elizabethan stage, and even there he would have needed in addition a poisoned rapier.

"There. You see what I mean."

"What about rouge?"

"You don't need rouge."

"What smell do you use, Beatrice?"

"Sous le Vent."

They have shot Hasselbacher, but I have no gun, Wormold

thought. Surely a gun should have been part of the office equipment, like the safe and the celluloid sheets and the microscope and the electric kettle. He had never in his life so much as handled a gun—but that was no insuperable objection. He had only to be as close to Carter as the door through which the voices came.

"We'll go shopping together. I think you'd like *Indiscret*. That's Lucien Lelong."

"It doesn't sound very passionate," Milly said.

"You are young. You don't have to put passion on behind the ears."

"You must give a man encouragement," Milly said.

"Just look at him."

"Like this?"

Wormold heard Beatrice laugh. He looked at the door with astonishment. He had gone in thought so far across the border that he had forgotten he was still here on this side with them.

"You needn't give them all that encouragement," Beatrice said.

"Did I languish?"

"I'd call it smoulder."

"Do you miss being married?" Milly asked.

"If you mean do I miss Peter, I don't."

"If he died would you marry again?"

"I don't think I'd better wait for that. He's only forty."

"Oh yes, I suppose *you* could marry again—if you call it marriage."

"I do."

"But it's terrible, isn't it? *I* have to marry for keeps."

"Most of us think we are going to do that—when we do it."

"I'd be much better off as a mistress."

"I don't believe your father would like that very much."

"I don't see why not. If he married again it wouldn't be any different. She'd really be his mistress, wouldn't she? He wanted to stay with mother always. I know. He told me so. It was a real marriage. Even a good pagan can't get round that."

"I thought the same about Peter. Milly, Milly, don't let them make you hard."

"They?"

"The nuns."

"Oh. They don't talk to me that way. Not that way at all."

There was always, of course, the possibility of a knife. But for a knife you had to be closer to Carter than he could ever hope to get.

Milly said, "Do you love my father?"

He thought, One day I can come back and settle these questions. But now there are more important problems—I have to discover how to kill a man. Surely they produced handbooks to tell you how? There must be treatises on unarmed combat. He looked at his hands, but he didn't trust them.

Beatrice said, "Why do you ask that?"

"A way you looked at him."

"When?"

"When he came back from that lunch. Perhaps you were just pleased because he'd made a speech?"

"Yes."

"It wouldn't do," Milly said. "I mean, you loving him."

Wormold said to himself: At least if I could kill him, I would kill for a clean reason. I would kill to show that you can't kill without being killed in your turn. I wouldn't kill for my country. I wouldn't kill for capitalism or communism or social democracy or the welfare state—whose welfare? I would kill Carter because he killed Hasselbacher. A family feud had been a better reason for murder than patriotism or the preference for one economic system over another. If I love or if I hate, let me love or hate as an individual. I will not be 59200 stroke 5 in anyone's global war.

"If I loved him, why shouldn't I?"

"He's married."

"Milly, dear Milly. Beware of formulas. If there's a God, he's not a God of formulas."

"Do you love him?"

"I never said so."

A gun is the only way; where can I get a gun?

Somebody came through the door; he didn't even look up. Rudy's tubes gave a high shriek in the next room. Milly's voice said, "We didn't hear you come in."

He said, "I want you to do something for me, Milly."

"Were you listening?"

He heard Beatrice say, "What's wrong? What's happened?"

"There's been an accident—a kind of accident."

"Who?"

"Dr. Hasselbacher."

"Serious?"

"Yes."

"You are breaking the news, aren't you?" Milly said.

"Yes."

"Poor Dr. Hasselbacher."

"Yes."

"I'll get the chaplain to say a Mass for every year we knew him." There hadn't, he realized, been any need to break a death gently so far as Milly was concerned. All deaths to her were happy deaths. Vengeance was unnecessary when you believed in a heaven. But he had no such belief. Mercy and forgiveness were scarcely virtues in a Christian—they came too easily.

He said, "Captain Segura was here. He wants you to marry him."

"That old man. I'll never ride in his car again."

"I'd like you to once more—tomorrow. Tell him I want to see him."

"Why?"

"A game of draughts. At ten o'clock. You and Beatrice must be out of the way."

"Will he pester me?"

"No. Just tell him to come and talk to me. Tell him to bring his list. He'll understand."

"And afterwards?"

"We are going home. To England."

When he was alone with Beatrice, he said, "That's that. The end of the office."

"What do you mean?"

"Perhaps we'll go down gloriously with one good report—the list of secret agents operating here."

"Including us?"

"Oh, no. We've never operated."

"I don't understand."

"I've got no agents, Beatrice. Not one. Hasselbacher was killed for no reason. There are no constructions in the Oriente mountains."

It was typical of her that she showed no incredulity. This was a piece of information like any other information to be filed for reference. Any assessment of its value would be made, he thought, by the head office.

He said, "Of course it's your duty to report this immediately to

London, but I'd be grateful if you'd wait till after tomorrow. We may be able to add something genuine then."

"If you are alive, you mean."

"Of course I'll be alive."

"You are planning something."

"Segura has the list of agents."

"That's not what you are planning. But if you are dead," she said with what sounded like anger, *"de mortuis,* I suppose."

"If something did happen to me I wouldn't want you to learn for the first time from these bogus files what a fraud I'd been."

"But Raul . . . there must have been a Raul."

"Poor man. He must have wondered what was happening to him. Taking a joy ride in his usual way. Perhaps he was drunk in his usual way too. I hope so."

"But he existed."

"One has to get a name from somewhere. I must have picked his up without remembering it."

"Those diagrams?"

"I drew them myself from the Atomic Pile Cleaner. The joke's over now. Would you like to write out a confession for me to sign? I'm glad they didn't do anything serious to Teresa."

She began to laugh. She put her head in her hands and laughed. She said, "Oh, how I love you."

"It must seem pretty silly to you."

"London seems pretty silly. And Henry Hawthorne. Do you think I would ever have left Peter if once—just once—he'd made a fool of UNESCO? But UNESCO was sacred. Cultural conferences were sacred. He never laughed. . . . Lend me your handkerchief."

"You're crying."

"I'm laughing. Those drawings . . ."

"One was a nozzle spray and another was a double-action coupling. I never thought they would pass the experts."

"They weren't seen by experts. You forget—this is a secret service. We have to protect our sources. We can't allow documents like that to reach anyone who really knows. Darling . . ."

"You said darling."

"It's a way of speaking. Do you remember the Tropicana and that man singing—I didn't know you were my boss and I was your secretary, you were just a nice man with a lovely daughter and I knew you wanted to do something crazy with a champagne bottle and I was so deadly bored with sense . . ."

"But I'm not the crazy type."

> *"They say the earth is round—*
> *My madness offends."*

"I wouldn't be a seller of vacuum cleaners if I were the crazy type."

> *"I say that night is day*
> *And I've no axe to grind."*

"Haven't you any more loyalty than I have?"

"You are loyal."

"Who to?"

"To Milly. I don't care a damn about men who are loyal to the people who pay them, to organizations. . . . I don't think even my country means all that much. There are many countries in our blood—aren't there?—but only one person. Would the world be in the mess it is if we were loyal to love and not to countries?"

He said, "I suppose they could take away my passport."

"Let them try."

"All the same," he said, "it's the end of a job for both of us."

Five

1

"Come in, Captain Segura."

Captain Segura gleamed. His leather gleamed, his buttons gleamed, and there was fresh pomade upon his hair. He was like a well-cared-for weapon. He said, "I was so pleased when Milly brought the message."

"We have a lot to talk over. Shall we have a game first? Tonight I am going to beat you."

"I doubt it, Mr. Wormold. I do not yet have to show you filial respect."

Wormold unfolded the draughts board. Then he arranged on

the board twenty-four miniature bottles of whisky: twelve Bourbon confronted twelve Scotch.

"What is this, Mr. Wormold?"

"An idea of Dr. Hasselbacher's. I thought we might have one game to his memory. When you take a piece you drink it."

"A shrewd idea, Mr. Wormold. As I am the better player, I drink more."

"And then I catch up with you—in the drinks also."

"I think I would prefer to play with ordinary pieces."

"Are you afraid of being beaten, Segura? Perhaps you have a weak head."

"My head is as strong as another man's, but sometimes with drink I lose my temper. I do not wish to lose my temper with my future father."

"Milly won't marry you, Segura."

"That is what we have to discuss."

"You play with the Bourbon. Bourbon is stronger than Scotch. I shall be handicapped."

"That is not necessary. I will play with the Scotch."

Segura turned the board and sat down.

"Why not take off your belt, Segura? You'll be more comfortable."

Segura laid his belt and holster on the ground beside him. "I will fight you unarmed," he said jovially.

"Do you keep your gun loaded?"

"Of course. The kind of enemies I possess do not give me a chance to load."

"Have you found the murderer of Hasselbacher?"

"No. He does not belong to the criminal class."

"Carter?"

"After what you said, naturally I checked. He was with Dr. Braun at the time. And we cannot doubt the word of the President of the European Traders' Association, can we?"

"So Dr. Braun is on your list?"

"Naturally. And now to play."

There is an imaginary line in draughts, as every player knows, that crosses the board diagonally from corner to corner; it is the line of defence. Whoever gains control of that line takes the initiative; when the line is crossed the attack has begun. With an insolent ease Segura established himself with a Defiance opening, then moved a bottle across through the centre of the board. He didn't hesitate between moves; he hardly looked at the board. It was Wormold who paused and thought.

"Where is Milly?" Segura asked.

"Out."

"And your charming secretary?"

"With Milly."

"You are already in difficulties," Captain Segura said. He struck at the base of Wormold's defence and captured a bottle of Old Taylor. "The first drink," he said and drained it. Wormold recklessly began a pincer movement in reply and almost at once lost a bottle—of Old Forester this time. A few beads of sweat came out on Segura's forehead and he cleared his throat after drinking. He said, "You play recklessly, Mr. Wormold." He indicated the board. "You should have taken that piece."

"You can huff me," Wormold said.

For the first time Segura hesitated. He said, "No. I prefer you to take my piece." It was an unfamiliar whisky called Cairngorm and it found a raw spot on Wormold's tongue.

They played for a while with exaggerated care, neither taking a piece.

"Is Carter still at the Seville-Biltmore?" Wormold asked.

"Yes."

"Do you keep him under observation?"

"No. What is the use?"

Wormold was clinging to the edge of the board with what was left of his foiled pincer movement, but he had lost his base. He made a false move which enabled Segura to thrust a protected piece into square 22 and there was no way left of saving his piece on 25 and preventing Segura from reaching the back row and gaining a king.

"Careless," Segura said.

"I can make it an exchange."

"But I have the king."

Segura drank a Four Roses and Wormold at the other end of the board took a Dimpled Haig. Segura said, "It is a hot evening." He crowned his king with a scrap of paper. Wormold said, "If I capture him I have to drink two bottles—I have spares in the cupboard."

"You have thought everything out," Segura said—was it with sourness?

He played now with great caution. It became difficult to tempt

him to a capture and Wormold began to realize the fundamental
weakness of his plan, that it is possible for a good player to defeat
an opponent without capturing his pieces. He took one more of
Segura's and was trapped. He was left without a move.

Segura wiped the sweat from his forehead. "You see," he said,
"you cannot win."

"You must give me my revenge."

"This Bourbon is strong. Eighty-five proof."

"We will switch the whiskies."

This time Wormold was black, with the Scotch. He had replaced the three Scotch he had drunk and the three Bourbon. He
started with the Old Fourteenth opening which is apt to lead to a
long-drawn-out game, for he knew now that his only hope was to
make Segura lose his caution and play for pieces. Again he tried
to be huffed, but Segura would not accept the move. It was as
though Segura had recognized that his real opponent was not
Wormold but his own head. He even threw away a piece with no
tactical advantage and forced Wormold to take it—a Hiram
Walker. Wormold realized that his own head was in danger: the
mixture of Scotch and Bourbon was a deadly one. He said, "Give
me a cigarette." Segura leant forward to light it and Wormold was
aware of the effort he had to make to keep the lighter steady. It
wouldn't snap and he cursed with unnecessary violence. Two
more drinks and I have him, Wormold thought.

But it was as difficult to lose a piece to an unwilling antagonist
as to capture one. Against his own will the battle was swaying to
his side. He drank one Harper's and made a king. He said with
false joviality, "The game's mine, Segura. Do you want to pack
up?"

Segura scowled at the board. It was obvious that he was torn
in two, between the desire to win and the desire to keep his head,
but his head was clouded by anger as well as whisky. He said,
"This is a pig's way of playing checkers." Now that his opponent
had a king, he could no longer play for a bloodless victory, for the
king had freedom of movement. This time when he sacrificed a
Kentucky Tavern it was a genuine sacrifice and he swore at the
pieces. "These damned shapes," he said, "they are all different.
Cut-glass, whoever heard of a checker piece of cut-glass?" Wormold felt his own brain fogged with the Bourbon, but the moment
for victory—and defeat—had come.

Segura said, "You moved my piece."

"No, that's Red Label. Mine."

"How in God's name can I tell the difference between Scotch and Bourbon? They are all bottles, aren't they?"

"You are angry because you are losing."

"I never lose."

Then Wormold made his careful slip and exposed his king. For a moment he thought that Segura had not noticed and then he thought that deliberately to avoid drinking Segura was going to let his chance go by. But the temptation to take the king was great and what lay beyond the move was a shattering victory. His own piece would be made a king and a massacre would follow. Yet he hesitated. The heat of the whisky and the close night melted his face like a wax doll's; he had difficulty in focussing. He said, "Why did you do that?"

"What?"

"You lose your king an' the game."

"Damn. I didn't notice. I must be drunk."

"You drunk?"

"A little."

"I'm drunk too. You know I'm drunk. You are trying to make me drunk. Why?"

"Don't be a fool, Segura. Why should I want to make you drunk? Let's stop the game, call it a draw."

"God damn a draw. I know why you want to make me drunk. You want to show me that list—I mean you want me to show you."

"What list?"

"I have you all in the net. Where is Milly?"

"I told you, out."

"Tonight I go to the Chief of Police. We draw the net tight."

"With Carter in it?"

"Who is Carter?" He wagged his finger at Wormold. "You are in it—but I know you are no agent. You are a fraud."

"Why not sleep a bit, Segura? A drawn game."

"No drawn game. Look. I take your king." He opened the little bottle of Red Label and drank it down.

"Two bottles for a king," Wormold said and handed him a Dunosdale Cream.

Segura sat heavily in his chair, his chin rocking. He said, "Admit you are beaten. I do not play for pieces."

"I admit nothing. I have the better head, and look, I huff you.

You could have gone on." A Canadian rye had got mixed with the Bourbons—a Lord Calvert—and Wormold drank it down. He thought: It must be the last. If he doesn't pass out now I'm finished. I won't be sober enough to pull a trigger. Did he say it was loaded?

"Matters nothing," Segura said in a whisper. "You finished anyway." He moved his hand slowly over the board as though he were carrying an egg in a spoon. "See?" He captured one piece, two pieces, three . . .

"Drink this, Segura." A George IV, a Queen Anne—the game was ending in a flourish of royalty—a Highland Queen.

"You can go on, Segura. Or shall I huff you again? Drink it down." Vat 69. "Another. Drink it, Segura." Grant's Standfast. Old Argyll. "Drink them, Segura. I surrender now." But it was Segura who had surrendered. Wormold undid the captain's collar to give him air and eased his head on the back of the seat, but his own legs were uncertain as he walked towards the door. He had Segura's gun in his pocket.

2

At the Seville-Biltmore he went to the house phone and called up Carter. He had to admit that Carter's nerves were steady—far steadier than his own. Carter's mission in Cuba had not been properly fulfilled and yet he stayed on, as a marksman or perhaps as a decoy duck. Wormold said, "Good evening, Carter."

"Why—good evening, Wormold." The voice had just the right chill of injured pride.

"I wanted to apologize to you, Carter. That silly business of the whisky. I was tight, I suppose. I'm a bit tight now. Not used to apologizing."

"It's quite all right, Wormold. Go to bed."

"Sneered at your stammer. Chap shouldn't do that." He found himself talking like Hawthorne. Falsity was an occupational disease.

"I didn't know what the h-hell you meant."

"I shoon—soon—found out what was wrong. Nothing to do with you. That damned head waiter poisoned his own dog. It was very old, of course, but to give it poisoned scraps—that's not the way to put a dog to sleep."

"Is that what h-happened? Thank you for letting me know, but it's late. I'm just going to bed, Wormold."

"Man's best friend."

"What's that? I can't h-hear you."

"Caesar, the King's friend, and there was the rough-haired one who went down at Jutland. Last seen on the bridge beside his master."

"You are drunk, Wormold." It was so much easier, Wormold found, to imitate drunkenness after—how many Scotch and Bourbon? You can trust a drunk man—*in vino veritas*. You can also more easily dispose of a drunk man. Carter would be a fool not to take the chance. Wormold said, "I feel in the mood for going round the spots."

"What spots?"

"The spots you wanted to see in Havana."

"It's getting late."

"It's the right time." Carter's hesitation came at him down the wire. He said, "Bring a gun." He felt a strange reluctance to kill an unarmed killer—if Carter should ever chance to be unarmed.

"A gun? Why?"

"In some of these places they try to roll you."

"Can't *you* bring one?"

"I don't happen to own one."

"Nor do I," and he believed he caught in the receiver the metallic sound of a chamber being checked. Diamond cut diamond, he thought, and smiled. But a smile is dangerous to the act of hate as much as to the act of love. He had to remind himself how Hasselbacher had looked, staring up from the floor under the bar. They had not given the old man one chance, and he was giving Carter plenty. He began to regret the drinks he had taken.

"I'll meet you in the bar," Carter said.

"Don't be long."

"I have to get dressed."

Wormold was glad now of the darkness of the bar. Carter, he supposed, was telephoning to his friends and perhaps making a rendezvous, but in the bar at any rate they couldn't pick him out before he saw them. There was one entrance from the street and one from the hotel, and at the back a kind of balcony which would give support if he needed it to his gun. Anyone who entered was blinded for a while by the darkness—as he himself was. When he entered he couldn't for a moment see whether the bar held one or two customers, for the pair were tightly locked on a sofa by the street door.

He asked for a Scotch, but he left it untasted, sitting on the balcony, watching both doors. Presently a man entered. He couldn't see the face; it was the hand patting the pipe pocket which identified Carter.

"Carter."

Carter came to him.

"Let's be off," Wormold said.

"Take your drink first and I'll h-have one to keep you company."

"I've had too much, Carter. I need some air. We'll get a drink in some house."

Carter sat down. "Tell me where you plan to take me."

"Any one of a dozen whore houses. They are all the same, Carter. About a dozen girls to choose from. They'll do an exhibition for you. Come on, we'll go. They get crowded after midnight."

Carter said anxiously, "I'd like a drink first. I can't go to a show like that stone sober."

"You aren't expecting anyone, are you, Carter?"

"No, why?"

"I thought—the way you watched the door . . ."

"I don't know a soul in this town. I told you."

"Except Dr. Braun."

"Oh yes, of course, Dr. Braun. But he's not the kind of companion to take to a h-house, is he?"

"After you, Carter."

Reluctantly Carter moved. It was obvious that he was searching for an excuse to stay. He said, "I just want to leave a message with the porter. I'm expecting a telephone call."

"From Dr. Braun?"

"Yes." He hesitated. "It seems rude going out like this before h-he rings. Can't you wait five minutes, Wormold?"

"Say you'll be back by one—unless you decide to make a night of it."

"It would be better to wait."

"Then I'll go without you. Damn you, Carter, I thought you wanted to see the town." He walked rapidly away. His car was parked across the street. He never looked back, but he heard steps following him. Carter no more wanted to lose him than he wanted to lose Carter.

"What a temper you've got, Wormold."

"I'm sorry. Drink takes me that way."

"I h-hope you are sober enough to drive straight."

"It would be better, Carter, if you drove."

He thought: That will keep his hands from his pockets.

"First right, first left, Carter."

They came out into the Atlantic drive; a lean white ship was leaving harbour—some tourist cruiser bound for Kingston or for Port au Prince. They could see the couples leaning over the rail, romantic in the moonlight, and a band was playing a fading favourite—"I Could Have Danced All Night."

"It makes me homesick," Carter said.

"For Nottwich?"

"Yes."

"There's no sea at Nottwich."

"The pleasure boats on the river looked as big as that when I was young."

A murderer had no right to be homesick; a murderer should be a machine, and I have to become a machine, too, Wormold thought, feeling in his pocket the handkerchief he would have to use to clean the fingerprints when the time came. But how to choose the time? What side-street or what doorway? And if the other shot first?

"Are your friends Russian, Carter? German? American?"

"What friends?" He added simply, "I have no friends."

"No friends?"

"No."

"To the left again, Carter, then right."

They moved at a walking pace now in a narrow street, lined with clubs; orchestras spoke from below ground like the ghost of Hamlet's father or that music under the paving stones in Alexandria when the god Hercules left Anthony. Two men in night-club uniforms bawled competitively to them across the road. Wormold said, "Let's stop. I need a drink badly before we go on."

"Are these whore houses?"

"No. We'll go to a house later." He thought, if only Carter when he left the wheel had grabbed his gun, it would have been so easy to fire. Carter said, "Do you know this spot?"

"No. But I know the tune." It was strange that they were playing that—"my madness offends."

There were coloured photographs of naked girls outside and in the night club Esperanto one neon-lighted word, *Strippteese.* Steps painted in stripes like cheap pajamas led them down towards a cellar foggy with Havanas. It seemed as suitable a place as any other for an execution. But he wanted a drink first. "You lead the way, Carter." Carter was hesitating. He opened his mouth and struggled with an aspirate—Wormold had never before heard him struggle for quite so long. "I h-h-h-hope . . ."

"What do you hope?"

"Nothing."

They sat and watched the stripping and both drank brandy and soda. A girl went from table to table ridding herself of clothes. She began with her gloves. A spectator took them with resignation like the contents of an In tray. Then she presented her back to Carter and told him to unhook her black lace corsets. Carter fumbled in vain at the catches, blushing all the time while the girl laughed and wriggled against his fingers. He said, "I'm sorry, I can't find . . ." Round the floor the gloomy men sat at their little tables watching Carter. No one smiled.

"You haven't had much practice, Carter, in Nottwich. Let me."

"Leave me alone, can't you?"

At last he got the corset undone and the girl rumpled his thin streaky hair and passed on. He smoothed it down again with a pocket comb. "I don't like this place," he said.

"You are shy with women, Carter." But how could one shoot a man at whom it was so easy to laugh?

"I don't like horseplay," Carter said.

They climbed the stairs. Carter's pocket was heavy on his hip. Of course it might be his pipe he carried. He sat at the wheel again and grumbled. "You can see that sort of show anywhere. Just tarts undressing."

"You didn't help her much."

"I was looking for a zip."

"I needed a drink badly."

"Rotten brandy, too. I wouldn't wonder if it was doped."

"Your whisky was more than doped, Carter." He was trying to heat his anger up and not to remember his ineffective victim struggling with the corset and blushing at his failure.

"What's that you said?"

"Stop here."

"Why?"

"You wanted to be taken to a house. Here is a house."

"But there's no one about."

"They are all closed and shuttered like this. Get out and ring the bell."

"What did you mean about the whisky?"

"Never mind that now. Get out and ring."

It was as suitable a place as a cellar (blank walls too had been frequently used for this purpose): a grey façade and a street where no one came except for one unlovely purpose. Carter slowly shifted his legs from under the wheel and Wormold watched his hands closely—the ineffective hands. It's a fair duel, he told himself, he's more accustomed to killing than I am, the chances are equal enough; I am not even quite sure my gun is loaded. He has more chance than Hasselbacher ever had.

With his hand on the door Carter paused again. He said, "Perhaps it would be more sensible—some other night. You know, I h-h-h-h . . ."

"You are frightened, Carter."

"I've never been to a h-h-h-house before. To tell you the truth, Wormold, I don't h-have much need of women."

"It sounds a lonely sort of life."

"I can do without them," he said defiantly. "There are more important things for a man than running after . . ."

"Why did you want to come to a house then?"

Again he startled Wormold with the plain truth. "I try to want them, but when it comes to the point . . ." He hovered on the edge of confession and then plunged. "It doesn't work, Wormold. I can't do what they want."

"Get out of the car."

I have to do it, Wormold thought, before he confesses any more to me. With every second the man was becoming human: a creature like oneself whom one might pity or console, not kill. Who knew what excuses were buried below any violent act? He drew Segura's gun.

"What?"

"Get out."

Carter stood against the whore-house door with a look of sullen complaint rather than fear. His fear was of women, not of violence. He said, "You are making a mistake. It was Braun who gave me the whisky. I'm not important."

"I don't care about the whisky. But you killed Hasselbacher, didn't you?"

Again he surprised Wormold with the truth. There was a kind of honesty in the man. "I was under orders, Wormold. I h-h-h- —" He had manoeuvered himself so that his elbow reached the bell, and now he leant back and in the depths of the house the bell rang and rang its summons to work.

"There's no enmity, Wormold. You got too dangerous, that was all. We are only private soldiers, you and I."

"Me dangerous? What fools you people must be. I have no agents, Carter."

"Oh yes you h-have. Those constructions in the mountains. We have copies of your drawings."

"The parts of a vacuum cleaner." He wondered who had supplied them: Lopez? Or Hawthorne's own courier, or a man in the Consulate?

Carter's hand went to his pocket and Wormold fired. Carter gave a sharp yelp. He said, "You nearly shot me," and pulled out a hand clasped round a shattered pipe. He said, "My Dunhill. You've smashed my Dunhill."

"Beginner's luck," Wormold said. He had braced himself for a death, but it was impossible to shoot again. The door behind Carter began to open. There was an impression of plastic music. "They'll look after you in there. You may need a woman now, Carter."

"You—you clown."

How right Carter was. He put the gun down beside him and slipped into the driving seat. Suddenly he felt happy. He might have killed a man. He had proved conclusively to himself that he wasn't one of the judges; he had no vocation for violence. Then Carter fired.

Six

1

He said to Beatrice, "I was just leaning forward to switch on the engine. That saved me, I imagine. Of course it was his right to fire back. It was a real duel, but the third shot was mine."

"What happened afterwards?"

"I had time to drive away before I was sick."

"Sick?"

"I suppose if I hadn't missed the war it would have seemed much less serious a thing killing a man. Poor Carter."

"Why should you feel sorry for him?"

"He was a man. I'd learnt a lot about him. He couldn't undo a girl's corset. He was scared of women. He liked his pipe and when he was a boy the pleasure steamers on the river at home seemed to him like liners. Perhaps he was a romantic. A romantic is usually afraid, isn't he, in case reality doesn't come up to expectations? They all expect too much."

"And then?"

"I wiped my prints off the gun and brought it back. Of course Segura will find that two shots have been fired. But I don't suppose he'll want to claim the bullets. It would be a little difficult to explain. He was still asleep when I came in. I'm afraid to think what a head he'll have now. My own is bad enough. But I tried to follow your instructions with the photograph."

"What photograph?"

"He had a list of foreign agents he was taking to the Chief of Police. I photographed it and put it back in his pocket. I'm glad to feel there's one real report that I've sent before I resign."

"You should have waited for me."

"How could I? He was going to wake at any moment. But this micro business is tricky."

"Why on earth did you make a microphotograph?"

"Because we can't trust any courier to Kingston. Carter's people—whoever they are—have copies of the Oriente drawings. That means a double-agent somewhere. Perhaps it's your man who smuggles in the drugs. So I made a microphotograph as you

showed me and I stuck it on the back of a stamp and I posted off
an assorted batch of five hundred British colonials, the way we
arranged for an emergency."

"We'll have to cable them which stamp you've stuck it to."

"Which stamp?"

"You don't expect them to look through five hundred stamps,
do you, looking for one black dot?"

"I hadn't thought of that. How very awkward."

"You must know which stamp . . ."

"I didn't think of looking at the front. I think it was a George
V, and it was red—or green."

"That's helpful. Do you remember any of the names on the
list?"

"No. There wasn't time to read it properly. I know I'm a fool
at this game, Beatrice."

"No. They are the fools."

"I wonder whom we'll hear from next. Dr. Braun . . . Segura . . ."

But it was neither of them.

2

The supercilious clerk from the Consulate appeared in the shop
at five o'clock the next afternoon. He stood stiffly among the vacuum cleaners like a disapproving tourist in a museum of phallic
objects. He told Wormold that the Ambassador wanted to see
him. "Will tomorrow morning do?" He was working on his last
report—Carter's death and his resignation.

"No, it won't. He telephoned from his home. You are to go
there straight away."

"I'm not an employee," Wormold said.

"Aren't you?"

Wormold drove back to Vedado, to the little white houses and
the bougainvilleas of the rich. It seemed a long while since his
visit to Professor Sanchez. He passed the house. What quarrels
were still in progress behind those doll's-house walls?

He had a sense that everyone in the Ambassador's home was
on the look-out for him and that the hall and the stairs had been
carefully cleared of spectators. On the first floor a woman turned
her back and shut herself in a room; he thought it was the Ambas-
sadress. Two children peered quickly through the banisters on the

second floor and ran off with a click of little heels on the tiled floor. The butler showed him into the drawing room—which was empty—and closed the door on him stealthily. Through the tall windows he could see a long green lawn and tall sub-tropical trees. Even there somebody was moving rapidly away.

The room was like many Embassy drawing rooms, a mixture of big inherited pieces and small personal objects acquired in previous stations. Wormold thought he could detect a past in Tehran (an odd-shaped pipe, a tile), Athens (an icon or two), but he was momentarily puzzled by an African mask—perhaps Monrovia?

The Ambassador came in, a tall cold man in a Guards tie, with something about him of what Hawthorne would have liked to be. He said, "Sit down, Wormold. Have a cigarette?"

"No thank you, sir."

"You'll find that chair more comfortable. Now it's no use beating about the bush, Wormold. You are in trouble."

"Yes."

"Of course I know nothing—nothing at all—of what you are doing here."

"I sell vacuum cleaners, sir."

The Ambassador looked at him with undisguised distaste. "Vacuum cleaners? I wasn't referring to them." He looked away from Wormold at the Persian pipe, the Greek icon, the Liberian mask. They were like the autobiography in which a man has written for reassurance only of his better days. He said, "Yesterday morning Captain Segura came to see me. Mind you, I don't know how the police got this information—it's none of my business— but he told me you had been sending a lot of reports home of a misleading character. I don't know whom you sent them to; that's none of my business either. He said in fact that you had been drawing money and pretending to have sources of information which simply don't exist. I thought it my duty to inform the Foreign Office at once. I gather you will be receiving orders to go home and report—who to I have no idea; that sort of thing has nothing to do with me."

Wormold saw two small heads looking out from behind one of the tall trees. He looked at them and they looked at him—he thought sympathetically. He said, "Yes, sir?"

"I got the impression that Captain Segura considered you were causing a lot of trouble here. I think if you refused to go home you might find yourself in serious trouble with the authorities, and under the circumstances of course I could do nothing to help you. Nothing at all. Captain Segura even suspects you of having forged some kind of document which he says you claim to have found in his possession. The whole subject is distasteful to me, Wormold. I can't tell you how distasteful it is. The correct sources for information abroad are the embassies. We have our attachés for that purpose. This so-called secret information is a trouble to every ambassador."

"Yes, sir."

"I don't know whether you've heard—it's been kept out of the papers—but an Englishman was shot the night before last. Captain Segura hinted that he was not unconnected with you."

"I met him once at lunch, sir."

"You had better go home, Wormold, on the first plane you can manage—the sooner the better for me—and discuss it with your people—whoever they are."

"Yes, sir."

3

The K.L.M. plane was due to take off at 3:30 in the morning for Amsterdam by way of Montreal. Wormold had no desire to travel by Kingston, where Hawthorne might have instructions to meet him. The office had been closed with a final cable and Rudy and his suitcase were routed to Jamaica. The code-books were burnt with the help of the celluloid sheets. Beatrice was to go with Rudy. Lopez was left in charge of the vacuum cleaners. All the personal possessions he valued Wormold got into one crate, which he arranged to send by sea. The horse was sold—to Captain Segura.

Beatrice helped him pack. The last object in the crate was the statue of St. Seraphina.

"Milly must be very unhappy," Beatrice said.

"She's wonderfully resigned. She says like Sir Humphrey Gilbert that God is just as close to her in England as in Cuba."

"It wasn't quite what Gilbert said."

There was a pile of unsecret rubbish left to be burnt.

Beatrice said, "What a lot of photographs you had tucked away —of *her*."

"I used to feel it was like killing someone to tear up a photograph. Of course I know now that it's quite different."

"What's this red box?"

"She gave me some cuff links once. They were stolen, but I kept the box. I don't know why. In a way I'm glad to see all this stuff go."

"The end of a life."

"Of two lives."

"What's this?"

"An old programme."

"Not so old. The Tropicana. May I keep it?"

"You are too young to keep things," Wormold said. "They accumulate too much. Soon you find you have nowhere left to live among the junk boxes."

"I'll risk it. That was a wonderful evening."

Milly and Wormold saw her off at the airport. Rudy disappeared unobtrusively, following the man with the enormous suitcase. It was a hot afternoon and people stood around drinking daiquiris. Ever since Captain Segura's proposal of marriage Milly's duenna had disappeared, but after her disappearance the child, whom he had hoped to see again, who had set fire to Thomas Earl Parkman, Junior, had not returned. It was as though Milly had outgrown both characters simultaneously. She said with grown-up tact, "I want to find some magazines for Beatrice," and busied herself at a bookstall with her back turned.

"I'm sorry," Wormold said. "I'll tell them when I get back that you know nothing. I wonder where you'll be sent next."

"The Persian Gulf perhaps. Basra."

"Why the Persian Gulf?"

"It's their idea of purgatory. Regeneration through sweat and tears. Do Phastkleaners have an agency at Basra?"

"I'm afraid Phastkleaners won't keep me on."

"What will you do?"

"I've got enough—thanks to poor Raul—for Milly's year in Switzerland. After that I don't know."

"You could open one of those practical-joke shops—you know, the bloodstained thumb and the spilt ink and the fly on the lump of sugar. How ghastly goings-away are. Please don't wait any longer."

"Shall I see you again?"

"I'll try not to go to Basra. I'll try to stay in the typists' pool with Angelica and Ethel and Miss Jenkinson. When I'm lucky I shall be off at six and we could meet at the Corner House for a cheap snack and go to the movies. It's one of those ghastly lives, isn't it, like UNESCO and modern writers in conference? It's been fun here with you."

"Yes."

"Now go away."

He went to the magazine stall and found Milly. "We're off," he said.

"But, Beatrice—she hasn't got her magazines."

"She doesn't want them."

"I didn't say goodbye."

"Too late. She's passed the emigration now. You'll see her in London. Perhaps."

4

It was as if they spent all their remaining time in airports. Now it was the K.L.M. flight and it was three in the morning and the sky was pink with the reflection of neon-lighted stands and landing flares, and it was Captain Segura who was doing the "seeing off." He tried to make the official occasion seem as private as possible, but it was still a little like a deportation. Segura said reproachfully, "You drove me to this."

"Your methods are gentler than Carter's—or Dr. Braun's. What are you doing about Dr. Braun?"

"He finds it necessary to return to Switzerland on a matter to do with his precision instruments."

"With a passage booked on to Moscow?"

"Not necessarily. Perhaps Bonn. Or Washington. Or even Bucharest. I don't know. Whoever they are, they are pleased, I believe, with your drawings."

"Drawings?"

"Of the constructions in Oriente. He will also take the credit for getting rid of a dangerous agent."

"Me?"

"Yes. Cuba will be a little quieter without you both, but I shall miss Milly."

"Milly would never have married you, Segura. She doesn't really like cigarette cases made of human skin."

"Did you ever hear whose skin?"

"No."

"A police officer who tortured my father to death. You see, he was a poor man. He belonged to the torturable class."

Milly joined them carrying *Time, Life, Paris Match,* and *Quick.* It was nearly 3:15 and there was a band of grey in the sky over the flare-path where the false dawn had begun. The pilots moved out to the plane and the air hostess followed. He knew the three of them by sight; they had sat with Beatrice at the Tropicana. A loudspeaker announced in English and Spanish the departure of flight 396 to Montreal and Amsterdam.

"I have a present for each of you," Segura said. He gave them two little packets. They opened them while the plane wheeled over Havana; the chain of lights along the marine parade swung out of sight and the sea fell like a curtain on all that past. In Wormold's packet was a miniature bottle of Grant's Standfast, and a bullet which had been fired from a police gun. In Milly's was a small silver horseshoe inscribed with her initials.

"Why the bullet?" Milly asked.

"Oh a joke in rather doubtful taste. All the same, he wasn't a bad chap," Wormold said.

"But not right for a husband," the grown-up Milly replied.

1

They had looked at him curiously when he gave his name, and then they had put him into a lift and taken him, a little to his surprise, down and not up. Now he sat in a long basement corridor watching a red light over a door; when it turned green, they had told him, he could go in, but not before. People who paid no attention to the light went in and went out; some of them carried papers and some of them briefcases, and one was in uniform, a colonel. Nobody looked at him; he felt that he embarrassed them. They ignored him as one ignores a malformed man. But presumably it was not his limp.

Hawthorne came down the passage from the lift. He looked rumpled, as though he had slept in his clothes; perhaps he had been on an all-night plane from Jamaica. He too would have ignored Wormold if Wormold had not spoken.

"Hullo, Hawthorne."

"Oh, you, Wormold."

"Did Beatrice arrive safely?"

"Yes. Naturally."

"Where is she, Hawthorne?"

"I have no idea."

"What's happening here? It looks like a court martial."

"It *is* a court martial," Hawthorne said frostily and went in to the room with the light. The clock stood at 11:25. He had been summoned for eleven.

He wondered whether there was anything they could do to him beyond sacking him, which presumably they had already done. That was probably what they were trying to decide in there. They could hardly charge him under the Official Secrets Act. He had invented secrets, he hadn't given them away. Presumably they could make it difficult for him if he tried to find a job abroad, and jobs at home were not easy to come by at his age, but he had no intention of giving them back their money. That was for Milly; he felt now as though he had earned it in his capacity as a target for Carter's poison, and Carter's bullet.

At 11:35 the colonel came out: he looked hot and angry as he strode towards the lift. There goes a hanging judge, thought Wormold. A man in a tweed jacket emerged next. He had blue eyes very deeply sunk and he needed no uniform to mark him as a sailor. He looked at Wormold accidentally and looked quickly away again like a man of integrity. He called out, "Wait for me, Colonel," and went down the passage with a very slight roll as though he were back on a bridge in rough weather. Hawthorne came next, in conversation with a very young man, and then Wormold was suddenly breathless, because the light was green and Beatrice was there.

"You are to go in," she said.

"What's the verdict?"

"I can't speak to you now. Where are you staying?"

He told her.

"I'll come to you at six. If I can."

"Am I to be shot at dawn?"

"Don't worry. Go in now. He doesn't like to be kept waiting."

"What's happening to you?"

She said, "Jakarta."

"What's that?"

"The end of the world," she said. "Further than Basra. Please go in."

A man wearing a black monocle sat all by himself behind a desk. He said, "Sit down, Wormold."

"I prefer to stand."

"Oh, that's a quotation isn't it?"

"Quotation?"

"I'm sure I remember hearing that in some play—amateur theatricals. A great many years ago, of course."

Wormold sat down. He said, "You've no right to send her to Jakarta."

"Send who to Jakarta?"

"Beatrice."

"Who's she? Oh, that secretary of yours. How I hate these Christian names. You'll have to see Miss Jenkinson about that. She's in charge of the pool, not me, thank God."

"She had nothing to do with anything."

"Anything? Listen, Wormold. We've decided to shut down your post, and the question arises—what are we to do with you?" It was coming now. Judging from the face of the colonel who had been one of his judges, he felt that what came would not be pleasant. The Chief took out his black monocle and Wormold was surprised by the baby eye. He said, "We thought the best thing for you under the circumstances would be to stay at home—on our training staff. Lecturing. How to run a station abroad. That kind of thing." He seemed to be swallowing something very disagreeable. He added, "Of course, as we always do when a man retires from a post abroad, we'll recommend you for a decoration. I think in your case—you were not there very long—we can hardly suggest anything higher than an O.B.E."

2

They greeted each other formally in a wilderness of sage-green chairs in an inexpensive hotel near Gower Street called the Pendennis. "I don't think I can get you a drink," he said. "It's Temperance."

"Why did you come here then?"

"I used to come with my parents when I was a boy. I hadn't realized about the temperance. It didn't trouble me then. Beatrice, what's happened? Are they mad?"

"They are pretty mad with both of us. They thought I should have spotted what was going on. The Chief had summoned quite a meeting. His liaisons were all there, with the War Office, the Admiralty, the Air Ministry. They had all your reports out in front of them and they went through them one by one. Communist infiltration in the government—nobody minded a memo to the Foreign Office cancelling that one. There were economic reports—they agreed they should be disavowed too. Only the Board of Trade would mind. Nobody got really touchy until the Service reports came up. There was one about disaffection in the Navy and another about refuelling bases for submarines. The commander said, 'There must be some truth in these.'"

"I said, 'Look at the source. He doesn't exist.'"

" 'We shall look such fools,' the commander said. 'They are going to be as pleased as Punch in Naval Intelligence.'

"But that was nothing to what they felt when the constructions were discussed."

"They'd really swallowed those drawings?"

"It was then they turned on poor Henry."

"I wish you wouldn't call him Henry."

"They said first of all that he had never reported you sold vacuum cleaners but that you were a kind of merchant king. The Chief didn't join in *that* hunt; he looked embarrassed for some reason, and anyway Henry—I mean Hawthorne—produced the file and all the details were on it. Of course that had never gone further than Miss Jenkinson's pool. Then they said he ought to have recognized the parts of a vacuum cleaner when he saw them. So he said he had, but there was no reason why the principle of a vacuum cleaner might not be applied to a weapon. After that they really howled for your blood—all except the Chief. There were moments when I thought he saw the funny side. He said to them, 'What we have to do is quite simple. We have to notify the Admiralty, the War Office, and the Air Ministry that all reports from Havana for the last six months are totally unreliable.' "

"But, Beatrice, they've offered me a job."

"That's easily explained. The commander crumbled first. Perhaps at sea one learns to take a long view. He said it would ruin the Service as far as the Admiralty was concerned. In future they would rely only on Naval Intelligence. Then the colonel said, 'If I tell the War Office we may as well pack up.' It was quite an impasse until the Chief suggested that perhaps the simplest plan was to circulate one more report from 59200 stroke 5—that the constructions had proved a failure and had been dismantled. There remained of course you. The Chief felt you had had valuable experience which should be kept for the use of the department rather than for the popular press. Too many people had written reminiscences lately of the Secret Service. Somebody mentioned the Official Secrets Act, but the Chief thought it might not cover your case. You should have seen them when they were balked of a victim. Of course they turned on me, but I wasn't going to be cross-examined by that gang. So I spoke out."

"What on earth did you say?"

"I told them even if I'd known I wouldn't have stopped you. I said you were working for something important—not for someone's notion of a global war that may never happen. That fool dressed up as a colonel said something about 'your country.' I said, 'What do you mean by his country? A flag someone invented two hundred years ago? The Bench of Bishops arguing about divorce and the House of Commons shouting Ya at each other across the floor? Or do you mean the T.U.C. and British Railways and the Co-Op? You probably think it's your regiment, if you ever stop to think, but we haven't got a regiment—he and I.' They tried to interrupt and I said, 'Oh, I forgot—there's something greater than one's country, isn't there? You taught us that with your League of Nations and your Atlantic Pact, NATO and UNO and SEATO. But they don't mean any more to most of us than all the other letters, USA and USSR. And we don't believe you any more when you say you want peace and justice and freedom. What kind of freedom? You want your careers.' I said I sympathized with the French officers in 1940 who looked after their families; they didn't anyway put their careers first. A country is more a family than a Parliamentary system."

"My God, you said all that?"

"Yes. It was quite a speech."

"Did you believe it?"

"Not all of it. They haven't left us much to believe, have they? —even disbelief. I can't believe in anything bigger than a home, or anything vaguer than a human being."

"Any human being?"

She walked quickly away without answering among the sage-green chairs and he saw that she had talked herself to the edge of tears. Ten years ago he would have followed her, but middle age is the period of sad caution. He watched her move away across the dreary room and he thought: "Darling" is a manner of speech, fourteen years between us, Milly—one shouldn't do anything to shock one's child or to injure the faith one doesn't share. She had reached the door before he joined her.

He said, "I've looked up Jakarta in all the reference books. You can't go there. It's a terrible place."

"I haven't any choice. I tried to stay in the pool."

"Did you want the pool?"

"We could have met at the Corner House sometimes and gone to a movie."

"A ghastly life—you said it."

"You would have been part of it."

"Beatrice, I'm fourteen years older than you."

"What the hell does that matter? I know what really worries you—it's not age, it's Milly."

"She has to learn her father's human too."

"She told me once it wouldn't do, my loving you."

"It's got to do. I can't love you as a one-way traffic."

"It won't be easy telling her."

"It may not be very easy to stay with me after a few years."

She said, "My darling, don't worry about that any longer. You won't be left twice."

As they kissed, Milly came in, carrying a large sewing basket for an old lady. She looked particularly virtuous. She had probably started a spell of doing good deeds. The old lady saw them first and clutched at Milly's arm. "Come away, dear," she said. "The idea, where anyone can see them!"

"It's all right," Milly said. "It's only my father."

The sound of her voice separated them.

The old lady said, "Is that your mother?"

"No. His secretary."

"Give me my basket," the old lady said with indignation.

"Well," Beatrice said, "that's that."

Wormold said, "I'm sorry, Milly."

"Oh," Milly said, "it's time she learnt a little about life."

"I wasn't thinking of her. I know this won't seem to you like a real marriage. . . ."

"I'm glad you are being married. In Havana I thought you were just having an affair. Of course it comes to the same thing, doesn't it, as you are both married already—but somehow it will be more dignified. Father, do you know where Tattersall's is?"

"Knightsbridge, I think, but it will be closed."

"I just wanted to explore the route."

"And you don't mind, Milly?"

"Oh, pagans can do almost anything, and you are pagans. Lucky you. I'll be back for dinner."

"So you see," Beatrice said, "it was all right after all."

"Yes. I managed her rather well, don't you think? I can do some things properly. By the way, the report about the enemy agents—surely that must have pleased them."

"Not exactly. You see, darling, it took the laboratory an hour and a half floating each stamp in water to try to find your dot. I think it was on the four hundred and eighty-second stamp, and then when they tried to enlarge it—well, there wasn't anything there. You'd either over-exposed the film or used the wrong end of the microscope."

"And yet they are giving me the O.B.E.?"

"Yes."

"And a job?"

"I doubt whether you'll keep it long."

"I don't mean to. Beatrice, when did you begin to imagine that you were . . . ?"

She put her hand on his shoulder and persuaded him into a shuffle among the dreary chairs. Then she began to sing, a little out of tune, as though she had been running a long way in order to catch him up.

"Sane men surround
You, old family friends.
They say the earth is round—
My madness offends.
An orange has pips, they say,
And an apple has rind. . . ."

"What are we going to live on?" Wormold asked.

"You and I can find a way."

"There are three of us," Wormold said, and she realized the chief problem of their future—that he would never be quite mad enough.